INTO THE PRESS OF WAR

Gripping his sword hilt, he powered the blade through the rest of the corpse's torso, it bursting forth through the other side. Entrails spilled out of the hollow half of the fallen enemy, his blade creating a stark, contrasting glow amidst the gore as it pulsed now brighter than ever.

In a wide stance, curved sword threatening any who dared to come in at him, he held his longsword back and to the side, warding off another flanking formation, nostrils flaring, slanted pursed lips hissing air violently in and out.

A sharp pain dug into his arm, causing him to drop his longsword, two more arrows bouncing off harmlessly along his breastplate.

The soldiers who had been waiting just out of attacking distance piled in, rushing him, and this time, he had to retreat, the press of dozens of flailing weapons quickly threatening to overtake him.

Lords of the Deep Hells Trilogy

Book 1

Shadow of the Arisen

You can contact me at:

authorpaulyoder@gmail.com

Visit me online for launch dates and other news at:
authorpaulyoder.com (sign up for the newsletter)
instagram.com/author_paul_yoder
tiktok.com/@authorpaulyoder
Paul Yoder on Goodreads
Paul Yoder on Amazon

ISBN:9798631048072

For Nikki, my wife,

Who has supported, loved, and stood by me in both my brightest days and my darkest nights.

LANDS OF WANDERLUST NOVELS BY

Paul Yoder

LORDS OF THE DEEP HELLS TRILOGY
Shadow of the Arisen
Lords of the Sands
Heart of the Maiden

KINGDOM OF CROWNS TRILOGY
The Rediron Warp
Firebrands
Seamwalker

LANDS
OF
WANDERLUST

Paul Yoder

Shadow
of the
Arisen

Lords of the Deep Hells Trilogy

Book I

The peoples of the
SOUTHERN SANDS REGION

JEENYRE
Jeenyre Monastery
Castle Sephentho
Dryad's Grove
Dover
Yellowstone

Ashfield
PLAINSCAPE
Sheaf
Viccarwood
Desolate Rift
Warwick
Barre
Highguard
Desolate Peak
Kitland
Nomadic Peoples of Highguard

CARIGANNIE
Death's Ride Pass
Grovine Ruins
Briggarden
Sansabar
Imhotep Pass
Fort Brockhill
Dolinger Crags
Badlands
Enclave of the Unclean

Alanth
Delath's Spire
Rochata-Ung
The Carigannie Dunes
Fort Wellspring
Ruins of Solstice

TABLE OF CONTENTS

1 Starlit Dunes

2 The Debt

3 Introductions

4 Company For The Road Ahead

5 Death's Cellar

6 Expanding The Senses

7 The Ancient Chambers

8 Reunion

9 The Soul In The Ring

10 Jadugarmok's Finest Spirits

11 Lurkers Under The Sand

12 Into The Worm Hole

13 The Little Farmhouse

14 Deliberations Of Sainthood

15 Eyes In The Dark

16 Face Of The Enemy

17 Servant Of Ash

18 Blessing Of A Saint

19 Headquarters And Deployments

20 The Expansive Grounds

21 Undone In The Dark

22 The Old Man In The Painting

23 Fading Light

24 Knock At The Door

25 The Last Light Of Day

26 Jaws At The Door

27 Into The Press Of War

28 At A Dagger's Distance

29 Hell's Crucible

30 The Broken Band

31 A Renewed Purpose

32 The Desolate Rift

33 The Climb

34 Trust And Sacrifice

35 Night Coach

36 A Royal Audience

37 Rearm

38 The Trail Back

39 At The Gates

40 Acid In The Dark

41 Dark Reunion

42 Grim Rendezvous

43 At Death's Door

44 Requiem Knell

45 Window Of Rest

46 Plaudits And Egress

47 Lingering Darkness

48 Solidarity

49 The Open Road

From The Author

Part One: The Journey of Sand

1

STARLIT DUNES

The metal rattle of gear against armor mixed with the entrancing sound of leather flapping from the violent wind droned on for what seemed to have been hours now. The lone traveler hunkered down in a dune depression in the middle of a vicious desert sandstorm with no shelter to protect him from the sting of the harsh pelting sands but a large, suede leather cloak he had wrapped around his body.

He was one no longer known by name, but by title, ever since he had left his homeland to the Far East. Since that time, others had just referred to the wanderer as "Nomad."

Though his gear seemed adapted to be suited for life in the desert, it was culturally an oddity among the arid nation he currently was traveling in.

Kneeling there at the bottom of a dune to take as little abuse from the storm as possible, he retreated into his subconsciousness, leaving his outer senses, mentally melting away.

In his meditative state, space, time, cause, effect, energy, all became one, his meditation bringing him closer to eternity, slowly drowning out any outside stimuli, leaving his consciousness in an endless space of both repleteness and nothingness—an equal measure of light and darkness.

Slowly, just after reaching his portion of meditative eternity, he began to come back to the physical realm. Though it had seemed as though he had just entered his trance, what was day before his meditation was now night. And though the sandstorm was dying down, a peek outside of his cloak that was wrapped around him like a small tent revealed that the unrelenting desert winds were still patrolling the endless dunes.

As he listened a moment, something instantly felt wrong. He put down his steel helm's visor, sliding two notches on either side of the eye holes, two crimson-tinted glass lenses closing the gap. With his face protected, he unwrapped his cloak and stood up, his cloak now wildly flapping behind him.

It didn't take him a great deal of concentration to single out what possibly could have pulled him out of his trance early—a sharp clang of steel on steel rung off over a distant dune, slicing through the din of the storm. He knew that sound so very well. It was the deathly beautiful interplay of weapons in the hands of combatants.

Sprinting in the direction of the clash, Nomad made his way up one dune and then another, stopping just at the crest of the second dune. Halting to listen again, he quickly determined that the fight was indeed over in the next valley.

By the sounds of it, the battle was a retreating one, and he guessed there to be only two combatants; the resounding steel sounded very similar each time and only sounded off once every few seconds.

Satisfied he wasn't going to be facing an army upon revealing himself, he marched over the dune's peak, exposing himself to an unconcerned duo, fighting through the harsh Tarigannie sandstorm.

The pair, though completely different in appearance, wore similarly heavy armor, both appearing as knights of differing factions. The oppressor, or advancing knight, wore full plate mail armor, tinted black. The banners and robes that hung down out of the slits and joints of his armor were dyed a dark pitch, with the hems being a rich mahogany.

With the oppressor turned to its prey, Nomad could only see the oppressive knight's back, but he could tell that he only wielded a large greatsword.

The prey seemed to handle herself confidently enough, but the fact that she was backing away from her opponent belied her conviction to the fight.

She was very beautiful—long, light-blonde hair parted to the side of a symmetric, clear-featured face. She seemed to be human, just as he was, though she was fair skinned, only lightly tanned, which was not a common skin tone in the harsh, sunbaked desert region of Tarigannie.

Her armor, in contrast to her opponent's, was a polished steel. A white tabard stretched its way down her middle over her armor, clearly displaying the mark of her faith, which Nomad recognized instantly as belonging to followers of Sareth—a rare, exclusive cult centered on the goddess of virtue and justice. Though their ways were a mystery to nearly all, and their presence unknown to most, Nomad had seen their influence, even as far as his distant homelands.

"A saren knight," Nomad whispered in wonder to see the recondite, elite holy warrior of Sareth standing before him.

The dark knight struck again, coming down hard with an overhanded strike, the saren bringing her large shield up just in time to deflect the blow off to the side, thrusting her long seax into the arm opening in her opponent's armor, sinking deep.

Nomad, who had been advancing to assist the saren, halted, seeing the deathblow just dealt, then watched in awe as the dark knight gripped the entrenched, sizeable blade, broke the grip the saren had on the hilt, and casually tossed it off to the side, lifting up its greatsword, beginning to advance once more.

Nomad began to race towards the two, seeing now that the saren fought against someone, or something, more formidable than perhaps even an elite saren was capable of dealing with.

She blocked another blow from the dark knight with her shield, unlatching a flail from the back of her belt as she did so. The blow forced her to her knees, though, and the dark knight took the high ground opportunity to lay into her with successive hard-hitting attacks, sword banging off of her upheld shield.

Allowing for one final slam of sword and shield, the saren flung her opponent's sword hard left with her shield, causing the dark knight to pause momentarily to steady himself for the next attack, but that moment was all the saren needed.

As she brought her flail in a wide arc, throwing all the force she could into the blow, the spiked, chained balls slammed hard into the dark knight's head.

The ferocity of the attack sent the knight's helmet flying off. The slam spun the knight halfway around, stopping just in time to meet a charging cloaked man who waited to draw his sword until the last possible moment, thumb releasing the curved sword from its sheath.

Nomad's sword came indiscernibly fast, slashing a crescent pattern across the dark knight's armor, clanging off steel the majority of the blow until the blade found purchase in the elbow joint of the knight's armor covering its arm.

A limb fell to the ground, the heavy gauntlet thudding into the sand. The attack had taken Nomad far past the knight, placing him next to the saren, who was justifiably stunned at the new addition to this private battle of theirs.

The last few attacks had happened so quickly that the battlefield stilled for a moment as all three combatants tried to catch up to what had just unfolded, and that's when Nomad and the saren simultaneously noticed something very concerning about their foe.

Under the whipping mop of black, ratty hair was nothing but bone—a skull atop a barren spine. The creature they faced off against was no man or other common race, but was strung together and animated like a macabre marionette.

With a grounding, though brief, glance at one another, Nomad and the saren established their immediate alliance against their now unified foe. Both came in at the dark knight fast—Nomad striking first.

Nomad's curved sword went high, aiming for the knight's unprotected head, but the knight bobbed just in time, the sword only lopping off a small slice of bone, dried skin, and hair.

The saren's attack, however, came in at the knight's blindside, pounding the knight back, this time off-balancing it completely, toppling it to the ground.

"Allow me," the saren commanded, for the first time revealing her voice, which, to Nomad, was so stern that it seemed to disagree with her fair, youthful appearance.

Nomad stood watching as the saren walked up to the downed foe, lifting her flail, ready to deal the deathblow.

Before the flail could fall, the knight shot his hand up, spoke in a profane tongue, and shot a green cloud of gas directly into the saren's face.

The saren stumbled back, the gas causing immediate respiratory fits as she choked her way out of the lingering gas cloud. Nomad sprang into action as he saw the knight working on getting back up.

The knight crouched over when an unbelievably sharp, curved sword sliced once, separating the top half of the knight's cranium, and then again after coming back around to decapitate the vile marionette.

The dark knight stayed down this time, and it appeared that with the decapitation of the skull went all ties to animation it once had.

The rush of thumping blood from the battle slowly handing back his senses to reason and awareness, Nomad began to notice violent coughing and wheezing behind him. Looking back, he could see that the saren was in a horrible state, grasping at her throat, fighting with everything she had for breath.

Kneeling by her side, Nomad could already tell the saren was not consciously aware of her surroundings. Her mind was wandering some distant corridors of pain.

He took out a tin container from one of his side pouches. Unclipping her tabard, he found a breastplate underneath. Undonning her armor, gently turning her over, he lifted up her undergarment to expose her back. He popped open the lid and dipped a finger in a gel-like substance, drawing a symbol in both areas over where the lungs were located. Concentrating for a few moments, he hummed in a trance-like tone, speaking in a language only his eastern kin would understand, caressing his middle finger over the now dried gel, igniting it in a faint green glow, heavy black fumes seeping from the flame.

Sitting there, his healing ritual complete, he swept the flames out in one motion and covered her back again with her undergarment.

"This is a sickness I cannot heal. Not completely at least."

As he sat her up, holding her head steady, there was a visible difference between her state of body and mind before his treatment and after. Her coughing had now completely gone away, and her eyes no longer receded up into her skull.

"Saren, can you understand my words?" he asked, knowing his heavy foreign accent probably made understanding him that much more difficult.

Luckily, she slowly nodded, indicating that she could hear him.

As she began to shake violently, dark colors seeped into her complexion even as they talked.

"We need to get you to the nearest town. What direction is that?"

"W—west," she was able to chatter out.

By now, the sandstorm had died even more so than before, and it only took Nomad a momentary glance up to orientate himself and locate a westward heading.

"Good. Try to stay conscious. If the mind wanders aimlessly through poison too long, there may not be much of your mind left after a cure is administered. I'll collect your weapons and we will be on our way," Nomad said as he got up and started to search for the discarded seax, shield, and flail, finding them all without too much trouble.

He sheathed her blade for her and strapped her flail and shield to her back, then hefted her over his shoulder and began to trudge to the nearest hill while traveling westward—the direction he hoped the nearest town was in.

2

THE DEBT

Nomad gave a clear knock on a private chamber door at an inn in the small desert town of Sansabar. He gently shifted the saren's weight on his shoulders, waiting for someone to answer his beckons, when, after a few moments, he finally heard footsteps on the old floorboards making their way to the door.

A lock latch slid and the door opened inward, revealing an utter mess of a room with all manner of scientific devices, papers and books, and specimens of all kinds locked and caged throughout the small chamber.

At the door was a short man, barely reaching past four foot, with nubby, pointed ears and a frazzled mop of light-green hair. Though Nomad hadn't seen many folk of the little man's race, he knew the man to be a praven—a curious and often unwittingly mischievous sort of people.

"Yes, can I help you?" the praven asked in a rushed tone.

Nomad, a little taken aback, expecting to find a healer of some ilk, stammered out, "I was told someone in this inn might be able to cure my friend's sickness, but perhaps I was misled. Sorry for interrupting your work."

Before Nomad could turn to go, the little man held up a finger and asked, "Sickness? What kind of sickness?"

Nomad turned back and answered, "She was poisoned by a dark knight—who was without flesh."

"Well now, that *is* interesting," the praven said, pausing for a moment to contemplate on Nomad's description of the knight, then added with a beckoning hand, "Come in, come in, please. You weren't misled. I've been known to cure poisons from time to time. I'm quite an accomplished chemist, and toxins definitely fall under my area of expertise. Determining what a toxin is composed of is no simple task; and beyond that, finding out if, or how, to construct a cure for the inflicted host is no small feat, I can assure you that."

Nomad had entered the praven's room, standing in the middle of it with the saren draped over his back while listening to the high-pitched voice continue to speak with little to no pause between statements.

"Ah, yes. Where to put the subject," the praven said, rapidly tapping his fingers on the table he was momentarily resting upon.

"Patient," Nomad corrected, a bit of worry seeping in at the practitioner's odd character.

"Yes, yes. Patient, subject, host—they're all quite the same. A problem manifests itself to us in this fine body we have before us, and it's up to us—well, me—to find a solution to that problem.

"Now, don't bother me with trifles further. We've got a job to do after all. I'll grab a table to lay out our subject—I mean patient—on."

With that, the little praven zipped off down the hall, continuing the one-sided conversation, yelling from the next room over.

"My name is Jadugarmok, by the way, but most here simply call me Jadu. I didn't catch your name. By the look of your facial structure, accent, and skin tone, you don't appear to be local. From the Far East, perhaps?"

Jadu was now making his way across the hall while dragging a table, all the while creating quite the ruckus. Nomad, putting the saren down on the disheveled bed, quickly went to help Jadu carry the table the rest of the way, answering the man's questions as they went.

"Surprisingly good eyes and ears, Mr. Jadu. I do indeed hail from the East. Many simply refer to me as Nomad, which I have been going by for some time now. You can call me by that name."

Back in Jadu's inn room, they set the borrowed table down on the hardwood floor.

"Place the patient on the table if you would and strip her of everything but her undergarments."

Nomad picked the saren up and gently set her down on the bare table, the saren letting out a moan of sickening pain as he did so. Nomad got to work at taking off the warrior's armor as quickly as he could, knowing that at this point, they had very little time left to spare, her condition and skin color having only worsened since the battle.

First he took her tabard off, revealing trim-fitting steel armor underneath. Unbuckling multiple latches attached to her breastplate, pauldrons, rerebraces, and vambraces, he slid all her upper torso armor off, one by one. He slipped off her gauntlets next, then started to unstrap her lower gear, starting with the cuisses, poleyns, then greaves and sabatons.

After all the heavy gear was discarded on the floor, Nomad then started in on the assortment of leather and padded clothes she wore, stripping her down to her undergarments, revealing very fair skin with lines of green trailing all throughout her body visible just beneath her skin—an ill sign of the dire nature of the consuming poison that currently inhabited her body.

"Now what?" Nomad asked, stepping back from the unarmored, disrobed knight.

Jadu looked up from his momentary silence while studying the condition of the prone, bare patient and answered, "Now you take a seat and let me get started with my diagnosis. I'll ask you questions if needed. I don't mind the company, but it may interfere with my work. I'll leave you with that word of warning in case this lady's life is of great worth to you."

Looking behind him, finding a chair, Nomad took a seat. Taking off a few articles of gear to get comfortable, he sat watching the peculiar praven perform some cursory tests—watching and feeling the slow rise and fall of the saren's chest, opening her eyelids and mouth, feeling around under her jawline and wrist.

After his assessment, Jadu began to shoot some seemingly disinterested questions in Nomad's direction.

"Do you know her?"

"I don't. She is a stranger to me," Nomad replied.

"Where did you find her then?"

"I came upon her in mid-combat in the dunes to the east of here," Nomad answered.

Tapping his chin in thought, Jadu asked, "Combatting what

exactly? You made mention of some knight without flesh—any more details than that?"

"Yes, very sinister in appearance, and as far as we could tell, he was all bone, no flesh or sinew," Nomad offered.

"Hmm. Indeed," Jadu mumbled as he took out a device from the folds of his robes and uncapped a turquoise cylinder, the tip of it producing a bright, white glow.

"That does help to narrow the types of poison this could be. How was this poison administered?"

"It shot forth some sort of gas from its hand after speaking some trigger word. It sounded profane in nature," Nomad replied.

"I see…," Jadu said, drawing out the phrase.

He opened the unconscious saren's mouth and peered in with his small light source inspecting as he talked. "Green gas. A corpse-like foe. Well, it's either good news or bad news then. She's either dead or alive depending on your answer to my next question. How long has it been since the poison entered her system?"

Nomad gave the question some brief thought before answering. "It has been eight hours now, give or take an hour or so."

Nomad waited for a response from Jadu, watching his facial features, which didn't lean one way or another. After a short pause lost in thought, Jadu answered, "Well, eight hours is generally the kill time for certusmortem, or as the locals around here call it, and aptly so, *the eight-hour death.*

"It's a toxin that is somewhat uniquely regional around these parts. It's a bacteria that sometimes is found in rotting carcasses. If a pustule explodes, those in the vicinity can find themselves quickly brought low with a respiratory infection, which can spread through the body at startling speed.

"You said the knight was all bone, but perhaps underneath its armor still remained decaying flesh with a large culture of certusmortem that popped and sprayed your friend here."

Looking to the faintly breathing saren on the table, Nomad asked, "Is there anything you can do for her?"

Jadu, taking pause from biting his lip, mumbled, "Yes. If I have the proper ingredients, I can make an ointment that should reduce the toxicity levels of her blood just enough so that she'll survive until her body takes care of the rest of the toxins."

Waiting for Jadu to continue, Nomad prompted him, asking, "Do you have the needed ingredients?"

Looking rather annoyed, Jadu returned Nomad's stare and said,

"I'm not sure yet. The recipe is in one of my study books somewhere, but finding it in any sort of timely manner is unlikely. I'm attempting to recall the recipe by memory."

Sitting back in his chair again, Nomad attempted to emotionally detach himself from the saren's fate. After all, he didn't even know her, but something about being able to take down the unholy knight and not doing so at her request, and potential demise, didn't sit right with him.

"Carlous bloom root! I'm pretty sure that's the medicinal ingredient that was slipping my memory. Alright, alright. Now hopefully I have the right amounts of everything," Jadu said while frantically scuttling around the small, cramped room.

It didn't take Jadu long to gather the small list of ingredients, ground them up, and combine them with a cream, producing a yellowish-orange paste.

"Here, help me coat this on her body," Jadu commanded, plopping a generous amount in a wooden bowl.

As they began rubbing the salve on the saren's body, Jadu kept talking, sometimes directed at Nomad and sometimes seemingly to himself.

"This salve is not so common a recipe. Well, might be common here, but not outside the region. Picked it up from a desert local around four months ago. But, what this is supposed to do is draw out the poison, almost like a sponge. So the paste, if it works, should start to turn brown, then black over the next hour or so."

Just as Jadu had detailed, even before they had finished coating all of the saren's body, the earlier coat began to turn a light-brown color, and by the time they had finished the coat and washed up in a washbasin down the hall, half of her covered body was a dark tint of brown, and almost visibly turning darker as they watched.

After making the intrigued off comment of "Seems to be working faster than the local described to me," Jadu went back to his desk where he had multiple books open and started reading from them disjointedly.

Flipping from book to book to scrap paper for a little more than an hour, Jadu finally looked sideways over to his patient, whispering, "That she still draws breath seems to indicate she's going to pull through. Feel free to wash that mass of black goop off of her and get her a room. Might take her a day or so before coming around, and a few days after that to recover her strength.

"Don't forget to clean up her armor a bit too. Wouldn't want any of the residue from the poison to cause any further problems with her in her weakened state. At the least, it'd be a skin irritant if any of it was left on.

"Thanks for bringing her in. I needed to prove out that local remedy sometime anyways before I could add it into my college's medical journals."

A bit confused at both the abruptness of the good news of the saren's expected positive recovery and the invitation to leave Jadu's room, Nomad stuttered out, "Th—thanks. What do I owe you for the care?"

Jadu placed a finger in the spot in his book and looked up to answer.

"Nothing. Unless you care to, that is. I have no issue taking a tip for the ingredients used. I found the experiment interesting. My college pays for my needs, so I'm well off with or without pay from you."

Nomad, feeling a bit incredulous towards the strange praven, fished through his purse and placed twenty gold strips on the table. It was a lot for him since he didn't own much monetary wealth, but it was nothing compared to performing such lifesaving medicine on short notice.

"That is what I can spare. Thank you, Jadu. Do you plan on staying here in this room for a few days?"

Jadu smiled and answered, "Ah, thank you for the tip! As to how long I'll be staying here, I'll be here a bit longer, more than likely. I have been boarded here for a month now collecting local samples, and I still have a bit more work to do in cataloging them."

Nomad began gathering his things and said, "Very good. I will see if there are any rooms open at this establishment then and get one for me and the saren. She will need someone to attend to her and a few days on my journey means little to me. I will be back to carry her to another room if the proprietor agrees to house us here."

A bit of gold later and with the keys to a room just down the hall from Jadu, Nomad began unloading all of his and the saren's belongings into the twin bedroom. He had spent a little extra and ordered a bath drawn for the saren.

Bidding Jadu thanks again, he lifted the unconscious saren off the table and made his way to the bathing room, which thankfully was not occupied, and the servant had already heated the water mildly in the time it took for him to transition his and her things to their new room.

Getting involved had cost Nomad more than half of the wealth he had on him, but he had never been one to worry over finances. The time spent nursing the saren would also cost him an extra week off the road on his aimless journey to wherever the wind took him. He didn't have reservations over his new dependent, but he did wonder, once she was to come around, how she would feel about his help.

She seemed, in the brief interactions he had with her, quite independent. At the most he supposed he expected a *thanks* from her—at the least, a claim that he should not have interfered with her affairs in the first place.

Either way, to be abruptly tied back into society and to someone needing his help, whether she would later admit it or not, felt good.

He had been without human ties for so long.

3
INTRODUCTIONS

Nomad was finishing up the meal the page boy had brought in when he noticed the saren rousing. Turning his chair to get a better look, he waited for her to open her eyes, which she did after a minute or two of slight movements mingled with moans.

She didn't start, nor did she seem overly concerned or frightened by the unfamiliar setting, though she did have a questioning look openly displayed in her features.

Nomad decided to take the initiative, asking, "Your color came back today. How are you feeling?"

She seemed to contemplate on the question for a moment before attempting to force her body into a sitting position, groaning, the effort straining her weakened muscles the whole way.

As she sat up, the bed covers slid down over her chest to her waist, exposing her upper torso.

Nomad quickly went for a sack on the table with a linen top wrap, handing it over to her to cover herself while averting his eyes, fumbling over an explanation of why she was naked.

"Your other undergarments were all but decomposed after the toxins in your body were expunged. I just got to the market this morning to get you new garments."

She made no attempt to take the cloth from Nomad. After a moment, she mustered an explanation, grunting through a throb of pain, "I don't think I could put it on."

Nomad, abashed slightly, and honestly not sure what to do, considered his next questions before mumbling out, "What would you like for me to do?"

Leaning against the wall next to the bed, she said, "If it's a distraction for you, clothe me, but I need water, and I need to be sitting up for that."

Wishing he had just clothed her earlier that afternoon when he had come in from the small-town bazaar to avoid the awkward situation he was now in, he took the long strip of linen and gently lifted her arms slightly and proceeded to wrap her chest, tying the excess in a knot on her side. Afterwards, he grabbed his bed's pillows and comforter and stuffed them behind her to prop her up in bed.

Going to the table, Nomad poured a cup of water from a clay pitcher and then brought her a drink, touching the mug to her lips, tipping it up slowly as she drank.

"Another one," she let out between breaths after the cup was emptied. Nomad complied.

"Would you like more?" Nomad asked.

Weakly shaking her head, she said, "Don't want to overdo it for now. Do you have any wafers or flatbread or anything? I'm starving."

Picking his leftover biscuit from his meal earlier, he handed it to her and added, "I will have a meal brought up soon for you."

As she began working laboriously on her bread, Nomad started to explain what had happened after she had gone down in the desert from the dark knight's poison; how he had carried her to the town, finding Jadu, administering the antidote just in time, cleaning her from the caustic goop, and setting them both up in a room so he could monitor her condition.

She finished her biscuit and asked for another drink, this time asking to hold the cup herself, some strength already coming back to her.

"Well certainly you didn't need to do all that for me," she scoffed, pausing to add, "but I'm glad you did. It seems I wouldn't be around right now if you hadn't."

Nomad could tell giving thanks was not her strong suit, and if he were to be honest with himself, gratitude wasn't his either, so he changed subjects for both their sakes.

"I do not know your name."

"Reza. And yours?" she asked.

Sitting back in his chair, he replied, "The few that have come to know me these last few years call me Nomad."

Reza seemed to pause, perhaps to consider asking about the origins of his odd name, but asked instead if Nomad could bring her her belongings. Nomad brought her a satchel and a belt strung with a number of pouches and watched as she unstrung a small pouch that sounded as though it carried coin.

After briefly counting through it, she looked up and said, "You haven't been through my stuff it looks like? If you had, I'm sure my gold would have been the first thing to go missing."

Perhaps in his younger years, his pride might have taken a blow at even the suggestion of theft. But after spending years on the unkind, open road, his pride now flapped like a torn and worn banner, and he took no offense to the suggestive reply. "No. Your possessions are yours, and I am not the kind of person to snoop."

"Well," she said, hesitating for a moment, "it seems you have integrity. That's an attribute my kind hold in high regard."

"Your kind cherish many principles similar to my own," Nomad responded.

Reza subtly crooked her head in curiosity and asked, "You know my kind?"

Nomad answered, "Saren. I wonder if you are but a follower of Sareth, or are a true born saren. By your fairness, I would guess you are indeed a saren. Few of that race walk upon Una.

"Only a handful of your kind have graced the land of my people, but those that have visited have been revered as honored guests and good omens. Your kind are considered heirs of the gods themselves, distinguished from mortal man. Your people possess spirits so strong as to defy death. Much of my culture has principles built up around what has been the core tenants of your kind for ages."

Though her body was slack, her eyes shone with curiosity and intent as she asked, "You know an unusual amount about my people. You are not from this region then? Your skin color doesn't quite disagree with the locals, but I do notice your facial features are not regional. Where do you hail from?"

Nomad nodded, confirming Reza's speculation of his heritage. "Silmurannon. I would be surprised if you have heard of my land. Even most of the well-traveled do not know of it."

Reza looked off for a moment as if searching her distant memory and slowly replied, "That place. It does sound familiar. Though, of any details, I am at a loss for. It's far to the east of here, correct?"

Nomad nodded. "Yes. Far to the east. It took me many years to travel to where we are. Most on horseback, some on boat, and recently, on foot."

"If I'm not prying too much to ask, what is the purpose of your long journey? It seems you've traveled far from your home for some purpose. What's so important?" Reza questioned.

"That," Nomad said between a long sigh, "is a long story. I suppose you could say I'm fleeing from something. A past that is too painful to face. Perhaps the further I journey, the more I hope to find the courage I lack to confront my demons. Distance has not seemed to ease my sorrows, but I know of no other path."

Reza didn't have a response for Nomad's cryptic answer, and it seemed as though she didn't want to press him on his history or purpose for being there. Nomad didn't allow too long a pause to pass before asking Reza the same question.

"And what of you? What brought you to our meeting place in the dunes? Where did that dark foe you faced come from?"

Reza did not hesitate in answering, "There is a cursed land southeast of here. As a traveler, you may have heard of Brigganden?"

Nomad shook his head, never having heard the name.

"Up until two years ago it was a prosperous trade city. It skirted the borders of the Tarigannie desert, which we're in currently, and the Plainstate, the territory you most likely just passed through to get here if you were traveling from the east. Brigganden refused to be subject to either the Tarigannie or Plainstate governance, and they fought for their freedom centuries ago and succeeded in winning their independence from either region.

"Well, a year ago, masses of refugees began migrating to either the Tarigannie or Plainstate regions with queer horror stories of the dead rising. Trade halted suddenly due to numerous raids to the incoming merchant caravans. The raids were not even for riches or spoils, but by all accounts, were simply a slaughter conducted by demonic beings. Some say there were corpses doing the fighting— talk of the arisen began to spread through the neighboring towns as the refugees continued to speak of nothing but the horror they witnessed as they were forced from their homes by the dead.

"It didn't take long for word to get out that Brigganden had been infiltrated by some sort of dark power—a necromancer, most rumormongers conclude.

17

"Sultan Metus, who's the sultan of the Plainstate, began contracting scout parties to investigate and gain intel on the current situation, but all but two of the first ten scout parties returned.

"He decided to hire more qualified, distinguished adventures and organized three squads of elite scouts. I was in one of those squads.

"We had tracked a suspicious band through the desert near Brigganden that was headed northwest. We were on their trail most of that day when a sandstorm hit and shortly after that we were attacked.

"I engaged that dark knight you saw. I got separated from my group in the midst of chaos. We were still fighting when you showed up."

Nomad's eyes widened at the story.

"I did not know I had wandered so close to such an unstable region. It has been a while since I had contact with locals. I passed through Plainstate with only one visit to a town, and even then, I did not loiter or ask about local politics."

Reza took a moment to chide Nomad's recklessness. "You travel through distant lands long enough without gathering basic regional information and it won't be long before you wander into a warring region, eat poisonous deadly fauna, or get lost in a wasteland without aid or supplies."

Nomad nodded his head in agreement. "Yes, there is wisdom in that. I agree."

Finding no argument there, Reza switched topics.

"My comrades—they'll be searching for me more than likely. I need to get out there and find them. I'm the leader of the group. This Jadu you spoke of earlier. Is he a competent physician? I need to know what happened to my body and when I can expect to have the strength to travel."

Nomad stood up and answered, stumbling slightly over his secondary language's vocabulary, "Yes, he would very much like to see that you are up. I will go let him know you are awake and call for the servant to bring up a meal for you."

With that, Nomad was out the door, leaving Reza in the room to rest.

Reza didn't have to wait long. Nomad entered the room with a short, little praven trailing behind him. Before he could even introduce Reza to him, Jadu began with a string of comments.

"Ah, you're looking much better if I do say so myself. That salve I concocted to save your life was a long shot if I am to be honest.

Local remedies often are less scientific and more placebo than anything, but I'm very glad to have had a successful experiment with this one. I'll definitely be interested in monitoring your recovery process over the next little while. Now that I've proven a cure, I'll need to document the after-effects of surviving such a potent poison."

Reza said nothing and didn't seem too concerned about Jadu's ramblings, leaving Nomad to jump in between Jadu's quick breaths.

"Reza, this is Jadu, the physician that cured you. Jadu, we were hoping that you might have an estimate on how long Reza would take to recover. She needs to return to a group she was traveling with as soon as able. It sounded like you do not have previous experience with this sickness, but do you have an idea of how long before she is ready for travel?"

Jadu considered Nomad's question for a moment, walked over to Reza's bedside, and threw back the covers from Reza's legs and began feeling muscle and fatty sections of her limbs. He then pushed firmly on her stomach and did a bit of tapping on the back. He inspected her arms, then listened with his ear to her chest as she breathed.

After looking down her throat and then looking in her eyes and ears, he broke the silence with, "I'm no physician, just an alchemist who's read some books on medicine by the way."

Reza gave Nomad a slightly confused look before Jadu continued.

"Well, that's not completely true. I do have an emphasis in health and poisons and remedies in one of my areas of study, but I wouldn't necessarily say that I'm a physician—perhaps an unlicensed physician's assistant would be a better term to describe my position on the subject."

Reza looked flatly to Nomad for an explanation.

Before Nomad could think of a response, Jadu jumped back to the main point of assessing Reza's health.

"Well, it seems you're a bit emaciated—maybe have lost ten or fifteen pounds since my first inspection of your body if I were to guess. That's a lot of weight, but plenty of water and a couple of meals will probably see that weight come partially back on. It doesn't take long for a body, especially an extremely fit body like yours, to recover from weight loss. You probably will be ready to travel by tomorrow with enough rest, food, and drink today."

Reza gave a slight smile of relief at hearing that news, but Jadu continued, "But, that's not the thing I'd worry about. That poison was quite exotic. I suspect—I mean, I've only heard local tales about it, and I know a thing or two about poisons. I'm guessing there could be moderate to serious after-effects of this poison, of which I'd be very interested to know of for my records—if you don't mind me shadowing you for the next week or two."

Reza, quite irked at the request, responded, "Two weeks? I plan on being up and out of here tomorrow, tracking down my scouting group, heading out to investigate Brigganden; which, by all accounts, is a horribly dangerous place to dwell near currently. You'd not be wanting to tag along in that place. And though I do thank you for your service, I surely don't plan to stick around here to pad your records with details of my recovery while leaving my comrades desperately wondering where I am. I need to return to them as soon as I can. They need me."

Jadu, not fazed by the off-putting tone of Reza in the least, pressed on. "Oh, you wouldn't even notice me. I was planning on packing up and moving on to other locations in the area anyways to continue research. I'm quite agreeable on the road, and while I would appreciate to finish my findings with this poison, you, I hope, would appreciate my company to care for any new developments or complications of the effects of this poison if it has not, in fact, completely run its course already."

Before Reza could reply, a knock at the door sounded. Nomad opened it to find the servant boy holding a hot meal on a tray. Handing the boy a few bits of silver pieces in exchange, Nomad closed the door and brought the tray over to Reza.

"Here, eat and drink and we'll see afterwards how you feel about standing and stretching. You must get your body used to working if you are to leave tomorrow into the desert."

Still eyeing Jadu, not forgetting the strange alchemist's intention to come with her to the treacherous Brigganden borders, Reza seemed about to start the argument up again when he suddenly spoke up.

"Well, I should be going—much to do! I'll check in later tonight and early in the morning, but do let me know if there are any status updates."

With that, Jadu left without leaving either Reza or Nomad time to respond.

Seeing that she now seemed a bit more stable sitting up, some of her energy already returning to her, and also noticing that she now appeared slightly frustrated, Nomad said, "I will leave you be now.

There are a few places in town I need to visit. I will be back in an hour or two. Do you need me to get you anything else before I leave?"

"No, thank you for everything so far. I'll be fine here," she said, taking a sip of water.

With that, Nomad turned and walked out the door, closing it behind him.

In actuality, he didn't have anywhere in particular to be, but he wanted to give Reza time to compose herself and dress if she needed it; though, she less than him seemed to care about her immodesty, under the current conditions at least.

Though he was no healer, he knew that even with a good night's rest there was no way she was going to be strong enough to travel any lengthy distance without help. Moreover, he gathered from their recent talk that she probably wasn't going to wait until she was better before shipping out, and she most certainly wasn't going to ask for help from anyone when she did.

4
COMPANY FOR THE ROAD AHEAD

Breakfast hadn't been the most pleasant of affairs for Reza. Jadu had shown up with food and drink for everyone, and the three ate and talked while sitting at the table in Nomad and Reza's room.

Jadu continued to assert his coming along with Reza on her journey to further study her as a test subject, and she had noticed that Nomad had packed his belongings earlier that morning as though he were going somewhere too. She hoped that he wasn't planning on coming with her since one tag-along would be enough trouble to deal with, let alone two; though Nomad, as she had witnessed, had seemed to be competent in taking care of himself in a tight spot.

Even still, she knew the place she was heading back to was dangerous, and to needlessly risk two random people's lives didn't set well with her. In her weakened condition, barely able to walk for more than a minute or two, she knew that having two travel companions would be helpful on the road, but their help was not worth the cost of their deaths on her shoulders.

Giving into a helping hand from Nomad, she gave him her coin sack to go buy a camel and some supplies at the stables and bazaar. He came back and loaded most of her belongings, including her armor, which she wasn't able to wear yet, on the saddlebags.

Coming back after loading everything up, Nomad began donning his travel gear while addressing Reza.

"Jadu seems quite set on studying you for a while longer at least, and I have no pressing matter to attend to, so if you would accept us, we both wish to see you along until you reunite with your group. I fear without us, if you run into any trouble out there in the desert, your fate will be left to those that find you."

Reza bounced up, a little too energetically, perhaps trying to overcompensate for her weakened condition, and said, "I don't see it necessary to ask that of you two, but if you insist, I'll at least pay you both for your escort services. I will refuse your company after I find my group, though. Where we're going has taken the lives of many scouts, and I won't have both your heads on my conscience."

"Understood," Nomad replied. He wanted to suggest that payment would not be necessary, but he knew paying them for a service might be the only way she would accept their company, not to mention that his purse was quite thin presently.

The two walked out of the room and knocked on Jadu's door on their way to the inn's front desk. Hearing a crash and some stumbling around, Jadu eventually opened the door. The room was a complete mess—bits, parts, and ingredients of his previous experiments still littering the room. They apparently weren't worth packing up and taking with him.

Hauling a heavy load in his various carry sacks strapped all over his body, he bounded through the doorway and into the hall with a smile on his face and green-tinted goggles over his eyes.

"Some fresh air could do me some good! I've not been out of my room for any reasonable amount of time in weeks now. Feeling better today, Reza?"

Reza, sending a scowl both Jadu and Nomad's way, responded, "This isn't an afternoon walk we're going on. Who knows where my comrades are? And if it takes me weeks to track them down, I will, and we'll be in what has been reported to be dangerous territory as well. I'm not responsible for your well-being for this trip, you know."

"No, we are responsible for yours. You are hiring us as your escorts, after all," Nomad cut in.

"Oh, is that so?" Jadu asked, hearing about his new job for the first time. Nomad gave him a stern look, but Jadu continued.

"Payment isn't necessary, Reza. I know I did save your life, and you are in no condition to brave the wilds, and without our help you probably would end up dead in the dunes within a few days, but I simply want to study your recovery—"

Nomad had his palm over his face by the time Reza interrupted.

"*You* follow me of your own free will."

Leaving the conversation at that, she turned and started arduously down the stairs and out the front door of the establishment.

Nomad stared demandingly at Jadu for an explanation. Jadu seemed unfazed at either Nomad or Reza's responses.

Scratching his chin, he shot a finger up in the air and exclaimed, "My toad! Goodness, almost forgot to bring him. Be right back. I'll meet you two out front."

Nomad opened his mouth, considering whether or not to have a talk with the eccentric, aloof praven before they were back in the presence of Reza, but decided against it. He closed his mouth and threw his arms up in resignation, figuring it more important to get back with Reza before she took off without them.

5
DEATH'S CELLAR

"So, how many lesions do you still have?" Jadu probed, opening the morning campfire conversation once Reza was up and sitting by the fire.

Instead of answering him, she gave Jadu a sideways glance, then went back to staring into the small little shrub fire Nomad had made earlier.

Jadu, after realizing she didn't intend on answering him, started to say, "My dear Reza—"

Before Jadu could start, Reza cut him off. "Don't call me *dear*."

Her tone even gave Jadu reason to pause before responding with, "Well, someone woke up on the wrong side of the sand dune today. We'll continue this conversation after you don't have sleep in your eyes," which again, got him another dirty look thrown his way for a moment before Reza tried to discreetly rub sleep away from her eyes.

"Tea is ready," Nomad said, some strain showing through his tone, being a bit frayed at the ends from Jadu and Reza's constant bickering over the past four days of traveling together.

He had considered briefly parting ways with the two since Reza had gotten back to sustainable health a day ago, but after giving the idea some thought, he determined not to. He did not like leaving things halfway done, and he surely was not willing to go back on his word—even if Reza would most likely be all for casting off the two's company if she could. He had promised her he'd help her find her friends, and he wanted to stick to that mission, even if he figured she could probably fare just fine out here without him and, most assuredly, Jadu's constant medical questions.

The rest of breakfast was held in relative silence, aside from the occasional curious verbal proddings of Jadu as he tried to eke out updates about Reza's physical condition.

Packing up camp, with Reza on her camel and the other two on foot, they began the day of travel heading southeast, Reza wanting to visit a location that her and her group had set as a fallback point. It had been quite a while since their separation, but she thought that the location would perhaps lead them to at least a clue as to where they should start searching for her comrades.

The next few hours were unusually quiet, even for Jadu, who usually always had something to converse about. Perhaps it was the foul mood that had settled over the group from the very start of the morning, but Nomad felt there was something else. Maybe it was the occasional shift in scents on the wind, or maybe it was the odd, chill wind that gusted by from time to time. Both were fleeting and barely perceptible, but off and disconcerting. Though no one spoke about it, they all were on edge.

"Look," Reza said as the three travelers crested a dune, breaking the morning-long silence for the group. "Gravine Ruins, our fallback point."

After the three took a moment to survey the ruins from a distance, Nomad commented, "It does not look occupied. Your friends do not appear to be here."

After moments more of silence, Nomad turned to see that Reza was lost in thought, seeming to stare past the ruins itself, perhaps trying to figure out her next move if her friends really weren't there.

The silence was too much for Jadu. He asked Reza, "What color did you say those lesions are now?"

Reza snorted in contempt, unloaded her weapons from the camel, and started down the slope towards the ruins, leaving the two behind.

"Blue? Green?" Jadu chirped after her, almost tumbling down the dune's slope. "Maybe a little of both with a dash of yellow? I bet that's probable from the coloring on your neck...."

Nomad tuned out Jadu's background chatter, like he assumed

Reza was doing, as something much more concerning occurred to them. The smell on the air had returned, and this time it was not drifting by. It was lingering and much more pronounced.

The smell, he could now tell, was some kind of corruption—something rotting perhaps—but it was mixed with something else. A strong preserving agent or something of the like. It worried Nomad. It was a smell he now recalled closely resembled the dark knight they had fought days ago. He started to jog to catch up to Reza, passing the camel's reins to Jadu as he passed him down the slope.

Catching up to Reza, he could tell she was on high alert as well, and the two moved briskly up to the ruins' crumbled shell of a perimeter watchtower and outer wall.

Reza took cover to assess the scene closer up while Nomad looked back to find that the camel was giving Jadu some issues, digging its heals in, refusing to move closer to the foul site. It was probably for the better since Jadu was still quite oblivious as to the escalated urgency of the situation.

Reza took a deep draw of the dry, sandy air, closing her eyes to help her focus exclusively on her sense of smell.

Reluctantly opening her eyes, she looked back at Nomad and whispered, "Same stink that the other knight had about him. Are you up for a fight? If there's even a chance my friends are here in danger, I need to investigate."

Nomad readily nodded in agreeance.

Reza turned and moved in past the outer walls with Nomad close behind her. They both now moved nimbly closer to the origin of the stench, closing in on the building that reeked most strongly of the embalmed deathly smell.

Sand on a cold, dry wind gusted over the steps that descended into a gaping maw of an entrance that led down to a subterranean room. A pungent malodor billowed out from the square-stone entrance of the large, lidless cellar. They could easily locate its source now.

Reza looked to Nomad briefly, readying her flail as Nomad gripped tight his curved sword. The two descended into the dark of the underground structure.

Resisting the urge to cover their mouths with cloth to fend off the overwhelming stench, they held their weapons up towards the enveloping darkness that was creeping in around them as they continued further down the stairway, which ended, delivering them into a large, but not very high, square room.

They could see multiple mounds on the sandstone floor. The scarce light made it difficult to see further into the room to make out exactly what the mounds were.

Looking to each other, Reza pointed to one of the mounds and led the way, closing the fifteen-foot distance to better inspect what it was they were surrounded by.

Bending down with Nomad standing at ready behind her, Reza poked the lump with the shaft of her flail as her eyes struggled to take in the dim scene.

A moan, derelict of emotion or thought, issued forth from what her eyes were finally deciphering to be a figure. Bone and sticky sinew shifted and slid apart as the body began to move and undulate, almost as if it were a grotesque puppet on strings, issuing another more forceful groan, sounding through mangled vocal cords emitting through multiple openings in the figure's throat and mouth.

Standing back up, and seeing enough to know that what they were standing before was no living thing, Reza loosed her flail's chain to let the spiked spheres dangle by her side.

Seeing Reza's intent, Nomad stepped back, giving Reza room as she arced her weapon high and then slammed it down into what was left of the figure's skull. The skull caved under the force of the blow and the body immediately went limp.

"Sarens have a natural talent—a sixth sense if you want to call it. Study a person or beast long enough and we can inherently know the heart or motives of an individual," Reza whispered. She paused before continuing, still considering the implications of what she was about to say.

"That thing…had no heart. Its motive was only to consume the light of others. I fear there's more of that down here—a lot more."

A sluggish slide to their left, then a woeful moan on their right, snapped both out of any thoughts they were engaged in. Nomad brought his sword to bear to the target on the right while Reza stood to face the movement to their left.

Realizing now that it wasn't just one or two things moving around in the darkness, but something closer to a dozen or more figures slowly standing and beginning to lurch towards them, Nomad whispered, "They hold the advantage in the dark. We should move to the stairs—"

Nomad cut his suggestion short as one of the figures lunged towards him. Reza snapped her flail around just in time to slam the rotted body on the shoulder, bringing it down to the ground.

Two figures made a move towards Reza. It was Nomad this time that stabbed over Reza's shoulder to impale an attacker's skull, while kicking the other in the chest, sending the walking corpse back a few steps, tripping, crumpling to the ground.

"I agree," Reza huffed, her voice briefly showing a tinge of worry.

The two only got a glimpse to see that the path to the stairs was already blocked by three more shambling bodies before they had to deal with another approaching figure.

Nomad withdrew to dislodge his sword from the skull of the dispatched attacker he had dealt with moments earlier while Reza brought around her flail, bashing the approaching body to the side, it managing to keep its footing this time.

With sword flinging gore to the ground as it came out of the attacker's head, Nomad now counted five figures walking towards them from the direction of the entrance with no idea of how many lurked in the shadows behind them. Then, a small figure came bounding down the steps.

Jadu, Nomad thought, but a shove a moment later by cold, spongy hands brought Nomad, and his sword, around to slice clean through the arms of the approaching corpse. Kneeing it down to the ground with no chance to prop itself up again, he brought his sword up through another groping figure's outstretched arms, and down through the thing's shoulder, dismembering it at the joint.

The whole room now sounded like a cacophony of damned wretches, and all Nomad could hear above the cries of the dead was Reza's relentless smashing flail hard at work to fend off the aggressors that now completely surrounded them both.

A deafening, orange-green explosion detonated between them and the entrance, laying not only Nomad and Reza prone, but also all the bodies that had amassed around them as well.

Holding his head with his free hand, attempting to stop the room from spinning and dipping, Nomad sat up and tried to look around to figure out what had just happened.

Knowing there was no time to linger, Nomad grabbed what he hoped to be Reza's arm and stood up, swaying horribly to the left once, twice, and a third time before finally being able to somewhat stable himself enough to get a good look at the direction he blurrily could tell light was coming from.

Stubbornly dragging Reza, he stepped, then jogged awkwardly towards the light at the entrance of the room, barely making it to the steps before smashing back to the ground, his head beginning to swirl terribly again.

After sitting back up, Nomad sat resting on the stairs, watching as Reza started to stir. He was in no condition to help her up, and all the two were able to do was lay there while their bodies worked through the waves of disorientation.

Even with the ringing in his ears, Nomad could hear the calls of the dead start up again, and he saw figures in the dark slowly rise up, approaching them.

As if a particular string of gravity pulled him to the left, he fell to the side, slamming hard onto the sandstone floor, immediately attempting to right himself, but failing to do anything other than flail against the ground.

Flame combusted and spattered, starting on the right side of the room, spreading to the center, and then to the left, enveloping the stalking figures that shambled towards him.

One small figure remained outside of the fire. It turned and walked up to him, lifting him upright, then Reza, and sat between the two, starting up a conversation in an excited tone.

"Got here not a moment too soon it looks like. What were those things? I've heard tales of the animated dead called *arisen*. I do believe that is what we just witnessed—fascinating!"

Nomad watched the deep-crimson fire now turn to a soft orange while listening to Jadu drone on about the arisen discovery as though the thought hadn't occurred to him that he and Reza were almost unconscious. This only added to the surreal moment Nomad was having while lying there, sickeningly dizzy in the dark room of an ancient ruins with burning arisen corpses all about them.

6
EXPANDING THE SENSES

Coming to, Nomad blurrily saw a fire in front of him. He stared into it for a moment while realizing that the ringing in his ears had greatly reduced. Taking in a sharp breath, he sat up and looked around.

"Ah, good! I have company again!" Jadu said from the other side of the fire pit.

They were outside in the center of a demolished building, some of the walls still reaching eight feet high around them. With no roof, he could see the cloudless night sky, the stars in their usual place.

"Reza—" Nomad started, but Jadu quickly followed up.

"She's resting. That explosion hit closer to her than you. It did a number on her. Her eardrums had burst from the concussion of the blast. I inspected and treated her. The perforation wasn't that bad, and her ears should recover in a week or so, though she'll be hard of hearing till then."

Seeing that Nomad was looking around again at their surroundings, Jadu added, "We should be safe tonight. I checked the underground chamber after the fire died down. Nothing but scorched carcasses down there—shame! I'd love to have studied one. I looked through the whole perimeter as well. No more arisen in the boundaries of the ruins."

Seeming a bit relieved, Nomad laid back down and closed his eyes, trying to not think about the pounding headache he had.

"What was that explosion, Jadu?" he said in an exasperated tone.

"Ah, yes. Interesting concoction that one is. A failed formula for a topical treatment for the tannerinth frog venom. Let's just say that patient didn't have much of a chance to get mad at me for not curing him. Well, to be fair, tannerinth frog venom is extremely deadly and he was good as dead anyways, but too bad about the explosion, though probably a better way to go than wasting away. One slip of the jar and he was no longer with us. Luckily I had left the room to get a cotton swab or I would have been whisked away as well!

"Anyways, yes. Terribly sorry about blowing you two over with that explosion. Extremely volatile that one is, mostly bark. All explosion with little flame. I would have chucked it further from you two but those arisen were all over the both of you; I wanted to make sure I hit them with it. I only had one, so I needed to make sure it worked, you see. I'll have to make sure I synthesize some more before we pack up camp. Might come in handy out in the hostile dunes it seems."

Jadu, seeing that Nomad had been rubbing his temples while he talked, added, "The headache from the blast is quite expected. Trauma so close to the brain usually results in feedback in the nerves. Here, drink some water and take this pill.

Nomad, seeing the large white pill in front of him, asked, "What is it made of?"

"It's just a composite of multiple herbs and minerals, bonded with some natural oils and fats. It's my own sedative to calm the nerves and also helps with headaches."

With the topical explosive balm fresh on his mind, Nomad bypassed the pill and took the waterskin. "Water will be just fine, thank you."

Taking a few swigs, the pain still quite intense, he patted Jadu on the shoulder and asked, "I could use something from my pouch on the camel, though. Would you mind retrieving a small, wooden cherry box for me?"

Jadu, happy to help, jumped up and started yammering on about how he hadn't seen cherry wood locally for quite some time while he dug through the camel's pouch that carried Nomad's gear. He found the box and returned to hand it to Nomad, then asked what the box contained.

"It is a—well, I do not know how to say it in your tongue. Where I am from it is called a *ko bako*. Here, let me show you."

Sliding the inner core of the box out, Nomad pulled out a small, sage-colored wad. Handing the wad for Jadu to inspect, Nomad said, "This is ko. You light the tip of it and let it slowly burn. Different ko treats different ailments. Some are physical, like this one. It does just what you said that pill does: relaxes the nerves and eases the mind. Some," he said while pulling out another red wad, "open the mind's eye—releases the spirit. Each is different, and each is either constructed by the user or inherited from ancestors. Recipes are always kept in the family, though. Methods are never shared; only the finished ko can be shared with others. To learn or steal another family's ko secret method brings a curse upon your family, and it is considered shameful to ask specifics about it."

Jadu, very enthralled by Nomad's culture, said, "Interesting! If I understand it correctly, we have similar substances in this and neighboring lands as well. We call it incense. This ko, could I try some? Is it something you inhale directly, or do you light it in the area to obtain these effects they're supposed to provide?"

"You can do either. Here. You can try this one," Nomad said, picking out a little wooden plate with a lump of lavender-colored material on it. "This is a mood balancer—aligning your mind, body, and spirit. This is a very old method passed down from fourteen generations of my family, the Kasaru clan. It has helped our people maintain a pleasant harmony with life and others for a long time now. I think you'll enjoy it."

Taking a burning twig from the campfire, Nomad first lit Jadu's ko, and then his own. Burning fast at first, then slowing to an incremental-moving ember, the lumps of ko began to burn downward, releasing multicolored smoke that rose to Nomad and Jadu's noses. Nomad deeply inhaled the sage-colored smoke with Jadu following suit.

Jadu's senses were immediately aware of multiple herbs and flora scents mixed with earthy hints of woods, oils, and components that were much harder to distinguish—bone perhaps, hide, fats…he wasn't sure. Whatever he had just inhaled completely opened up his olfactory, absorbing every minutia of scent that entered.

Taking another draw of the smoke again imbedded every particle of smell into his receptors, penetrating straight through to his mind, opening up a vast ocean of understanding he had happened upon here and there throughout his life, all coalescing into one great body of peace and attunement.

He opened his eyes to see the sky, a few backlit clouds floating past Phosen, the only moon visible in the night sky at the time, the stars all scattered like twinkling gems strung up in the firmament. Stars at some points were so dense that they formed a very dim heavenly glow, almost seeming like a pearlescent span, an incomprehensible, undeniable display of life in the great beyond. The vastness of the universe and the beauty of it all stretched out before him, overwhelming him.

He could feel a warm tear roll down his cheek. Looking down to the small wooden tray that held the ashes of the long-spent ko, he slowly looked over to Nomad, who wore an understanding smile and smiled back, gripping his forearm as he whispered, "Thank you."

Nomad nodded, headache not even a memory at that point, and lay back to soak in the warmth of the campfire, the night air as still as death.

7
THE ANCIENT CHAMBERS

"What happened?" Reza groaned, slowly sitting up. He looked around to find Nomad and Jadu enjoying a light breakfast.

"Ah, good. My dear Reza is awake," Jadu chirped, adding after a moment, "How are those lesions coming along?"

Reza held her head and moaned, "My head—why does everything sound muted?"

Jadu pulled the same white pill he had offered Nomad the night before out of his pack. He handed it and a tin cup halfway filled with herbal tea to Reza.

"The pill will help with the headache, and I can help with the hearing after breakfast. There's a liquid medicine I have that helps heal tissue faster that'll help with the burst eardrums. Here, enjoy the tea first, though. Take a moment to acclimate."

Taking the cup and eyeing the pill and Jadu suspiciously for a moment, she breathed sharply and put a hand to her forehead, trying to stop the pain. After snatching the pill and slapping it into her mouth, and taking a swig of the tea to help the pill go down, she pinched the bridge of her nose and sat back with eyes firmly shut, a clear grimace on her face.

Nomad slid a wooden plate with some spiced hashed potatoes on a stone slab next to Reza.

"You should eat a bit too when you're ready. You were out all afternoon and night. Good thing Jadu found us down there when he did, without his explosive concoctions—the dead would have overwhelmed us."

"Are there any left?" She groaned.

"He said he checked the grounds and found no evidence of more dead, and we had no troubles last night either. Just get as much rest as you need—we'll stay watch. We can camp here for another day till the headache subsides."

Not wanting to stay put simply due to her condition, but also not having a plan of where they should look for her group next, Reza let out a defeated sign and put a cloth over her head, blocking out the blinding morning sun.

After finishing up breakfast, Jadu and Nomad started to unpack some camping supplies and equipment from the camel, Nomad setting up the sunshade over Reza while Reza took bites of her potatoes every few minutes and finished off her tea. Jadu went to work at arranging his belongings, rummaging through container after container until he found the liquid he had been looking for.

Nomad watched Jadu administer a few drops of his medicine in each of Reza's ears, explaining to her that she'd be hard of hearing for a few days while the medicine did its work.

Looking up over the ruins and dunes, he went to retrieve his pack and told the two he was going to take a look around for a while and to call if they needed him.

He first walked the perimeter of the ruins and determined that he suspected the place to be more than a settlement—maybe a fort or military town since it wasn't large enough to be a city or keep. There was a number of hollowed-out watchtowers and structures along the outer wall. In the places that the wall still stood intact (which were only two twenty-foot-long sections) the wall stood ten feet high.

Weaving his way back in through the crumbling structures, he found three buildings that still stood—all others were crumbled and shells, the sandstone succumbing to years of the harsh desert winds.

The three standing structures were in poor condition, and there was nothing in their rooms anyways, so he proceeded to make his way back to the underground room Reza and he had encountered the arisen dead.

Standing before the mouth of the tunnel, Nomad took off his

pack and got out a small hand torch, doused it in some oil, then struck it alit with his flint and steel kit. Putting everything but the torch back in his pack, he started back down the stairs of the still, dark tunnel.

The stench that was there before had thankfully, for the most part, improved. There was still the slightest smell of lingering putridity, but the overwhelming scent now was burnt hide, meat, and bone, which he could handle with little issue.

The torch crackled, consuming the surface oil ferociously, slowly mellowing as its surface fuel began to diminish. Casting light on all four corners of the large, square room, Nomad stepped out into the center to get a good look at the destruction Jadu had unleashed.

Thirty bodies, or what was left of them, lay crumpled, completely burnt black to the bone. The heat for some had been so intense that even the bone had crumbled to powdered ash.

Had Jadu saved their lives? He stood there considering the odds, weighing favor, when a clank of armor at the top of the stairs turned his attention to the entrance.

Clanking all the way down until coming into view, Nomad confirmed that it was indeed Reza that approached. Standing at the foot of the stairs now, waiting for her eyes to adjust to the darkness, Reza slowly headed towards Nomad's torch.

He considered if he should voice his concerns with her being in pain and injured and still being down in a potentially dangerous place. Considering how strong-willed Reza was, though, experience cautioned him to keep silent on the issue, knowing that she would more than likely do as she wished.

"I wanted to inspect this underground structure further. Jadu said he glanced over it and found no threat, but…you know how attentive Jadu can selectively be."

Reza, who had seemed to have been studying Nomad's reaction to her arrival, replied, "Yes. I thought it best to double-check as well."

"Did you bring a torch?" Nomad asked, apparently a little too gently since Reza crooked her ear, indicating for Nomad to ask again louder, which he did, this time Reza answering that she hadn't.

"Come," Nomad said, beckoning her over. "We'll share mine."

After entering into the light of the torch, Reza wasted no time, suggesting they begin by searching the perimeter, the room being so expansive that even with the torchlight, they still couldn't discern the ends of the room.

Stepping around burnt corpses, the two leisurely made their way to the left wall. It was a good thirty paces, and the walls had been scorched from Jadu's chemical fire, making it hard to tell it was a wall and not just the darkness.

Putting a hand on the wall, Reza scratched a bit of soot and sand off, finding that the walls were chiseled sandstone, and said, "Follow the wall. See where it leads."

Another thirty paces marked the corner of the room. Turning and starting to walk down the far end of the room's wall soon brought them to an arched portal leading down a narrow tunnel.

Both looked down the dark stretch for a moment before turning to one another. Reza, putting a hand out for the torch, said, "I'd feel more comfortable in the front. My armor is a lot more inclusive than yours."

Nomad didn't like the idea of having the half-deaf one leading them into the darkness, but not wanting to actively defy her command-like request, he reluctantly gave her the torch. Reza turned and started down the one-person-width tunnel first with Nomad close behind her.

Not far in, a dropped ledge on the roof of the tunnel with an inscription on it led Reza to stop and inspect the tablet.

Nomad, looking at the foreign symbols, said, "I don't recognize that writing."

Reza, who had been studying the inscription, broke her silence and replied, "I barely can interpret it, and I've lived around this region for many years. It's some kind of old, local dialect. I believe it translates to, 'Our dead rest lightly here. Respect those that slumber within these halls.'"

"Are they speaking of the dead that attacked us back there?" Nomad questioned.

Reza, giving the inscription further thought, replied, "No. I believe the writing refers to what's ahead, not behind. That symbol," she said as she pointed to two crossed square marks with two wavy lines in them. "That, I think, stands for tomb or mausoleum. It might be that this tunnel leads to some sort of burial chambers."

"Burial chambers…. The best way to honor the dead is by leaving them be. Perhaps we should turn back," Nomad said, ready to return the way they had come.

"Hold on," Reza started, turning to eye Nomad. "The best way to honor the dead in this case would be to make sure nothing had desecrated their resting places. Who knows how long those monsters in the front room had lingered here."

A cold sweat broke out across Nomad's brow. Looking nervously back the way they came, Reza could tell something about gravesites and the subject of the hallowed dead bothered the man.

"Come, don't leave me lightless. Let's go in a little further to make sure that the dead rest in peace here."

With that said, Reza turned to start walking down the black corridor, relieved that it didn't take Nomad too long to start up after her to light her way.

It wasn't far before Reza noticed two portals to the left and right on either side of the hallway.

Quietly putting her hand around the hilt of her seax, Reza quickstepped into the room to the left with Nomad following suit.

Though the room was long, it was only twice as wide as the one-person-wide hallway, causing Nomad to almost crash into Reza as he entered, not expecting the tight squeeze.

Shelves of the remains of the long-ago deceased lined the wall. Much of what must have once been an orderly scene now only looked as if years of grave robbers and animals had picked through the shrines of anything but bone and tattered cloth—broken urns and fragments of clayware strewn across the floor and shelves.

"Ransacked catacombs," Reza said, inspecting the floor and shelves while she mumbled, "Which appear to have not been disturbed recently either. Simply by the amount of dust film in this room, I'd suspect we are the first ones in here in months, possibly years. Not so with the hallway, though. Excuse me."

Nomad moved back out into the hallway, giving Reza room to stoop down to inspect and compare the floor of the burial room and the hallway, the hallway appearing quite a bit cleaner than the burial room.

"You think someone has used the main hall recently?" Nomad asked, trying to reason through what Reza was thinking.

"Perhaps…," Reza replied, drawing the word out, "but there could be other explanations. The wind could have blown in from the open entrance and blown all the settled dust away down the main corridor. We'll have to investigate further for answers. We're not going to learn much from dust."

Poking her head into the adjacent burial room to the right, and finding nothing different from the room to the left, she ushered Nomad to lead the way down the tunnel until they reached another pair of adjacent portals.

After leaning into each of the rooms for a moment, he looked back and said, "Same as the other two rooms," then moved farther down the hall, which eventually opened up into a large room lined with four columns of pillars reaching from floor to ceiling, extending all the way down to the end of the chamber.

The torchlight reflected back off of multiple mirrors angled in different directions imbedded in the pillars, scattering light all around the room, lighting it up quite nicely.

Finding that some of the pillars held mounted, unlit torches, Nomad lit a few that appeared to be in more a condition to hold a flame for a while. The room now was well lit, and Nomad and Reza walked down to the end of the room, past seven rows of shimmering pillars, and approached the altar at the end of the path.

The two stood still in silence for a few moments admiring the ancient, elaborately carved sandstone altar that lay before them.

"I wonder," Reza whispered, barely audible above the gentle crackle of the old torches farther back in the room.

Blowing the grit and dust off of a stone tablet at the base of the altar revealed more of the same ancient language symbols, which Reza began translating.

"Tungéun Haukchék rests here, head of the Haukchék name, awaiting the breath of Dannon to restore life to him and his family who reside in these halls."

Finishing reading the stone, she added, "Well then, this must be a sarcophagus, not simply an altar. I'm surprised it hasn't been tampered with all these years, but then again, this dialect is an uncommon one other than for those that live around here, and most locals are more than superstitious to risk angering the dead, especially dead with renown status and power."

Nomad remained silent, and Reza turned to assess his demeanor. Turning around to look back the way they had come, his attention clearly not on the sarcophagus before them, Reza could tell Nomad was uncomfortable being in the tomb.

A bit disappointed in her company's lack of interest in such an interesting find, she was about to suggest they leave, for she saw nothing of actual help to solve why there had been a small horde of risen corpses in the front room. But then she noticed a small, dark shape through two of the pillars at the far-right end of the room. Nomad snapped back to attention as Reza got up and headed over to the dark object across the room.

Kneeling down, Reza picked up a dark scrap of cloth, noticing the ground around it had been freshly trodden upon by something hard and sharp. Two recent scrape marks had been lightly scarred into the soft, sandstone floor.

"Sabatons perhaps? Looks recent, don't you think?" Reza asked to a finally interested Nomad.

"Hmm. Yes. It does appear like it. The two marks are a pace apart. Seems their path points to the exit," Nomad responded.

"If that's where they were going, where were they coming from?" Reza questioned, trailing off as she followed the direction of the marks back to a dimly lit portion of the wall.

The whole length of the wall was not flat and smooth. Rough carvings, most in seemingly abstract shapes and designs with some representing human and animalistic figures, decorated the whole of it. The point on the wall where the tracks led to depicted a more elaborate scene than most of the other carvings and was enclosed in an arch. The scene was of two women, one older and one noticeably younger. They both wore veils covering their faces and there was a flying beast in the air above them looking down upon them.

"That's Dannon," Reza said, pointing to the beast in the air. "I've only seen him depicted in a few older records, but I do believe that's him. The Tarigannie people are quite secretive of their history to almost all outsiders. Being a saren, though, has its advantages among most races. That's how I know a bit of their more aged dialects and forgotten deities. I've had open access to some renowned libraries here in Tarigannie for a while now. Most people here now worship Gothganna. A sun goddess. Few even remember the old gods like Dannon—"

"Reza," Nomad cut in, "look here."

Nomad, crouched over and pointing to the floor at the crack of the wall, mumbled, "Heavy wear marks in the grooves at the base of the carving."

Reza, looking over the whole carved slab of wall again, noticed that it was slightly depressed from the rest of the wall, and there were two deeply carved pockets in the stone on either end of the slab.

"Perhaps this is more than just a nice wall carving," she said as she gripped the handhold in the slab, pulling sideways. With some effort, the large slab of wall began to slide, rolling on a narrow track of hard-stone cylinders.

Reza, slowly opening wide an entrance to some dark room, stepped back. The two looked in awe at the hidden room they had stumbled upon, imaginations going wild with theories of what could lie within.

The one with the torch, Nomad, stepped into the small shrine room first, shedding light that glinted and shone off of broken, golden pottery and tipped over braziers. Scattered coin and jewelry and different colored powders covered the floor and shelves, reflecting a golden hue back at them.

So claustrophobic and displaced were the contents of the room that Nomad didn't notice at first the free-standing skeleton to the left of him until its jaw hinged open and let out a multi-toned scream, immediately drawing the startled attention of Nomad and Reza.

It fell forward towards Nomad as if falling off of a frame. Instead of crumpling to the ground, however, it dipped and then lunged upward, its dark eye sockets remaining fixed on Nomad, claw-like hands reaching up to dig into Nomad's face.

Nomad was yanked back, Reza throwing him behind her like a ragdoll, quickly drawing her seax, holding it between her and the unsteady, but determined, animated skeleton.

"Shit—" was all Reza could blurt out, cursing her curiosity that had led them this deep into the tomb as the skeleton made another, more resolved lunge, this time at Reza.

Bringing her free hand around, she slammed the skeleton's skull with the back of her gauntlet, sending the shambling bones crashing back against the corner of the desecrated hidden room.

Nomad was up now, drawing his sword, when he heard a grinding sound far behind him. Four boney hands clenched around the edge of the sepulcher's stone slab, revealing another secret room on the far wall.

"Two more behind us!" Nomad shouted above the persistent echoing grind of the stone slab.

Just as the skeleton Reza had struck began to right itself, another, smaller, skeleton began to mindlessly walk out of the sepulcher's shadows, not yet seemingly interested in Reza and Nomad.

Seeing that the two skeletons were close to finishing opening the other secret portal, Nomad bent down and picked up a sizeable chunk of sandstone at the base of one of the crumbling pillars.

The two skeletons leapt out of the dark room, galloping headlong towards Nomad, their skeletal structure jostling violently, but their skulls remaining dead-locked on Nomad.

Nomad launched the rock at the lead skeleton's skull, the rock shattering into dust upon impact, the skeleton not even acknowledging the assault.

Gripping his curved sword, Nomad got into stance to receive the first assailant.

Reza brought up her seax to block a downward slam from the skeleton she had backhanded, but without her shield or flail, all she could do to stop the second swipe to her midsection was grab the skeleton's wrist, locking the two up in a bind, allowing the skeleton in dangerously close.

Aged, white, gnashing teeth nipped in towards Reza's face, clamping down on some of Reza's loose hair, ripping a small clump out as Reza pushed the skeleton away.

It recoiled fast and leapt back in, leaving Reza no time to present a strong defensive front. Reza held out her free hand to push at the skeleton's ribcage, successfully keeping the thing at bay for a moment, it jostling violently all over, trying to get around its impediment. But as Reza focused on her immediate threat, the smaller skeleton had oriented itself, seemingly finding its sinister charge, leaping into the fray, biting in repeatedly at Reza's unprotected neck and side of her head, smearing fresh blood all over the child-sized, vicious skull.

The sharp pain to her most vital region caused Reza to muster the speed and strength needed to forcibly throw both attackers a good distance away from her, both skeletons hitting the wall with enough force for their bones to hollowly clank and crack. Reza still stood, but was visibly shaking, feeling incredibly vulnerable with every second that went by without the full protection of her armor, shield, and her flail. Her seax was short, and on top of that, stabbing and slashing at bones wasn't going to prove very effective.

Two claws that came in at Nomad to choke the life out of him were lopped off with one sideways cut, spinning to follow through with another horizontal cut that landed hard along the spine between the attacker's skull and ribcage.

The skull spun twice in the air before coming down on the sandstone floor, the body toppling forward from its own momentum, sliding well past where Nomad stood, giving Nomad a clear view to his next attacker—a bony frame that stood a good two and a half heads over Nomad.

Wide shoulders and narrow hips. Nomad assumed the giant striding towards him was once a strapping man, intimidating most definitely in life, as well as in death.

Nomad's brief hesitation was enough for the giant to take advantage of. Swatting him aside, the large, bony hand easily sent Nomad flying two yards into a crumbling pillar, the impact sending dust and sand everywhere.

He attempted to recover quickly, but the giant was to him in a single stride, clenching its hand into a fist of bone, bringing it down hard on Nomad's back, sending him down to the ground again before he could even fully get back to his feet.

Feeling the second hit land hard, knowing he couldn't afford to be pinned by his colossal opponent, he kicked out as hard as he could, popping the giant's left leg out from under him, sending the skeleton down, it now struggling to steady its massive weight, leaving Nomad the chance to roll away and bound back to his feet.

The giant still stumbled, appearing slightly injured at the last scuffle and fumble. Seeing a line of attack in, Nomad stepped swiftly towards the skeleton, shuffling to the giant's left, then striking hard from the side with his sword.

The giant was swift enough to bring up an arm to block the incoming attack, but the blade shattered right through the two thick bones. Making a swift adjustment to his arc, Nomad swiveled and threw his blade back up to the skeleton's right, connecting with the giant's right elbow joint, coming through, leaving the giant holding out two broken arm stumps, reeling backwards, not even sure at that moment what had taken place in Nomad's last attack.

Stepping up, Nomad pressed forward, throwing all of his strength into a clean, horizontal cut, severing the giant's lower spine, the upper torso landing upright on the ground before him. He came back around with his blade, decapitating the giant with another horizontal cut. The dismembered giant toppled to the ground, its hollow skull landing on the sandstone floor with a clunk.

The child-sized skeleton, with face smeared red, let out an explosive scream, bellowing at Reza, the sound shaking her to her very core, tearing from her what was left of her morale.

A red trailing glow sparked to life in the eye sockets of the child skeleton as it let out another bellowing howl from beyond, arms violently shaking at its sides.

Reza could see both skeletons recoil, getting ready to pounce. Backpedaling before the two attackers could get the jump on her, she pivoted around the closest pillar, narrowly dodging the twin attack.

The skeletons split paths and Reza intercepted the adult skeleton coming around on the left side of the pillar, hacking as hard as she could at the flailing limbs of the skeleton.

The seax was short, and primarily a gouging weapon, but Reza was now swinging with enough frantic power to unhinge the skeleton's left arm, putting the creature at an extreme disadvantage.

Not seeming to care at all about its lost limb, the skeleton crashed into Reza, skull nipping desperately at Reza's face.

A jolt from behind caused Reza to drop her short sword, it clanging across the sandstone floor out of reach.

Small hands spastically searched for handholds as the small, blood-lusting skeleton skittered up Reza's back while the skeleton in front continued to jerk upwards, trying to get at her face.

Focusing on the maimed skeleton in front of her, ignoring the cruel bites the child skeleton was attempting to land on her neck through her long, platinum hair, Reza latched both hands on either side of the adult skeleton's skull and began to squeeze.

The thing at first simply continued to struggle to rake at her face, but after a few more moments of Reza pumping energy into the squeeze, the skull began to crack. The figure, realizing it was about to be crushed, began to writhe wildly, now pushing to get away from its captor.

The vise-like effort Reza was making came at a cost. The blood-frenzied skeleton on her back had mangled her hair and gotten through to flesh, and now it bit down hard, slicing out a chunk of Reza's neck, blood spraying it in its welcoming, evil visage. Boney craters that pocked its skull filled with blood and it let up momentarily to revel in the gory accomplishment.

Reza, spurred on by pain and understanding that her last wound gave her little time to take care of the two threats before she fell due to loss of blood, pressed with phantom strength that her body freely gave, crushing the skull between her hands all at once.

Immediately dropping the powdered remains of the now-lifeless skull, she reached back and gripped the face of the skull of the bloody skeleton and ripped the creature off of her back with one hand, her upper body muscle bursting with power as a last-ditch effort to end the wicked child. Its skull smashed into the crypt wall, cracking the skull enough to render the rest of the body limp.

Reza's body, seeing the immediate threat averted, instantly dropped its emergency energy ration, dropping her to her knees, trembling as she weakly sat with back against a pillar she was next to, just as Nomad came sprinting up, seeing Reza in dire condition.

No words were exchanged as Nomad quickly ripped cloth from his hem below his armor. Making a pad with the cloth, he moved Reza's hand, which had started to come up to staunch the blood spurting from her horribly mangled neck, placing it over the wound, applying pressure that made Reza jolt uncontrollably from the pain.

She began to shake unintentionally, her eyes rolling back in her head. Nomad was losing her.

He began to chant in a monotone, but firm, droning foreign tongue, his eyes penetrating past her surface features and looking further into her core.

Quickly the shaking turned to trembling, and her eyes began to descend, coming into focus.

Sluggishly coming back around, Reza began to raise a feeble hand, which Nomad grabbed, attempting to tell her to rest.

"No," she whispered, barely audible, even in the silence of the crypt. "Leave me be."

Nomad stopped his chanting, confused by her request, but released her and watched as she rested her unbelievably white hands, almost seeming like marble after so much lost blood, on her blood-soaked bandage.

Looking her swiftly fading body over, Nomad began to feel panicked—much more so than when he was fighting the restless dead.

Fighting was an activity he was at home in, no matter the enemy, but pending death was a foe that ever had him and his loved ones at its mercy. If the fates wanted her that day, they would have her, with or without his say.

There was nothing he could do at that point to save her; and, though their paths had just intertwined days before, he had had more human connection with Reza than he had with anyone in many, many years. Seeing her spirit's slow flight from her mortal frame was bringing back a panic he knew so well from when his wife died another lifetime ago.

"Reza—" Nomad began to tenderly whisper, but a tightening knot quickly was making it difficult to speak.

Just as he began to realize that Reza was likely not leaving that tomb alive that day, he began to notice a faint, milky glow start to surround Reza's hand over her wound. The glow continued to brighten into a pearlescent, soundless light, enveloping Reza and him in an aura of hopeful peace, instantly calming and abating his dread and trepidation.

The light held for a few seconds, and then receded, leaving them in the dim torchlight once more.

Exhausted, Reza's hand fell to the stone floor, the bandage falling with it.

Nomad's eyes went wide at seeing the flesh perfectly smooth and blemish-free where moments before it had been mangled and exposed.

Reza, though still dangerously pale, was awake and looking at Nomad, weakly smiling at his astonishment, letting out a humored grunt as Nomad fell over her, laughing and embracing her tightly.

Releasing her from his bear hug, Nomad sat back, resting on unreliably trembling arms. His overwhelming smile clearly spoke his relief that she had stepped back from death's gate.

"I would have tried to fight better if I had known you would have almost lost it over me nearly blacking out," Reza hoarsely said, trying to lighten the mood, seeing how deeply affected Nomad must have been at her mortal injury.

"Yes, you make sure to do that next time," Nomad chuckled, trying to relieve the emotionally mixed tension that still lingered with him.

"How are you still alive? What was that light?" he pressed.

Reza taxingly closed and opened her eyes and let out a sigh. Nomad closed his hands around hers, answering for her, "We can worry about that later. We should get you above ground—"

Nomad halted, noticing that Reza had gone stiff.

He looked over his shoulder at something that had caused her to widen her tired eyes. Looking behind him, he snatched his sword, facing a spectral outline of a girl, faintly glowing icy white.

She was holding a ring in her hand, which was barely discernable through her translucent fingers. Stretching it forward, she was about to open her hand to offer it to Reza when she disappeared as an angry fizzing sound popped and sputtered from the bloody skeleton's skull.

The skull fell forward, knocking off the ground, and rolled to a stop, black smoke issuing from a burned rune carved into the base of the skull.

The old silver ring bounced and rolled on the gritty sandstone floor and tinked against Reza's cuisse plate. Giving a curious look, Reza picked it up and inspected it. It looked as old as the tombs they were in, its silver sheen long lost to time, now coated with a bluish-gray film. Mounted on the top was a rounded diamond, gleaming in the dim light, seeming to defy the taint of age all other materials are subject to.

"We should get above ground. We have disturbed the dead enough this day," Nomad said, helping Reza to her feet, lifting her arm over his shoulder to aid her as they made their way back to the surface.

8
REUNION

The noonday sun bore down on the two, causing them to shield their eyes to the blinding desert sunlight. The two made their way back to camp a few blocks away from the open crypt, eyes still trying to adjust from being in the dark underground for so long.

Slogging into camp, Reza almost collapsed with Nomad barely holding her up, both squinting, trying to make sense of the scene of Jadu chatting with someone partially obstructed behind the remains of a stone wall.

Sliding his hand to his sword hilt, Nomad—with Reza—quietly stalked up behind Jadu, putting into clear view the camp's visitors.

Jadu conversed with a woman who was in her later years, her skin showing her vast experience mapped out through age lines and scars. Her hoary, fine hair hung down in a braid that trailed along her shoulder and then down her back. Her eyes were an intense grayish blue, which stood in striking contrast to her warm, creased smile and worn skin.

Surprising to Nomad was what she wore. Like Reza, she wore a mix between half and full plate, and on top of that, she wore it with ease, not seeming to be bothered by the weight of it.

Directly behind her, a man turned his hawk-like gaze to Nomad as soon as he and Reza shuffled into view. The man was adorned in an assortment of daggers, ranging from thin, long ones to thick, stout ones, latched in various fashion to his trim leather outfit. He was tall, with short, swept brown hair. The occasional deep scar littered his copper-tanned skin, but his face was smooth and handsome.

There was another man lying down sprawled out asleep on a blanket behind the dagger enthusiast. Huge plates of armor partially buried in the hot sand lay next to him. He was stripped down to light garments, exposing his massive physique.

Cords of muscles, toned even in rest, braided all along his silhouette. A huge greatsword lay sunk into the sand next to him, which Nomad guessed by the projection of the blade's taper to be close to over half the length of the man himself, who seemed to be well over six feet tall. He had a wide jawline and a tuff of crow-black hair above his forehead, but it was shorn everywhere else. Every slow resting breath he took raised his barrel-like chest many inches.

Reza patted Nomad on the shoulder and pointed to the group of three and quietly voiced, "These are my friends I told you about."

"Reza, you half-pint, where have you been?" the man excitedly shouted when his gaze turned from Nomad to Reza. Coming over to her side, he unloaded her from Nomad's shoulder to his.

"You don't look so good. Here, have a seat," he said, helping her to take a seat on a boulder by the put-out campfire, taking off her pieces of armor as she responded to him.

"Good to see you managed to survive without me to protect your back," Reza replied, smiling at him as he assisted her, adding, "and front and sides."

The older woman held a hand up and paused her conversation with Jadu, who continued to talk at her, and strolled up to Reza. She crouched down to cup Reza's face in her hands, the two smiling a wordless greeting between them.

Shifting to a relaxed stance, Reza noticed Nomad and said, "Ah, everyone, you've apparently met Jadu already. Well, this is Nomad, who I'm greatly indebted to. It's only been a few days that we've traveled together, but already he's saved my life multiple times."

Nomad bowed his head in greetings, the dagger man replying to the introduction with, "Taking care of this one ain't no small feat. Young and foolish she can be. Takes our whole attention to keep her out of trouble and alive."

Reza jabbed the man hard in the ribs, her elbow still having unforgiving steel armor strapped to it.

The man let out a yelp and mumbled, "Should have known to take off your vambraces first."

Ignoring the sibling-like rivalry between the two, the old woman walked over to Nomad and gave him a short embrace and said, "Jadu told us about your care for our Reza. That she is alive and praising you is testament to your strength and character. You have all of our heartfelt gratitude, Nomad. It's refreshing to know there are those in the world that still give to those in need unconditionally.

"My name is Bede. The loud one over there is Finian."

"Call me Fin," the man cut in with a flinty look. "Only Bede calls me Finian and gets away with it."

"Finian, don't interrupt, it's rude. Excuse him if you would, Nomad. His manners are still a work in progress. But that big lump over there," she said, stretching a hand out in the direction of the sleeping, muscly man, "he's Cavok. He might look intimidating, and believe me, he can be if you get on the wrong side of him, but he's really a humble, loyal man.

"If you need anything, we're at your service just as you were for Reza. We welcome your company."

Bowing slightly, Nomad managed a *thank you*.

Fin helped Reza to her feet, helping her to lay down in the shade of the half-tent to the side of the camp. Nomad had wanted to speak with Reza about the healing light she had produced in the crypts, but he knew she needed her rest now, and he also knew that she was in good company.

Bede, seeing his concern for Reza as he watched her gently lie down on the mat, spoke softly to him. "Poor girl seems exhausted. Speaking of that, I'd like to talk with you a bit on recent events if you don't mind."

Nomad, recognizing the prod for information, raised an eyebrow and turned to Bede, giving her his attention.

"Certainly. What would you like to talk about?" Nomad asked.

Bede was quick to ask a question in reply. "What's got both of you so winded? Reza looks as though she's ready to collapse, and it's not but midday."

Summarizing their eventful morning, Nomad explained, "These ruins have many lingering dangers to them. Against my advising, she insisted on investigating an old burial site. The spirits that resided there did not appreciate our presence. We were attacked and Reza barely made it through the encounter alive. She was mortally

51

wounded and was slipping away when…" Nomad paused, fumbling for words as he tried to describe what he truly did not understand. "I am not entirely sure what she did, but there was a bright, calming light, and then her wounds were gone, but her strength all but left after that."

Bede, showing open concern when Nomad had mentioned the almost tragic story, asked, "What became of the spirits that harmed Reza? Do we need to leave this site or are we safe where we are?"

Nomad was quick to answer her concerns, "As long as no one enters that burial hall, I believe we are safe here. Their lychgate warned us upon entering to not loiter," Nomad said, lowering his voice and looking over at Reza, who appeared already asleep.

Bede looked to Reza now too, lost in thought just as Nomad was. She whispered to Nomad, "She's an interesting creature, that girl. Will made of iron and fire. Seems she's had a rough few days since getting separated from us."

Bede turned and looked out over the endless dunes past the old town's borders and continued, "She's like a sister to them and a daughter to me. We've been together for a few years now, but the ties that bind our spirits and friendship make it feel like lifetimes."

Looking to Nomad, Bede asked, "Have you ever heard of a people called the saren?"

Nomad nodded, cleared his throat, and said, "Yes. Saren are exalted gifts from the gods to my people. They are more than respected. There is even one in my land that has a whole city devoted to her. Wherever they tread is considered sacred ground. Her crest shows her allegiance to the goddess Sareth. Only sarens themselves are allowed to wear that banner, and she does share the same features of the saren I've heard about in myths—hair like the finest white gold, features delicate, more fair and beautiful than any human could hope to be…."

Nomad had wandered off in thought as he spoke. Bede smiled and brought Nomad back to the conversation with, "In all the years I've known her, I've never discussed deeply her heritage. She, for whatever reason, doesn't like to talk about her people, and hardly ever brings it up, even with those she's close to.

"You are right, though, that she is a saren. Her people are said to have the blessing of an eternal life cycle. An exclusively female race, they age slower than humans, and when they do die, be it in battle or by old age, they come back to our realm in the form of a young girl, with the faintest of memories of their past lives. Some retain their past lives' memories more clearly than others.

"They are the handmaids and, some believe, literal offspring, of Sareth. We may die and depart from this realm, but they are destined to return to it through the ages."

Pausing for a moment, Bede met Nomad's eyes and said, "That healing light you said you witnessed, I've only seen her use it one other time. That's an inherent trait the saren are said to possess. A healing power that can bring life back to those who are well on their way to the other side. I myself am a healer. I grew up in monasteries learning the sacred practice of mending wounds through the holy powers of the God Elendium, whom I've pledged my whole life in service to. Even the powers granted to the highest line of priests don't amount to a portion of the healing touch of a saren. But their healing comes at a price, as we see," Bede said, pointing to Reza, collapsed and deep in slumber. "She's likely to be out the rest of the day and night. That's what happened last time she used her power…" Bede paused for a moment and tenderly added, "…to heal me."

"I see," Nomad whispered, looking down, considering it all.

"Oh, you're bleeding!" Bede said, eyes widening, pointing to a deep-red stain on Nomad's dark linen smock beneath his chain shirt.

"Ribs might be bruised, but nothing that I can't sleep off," Nomad said, holding a hand to the bloody spot, patting a bit too hard, causing him to wince in momentary pain.

Bede gave him a stern look for a moment, considering whether she should press the point with a person she had just met moments ago. Putting a hand on Nomad's back, she guided him over to a fallen sandstone slab, asking him to lay on it. Nomad obeyed, though hesitantly so, and started to lay on the slab.

"Lie your head on this cloth on the decline, please," Bede said, placing a bundle of fabric on the lower end of the rock while helping Nomad to adjust in the position she wanted him in on the slab.

Lifting up his chain shirt just enough to clear the area that was stained with blood, she carefully peeled back the blood-soaked cloth from Nomad's lower rib area, revealing a harsh scratch along his side and front.

"Hmm," Bede hummed. "The scratch isn't serious."

Opening a pouch to her side, she took out a clean, white fabric and a bottle of a clear liquid. She dabbed the cloth with the liquid and then touched it to the wound.

Nomad knew it was alcohol that she had placed on his open sore upon contact, and though his face didn't show his discomfort, his muscles tightening did.

Bede was quick, albeit gentle, about her work, wiping the blood from the skin and picking out fabric from his open wound.

After the wound was clean, Bede started to lightly press on the areas around the open wound, feeling, at first, the muscle and tissue. Once Nomad made no protest to that, she dug deeper to the bone, finding the ribs. This did cause Nomad to hold his breath. An action that Bede took note of.

Bede let up and cleaned her hands of blood and got another white fabric out along with a close-lidded saucer. She opened it and scooped out a bit of white, silky cream and gently applied it to Nomad's side. She then placed the cool, fine fabric over it, wrapping a few bandage rolls around his torso to keep the cloth in place over the wound.

"Medical cashmere that is. Laced with healing properties that'll mend that wound and even ease the soreness of the muscles beneath in no time," Bede said, cleaning up the used fabric and her supplies she had gotten out of her pouch, adding, "No broken ribs, thankfully. You should be all mended in a day or two."

Sitting up, tenderly trying to avoid using his bruised side muscles, Nomad kindly replied, "I appreciate your aid. You did not have to mend me. It is a great kindness I will not forget."

"Don't mention it," Bede said, hand raised. "It's *I* that owe *you* for being there for Reza when she needed help. Now come, let's go join the group before your talkative friend Jadu yaks Finian's ears off."

9
THE SOUL IN THE RING

The twin moons of the night sky bathed the desert dunes in a pale-blue shimmer. Reza, groggily coming to, lifted herself up on her elbows, looking out past the low-burning campfire and sleeping bodies to the silhouettes of the ruined buildings of the town.

Her mind slowly sorted through how she had gotten there, remembering the wicked bite of the small skeleton and her having to use her ancestral powers. Nomad had seen her use those powers she worked so hard to conceal. Having her heritage as public knowledge had never done her any favors in the past, and she began to think fixedly on how she was going to explain the occurrence off to him.

Lost in thought, laying back down, still feeling quite drained from the use of her power earlier, she became aware of a trinket she was fingering. She had completely forgotten about the ghostly little girl that they had seen before leaving the tomb and the ring that the girl had dropped before her. She had picked it up, not considering if that was a good or bad move at the time.

She held it up in the moonlight, appreciating the brilliant shimmer the cut diamond emitted as it refracted the moon and starlight in all directions.

Inspecting the delicate bluish-gray hoop of metal carefully, she thought she caught the hint of an engraving on the inside of the ring. Sitting up, she turned the ring's back end to the fire and clearly saw that there was writing on the ring's underside.

The symbols were written in the same ancient Tarigonniean runic dialects that she and Nomad had come across at the entrance of the tombs. Whispering, she began to read aloud, sounding out syllables as she went along.

"Sa-ahlorn tulleip—decant ethül-long." She let the cryptic words hang in the air for a moment, piecing the ancient language back together in her tongue. "Our love shall bind us—in this life, and the next."

A glow, at first only degrees lighter than what normally glimmered from the diamond on top, started to emit from the masterfully crafted clear stone. Glowing with unnatural brilliance now, Reza looked around at her sleeping comrades to see if anyone else had noticed her little growing light source, surprised and concerned with the magic she had unwittingly activated.

After the glow leveled out, no longer increasing in brightness, Reza turned the ring over in her fingers, staring deeply into the source of the light, the diamond. Almost mindlessly, she slipped the ring onto her right ring finger. It was a perfect fit.

Within a blink, Reza could tell something was different. Her vision seemed to have incorporated a new spectrum of sight. The ring's glow was now twice as bright. As she looked out into the relative dimness of the night, the light from the diamond seeped out through the ruins, lighting the derelict town with a spectral teal-white glow.

As Reza's gaze rose, she jumped when she noticed a translucent woman standing in the midst of their camp, staring fixedly at Reza.

Reza looked around the camp to find no one—even Fin, who was the lightest sleeper she knew—stirred from their slumber due to the incredible illumination that now filled the camp.

Reza stared wide-eyed at the ghostly figure dressed in a tight gown—sheer, flowing robes, with metal cuffs adorning revealing areas of her body. The ghostly figure started walking towards her, smiling, speaking a sentence in ancient Tarigonniean, which Reza translated instantly with unusual ease.

"I thank you for freeing my family from the curse placed upon us."

The figure knelt down and embraced a still frozen Reza, not yet sure if she should attack the specter, call out to her comrades, or hear her out before making a judgment.

The touch of the spectral figure came first as a chill, her skin rippling in waves of goosebumps. It wasn't a physical touch; it was more like a light pressure of an unseen force that penetrated through the skin, making contact with something deeper. Though the feeling was very strange, it wasn't exactly unpleasant. She felt surprisingly calm—more curious now as to the figure's purpose and motives than threatened by them.

The figure sat back and looked warmly at Reza, the two studying the features of the other. Reza now noticed hues of colors through the vibrant phosphorescent glow that surrounded her.

Her gown seemed white, and the jewelry and metal adorning bands clasped around her arms, wrists, and legs were engraved gold. Her hair was dark and finely braided with bangs cut in straight, perfect lines. She had an elegantly long face and nose, and her complexion was flawless, with heavy eyeliner along the slits of the eyes. Her skin tone seemed not light, but not overly dark either. Her lips were full and her eyebrows were well outlined. Taking in her presence, Reza thought that perhaps she was the most exotically beautiful woman she had ever seen.

Reza looked over to her sleeping comrades once more and then whispered to the specter two feet before her, speaking in unusually fluent ancient Tarigonniean, the ring somehow enhancing her understanding of the dead language. "You—are you a spirit?"

The spirit nodded and replied also in tongue, "Yes. One that you recently partially set free, along with my children—my two sons and my precious daughter."

Wondering if the spirit spoke of the skeletons that she and Nomad had fought and destroyed in the tombs, Reza asked, "Was that apparition that gave me this ring your daughter, or was that small skeleton I—" Reza hesitated, looking for a way to respectfully ask the difficult question. "I defended myself against, your daughter?"

Thankfully for Reza, the spirit didn't seem offended by the question in the least, and the spirit's answer was in the same, appreciative voice.

"They were both my little one. My family's remains, save for my husband, were recently hexed by a powerful and dark cleric, giving a remnant of life back to those bones we once inhabited. He used us as his playthings while he stayed here performing duties that we didn't have the mind to decipher. His hex gave us just enough life to follow commands, but not enough to function of our own free will. You saw my daughter's animated remains, but you also saw her spirit manifest one last time before the hex was broken, departing her spirit from this realm for good.

"I remain not due to the hex, but due to this ring, which my husband had imbued with a portion of my soul upon my sacrificial death. Unlike my children, hex or no hex, a part of me will remain upon this earth, awaiting my husband's return, as long as the enchantment on this ring holds and this ring exists."

Reza, almost hypnotized by the woman's ice-blue irises, gazed into her eyes without looking away, reflecting over the spirit's story.

"So, when my comrade and I destroyed your family's remains, that broke the hex for your family, but what *this* contains—" Reza said, holding up the hand the ring was on, "is a different kind of magic. A magic that chained part of your soul to this ring long ago. Do I understand all of this correctly?"

The woman again nodded and responded, "Yes. Many of the pharaohs employed the skills of death priests to ensnare their wife's soul in their prime to anchor their most choice wife to this realm so that upon their return, after our God, Dannon, restores them to this realm, they would have their choice wife there with him to begin ruling over his domain again."

Breaking away from the woman's entrancing, unblinking gaze, Reza looked back into the ring's light and asked, "So, this dark cleric. How recent did he visit your family's tomb, and what other things did he do while here besides hex your family? Do you know anything of his motives?"

For the first time, the spirit's countenance seemed to turn slightly sorrowful, and the woman answered in a somewhat reduced tone.

"Our weak spirit link to this realm was tentative and easily dominated by his twisted will during the hex, and looking back through those fragmented memories is like looking through a mist. Of what little I remember—and even then it feels like memories of another—but what I remember is a great army of the dead. There were many foul and mutated constructs. Creatures either altered so horribly that they did not resemble any living thing, or creatures, like my family, that had been brought out of a sleep that was meant to be permanent.

"He did horrible things to the living he brought into our tomb, and even the dead—" The woman paused, reflecting on the horrible acts of the one she spoke of, or composing herself, Reza didn't know

58

which, but she continued to finish her story.

"I resisted his perverse ways once when he attacked me and my daughter. Perhaps the proximity to the ring you now wear aided to bolster my spirit to unexpected levels of sentience, but that scared him enough to leave our resting place. He has not returned for some time now. How long, I cannot be sure."

Reza could see in the woman's eyes a suppressed pain and hopelessness. She wanted to help her in some way, but didn't see how she could currently.

"Do you know anything else about this cleric? Where he came from or his name?" Reza whispered as gently as she could.

The specter for the first time looked away, visibly thinking hard on Reza's question.

"I recall him speaking of a taken city many times. A city that now belonged to the dead. He also spoke of a master of the master. I do not know what he referred to, but he talked of this master of the master more than once.

"I do remember the cleric's name, though," she said, voice now firm as she looked decisively back into Reza's eyes. A curl of disgust and a snarl sounded as she spat out the name.

"Lashik."

Holding onto her spite for a moment longer, she sighed and appeared to calm, closing her eyes momentarily before reverting back to her usual, haunting balance between a melancholy and sweetly appreciative demeanor.

"You have done my family a great service in releasing them from the taint of that hex. I cannot see," she said, slightly frustrated. "Are we near my family's burial tomb?"

Reza, slightly confused by the question, answered, "Yes. The tombs are not but a few hundred paces from here. What do you mean you can't see? You can see me, right?"

"You are all I can see. The wearer of this ring. Other than the faint auras of life forces around you and the occasional window into your perception, I am connected to this realm only through you. I am blind. No other soul can see or interact with me either. You are the only one that can visit this strange rift between realms."

Reza looked at her sleeping comrades, seeing that the bright light that had lit up the camp seemed to not affect them in the least, understanding why no one but she was startled when she had put on the ring.

The spirit began talking again.

"My name is Isis. I instructed my daughter to give you this ring, Reza. It was her final act before our great parting—" she said, this time clearly emotionally struggling to finish her statement.

Tender moments and topics were areas that Reza felt ill at home with, and she didn't know how to respond, but after considering her last statement, she asked, "How do you know my name? I haven't given it to you."

Placing a spectral hand on Reza's knee, Isis said, "There was a moment between the release of the hex's power and the transfer of my spirit catching hold of this ring's enchantment when you were upon your deathbed from my daughter's mortal attack. At that moment, I heard someone whisper your name as tenderly as I've ever heard a name spoken. As reverent as a loved one voicing a burial rite. That man that spoke your name, he cares greatly for you. Of that I know."

Reza turned away, not sure how she felt about the opinion or wanting to consider it at the moment. Seeing Reza's obvious awkwardness towards the subject, Isis shifted and stood up.

"I feel the age upon this enchantment is great. I don't know how much further I can stay with you, but I do hope you call me forth again. It has been many ages since I've been given a companion and have been given control of my own mind. I am glad the ring has fallen upon you, Reza."

Reza wanted to keep her there with her, to learn more about her or of the enemy they faced, but when she finally opened her mouth to speak, the specter began fading in with the phosphorescent mist that weaved in and out of the camp.

Isis now indiscernibly intermingled with the currents of spectral flow, Reza lay back, keeping the ring on, reflecting on the unexpected conversation she had with the ghost of a woman whose remains she had just crushed into powder earlier that day.

Thinking on Isis' story while watching the glowing mist weave in and around her, she whispered one word into the night sky.

"Lashik."

The mist seemed to whirl angrily at the mention of the dark cleric's name.

10

JADUGARMOK'S FINEST
SPIRITS

It had been a long day of rest, but with the fall of the starlit night, the camp was well lit. Raucous laughter and singing, especially from Fin, Cavok, and Jadu, resounded all through the empty shell of the ruins.

"To my new friend, Jadu! What tongue you have for fine spirits, little one!" Cavok bellowed, raising a chipped mug a little too enthusiastically high into the air.

Some of the liquor sloshed out of the mug, flinging next to the campfire, lighting the drizzling alcohol aflame in dramatic flashes of green, orange, and red, causing a renewed round of laughter from most present at the fireside.

Reza watched the folly in disapproval, seeing that even Bede, usually the most sensible one among her comrades, was more than just a little merry at this point.

"What is this stuff, Jadu?" Fin asked, badly slurring his words.

"Ah, yes. The contents of my intoxicant. That, unfortunately, is a closely guarded secret—one which I cannot divulge. You see, I made that mistake once, telling a colleague of mine the recipe. Soon I was out of a drinking buddy and colleague! He went and started a very successful bar showcasing my drink as his own! Never again. This little beauty's secret goes with me to the grave," he said between hiccups, leaning forward to kiss his beaker he had been drinking from.

The giggling died down for a moment, Reza just letting out a sigh of relief when Cavok let out a belch so powerful, that the bass of the proclamation vibrated through everyone around the campfire, with Reza quickly covering her still recuperating ears.

Fumes from Cavok's breath mixed with the heat of the fire, lighting aflame a trail leading back to the man's open mouth, exploded the air around the group momentarily, strong enough to blow Cavok off the boulder he sat on, landing him on his back in the sand. The rest were on the ground soon after, not from the flash, but from Cavok's antics.

Reza seemed to be the only one concerned for Cavok's well-being, but soon after the explosion had felled him, she could see a large hand reach out and grab Jadu, easily picking up the little figure, whose sleepy eyes opened wide as soon as he realized his feet weren't on the ground anymore, shouting, "I'm flying! By my chin, I'm flying!"

Holding the small man above him, placing a silencing finger to his mouth, shushing him, Reza could hear Cavok mumble in his deep voice that could be heard even over the continued roar of laughter from the others, "I like you. You're staying with us."

With his most important message declared, the large man released Jadu, who plopped down on his head in the sand, flipping upright to spray a mouth full of sand all over an audience who found the scene to be hilarious. All, that is, but for Reza.

Getting up, having had enough *entertainment* for the evening, she began to walk out of the firelight, thinking to stroll the ruins one last time before they packed camp on the morrow and headed out.

"Easterner, from what I've heard, you'd make a great addition to our group. What do you say about coming along with us, hmm? Reza can always use another pair of eyes watching out for her," Fin chuckled.

Though Reza didn't quite know if he was seriously extending an invite to their scouting party, or if it were the alcohol talking, she had had enough of the folly being had at the expense of their deadly serious mission.

"Who are you to offer him a position with us? Are you Sultan

Metus, who hired us for this job, Fin?"

Reza's harsh tone seemed to mostly go unnoticed, Fin answering in an overly dramatized regal voice, "Sultan Metus, I am not. King Fin—yes. With the powers vested in me, I remove the leadership of this daring adventuring group," he said while taking off an imaginary crown from Reza's head, placing it over Nomad's, "and turn over this task to—what was your name again?"

"Nomad," Nomad said, mildly humored, though trying to keep a straight face, aware of Reza's extreme dissatisfaction with the lightheartedness of the group, though having a very hard time due to the alcohol.

"Nomad! There we have it. Look how he fits right in. And just think, you would have been dead a few times over without having him around. So out of anyone, you should be the one begging him to come along with us. We'd be better served to have him with us! And that little one over there," Fin said, looking sideways at Jadu, whispering the last of his speech, "Well…he makes *very* good liquor."

"That he does!" Cavok agreed from his spot, which was still on the ground.

Reza looked around momentarily, noticing that only Nomad and Bede were making eye contact. Realizing that she was furious sobered the two up a bit.

"We're heading to Brigganden. A whole city rumored to have been sacked a year ago and occupied by an arisen army; which, due to recent events that we've witnessed, I would say has quite a bit of validity to. On top of that, Bede, Fin, Cavok, and I are being paid very handsomely by Sultan Metus, the sultan of the Plainstate himself, to infiltrate and scout out the city in the most hostile of conditions. Eight of the first ten scouting parties he sent out didn't return, and the two that did return came back gravely wounded with little of their sense intact. We're veterans. Elite Scouts if you've forgotten our official title. Seasoned experts in our trade. How could we responsibly allow two civilians we just met to join us in such a dangerous venture?" Reza fumed, stirring herself up even more the more she spoke.

The mood around the campsite had turned quickly. Fin, realizing fun wasn't going to be tolerated further in her presence, met Reza's glare once, stood up, took a jug of Jadu's moonshine, and walked off into the night, mumbling loud enough for Reza to hear.

"Ever the life of the party—eh, ol' girl?" then issued a command to an almost comatose Cavok, "C'mon, Cavok. You'll have no fun drinking that flagon here. There's a guard tower a hundred paces back calling our name."

The hulk of a man slowly got up, heeding his companion's call, marching off out of the camp's glow, Jadu perking up from his sand bed.

"Think they aim to deconstruct my brew? I'd better go watch them," Jadu slurred, weaving dizzily off after the two departing men.

"Reza, this is a subject that could have been brought up in the morning," Bede said, hand held over her eyes, either to express disappointment with the way Reza handled the situation and escalated the conversation, or to hold her dizzy head still.

"You should have distributed that bit of wisdom to Fin then. He's the one that brought adding new party members up," Reza snapped, turning her glare to Bede.

Bede sighed, contemplating her answer for a moment.

"I don't know if Fin was joking about inviting Nomad and Jadu along or if it was his way of seriously broaching the question, but to be honest, I had been thinking along similar lines. Perhaps the fates brought these two along our path for a reason.

"I set forth with you, Fin, and Cavok on this mission not for the pay, but because whatever it is that's within those city walls should not be allowed to fester. Getting Sultan Metus information of the threat he faces is essential for him to formulate a strategy of attack. Until he gets good intel, he feels it to be unwise to launch a military campaign against the city takeover. The more help we have to infiltrate Brigganden, the better, in my opinion. And Nomad has already shown he's more than capable of taking care of himself. He hasn't shown it to us—he's shown it to you, Reza."

Reza released her stare, looking off over the dunes, features hard, obviously frustrated with how the evening went.

Nomad, along with Bede, hadn't partaken nearly as much as the other three, but he had had enough to know to watch his words. He put a hand on Bede's, thanking her for her words, and sat up straight, knowing to stand would have put his credibility into question, and said as soberly as he could, trying to answer Reza's reservations with having him in the group.

"Though I felt the question of me joining your path lingering in the air today, no one has issued an invite to join your group on its mission until now, if all that could be considered an invitation. This is not my first language after all.

"If your concern is how you will pay me, I do not require

payment. And if your concern is how I can take care of myself—you saw firsthand that I can.

"Without promise of payment or knowing the fine details of your mission, my motives may concern you of why I would choose to join a group facing very steep odds.

"I hold this name for a reason. *Nomad*. It is what I have been for so long now. No one even knows my name anymore. I have been an outsider, with no ties to others for so long, I almost forget why I travel on at times. But I found something I once had in you and Jadu, and I am quickly finding in Bede and the others. A human connection. I forgot how reassuring it is to be with others that have your concern in mind—that do not look at you as just a passerby.

"I have my issues—my demons that follow me—but it seems you all understand demons. If I could travel with you good people for a time, even if it is just for this mission of yours—well, it would mean a great deal to me, and I promise to help you see your objective through to the best of my ability. I need to reconnect with someone, something, if only for a while."

Bede put an arm around Nomad and squeezed him tight. Nomad thought he saw Reza's lips twitch slightly, trying to assess how his response had affected her. Perhaps it was a trick of the flickering firelight, but he thought he saw moistness rim her eyes as she turned away from the two, mumbling, "We'll discuss this in the morning," as she stormed off.

Watching Reza walk out of the firelight, Bede waited a moment before turning back to Nomad, gently asking, "What's your real name?"

"Loved ones knew me as Hiro. My formal name is Kazuhiro Kasaru. The Kasaru family are one of the older houses in my homeland. Though we never extremely wealthy, my ancestors have had great influence and the occasional spotlight in my people's history. It is a family I could be no prouder of."

Bede smiled warmly and said, "It's a lovely name, Hiro."

Bede patted him on the back and then stood up to stretch, letting out a long yawn.

"Well, it's far past my bedtime. I had better turn in," she said, looking to see that Nomad had not looked away from the direction Reza had stormed off in.

"Don't you worry about Reza. I'll have a good chat with her tomorrow once everyone's head is a bit clearer. I talked to the boys and they seem enamored with you two, and I think Reza agrees, it'd be nice to have a man in the group that didn't always behave like a child for once," she said, chuckling a little at her own comment.

"We'd love to have you and Jadu in our company."

Bede met Nomad's eyes once more, then turned to head to her bedroll, leaving Nomad to reflect on the evening's light, and heavy, conversations.

11

LURKERS UNDER THE SAND

The next morning, the camp was quite still, most waking up well after sunrise, with the exception of Reza. Nomad had prepared a breakfast enough for the six of them with the last of the victuals he had in his stores.

Jadu's firewater had done a number on Fin and Jadu in particular, who, besides Cavok, had drank the most. Neither spoke much during the early part of the morning, which in Jadu's case was a noticeable oddity to the rest of the group.

Cavok, as soon as he was up, began packing his things for the road, helping Bede to clean up the rest of the site as if the amount of drinking the previous night hadn't even occurred.

By the time everyone had eaten and finished packing up, Reza was chomping at the bit to get the group moving away from the ruins as soon as possible, multiple times looking up to see the sun rising higher and higher, signaling their tardiness of getting on the trail again.

Strange to Nomad was the lack of talk regarding his and Jadu's joining the group. They hadn't reached a firm agreement last night with Reza, who Nomad understood to be the leader of the band. But with no resistance met when they finally shipped out of camp as all of them headed in the same direction over the first few dunes, leaving the ruins behind, he figured a silent agreement had been struck between her and the two new members of the traveling company.

"Brigganden is to our south, sixteen leagues from the ruins. It'll take a full day to cover half that distance. We'll camp tonight once the sun has set. No drinking—" Reza commanded. She paused to meet eyes with Fin, Jadu, and Cavok, then continued her briefing.

"Tomorrow, we'll finish covering the rest of the distance to bring Brigganden into sight. We'll need to remain on high alert tomorrow. No more campfires or lights. Though rumors speak of the threat we are to assess as being the arisen, we must not assume that to be the only threat we find present at Brigganden.

"We'll send Fin ahead to scout a safe path to the city gates. Once he returns with a clear route there for all of us, we'll make our way into the city and investigate. I have detailed maps of Brigganden which we'll all look over tonight to construct a detailed list of locations we'll want to work through and discuss our overall goals more clearly, but in general, we are to collect as much information about our enemy currently occupying Brigganden as we can."

"To observe the arisen go about their daily routine would be quite the scientific opportunity!" Jadu piped up, realizing, perhaps for the first time, what their broad mission's aim was to be.

"This is not a scientific field trip," Reza almost shouted back, which caused a silence in the marching company for a few moments until Jadu had another thought he felt he needed to voice.

"How are those lesions coming along, Reza? There were some on your lower regions when you were under my care that concerned me. Might be permanent disfiguration down there—never know. I'd very much like to update my notes—"

Jadu didn't get far in his inquiry as Reza halted, grabbed Jadu by the collar, and dragged him, his little legs doing their best to keep up with the almost frantic rate of pace Reza kept as she walked away from the group until they were over a dune out of everyone else's sight.

Besides Fin and Cavok's humored chuckles at the little man's audaciousness in the face of Reza, the group halted their march and worriedly waited, all muttering silent prayers for Jadu's safe return.

Reza marched along back up the dune, returning to the group looking just as she had left, very disgruntled. Worry spread through the ranks, being voiced aloud by Fin when he whispered a sincere, "Rest his soul. He was a dumb, smart, brave, little man—and we shall all miss his legendary drink."

Just as Fin finished his eulogy, Jadu came popping over the sand dune, writing fiercely in his leather-bound notebook, making his way back to the group.

Pleasantly confused, Fin slapped Jadu on the back once he was back to the group and said in a jesting tone, "Unscathed! But how?"

Jadu looked up from his notebook to see all eyes on him. Always excited to talk, given the platform, he lifted his finger up in the air and was about to speak when Reza turned around and gave him a glare that could have made any sentient being uneasy. Curling up his finger, he dove back into his notes and started writing again.

Attention turned to Reza, who now looked back at the group with an unconcerned look.

"Smartest thing I've heard him say," she said, turning around, leading the camel forward again.

"But I *didn't* say anything," Jadu piped in, looking up from his notes, skipping to catch up to the moving caravan, causing a facepalm from most in the group. Cavok, however, laughed and picked Jadu up, giving him a seat on his shoulder, the whole group picking up the pace once more along the endless dunes.

"Good spirits and good humor. I like this one," Cavok said, getting an agreeing smile from Fin and a disapproving, but humored, stern look from Bede.

The dunes were a rusty orange color as the sun hung low in the sky, still persistently beating upon the traveling group as they made their way over what must have been their hundredth dune that day.

Conversation had long since ceased, as the group silently made one final push to gain as much ground as they could before nightfall forced them to pitch camp.

It was Cavok who caused everyone to pause momentarily when he stood up straight, almost pitching Jadu off his shoulder, saying in a deadly serious, low tone, "Stench on the air."

Jadu and Nomad didn't know if Cavok was aiming to lighten the mood with an odd joke, but looking at the others who were just as pensive as he was, Nomad thought to put a reassuring hand over his sword hilt and scanned their area for any perceivable danger.

"There." Cavok pointed to a sinkhole in the dip of the next dune. Putting Jadu down on the ground, the large man sprinted over to the hole in the sand, slowing up as he neared the crest of the pit.

Reaching in, he scraped his fingers along the hole's roof and held up his hand that was now covered in black, greasy sludge.

"Waste worms," Cavok proclaimed. "They burrow under dunes and line their tunnels with slime to harden the sand to make large dens underground. This slime is fresh."

The group halted. They looked to one another, not sure of the next move they should make. They listened as Cavok wiped his hand of the sludge and continued.

"They often make their tunnels purposefully close to the surface of the sand so prey will fall in. As long as we don't tread on thin crust and fall in, we should be fine. They aren't much of a fight above ground," Cavok called out as he started making his way back to the group.

"Well how do we know if we're walking on thin crust?" Reza asked Cavok, who was being very deliberate to retrace his footsteps back the way he had come.

"We don't. Unload the camel and send it in front of us. Light some torches. They hate fire. Even the smell of it they'll avoid—unless they're starving. They've been known to surface for food if they're desperate enough," Cavok called out as he made it back to the top of the dunes the group had halted on.

"The sun is midway over the horizon. It'll be dark within a quarter-hour. Do we do as Cavok advises and send the camel ahead of us and travel into the night to get out of these waste worms' territory, or do we set camp in a valley and make sure to light a large campfire tonight?" Bede asked, holding a hand over her eyes as she assessed the sun's position.

Reza looked to the setting sun, large, expanding shadows already stretching across the dune beds below them, answering her own question before anyone else had the chance to reply.

"I don't like the idea of walking through the night with the chance of one of us falling into a worm's den. Let's set up camp in a trough and use the rest of the firewood we have. We won't be using it after tonight anyways."

With no objection offered to Reza's decision, Cavok swatted the camel forward, leading it down into the closest dune valley, finding a relatively level area to start pitching camp.

The camel still carried two large bundles of firewood, which Cavok unlashed and tossed over in a pile in the middle of the depression.

The bundle hit the dune floor, breaking through the surface of the sand, instantly opening up a widening sinkhole.

All but Cavok and the camel were still only halfway down the slope when the dune bed started to crumble, the hardened sandy crust breaking away in slates, falling into a large, dark pit.

Bede and Jadu started to rush down to Cavok, who stood pensively next to the camel when Nomad, Fin, and Reza grabbed and halted their rush to assist a stranded Cavok, who stood paces away from the lip of the pit.

"Hold!" Cavok commanded, looking up to make sure Bede and Jadu heeded his order, then looked back to the newly formed hole in the ground, which seemed to have ceased growing.

The camel pranced uneasily. Cavok looked at the beast with a threatening glare, grabbing the shaggy flank in an attempt to calm the beast. The gesture did the opposite, the rough grip of the burly man only causing the camel to start back-treading away from the newly formed hole.

Cavok turned and readied himself to leap back to the base of the dunes, but as he crouched, readying himself to spring to the others, the whole hollow ledge he and the camel were on collapsed, dropping them both into the blackness of the freshly opened cavern.

"Cavok!" Bede cried out as Reza leapt past the group towards the edge of the cavern's roof.

"Rope!" Reza called out, extending a hand to the gawking group.

"All our rope is on the camel," Fin hastily replied.

With that, Reza dropped her shield in the sand, turned, and jumped into the black mouth of the pit.

12

INTO THE WORM HOLE

The landing was rough since she couldn't see the floor until she impacted it. Hitting the ground, she managed a rough roll, throwing off a bit of her gathered momentum.

Standing up on uneven ground, slabs of ceiling causing her to almost topple, she squinted her eyes to look for Cavok through the settling fine sand that now lingered in the air.

The cavern she was in was large, but the dust and darkness made it difficult to see anything past a few paces in front of her. Looking up, she narrowly managed to dodge more falling crust followed by a flow of sand, which added more dust in the air, making it hard to even judge the height of the roof.

Pitching forward, tripping over another slab of crust, she landed hard on the sandstone floor. Pulling her head up, she started to crawl on her hands and knees, feeling her way until she grabbed on to something large and hairy.

Groping around, she felt what she knew to be the camel's assorted pouches and bags with their belongings.

She searched for the head but instead felt something wet and sharp. Bringing up her hand to her face, she saw that blood now heavily coated her hand.

Must have broken its neck in the fall, she thought, wiping her bloodied hand on the nape of the camel's thick coat.

In need of light badly, she fumbled around with the saddlebags that lay slumped over the camel's back. Unlatching the pouches that she could get to, she felt for the torches in the dark of the cavern.

Pausing a moment, a thought coming to her, she hurriedly slipped a hand in a side pouch on her carry sack strapped to her back. She pulled out Isis' ring and put it on.

The phosphorescent teal mist instantly flowed from the ring, penetrating through the dust cloud, expanding out through the tunneled-out room, outlining the walls and flowing deep into numerous tunnels that entered into the cavity she was now in.

Looking down to the pack, she began the search anew, this time looking for rope. Flipping open a pouch, she grabbed the coil of rope that had a grappling hook attached to it. Holding it up, she started to scan the room again to look for Cavok.

She spotted him on the far side of the cavern, standing with sword out in front of him. It appeared as though he was facing a foe, but she saw no immediate threat.

The camel lifted high into the air, straps catching momentarily on her armor, sending her rolling backwards. She turned to see the camel lifted in the air, bringing up her arm just in time to shield her face from a spray of gore as something crunched down into the midsection of the camel. The massive pressure of the maw that held the camel aloft sent innards spraying forth from punctures in the camel's stomach, a red mist now hanging in the air as a moist stench blew over her.

With the camel rent in two, the hindquarters were drug off, leaving Reza reeling backwards, away from the bloodbath in the dark.

Flinging entrails from her armor, standing up, she spotted Cavok again, this time making a sprint to him, knowing that if whatever so effortlessly severed the camel were to face him, even Cavok would stand little chance of defending against such a creature.

A bill, shovel-like and as large as Cavok himself, came out of the tunnel he stood in front of. The head of the worm writhed out in front of him, rearing up in the same fashion as that of a snake about to strike at its prey.

Cavok looked poised, ready to defend or dodge the attack, but out of a side tunnel came another worm head that Cavok didn't see. It slithered along the ground, making its way to its unwitting prey.

Reza pulled out her seax mid-sprint, leaping a dozen paces in a single bound, coming down hard on the worm, blade sinking as deeply as it could.

The worm's death throes were instant, and Reza barely got her blade out in time before being launched off right into Cavok, sending them both crashing to the ground just as the reared worm that had been studying him came crashing down where he had just been standing.

Seeing that Reza hadn't fully evaded the worm's lunge, Cavok kicked the side of the worm's head, shoving the massive cord of muscle over just enough for Reza to crawl up from being pinched under it.

Favoring her left leg, which had been pinned under the multi-ton worm, she immediately began to stumble back over to the opening of the cavern, unslinging her rope from around her shoulder. With a grunt, she tossed the coil up and over the roof of the cavern, onto the surface. Waiting for a moment to make sure the rope didn't tumble back into the hole, she turned to check on the worm and Cavok, realizing she had dropped her seax over by the two in the aftermath of the collision.

Cavok was hacking violently at the base of the worm's head with his massive greatsword, the worm frantically attempting to recoil back into its tunnel, rearing up one last time to try to maneuver itself backwards.

Cavok, with a final furious cleave, severed most of the core of the thick worm's neck, leaving the head to slough off to the cave's floor from its own dead weight. The body of the worm thrashed about, still attached to its limp head by a few flaps of skin and tissue.

Reza, seeing the ferocity of the bloodied man, heaving, eagerly looking for the next fight with only death in his eyes, hesitated for a moment.

A glint of steel shone to the right of Cavok. Charging over to recover her dropped blade, she snatched it up and looked back to the entrance to find more waste worms entering the cave from the tunnels to the rear of the room.

"Cavok, away from the walls. We take them as they come. Take care of the right flank," Reza ordered, unlatching her flail from the back of her belt, holding it in her right hand with her seax in her left.

The order appeared to sink in past Cavok's frenzied state of mind enough for him to give a nod of understanding Reza's way before turning, with sword feverously gripped in both hands, teeth grinding in anticipation of the upcoming slaughter.

As the dust finally settled enough for Reza, even without the aid of Isis' ring, to see clearly the horde of thirty-foot-long worms making their way to the two small trespassers, she noticed a silhouette above the rim of the cave's ceiling, tossing a bottle down into the midst of the worm horde.

An explosion, twice as potent as the one that had blasted her down in the crypt ruins, erupted in the center of the mass of squirming carapace. The thin cave roof shuttered and threatened to break apart atop them even as hunks of husk flew out from the epicenter of the blast, bits slamming into Reza, knocking her back, forcing her to shield herself from the shrapnel.

Before she could look back at the damage done to the worms, another explosion, no less as powerful as the first, ripped into the horde once more, downing the worms closest to the blast, the rest of the worms scattering, wriggling back into the tunnels they had just come out of in search for food.

A rope was tossed down over the ledge, the end of it landing on top of one of the half-blown-apart worm carcasses. Looking over, Reza thankfully saw that the blasts had snapped Cavok out of his crazed state. He latched his greatsword into its harness on his back, then jogged over to Reza's side.

"Too many in the shadows—we need to leave," he said, reaching to aid Reza, seeing that she now favored a leg. Reza waved his offer off with a held-up palm.

"You climb that rope out of here. I'll check to see if we can salvage anything from our camel. It was carrying a lot of our gear. Go. I'll meet you at the top."

Without hesitation, Cavok jogged off, leapt onto the worm carcass, and started climbing the rope out of the cave.

Reza, still with her illuminating ring on, headed over to the mess that was the tangle of dead worms. Tens of thousands of pounds of worm flesh littered the room, and after a minute of searching hopelessly for the half of the camel's body that hadn't been taken back into the tunnels to be consumed, she made her way to the rope.

Looking around from her vantage point atop the downed worm, she still could spot no camel half, but a sound echoing from the tunnels behind her caused her to turn around. She spotted the slithering mass of another worm working through the labyrinthine tunnel system that riddled the ground around them.

She knew her window to find what she looked for was over.

Taking off her ring, she slipped it back into her back pouch. Tugging on the rope to make sure whoever was holding it for her topside was ready for her weight, she began climbing up and over the crest of the cave roof.

A large arm grabbed her by the back of her armor and hefted her up and over the sandy rim. Cavok led her over to the bank of the sand dune and sat her down, taking a seat next to her himself, letting out a large breath.

Slick with worm blood covering every inch of her armor, Reza, after catching her breath a bit, could see the concerned look in everyone's expression, besides Cavok, who wore a large grin due to the victory and excitement of the worm encounter.

"Hope you enjoyed yourself. We just lost most of our gear," Reza said to Cavok, laying back on her bed of sand, closing her eyes to consider how they were going to get by without their supplies.

13

THE LITTLE FARMHOUSE

The night had been a long one for them all. Two in the group had stayed up on a rotating watch the whole night through, and the sound of the feasting of the worms on their own fallen kind did little to ease anyone's nerves.

Bede had attempted to get Reza not to take part in the night watch, but she had refused, busying herself with the task of assessing what was left of their inventory.

They had lost a great deal of gear with the camel's loss. All of the group's combined foodstuffs and most of their water had been lost. All of their bedding and tent canvasing was gone. Their cooking gear, tools, city maps, notes, most of their rope, candles, torches, and an assortment of odds and ends now probably all resided in the belly of a worm.

The rest of the group had woken up with the rise of the sun to find that Fin and Cavok had cleverly fished out a large chunk of worm meat from the feeding frenzy in the cave along with a bundle of wood. They had started a small campfire, cooking chunks of worm meat spread out all around the borders of the fire, placing the flesh atop overturned husk to keep the meat out of the sand since they had lost their roasting spit with the rest of their gear.

Breakfast had not been a pleasant experience. Not only was the worm meat beyond chewy, but Reza's foul mood from the previous day's events only worsened as she did her best to hide an injured knee while still covered in dried worm blood, which was now chafing her beneath her armor and matting her hair.

The hike that day was savage. Reza pushed their pace harder than little Jadu's legs could keep up with, Cavok having to shoulder the man as he had the previous day. Even with Bede trailing slightly behind, Reza insisted on keeping the trail without breaks.

Breaking camp early that morning and double-timing their journey landed them shortly after midday on the last of the large dunes before the desert flatlands that stretched out for a few miles, putting the dark city of Brigganden and its sprawling, rural shanty districts outside of the city gates into view.

The city was too far away to determine anything about the state of the place, but some of the shanty homes and croplands stretched out closer to them, and from what they could see from their vantage point, disheartened them.

Pastures were littered with numerous carcasses of all manner of livestock. A few fields and buildings had been scorched to the ground. Upon the long stretch of dry farmland that reached out to the horizon line of the vast plains that lay between Fort Wellspring and Brigganden's great city gates was a scene of rot and ruin.

Along the highway lay a grouping of bodies, a few horses mixed with a large number of humans, lying in the scorching sun, still and lifeless around four large wagons.

"A caravan. Perhaps that's our opportunity to resupply on some of our lost gear," Reza said while turning her waterskin upside down to confirm it was dry, an action she had subconsciously performed twice earlier that hour.

"We'll need water and food before the night comes on—"

Halting her thought, Fin held up a strip of rubbery worm jerky in front of her face. Shoving the detestable meat away from her, she continued with what she was saying.

"After we secure food and drink, we need to see about shelter. A good option may be one of those farmhouses or a hut in the inner shanties. There we can get some good rest and plan how we're going to infiltrate the city on the morrow."

"Do you want me to go alone to see what I can scavenge from the caravan?" Fin asked.

"It's far enough away from the city and close enough to us that I don't think we'd be risking too much just hitting it on our way to the farmlands," Reza replied, already starting down the last sand dune on her way to the caravan a mile into the open plains.

Reza increased their pace now that they were on flat, solid ground, and though the group was worn out from the light sleep they got the night before coupled with the torturous pace Reza had held them to that morning, seeing their destination helped keep complaints at bay as they hastily jogged the last mile to the caravan.

Wind blew in powerful, sporadic gusts, almost toppling Jadu off of Cavok's shoulder once or twice, forcing Cavok to put Jadu down to tough out the last stretch of their march on his own.

As they neared the open grave that was the slaughtered caravan, a lingering, rotting smell gusted their way; and though it was a noticeable smell, it was not overwhelming as it would have been if the slaughter had been more recent.

"Check the wagons for food or drink," Reza said, jumping into the closest one, leaving the other three to the rest of the group to inspect.

Nomad split off and headed for the far-right stagecoach as Jadu, Bede, Fin, and Cavok went for the other two wagons.

Opening the large coach door provided a view to the horror story written in crusted blood all over the interior of the coach.

A mummified leg slid and fell out on Nomad, causing him to back up slightly, hesitating a moment before hopping up on the step to get a better view of exactly what was in the coach.

Curtains over the window had been clawed at and the window frames on the other side of the coach were splintered and broken. It looked as though something, or someone, had gained entrance to the coach by brutal force.

Body parts were scattered across the upholstery, bloody trails and handprints decorating the seats, floor, and walls in horrid abundance. How many bodies did it take to so fully coat the space, Nomad didn't know, but the amount of blood spilled there seemed to suggest more than one.

Seeing nothing more than blood and parts of people, he jumped down off the coach and returned to Reza, who was throwing sacks of something out of the interior of her wagon.

"Nomad, take a bag of the flour and one of the rice. I'll carry the two bags of oats. Everything else in here looks spoiled."

Hefting the rice and flour, Nomad waited for Reza to jump out of the wagon with her oats before heading over to Bede and Jadu, who had just finished picking through the contents of their wagon.

"Flint and steel, a few blankets, a lantern, a few candles, some soap and clean rags, cutlery knives, and a crowbar. Nothing else is of value to us or is bloodied and ruined," Bede said, getting out of the wagon with all the gear they found, smiling as she helped Jadu down after her.

"Good. We can use that stuff. Let's go check on Fin and Cavok and then get out of here. I don't want to spend more time than we need to out in the open on the highway like this," Reza said, corralling everyone to the last wagon.

They came around the side of the wagon to find Fin counting strips of gold from a purse, cinching up the drawstrings, looking up to find Reza, who wore a disapproving look.

Seeing that looks weren't enough to deter Fin, Reza issued in a stern voice, "We don't steal from the dead."

Arching one eyebrow, holding up his newly acquired purse, Fin replied, "Then why are we here? Looks like you had a good haul. How is what you're doing any different than this?"

"We *need* food and supplies. Oats and rice isn't going to do them any good, but it'll save our lives," Reza shot back, wanting to say more, but stopping with that.

"Gold isn't going to do them any good either," Fin said, tucking the sack in his carrying bag, done with the conversation.

Reza's scowl was lost on Fin, who had moved on to help Cavok unload a few bottles the large man had handed out of the wagon's side.

Turning the bottles around so that he could see the labels on the front, Fin's face lit up.

"Ah, a Bolionnay and a Zandival. Now those are some sweet wines. Hopefully the heat hasn't spoiled them."

Cavok handed Fin one more bottle of clear liquid with no label. Fin uncorked it and took a sniff.

"Whoa! That's strong stuff, whatever it is. Maybe too strong to drink. You might could use this for treating wounds, Bede. Why don't you hold on to it?"

Jumping down out of the wagon, causing it to rock violently, Cavok held on his shoulder, where he usually held Jadu, a small cask with a brass spigot on the end of it and a cork on top.

Uncorking the cask, Cavok took a long draw of the aroma, letting the smell linger in his sinuses for a moment before casually proclaiming that it was old ale.

The discovery of alcohol had not improved Reza's scowl, but with both men ignoring the wicked glare she issued at them, knowing she didn't have time to argue the men's priority in resupplying, she turned and started heading for the nearest farmstead, mumbling over her shoulder, "We need to get off the highway. Keep an eye out for trouble and a farmhouse that will suit us."

The whole group packed up and headed off the road through fields of golden hay, eventually leading them into a cow pasture filled with cattle carcasses, skipping over to a country road with a few farmhouses along it, most in disrepair, either scorched or windows and doors being broken down.

"Look. That one might do," Fin said, pointing to a smaller farm cabin that didn't bear any damage to its facade.

"Let's check it out," Reza nodded, leading the group down the long path from the main road to the farmhouse tucked back behind a long row of tall, scraggly cypress bushes.

Coming up to the front steps, Reza pointed to Fin and Nomad and curved her hand around her fist.

Fin saw it as a visual cue he apparently was familiar with, instantly trotting around the side of the building. Nomad followed behind, figuring she was asking them to flank around back as they inspected the front.

Fin quickly swept around the side of the house, ducking below the side windows, slinking up to the back door. Nomad positioned himself quietly beside Fin, waiting for him as he checked the door handle, finding it to be locked.

A smile now on his face, Fin reached in one of the many pouches along his leather vest and pulled out a small looped chain of fine picks and curved, flat tools. Cycling through the chain, picking a thin flat-head wedge and a crooked, narrow spike, he inserted the two metal tools into the small lock above the handle.

Within seconds, a soft metallic click sounded and Fin pulled his tools out of the lock, swiftly putting them back in his pouch. Drawing a dagger from the back of his belt prompted Nomad to draw his curved-blade sword and the two entered as Fin swiftly opened the back door.

The back door had led them into a short hallway, with a doorway leading into an empty, well-kept bedroom to their left. Moving past the room after a short cursory glance, Fin crept past a closed door to their right and into what appeared to be the kitchen and sitting area just as Reza and the rest of the group came in the front door a room over in the living room.

Making eye contact with Reza, Fin held up his finger to his lips and went back to the closed door they had just passed.

Opening it, he looked down into the darkness and said, "A cellar. We'll need a light down there, but I doubt we need to keep quiet. They already know we're here by the footsteps on the floorboard if there is anyone down there, which I doubt there is."

Closing the door to the cellar, Fin pointed back down the short hallway leading to the back door, saying, "A bedroom back there. Place seems to be deserted."

"A small guest room over here," Cavok said, coming out of a room that led into the living room.

"Not the biggest place, but nice and quiet and out of the way. Who knows if we're going to find many other places not savaged by whatever mayhem ran through this land. This army that invaded Brigganden sure is thorough, if nothing else," Fin said, looking to Reza, who was already headed to the back door, looking out the windowpane, not seeming too interested in Fin's assessment.

Looking back to the group who waited in the living room, Fin turned back to Reza, who opened the door and said over her shoulder, "This'll do," and took off out of the house, running past the backyard into the corral.

The group looked on in confusion as Reza frantically went from horse trough to horse trough, finding one that was cleaner than the rest, jumping in, undoing her armor, and dunking her head all the way under.

"That's what she was looking for," Bede said with a smile. Remembering the soap and clean rags she had fished from the wrecked caravan, she pulled them out of her pack and headed over to Reza to hand them over.

"Look," Fin said, pointing out into the field, spotting a group of horses galloping up to the trough where Reza bathed.

Reza resurfaced just as the group of five horses came trotting up to the trough, all poking their overjoyed, long snouts at the wet mop of hair that protruded out of their water trough.

Jerking as far back as she could in the tight trough, Reza let out a hiss of surprise at the sudden sight of the large animals inches away from her face.

While Reza looked back at the gawkers in the farmhouse, Fin and Cavok laughing hysterically at the predicament, one of the horses took advantage of the distraction and champed at her hair as the other horses brayed mischievously at the deed.

She swatted the large snout away, ready to rush back to the house even though she was nude, much more concerned with the overly frisky nippiness of the horses than being exposed in front of her comrades.

"Shoo! Shoo, you naughty beasts!" Bede said, waving the group of horses momentarily off, giving Reza some space in her tub.

"Here, you poor thing. Take the soap and a washrag and clean up. I'll keep these jokers at bay—"

Bede cut off midsentence, looking back at Reza to find horrible red chafe marks all over Reza's body where the dried worm gore had worked her skin raw throughout the long day of travel.

"Oh, Reza, why didn't you let me know your filthy armor was chafing you so badly? I'll have to take a look at those sores once you're all washed up. You'll get infected if we don't tend to them properly."

"Bede—" Reza started to protest, but Bede shot her an uncompromising look that only a matron could give. Reza, realizing it pointless to protest the point, took the soap and began untangling the massive knots of dried blood from her hair and rubbing off the gore caked to her face and body.

Seeing that Bede had contained the horses and that the fun was over, Fin and Cavok went back inside, with Nomad and Jadu following out of respect for Reza's privacy.

Finding that the stove already held a large basin of water next to it, Fin exclaimed, "Looks like we'll be having cooked rice and oats tonight— maybe even some flatbread."

Jadu, quite famished with not having anything to eat since their worm meat breakfast that morning, suggested, "Why don't we start cooking the food now?"

Shaking his head to the suggestion, Fin answered, "Smoke is a lot easier to see during the day. We'd be giving away our location to anyone on duty even looking this direction from the city. We'll start cooking well after sunset. Here's some worm jerky, though. Go look for spare blankets so we can drape them over the windows tonight. Being the only home with lights on inside will point us out like a sore thumb."

Jadu caught the, what he believed to be, inedible worm jerky, and gave a long sigh at the prospect of being put to work on an empty stomach. Sulking off into the bedroom, the group could hear another heavy sigh as he opened chests and closets to find extra linen to drape over the windows.

Pulling out a candle and a striker, Fin lit the candle and opened the door that led down to the basement.

It took him a while, but Fin came back up to a resting Nomad and Cavok, who were laying across the two padded benches in the room to announce that there wasn't much in the basement that they could use, it being filled with mostly farm tools, animal hides, and other hunting gear.

"Well then, what's that?" Cavok asked, looking at the ceramic jug Fin had looped around one of his fingers.

Fin uncorked the jug and recoiled slightly.

"Lighter fluid is what we're going to use it as, I'm thinking. I doubt that's what the previous owner had it down there for, though."

Fin placed the jug down by the stove. Cavok picked it up directly after, taking a sniff and a swig, then placing it back on the stove, letting out, with a cough, "Yeah. Lighter fluid."

A mound of blankets atop a small praven's legs entered the main room, the rest of the men turning their attention to the silly little moving bundle of comforters. Dropping the pile of blankets, Jadu flopped onto the large mound, looking exhausted from the poor sleep and long morning they had.

Just as Jadu let out a sigh on his mountain of fabric, Bede hurriedly came in from the back door and snatched one of the blankets Jadu was laying on top of, toppling the little praven off the pile onto the ground

"Sorry, Jadu!" Bede apologized, rushing back out the door, leaving Jadu on his back on the floor like a flipped-over tortoise, not sure what had just happened.

Bede went to cover up Reza. Wrapping her up, Bede ushered Reza inside, assuring her as she eyed her gear that she would clean and dry her clothes for her once she was in and mended.

Taking a step up the back porch caused Reza to let out a low hiss of pain. Pausing a moment, she stepped up the second step to enter through the back door.

"What's the matter? Does the chafing hurt that badly?" Bede asked, looking down to the leg Reza was favoring while they headed down the hallway.

With Reza and Bede's entry into the little cabin, the men looked up to see their dripping-wet comrade, obliviously letting slip her barely covering blanket down past areas that made Nomad and Fin blush, Cavok smile wide, and Jadu look on in confusion as to why he had been flopped on the hard wooden floor.

"No, the chafing's nothing," Reza got out as Bede fell over herself to try and cover up Reza with the small blanket that was mostly wrapped around her.

"I was crushed by a worm last night during the battle. It might be more serious than I had thought. It's been getting worse all day."

Leading Reza into the master bedroom, to Cavok's disappointment, Bede shut the door and sat Reza on the bed, unpacking an assortment of medical supplies from the satchels she wore.

Gently handling Reza's leg, Bede lifted up the injured limb and slowly turned it from left to right, slightly rotating it until she saw Reza flinch.

"Does it hurt when I twist or turn it?" Bede asked.

Reza was silent for a few moments but then reluctantly admitted, "Both."

Resting her leg back against the bed again, Bede pulled out a talisman. Reza knew it to be the symbol of Bede's faith.

"Your knee is inflamed, and it seems deep bruising and perhaps even some fracturing is at the route of your pain. This isn't going to go away anytime soon. You might have pushed through it today, but your body is going to make you pay for that course of action tonight and tomorrow. You can't continue like this," Bede said, holding her talisman cupped in her hands.

"We can't stay here for days or weeks waiting for my knee to get better. I'll have to go on regardless of the pain," Reza said, stubbornly refusing the verdict Bede had given her.

"Settle down," Bede said in a motherly tone, holding Reza by the arms as Reza started to get up off the bed.

"Not only would you likely run your leg into infection and likely amputation, it's not necessary. I can heal the wound. Elendium has been close today. I feel a faith healing to be the answer to our dilemma if you would allow me to pray over the wound."

Reza knew more about Bede's god Elendium than any of the other deities besides her own goddess, Sareth. Often, the followers of Sareth and the high priests of the followers of Elendium worked together in various capacities, giving Reza and Bede a unique insight into each other's faiths. Though Reza wasn't overly fond of Elendium, Bede had high regard for Sareth.

Looking down, Reza mumbled loud enough for Bede to hear, "A

god that only heals when convenient for him does not seem like a god of compassion."

Bede shook her head and replied with a genuine smile, "Elendium has his timeline. True, Sareth allows access to her divine powers to her followers at all times, but in my experience, some things are better reserved and used sparingly. All the brighter is the answer to prayer when Elendium himself answers a call, deeming the follower, and cause, a worthy one."

Reza was about to reply, but decided not to get into debating over religion just then, knowing that though she disagreed of the disconnected and limited support Elendium gave to his followers, power was occasionally with his priests and priestesses. Bede had divinely healed her wounds in the past, and it was usually when Reza herself had been in better terms with Elendium.

Reza sighed and said, "Well, if he is with us today, then I welcome the aid. I will pray with you."

Bede smiled, seeing that the more agreeable side of Reza had given in and was now willing to ask for healing and health from her god.

Holding Reza's hands in hers, Bede clutched with Reza the talisman of Elendium, focusing on the holy figure, both meditating for a minute to clear their minds before beginning the prayer.

Bede parted her lips and began to utter a prayer.

"Elendium. Unworthy in many ways though we are, we come to thee in supplication, seeking both healing and safety on the road ahead.

"Reza, a dear daughter of Sareth, the high-queen Eleemosynary to our realm, is in need. Injured in battle, her injuries now require quick mending.

"There is a great evil very close to the place we now reside. An evil that we must not linger long near. An evil that must be driven hence without delay. For this reason we call upon thy divine powers of healing. Please mend both bone, blood, and sinew and recover Reza's body and spirit. Provide peace and clairvoyance to her that she may lead us along the holy path.

"Great is thy name and eternal is they throne in the heavens above. Amen."

With the prayer ended, Reza opened her eyes, inspecting her body, testing her still hurt leg.

"Do you think he wasn't listening to your prayer? My injury is still there," Reza said, as reverently as she could, seeing that Bede was still meditating with eyes closed.

Bede seemed not to hear Reza's question, remaining still for some time.

Reza rested her heavy hands on the bed. She wanted to lay back on it, being completely exhausted from the rough last leg of their journey, but refrained from doing so out of respect for Bede. Letting out a sigh, she looked down at her swollen knee. It had only gotten bigger and more painful since she had taken her tautly cinched armor off.

Though she herself had the capacity to mend wounds, she had not spent the necessary study and practice to master her natural skill of healing. She only used her talent in times of great need, and rarely on herself at that. She was now much regretting her choice to neglect that area of study during her stay at the Jeenyre monastery.

She was thinking of if she'd make good on her original intentions of pressing forward regardless of the wound, or stay and rest, when Bede raised her hand and uttered words that Reza was not familiar with.

A soothing feeling lightly touched down in the center of her chest and then spread outwards to the tips of her limbs. Her flesh and bone seemed to respond to the feeling, and she could see her abrasions were healing over right before her eyes.

Something in her knee began to shift and squeeze, and she could feel that under the pressure, her knee's inflamed state began to reduce, the pain slowly leaving.

After a pause of surprise, Reza whispered, "Wow, Bede. You've healed me by a prayer of faith before, but never like this. I think my leg and chafing are completely healed up. Seems like Elendium had both ears open to hear your prayer today."

Bede opened her eyes, looking to Reza, seeming to wake up from a lapse of consciousness. Her expression turned to one of jubilant surprise when she saw that Reza's injury, along with her bad chafing, had vanished.

"What's that light?" Reza asked, opening up Bede's hand that held her talisman to find that it now took on a pearlescent glow about it, lighting up half of the room.

"Oh my god!" Bede let out, seeing her lit talisman for the first time.

Breaking the silence, not sure what the omen meant, Reza shifted in her blanket and asked, "Bede, what's it mean? It's never done that before, right?"

"Never," Bede started, looking for words to form the next part of her sentence, slowly getting it out.

"And it shouldn't be shining now. But it is. This sign is reserved for a high position in my church, not a simple cleric like myself."

Now more interested than worried, Reza gently shook Bede's arm and asked, "Bede, what position in the church is this sign meant for, and what does it mean?"

Bede looked up to meet Reza's eyes and whispered an answer in disbelief.

"Only special followers of Elendium are gifted with his personal seal, the illuminating of a talisman. Very few ever attain this position even through a lifetime of service. That sign is reserved only for saints, the regional representatives of Elendium himself. To attain sainthood is to assure a place in Elendium's favor—forever."

14

DELIBERATIONS OF SAINTHOOD

Reza now understood the reason for Bede's incredulity. She knew enough about Bede's faith to know that saints were very high up in the faith's hierarchy. Though the cardinals oversaw most of the quotidian functions and operations of the church on a regional level, the saints were the church's stationary figures, being seen as regional representatives of Elendium, with only the high priests and prophet being above them in authority.

Bede and Reza sat there, their gaze fixed mesmerizingly to the small, circular talisman etched with symbols of stars, moon phases, and the sun.

"Word from a saint is to be taken as the direct word and will of Elendium himself. He chose me to be one of his select handmaidens in this realm," Bede whispered wistfully.

Reza seemed to mull over the information for a moment before breaking the silence.

"Is it often for lower-ranking clergy to be chosen and called to sainthood?"

"Not usually these days, no. In the past, it wasn't so uncommon, but these last two centuries, often there is a direct progression through the ranks without any skipping of positions. It seems more curated these days than those in the records. Rarely are women, and even more rare are field clerics like myself, to be called to such a position," Bede answered, stringing the chained talisman back over her neck.

"So Bede, what you're telling me is that in your church, you just became the leading authority over this region?" Reza asked.

"It appears so—but—I don't know. It would be unprecedented in the church today as far as I know," Bede said, obviously still confused herself with what the glowing symbol meant for her standing in the church, eyebrows raised, eyes still locked onto the glowing talisman.

Standing up, Reza took the blanket that was wrapped around her and started drying her hair with it, continuing to ask Bede questions as they came to her.

"What's the procedure for new saints? Do you need to report to your order immediately? How will this affect our current mission?"

Bede looked up from the talisman long enough to notice Reza still patting her hair dry with the small blanket.

Getting up, Bede remarked, "Oh, you poor thing. I was completely thinking of myself this whole time while you've been wet and naked. Here, I'll be right back with your clothes. With any luck, that dry desert heat will have already dried your undergarments."

Bede left the room and was back with Reza's sunbaked undergarments within a minute, handing Reza her clothes.

Putting them on, Reza asked the question to Bede again about when she would need to ship out to report to her order about the new spiritual development.

Bede answered without hesitation, having had time to think over the question while retrieving Reza's garb.

"If Elendium had not wanted me here to help in fulfilling this mission, he would not have called me to sainthood at this moment, asking me to forsake my friends the night before completing our objective. Let's carry out our mission as planned. Afterwards, I'll report to the council for guidance."

"Have you considered—" Reza started, pausing to consider if she wanted to finish her thought, "that perhaps this sign is your god warning you against this mission?"

Bede shook her head and answered, "No. I know you well

enough to know regardless of my leaving or warning against carrying through with this mission that you would still press on. Elendium would know your heart on the matter too. He wouldn't ask me to forsake you and the others.

"I think that what is more likely is that our mission is more vital than we think it is. Perhaps the evil within those walls—" Bede said, pointing in the direction of Brigganden, "may play into a larger scheme in the fight against evil. Maybe this is bigger than just a sacked city. Why else would he call me to such an honored position on the eve of us infiltrating the city of the unknown enemy?"

Reza sat on the bed next to Bede and sighed. "I don't know, but the timing doesn't set well with me. We'll have to be extra careful tomorrow. Who knows what we're going to find within the walls of that graveyard of a city."

Bede leaned shoulder to shoulder with Reza, looking blankly at a framed oil painting on the wall in front of them and agreed, saying, "I know. Hope those boys can keep out of trouble. Finian is sneaky enough and Hiro is wise enough for them to both keep well hidden and safe, but that big lug Cavok fancies himself invincible. And Jadu—" Bede laughed. "Well, that one's a piece of work. Clueless. *Smart*, but clueless when it comes to the big wide world."

Reza looked over to Bede and said in a questioning tone, "Hiro?"

"Oh, yes. Nomad's real name is Kazuhiro Kasa-something-or-other. He told me his loved ones back home call him Hiro," Bede replied.

"Hiro," Reza whispered, looking off at the same oil painting that Bede had been staring at for the past little bit, then added with a chuckle, "Bede, a saint."

Bede broke her stare at the painting and looked playfully at Reza, gently shoving her arm.

"Well don't act *too* surprised," Bede said in mock offense.

"As you command, your Saintliness," Reza replied whimsically with sweeping hand motions, a grin poorly concealed on both of their faces.

Part Two: City of the Dead

15

EYES IN THE DARK

Fin and Nomad slid across a sandy granite slab, landing on a cobblestone walkway. Pushing back against the granite wall, both held still as they huffed quietly, slightly out of breath.

"Think they saw us?" Fin asked, looking to Nomad.

Nomad slinked around the granite wall to the steps that led up to the raised archway they had been rushed across. He slowly poked his head up high enough to get a view of the watchtower that they had seen man-shaped figures moving around in. Finding that the movement had now settled, the figures appearing to be looking out over the farmland, Nomad let out a sigh.

Scooting back over to Fin, Nomad said in a quiet voice, "I don't think so. Seems they're looking out over the farmlands."

At the news, Fin let out a heavy breath and pushed off from the granite wall, with Nomad close behind, moving to the shadows of a side alley leading them closer to the city walls, which stood towering over them thirty feet tall, with the towers along the wall reaching another twenty feet above that.

The night before, Reza had briefed the group on the details of their mission and everyone's roles the following day. The first move of the plan was for Nomad and Fin to scout a trail and find a way for the group to enter the city. The task was proving more difficult than Fin had expected, finding shambling figures donned in armor posted at every main city gate leading into the city. They had looped back around and looked for smaller, concealed entrances with no luck so far.

Though it had been many years, Fin had visited Brigganden a few times in the past and had heard of underground passages from the outside of the wall leading in, and though he knew the tunnels were for military use, he didn't know much beyond the thin rumors he had gleaned fraternizing with off-duty military.

"If I recall, the military district inside the city is somewhere on the other side of this stretch of wall. Now we just need to find a portal or building that might house a tunnel that leads into the city," Fin whispered to Nomad as he brushed his hand up against the cool stone wall's base.

"So we are looking for a military building?" Nomad asked, looking off down the lane.

"Maybe—not sure. I don't even know for sure if the officer that told me of the secret entrance was telling the truth," Fin replied, turning to look at Nomad, who was pointing at a building down the street that stood only a story tall, but took up a quarter of the shanty street.

"Now that's a building a bit out of place. No slum shack owner has coin enough to own that much land, and no investor would care to invest so much into an estate out in the slums. Good catch," Fin said, moving past Nomad towards the building.

The building was of simple make, but as opposed to the surrounding adobe two-to-three-story shanty buildings, which seemed to tower above it, it was constructed of hewn sandstone.

Traveling along the side of the building, Fin and Nomad didn't notice any windows or side entrances along the perimeter. It seemed like a large block of stone rather than an inhabitable building save for the minimalist line designs that stretched along the walls and the rooftop canopies.

Tiptoeing along the front of the building, Fin quickly made his way to the front door, which was thick oak—iron strips reinforcing the planks with a latch and keyhole to the side.

Testing the door, pulling the latch, finding it locked, Fin pulled out his chain of lock-picking tools, quickly going through and testing different-sized wedges and picks in the lock.

Nomad turned his head, then looked down the street, hearing some faint commotion a few blocks away.

"Better hurry. Sounds like footsteps approaching," Nomad whispered, keeping an eye on the direction of the marching that continued to become more recognizable.

"Tough lock—and I don't say that often," Fin mumbled as he fidgeted with another pair of tools on the chain.

A loud metal click brought Nomad's attention back to the door with Fin swinging open the heavy door just wide enough for the two to slink in before shutting it behind them.

"They weren't around the corner when we entered, right?" Fin asked, to which Nomad shook his head.

That seemed to temporarily ease Fin's mind, but after a few moments, they began to hear the marching of a troop, perhaps ten or so pairs of boots, march up to the squat building, and thankfully for Nomad and Fin, continue past.

"Thank the gods," Fin sighed, standing up, turning his attention to the large, dark room.

Nomad followed suit, walking around with limited light coming in through vents in the ceiling that appeared to lead to the roof.

Seeing that Fin had already moved ahead down the hall, Nomad hurried to keep up, shielding his face from an unexpected burst of flame from a chemical striker Fin struck. Putting the flame to a candle, Fin led on past doorways opening to rooms with beds, tables, files, bookshelves, and other furnishings that were not even worth a second glance to Fin.

Stopping dead in his tracks, Fin held an arm out, stopping a bewildered Nomad, Fin's gaze locked on a glint dimly shining in one of the side rooms.

"I'd know that hue of metal even if I was born blind straight from the womb," Fin said in a reverent tone.

Moving into the room, Fin shone the candle's flame across a few strips of gold laying on a table behind a stack of parchment.

"How did you…" Nomad started to say, not sure how Fin had been able to perceive the small bits of gold amidst such clutter.

"Have you heard of that saying, 'You know when a loved one is near by the tug of the heart'?" Fin said with a mockingly tender look.

"No. I have not heard of this saying," Nomad admitted.

"Well," Fin murmured as he plucked up the five strips of gold, "you should get out more."

Reaching over the desk to get the last strip, Fin let out a stifled chuckle.

"Hellooo," he exclaimed, a wide smile etching across his face.

"What?"

"Have you heard of this other saying, 'Where there is a little gold, there is *always* more nearby'?" Fin asked as he stepped behind the desk and pulled open a cracked drawer, revealing three large gold bars with a few bags full of gold strips along the drawer walls.

Fin couldn't contain a giggle this time, and he was only humored more when he looked at Nomad's expression of surprise.

"Now *this* is what I signed up for," he said, hefting the large bar of gold in his hand, stuffing it into his carry sack.

Nomad didn't know what to say to the man who seemed beside himself with delight.

Two jangling coin pouches were tossed Nomad's way, which he snatched up reflexively. Fin had cleaned out the desk in no time and picked up the candle again from the table. He headed back out into the hallway, smile still comfortably on his face.

"I like going on reconnaissance with you, Nomad. For once I've got a partner as discreet and quick as me who doesn't turn down a bit o' gold when it's there for the taking," Fin said, taking a look back at Nomad, who still looked slightly confused with two sacks of gold in each hand.

Fin started back down the hallway, talking quietly over his shoulder to Nomad as they continued.

"Cavok would have had the whole enemy forces bearing down on us by now because of how loud he is, and Reza would have said something that don't make any sense, like *that belongs to someone else*, even if it's gold left behind in an abandoned city like this."

Fin had been casually inspecting opened doors as they passed rooms along the hallway, but halted once more, leading with the candle into a large side room.

The room was filled with all sorts of armaments lining the walls and mounted on shelves and frame mounts.

"Looks like a military armory," Fin said, picking up a dented, poorly constructed breastplate. "Only the military would keep such a mass quantity of shoddy equipment like this lying around."

"This is a good sign then. If we were looking for a military compound outside of the city walls, then this must be it," Nomad suggested.

"Yes," Fin said, placing the breastplate back on its stand. "Perhaps that rumored tunnel does exist. We'll see. Let's keep moving."

The hallway passed two more sets of doorways before coming to a stairway leading down into a basement with a few boxes and storage crates lining the room. The faintest light from the wavering candle did little to illuminate the mid-sized room, playing tricks amongst the clutter, casting shadows sporadically across the cold stone walls.

The path leading down another flight of stairs led them to an iron-barred gate, blocking their way to a long, dark tunnel.

"I do believe we have found what we were looking for. Better head back and let Reza know we've got our way into the city," Fin whispered, and it seemed to Nomad that his voice carried much farther down the long, dark tunnel than it naturally should have.

Fin was quick to sprint back up the stairs, having completed his objective, but Nomad was slow to follow.

As the dim light of the candle ascended the steps, Nomad kept his uneasy gaze hesitantly fixed on the deep tunnel that lay past the gates.

Just before the light was almost completely withdrawn, he thought he saw two moving glimmers in the dark a few paces past the bars.

Resting a hand on his sword hilt, he backed away from the gate, back-treading up the stairs.

Something was there—close and silent—at home and lurking in the pure darkness.

16
FACE OF THE ENEMY

"Bede, feeling alright my dear? I haven't known you for too long, but even I think you've been quite subdued this morning," Jadu said, breaking the, what was supposed to be, tactical silence Reza had ordered during their travel from the farmhouse to the military compound outside the city walls Fin and Nomad had discovered.

"Jadu. Quiet!" Reza whispered sternly, to which Jadu momentarily complied with, but even Reza noted a worrying look from Cavok at the comment, Jadu seeming to give voice to the large man's inner thoughts as well.

Reza, looking to Bede, could see the strain clearly on the mature woman's face, and she could only guess the cause of her unusual solemnity to be her previous day's divine calling that so far, only Bede and her had knowledge of.

The group kept moving in silence towards the wall.

"Cheer up! It's not every day that one gets to study the presumably walking deceased go about their daily routine! Exciting, isn't it!"

"Jadu, shut up!" Reza scolded through clenched teeth, lightly slapping him on the back of the head to drill her point into the little, oblivious praven's head.

Fin, at the head of the line, halted, holding up a hand of warning to everyone. With everyone's attention on Fin, he held up a finger over his lips momentarily, then pointed to a building's side door that was slightly ajar.

Nomad led the group into the door with Fin entering last, quietly closing the door behind them, motioning for everyone to get down or hide behind something once they were inside.

The building seemed to be an inn or apartment establishment, with the room they had entered being the main lobby. The windows of the lobby faced the streets, giving them a good view of the surrounding area.

Just as Reza was about to ask Fin what this was all about, the sound of a sloppily coordinated march began to come clearly discernable in the distance.

The marching came closer, and the group knew that the march was on their street and headed in their direction.

It wasn't long before the leader of the march came into view, followed by the leader's division, passing by on the street outside of the abandoned building Reza's group had hid in.

The sight was almost unbelievable, and everyone's mood, except Jadu, had shifted to grim, as they now realized the horribly twisted nature of the enemy they faced.

It was a parade of the dead. Male or female once in life could no longer be discerned as such due to all the dead now donning the same, leveling aspect of corruption. Flesh molting and sagging, tugging at the bone, stubbornly refused to completely decay.

The division of the walking dead seemed to follow the leader of the band, taking a lazy right at a street corner, turning out of sight, their unbelievably tired march slowly dying off, leaving the hidden group quiet and still, each processing the sight they had just taken in.

"It seems the preliminary reports were true. Our unknown enemy does appear to be an arisen force," Reza whispered. Everyone remained still in their hiding spots, listening to her talk, hesitant to respond even though the arisen troop was far out of sight now.

Standing up, Reza announced, "Alright, let's get back on the trail. Fin, how far till we reach the military building?"

"Just down the street. Here, I'll lead. Everyone keep close to the buildings closest to the city wall. There are guards posted above. Stay silent till we get in the building," Fin ordered, then led the group out of the broken building across the street, keeping within the buildings' shadows until they arrived at the garrison.

With the last of them in, and after closing the large door behind them, Nomad approached Reza and whispered something into her ear, the rest of the group waiting for Reza's commands.

"What did it look like?" Reza asked quietly back, garnering attention from everyone else in the room who stood awaiting orders.

Nomad replied openly, seeing that Fin was about to ask what it was they were discussing, "I did not get a good look at it, but I am sure there is something lurking beyond the gate down in the tunnel system we are about to enter. I suggest caution. And we will need light. It's pitch black down there."

"I didn't see anything down there. When did you spot it?" Fin asked as he came back to the group from across the room.

"You were halfway up the stairs when I noticed its eyes shimmer in the dark," Nomad replied.

"Why didn't you tell me about it?" Fin asked with his head tilted slightly.

"It was behind bars. It didn't pose a threat to us and I didn't know what it was. I bring it up now to advise everyone to be on guard since we will be traveling in that tunnel with it—be it a real threat, or harmless."

Reza stepped into the forming circle and stated, "We face unknown threats either way we go, but we know the other entrances to the city are much more public. This seems to be our best way in, so just have your weapons out and be on your toes. Those who have light sources, light them up now.

"Fin, you'll lead, followed by Nomad and myself. Bede and Jadu will follow behind. Cavok, you're rearguard. Everyone clear of their roles?"

With understanding nods from the group, Bede lit up her lantern, Fin lit a candle, Nomad lit his small torch, and Jadu dug from his robes a turquoise cylinder that shone a faint white glow.

Taking the lead again, Fin started them down the hallway, then down the stairs that led to the iron-barred gate.

Testing the gate, finding it locked, Fin placed his candle on the flat of the gate's horizontal support bar and pulled out his lock-pick chain.

Laying a finger on the rim of the keyhole, Fin inspected the small opening. Sliding two slender picks in, he felt the light tug and pull of the delicate device's inner parts, holding his breath to keep a steady hand as he manipulated it.

A few moments of fiddling with the lock and a mechanical click later, the door creaked ajar slightly.

"Too easy," Fin said with a smug expression on his face. He opened the door completely, revealing the long, black tunnel that stretched out before them.

A moment of hesitation swept through the group as they waited for Fin to move through the iron gate.

"Weapons out," he issued in a low voice, unsheathing a long, cross-hilted stiletto, moving past the bars of iron, silently retrieving his candle as he passed.

Leading with his candle, Fin slowly parted the veil of darkness at the mouth of the cave.

17
SERVANT OF ASH

Nomad put on his helmet and drew his curved sword as he followed Fin—Reza drawing her seax close behind. Bede unlooped a rounded mace as Jadu and Cavok took up the rear.

Thankfully, the tunnel was rather consistently shaped, which freed up the company's attention from worrying about knocking their heads on the cave ceiling and allowed them to focus their attention on the nooks and crannies along the cave walls.

Nomad nudged Fin and pointed at a small object hanging from a string a few paces ahead of them.

Moving up to the shriveled object, Fin plucked it from its noose, bringing it closer for inspection in the candle and torchlight.

Hair began to singe as Fin brought the little noose closer to the flame, causing the two to realize what they thought had been a ratty hempen string was actually a tangled line of hair that was wrapped around a chunk of skin and meat.

Flipping the giblet over, Fin dropped it as he and Nomad saw a half-ripped-off fingernail on the other side of the nub of flesh.

"Eesh. A fingertip strung up by hair," Fin murmured under his breath, loud enough for Reza to hear as she had come up to them to see what they had stopped in the middle of the cave to inspect.

"Let's not tarry," Reza said in a low voice, looking around for potential threats as she waited for Fin to start the slow, quiet march up again.

Only a few paces further down the tunnel, Fin and Nomad spotted two more hanging fingertips. Coming up to them, they could see a whole grouping of suspended fingertips beyond that.

Grabbing at the hair string of the closest one, Fin yanked it from the tunnel roof, dislodging it easily. The rest of the network of strung fingertips jerked his way, all being strung together with fine hairs that Fin hadn't seen before the tug. The chunks of meat and nails bobbed grotesquely up and down as he dropped the strand of hair Fin had in his hand.

"It's a web of hair," Fin said, disgust thick in his voice.

Nomad placed a hand across Fin's chest, pushing him back a step, and offered his torch to Reza, who took it readily. Sweeping his foot out, gripping his sword hilt with both hands, he quietly drew a wide stance. Nomad quickly brought his sword swathing across the network of hair, cutting down numerous fingertips with the action.

Continuing to arc his blade through the hair in front of him, Nomad carved a path through the web, leading the group further into the cave system with everyone following in a single-file line, surrounded by fingertips and hair on both sides of them.

Fin, looking down to the cave floor to attempt to not step on the crunchy bits of bone, nail, and dried flesh, abruptly bumped into Nomad, looking up to find that Nomad had stopped and was looking off to the side.

With one glance, Fin could see that Nomad was at full attention. Though he had not known the man for very long, Fin naturally trusted Nomad's acuity, and he brought up his stiletto just as he saw a small outline of a head, two small black eyes whisking in and out of the candlelight.

Knowing they had company that was well aware of them, Fin spoke clearly to the rest of the comrades behind him.

"That thing Nomad said he saw earlier in the dark—it's close by. Ready yourselves. It looked desperately hungry, whatever it is."

The march halted, each member of the group pointing their weapons into the mass of hair, flesh, and darkness that surrounded them, probing for their unseen stalker.

"Curse this darkness," Bede breathed, trying to hold high her lantern to allow for more illumination for the whole group.

Reza swayed her torch in a wide arc, sizzling the hairs that hung down from the ceiling, plopping countless fingertips to the floor in a sickening rhythm.

"More light? I could help with that," Jadu suddenly piped up, frantically digging through one of his many satchels that hung across his robes.

"Now's not the time for antics, Jadu," Reza replied, sweeping her torch to her other side to give her a large circle to stand in, clear of the mortifying web.

A few bottles began clinking together. Jadu was set on whatever task he had assigned himself to.

"Wait. Jadu—" Reza began, turning to glance at the little figure of robes and satchels, just then realizing that Jadu had vials of different colored liquids out, mixing substance with substance. If they were volatile substances the little praven played with, she had no way of knowing, but seeing how the last two times she had seen him with glass vials filled with unknown liquid, events had ended with a bang. She guessed the third time would be no different.

Rushing past Bede to get to the little alchemist, she was a hand's reach away when he dropped in a silver cube into a clear white liquid, igniting a chemical reaction before Reza could snatch it from him.

The tunnel, which now was shown to be twenty-five feet across, lit up in a brilliant, penetrating silver light. The vial shone down through the tunnel, weaving around the network of hair, digging into each little crack along the wide tunnel's walls.

A hellish shriek sounded up ahead of them, and while shielding their eyes from the intense light, they could make out a small, gray figure scurrying and tripping over itself, running into walls as it tried to escape Jadu's light

"Grab it!" Fin called to Nomad, holding his sword for him as the armored man put his visor's crimson eye guards down, helping to cut the unnatural brilliance of the light by many degrees.

Nomad rushed the creature. He knew that he would have to come in fast and hard. The thing was in a frenzy, and gently handling it was only going to result in his own injury.

Stepping up to the creature, Nomad slammed the side of its head with an open palm, disorienting the thing even more, adding to its hysteria. It writhed on the ground shrieking and swiping with its clawed hands, showing its tormented visage to Nomad.

It could almost pass for being praven, save for the sagging, unnatural features and ashy, drooping skin. The area around its eyes now glinted with blood and gashes, and Nomad could see it was adding more cuts to its eyes with its sharp, long claws as the light burst through to hit its face directly as Nomad stepped out of the way of the light.

It flipped back over on its front, trying to scuttle out of Nomad's presence.

Snapping out of his momentary awe, wondering if it was a living creature rather than an arisen, Nomad snapped an arm around its neck, locking his arm in a chokehold on the thing.

The creature raked violently at the assailant, and if it were not for Nomad's armor protecting him, the vicious claws might have cut him to the bone.

Squeezing the little creature's neck even tighter, muscles straining, Nomad shook the unbridled fight out of the little figure as it suddenly went limp in Nomad's grasp.

The fight had been violent and intense, but was over as quickly as it had started.

The rest of the group finished making their way through the tangle of hair, arriving by his side, looking over the strange creature that lay unconscious on the tunnel floor.

"This thing is living," Nomad said between breaths. He took his helmet off, strands of long hair clinging to his brow from the light perspiration he had worked up.

"Sure is," Fin agreed, looking uneasy at its mangled eyes. "Seems to not be the biggest fan of light either."

Jadu partially concealed his light vial and stepped forward, getting a better look at the figure that closely matched his size.

Jadu's features slackened in distraught, showing an expression very rarely assigned to his face. Bede mirrored the same horrified expression. They alone seemed to recognize the identity of the creature.

"Greyoldor," Jadu whispered in a voice that almost sounded like a chant.

"What is that, Jadu?" Reza asked in a worried tone, looking at the little praven.

Bede cleared her throat, answering for Jadu. "It's what becomes of a praven when given to the powers of one of the lords of hell: Telenthlanor—lord of ash."

The tunnel, strung with its macabre drapings, was silent, save for the crackle of torchlight.

18

BLESSING OF A SAINT

"Telenthlanor?" Fin said incredulously. "We're in big trouble if our enemy has one of the lords of hell backing them."

"This does not bode well for our mission," Reza agreed, still fixated on the small, ashen figure.

"Or…" Fin started, reasoning through an idea silently before continuing, "perhaps it does."

"How in the lower hells does this revelation work for us, Fin?" Reza shot back, audibly annoyed with the man she knew like a brother, knowing a shifty scheme was working its way through his mind.

Turning to discuss the matter with the whole group rather than just Reza, Fin replied, "Well, we've got what we came for, right? We've confirmed that the troops at least are arisen abominations, just as former unconfirmed accounts asserted. We've found ties to a specific sect—followers of Telenthlanor. The city is occupied and their forces are mobilized. Their motives are obviously hostile to anyone not of their twisted ilk. That's plenty to report back to Sultan Metus with. We would be presenting him with more information than any scouts before us—much more."

Reza was shaking her head, even before Fin had finished his argument.

"We don't know the enemy's number. We don't know who their leader is. We don't know if Telenthlanor is the only deity worshiped among our enemy. There could be an alliance we're not yet aware of. We don't know their intentions. Are they actually mobilized and ready to stage an attack? If so, where and in how many numbers? Where within the city are their strongholds? Where are their leaders stationed?

"I have many questions I would like answered. Perhaps we don't get to all of them, but we need more information than what we currently have. Sultan Metus would not appreciate a lazy report. He hired us for this mission because he knew he could count on us to be thorough, not to show up at the walls and then turn back."

Fin, looking a bit deflated, glanced hopefully at the rest of the group for their thoughts on the subject.

"I still haven't gotten to dissect one of those arisen subjects," Jadu offered, sounding a bit neglected, Fin staring the little praven down before Bede spoke up.

"I side with Reza. This morning, there's been a dread feeling come over me. This enemy we face, I feel, is part of a larger problem than perhaps anyone might believe to be. I sense…evil, very strongly in this city. We've seen hints at what wickedness resides here through the arisen army that passed us by and this servant of Telenthlanor, but I fear there are even bigger bugs under the floorboards of this city. We need a clearer picture of what's inside these walls. To deliver an incomplete report to the sultan may undersell the dire threat that may reside here, which may cause him to misstep in his future decisions regarding how he is going to go about sieging Brigganden, if he so decides to, which could result in the loss of many lives. To underestimate your foe is the greatest mistake a commander can make."

With everyone siding against him, Fin gave a defeated smirk, twirled his stiletto once before sheathing it, and said, "Indeed," leaving the conversation at that.

Nomad, slightly distracted with the group's conversation deciding their next move, snapped back to the greyoldor as it explosively came to, catching Nomad across the face with its surprisingly powerful arms, its claws digging in deep, hooking Nomad in the eye as it jumped up.

Nomad covered his face immediately, clutching his gouged,

bleeding eye socket as the greyoldor bolted away from the bright light that Jadu held.

"Do I follow?" Fin asked Reza hastily, seeing the shadowy figure darting around the tunnel corner, out of sight.

Nomad, lifting his hand away from his face for a moment, showed that his eye had been completely mutilated, which the others could see now, blood streaking down his face in a long, bone-deep laceration.

Nomad's scream of agony was enough to answer Fin's question. Reza quickly turned to Bede for consultation.

"What can you do for him?" she asked, Bede already bending down to inspect the wound.

Nomad had stilled somewhat, allowing Bede to confirm that the wound was as bad as it had originally appeared. The whole man's face had been laid open by the scratch, and his eye had either been gouged clean out or was so lacerated that it appeared only as a mangled ball of slick, bloody tissue.

A moan, agony mixed with sorrow, issued from the incapacitated man followed by a solemn silence amongst the group as they waited for Bede to act as Nomad tensed in pain.

Whispering something only audible to Nomad, Bede lifted up her glowing talisman out from behind her tabard, then, speaking in a tongue none in the group could understand, she began to commune with her god.

The light of the talisman grew, shining brighter and brighter until it overtook even Jadu's glowing vial, becoming so brilliant, the rest had to turn away, shielding their eyes to the light.

Bede held the light, looking down at Nomad, Nomad looking up at her, both not seeming to be affected by the blinding light that was between them.

Slowly, Bede, who seemed to be for a moment transformed into a being more heavenly than anything he had laid eyes upon in his life, came into focus in Nomad's vision, the pain and blood sifting away.

Reza and Jadu gasped, and Fin and Cavok stood staring, mouths agape, to find Nomad, whose eye and face had been destroyed a moment before the bright light, now appearing completely healed and intact.

"Interesting…" Jadu murmured, pulling out a small journal and pen to scribble something down.

Reza, eyes wide, knelt down to inspect Nomad's healed face, tracing with her fingers over the area that had been repaired.

"Bede, how—" Reza started, but then glanced at the glowing talisman, instantly being reminded of the revelatory night before between the two. She paused, finding her answer as to how she had healed Nomad's wound so completely.

Seeing that the rest of the group still stood in confusion, Bede smiled and answered, "It seems Elendium saw it vital for Hiro to have his vision for this mission."

"Hiro?" Jadu asked as Nomad started to stand back up.

"That's Nomad's real name," Reza answered, helping him to his feet.

"Hmph. You think you know a guy," Jadu said with a teasing smile, then added, "Well, I must say, quite an impressive display of divine healing, Bede. From what I've learned in my studies concerning gods, if a deity is willing to perform such a display of restoration on a person, that means that either the cause or the subject is of great importance to the said deity. So either this mission somehow is quite important to Elendium or Nomad himself holds some key purpose in Elendium's eyes. Interesting turn of events whatever the case. Glad I'm here to document it! A chronicler I am not, but for such a potentially important event, I wouldn't mind taking a few notes here and there to hand over to my colleagues in the proper department in my college."

"There's another reason such a miracle could be performed," Reza said, catching Jadu's attention, the praven very interested in hearing what other possibility he might have left out of his hypothesis.

"The servant that performed the healing could be in great standings with Elendium."

Jadu tapped a thoughtful finger to his jaw.

"Doubtful, but a possibility I suppose. No offense, Bede—but as I recall, generally speaking, Elendium is not a god known for a free use of his powers amongst most of his followers, but only to the most senior members of the faith. My conclusions are much more likely."

Reza, slightly annoyed at the blasé shrug of her answer, turned to see what the others thought, finding Fin still with his mouth gaped open.

Fin, looking at Bede, finally spoke. "Bede. Remember all those times I twisted ankles, pulled muscles, got bruised, cut up, broke bones, and you just put bandages and splints on me?"

"Yes," Bede answered, patting Nomad on his back as he picked up his helmet, tucking it under his arm.

"Well?" Fin pushed, seeing that she wasn't following where he was going with his claim.

Showing that she had gotten his hint, Bede answered, lightly patting Fin's cheek, "Well maybe next time you stub your toe, I'll hand the bandages to Cavok to nurse your wound. Sound good, dear?"

Bede's sly remark got a chuckle out of Cavok, who was standing behind Fin.

Stooping down to reach for a leg, Cavok asked in a motherly tone, "Which toe did you stub, dearie?"

Fin swatted him off vexingly, still confused as to the sudden miracle Bede had seemingly pulled out of nowhere.

Nomad reached an arm out to Bede's shoulder, causing her to turn around.

Meeting eyes, he said in a tone that most missed over the banter of Fin and Cavok, "Thank you, Bede. The healing you performed, and those words you spoke, I shall cherish till the day I die. I am in both you and your God's debt."

Bede returned Hiro's compliment with an understanding smile as Reza stepped forward, speaking to the group.

"That wretch that scuttled away may be off to alert someone of our presence. It'd be best if we kept moving now that Nomad is healed.

"Fin. Nomad. Would you mind getting us out of this hole?" she said, swatting away a hanging fingernail that swayed a little too close to her face for comfort.

"My pleasure," Fin agreed, slapping at a still chuckling Cavok for good measure.

As Nomad put his helmet back on and Fin unsheathed his stiletto once more, the two pressed the group onward through the network of hair and nails.

19

HEADQUARTERS AND DEPLOYMENTS

The mechanical click of the iron-barred gate echoed through the tunnel as Fin unlocked the path leading up a flight of chiseled sandstone stairs.

Fin slipped through the opened, creaky gate and held up a finger, signaling the group to wait where they were for a minute. Sneaking up the stairs without a sound, he disappeared from the rest of the group's sight, leaving them waiting there in the dank tunnel.

They had only been a hundred feet or so from the tunnel entrance when they had run into the greyoldor, and though it had scuttled off in the direction of the exit, the gate had been locked upon them arriving at it, leaving the group guessing as to how it had stayed out of detection as there didn't seem to be any other way along the tunnel system where it could have escaped.

Fin wasn't gone long before he strolled back down the stairs he had ascended moments ago.

"Leads up into some kind of officers' quarters—quite abandoned so it seems. I still advise discretion," Fin said, eyeing Cavok with his last statement, "but I see no immediate threat in the building above."

"Alright, let's move," Reza said, already slipping around the partially opened gate, moving to pass Fin.

Keeping her seax readied, Reza marched the group up the stairs, which led into a short hallway that opened up to a large corridor that was lined with officer chambers on either side.

Cautiously approaching one of the windows along the outer hallways at the end of the officers' corridor, Reza peeked out the thick, glass windowpane to find that they were on the second floor of a building that was one of many lining a large courtyard. Taking in their surroundings, she sat down, back against the wall, and ordered the rest of the group to get low and out of sight as well.

"Well, where are we and what's out there?" Bede whispered, asking the question everyone else was wondering.

Reza sheathed her seax and said, "The stairway let us out on the second floor of a building attached to a line of similar buildings. If they're all somehow connected internally, I'm not sure, so we'll need to be cautious in here.

"There's a large courtyard down there. Looks like some military or ruling class wing of the city.

"What's in the courtyard? I'm assuming you wouldn't have had us get out of sight if you hadn't seen anything down there," Fin asked, trying to push Reza to her point.

Reza eyed Fin for a moment and said, "I was getting to that, Fin. There are a few ranks of arisen down there—"

Fin jumped in, asking, "How many we talking?"

"Fin!" Reza whispered a little too harshly, taking a moment to recompose herself before continuing. "Stop interrupting. Let me finish my thoughts. There were two troops marching out of the courtyard—maybe twenty in each. There's some kind of opened, covered structure on the other side of the courtyard with two more divisions just standing there in file—forty tops in each division."

Fin now had his hand raised, trying very hard to look like a schoolboy waiting for his teacher to call on him to comment. Reza slapped Fin's hand down and huffed out an exasperated "What?"

"So what you're saying is, there's a hundred and twenty soldiers— give or take—right outside the window," Fin said in a mockingly calm voice.

"That's exactly what I'm saying," Reza responded, not appreciating Fin's mocking tone in the least. "Looked like they are also accompanied by some of those heavily armored dark knights me and Nomad fought back in the dunes. By the looks of their formation, those knights might hold rank over the grunts we saw patrolling the streets. If there's rank and order among this army, that means there's intelligence somewhere up the line that's organizing this army."

Seeing his sarcasm wasn't doing him any favors, Fin attempted to level with Reza.

"Reza, that is a force sizable enough, just in that courtyard alone, to merit us packing up and heading out. One misstep from any one of us and we'll have a whole city of arisen bearing down on us.

"We now know, as you said, there's order and leadership and that their numbers at the least number in the hundreds. Let's add that to the things we've already found out about this enemy and head back to the Plainstate before we get in over our heads. Need I remind you we already have an escaped prisoner who ran off to who knows where to alert leadership of our presence."

Reza, about to argue back with Fin, stopped herself and took a look around at the other group members, trying to assess if more seemed to share Fin's reservations about the mission.

"How does everyone feel about our mission at this point? I am very determined to get what we came for, but if the majority of the group should agree with Fin, that we shouldn't continue further, perhaps we could split the group if necessary."

No answer immediately came, and Cavok went from a kneeling position to laying down, resting in the back of the group, seeing that they might be there for a while.

"I'd love to stay—at least until we capture one of those arisen specimen. I've never been able to analyze this particular brand of dark magic up close and would very much like to do so," Jadu said, tapping his fingers together in an unconsciously scheming manner.

Not happy with Jadu's reasoning, but willing to take the vote to stay and continue with their intended mission, Reza nodded her head in acceptance of the vote.

"Nomad, what about you?" Reza asked, seeing that no one else was jumping to answer the question.

Taking a moment more to consider his answer, he took a seat on the floor, cross-legged, and answered.

"I pledged myself to your cause and to you back in the ruins. You are the leader of this group. I trust your judgment either way."

Reza lingered on Nomad's words for a moment before she turned to Bede and asked her the same question.

Bede had her eyes closed and clutched her talisman. She seemed desperately internally struggling over the issue, and the long wait for an answer began to cause everyone's curiosity to pique, including Cavok, who took his hand off his eyes to glance at the deliberating woman.

Her answer came in a weak voice, the answer seeming to weigh her down.

"There's something—something here that—I don't know how to describe. We are meant to be here, I feel. I'm sorry Finian, but I'm going to have to side with Reza, though perhaps not for the reasons she wants to stay for."

The answer had left most slightly confused, including Reza. But seeing Cavok's attention waning, Reza vocally prodded the man, saying, "Cavok, speak."

Slowly sitting back up, he answered the terse invitation to offer his opinion on the matter.

"As Nomad said, I follow your orders—"

Reza, thinking Cavok was finished, turned to Fin and was about to address him when Cavok cut back in.

"But, if Fin is to leave us, I stay with Fin."

Turning one more time to consider his additional stipulation, Reza issued a, "Fair enough," then turned to Fin to ask, "Well, Fin?"

Fin looked sideways at the rest of the group to his right, issuing a disappointed sigh before shrugging his shoulders.

"If we're going to stick around a city that houses an army of the arisen, you had better have a good and very specific plan for us to follow. This isn't a job we're going to be able to haphazardly improvise our way through. What do we need to accomplish before we can leave? How are we going to accomplish those objectives? And we'll need to draw a line in the sand for when the risk factor becomes too high and we decide to abort the mission."

Reza nodded her head and replied, "That's a very reasonable demand. I do have in mind two specific things I'd want to know to call this mission a success. I want to know who is at the head of this army and a little bit about them, and I want to know how big approximately the army is. To know details on the motivations of the leader would be nice, but not necessarily imperative.

"If we're spotted or our presence is given away at any point during accomplishing those two objectives, we pack up and head out immediately."

Fin stroked his chin, considering Reza's proposition, then said,

"Alright. Hunt down the boss of this joint and do a little spying on them, then do some surveillance of the troops scattered about the city. It's a tall order to fulfill, but as long as that's it—as long as we pull out as soon as we complete those two objectives—I suppose I'm in."

"Good," Reza said, with the faintest smile showing for a moment before continuing.

"I suggest we split up to carry out both objectives simultaneously."

"Split up?" Bede blurted out, following up with, "Reza, we're deep in enemy territory. Splitting up doesn't sound like the most sensible solution."

It was Nomad who spoke up next, saying, "It makes sense. Larger numbers may help us take on a trial when trouble has found us, but fewer numbers helps us to avoid being found by trouble in the first place."

Fin raised a finger and added, "I agree. I'd much rather us travel in small numbers and light if scouting and spying is all that needs to be done. Myself and Nomad alone could more than likely take care of both objectives, and the rest of the group could stay low and hidden here, securing our escape route while we gather what information we need to gather."

"I don't like sending you two out alone. Not that I don't trust either of your capabilities when it comes to stealth, but if you got in over your heads, you'd have no way to call for backup," Reza responded.

"I don't like the idea of being alone in a city of arisen either, but if we get into trouble, backup of four more people won't do anything against an army. Our only advantage currently is that we have not yet been detected, and even that might be untrue since we let that twisted praven go earlier. I'd keep hidden ten times better without any of your company, and I think Nomad would agree with me on this. If stealth is our clearest shot at accomplishing these two objectives timely and successfully, then this is what needs to be done."

Reza scowled at the stone floor, deep in thought, thinking through the various options open to them and the probability of success for each. After a few moments, she looked up to address the group collectively.

"We'll split into three groups of two. Cavok and myself will stay here to ensure our escape route remains open, Nomad and Bede will make their way to the king's court to locate and gather more information of the leaders of this army, and Fin and Jadu will head into the center of the city and ascend Darendul Tower to survey the activity and numbers of the enemy from a vantage point.

"Cavok, our job here will be to occupy one of these officer's quarters and maintain a basecamp. If either one of the two deployed parties needs assistance, we'll do our best to keep an eye in their general direction and move to assist if we can. We'll also do what we can to eliminate any passing threats in this area if we think it necessary, but for the most part, we're just going to try and keep out of sight and stay put and provide aid if we see the need.

"Nomad and Bede. I wish we still had the maps of the city, but we don't. They were on the camel when it was eaten. Do you know where the king's court is from this location, Bede?"

Bede carefully rose up to peer out the window, past the courtyard below them, out into the city beyond. Bobbing her head for a better look, she whispered, "Should be past the noble and court buildings on the other side of this courtyard, shouldn't it?"

"You got it. It's not that far to travel, but you two will be moving through, what we can see to be, active enemy territory. You'll need to take your time getting there and figuring out if indeed that is where the leaders of this army have set up camp. They might have chosen a different location to campaign from. You might even end up stumbling upon it en route. If you get there and find no evidence of a headquarters, then you might check in surrounding areas. If there's nothing there, come back to us and we'll regroup and talk about leads and assess our options.

"Also, Bede, I've seen how efficient a stalker Nomad is, and I'm confident that he can avoid detection in full gear, but I'd advise you to travel light, perhaps even traveling without your armor. Plate armor and chainmail can get pretty loud, regardless of how agile one is, so perhaps stripping down to light armor would be best for this mission."

"Understood," Bede responded without reservations.

"Fin. I'm assuming that you know where Darendul Tower is? It is the tallest structure in Brigganden after all."

Fin, who appeared quite distracted, almost didn't hear Reza's question. A gentle nudge by Bede brought him back to the conversation.

"Oh. Umm, yes. I know where it's at."

Reza paused, looking at both Fin and Jadu now, seeing that Jadu looked just as distracted in secretive thought as Fin did.

"What's going on here?" Reza asked, voicing her thoughts aloud with more than a little annoyed curiosity in her tone.

Fin, seeing that everyone's attention now was on the two's peculiar mood shifts, came forward with a short answer.

"Nothing. It's just that it is a renowned enchanters association tower that's more than likely riddled with deadly traps to keep out those who don't belong."

"Oh," Reza said, considering the new information. "Well then, survey from another tall building."

"No!" both Fin and Jadu said simultaneously, with Fin letting out a nervous chuckle, following up with, "It's nothing we can't handle."

"Nothing at all!" Jadu added, causing Bede and Reza to exchange very confused looks between one another.

"Tallest building and all, right? Best chance at getting a good look out into the city, that's for sure," Fin added unconvincingly.

Reza knew both had an ulterior motive for wanting to stick with surveying from that particular tower, and though she could guess at what that motive was—Fin being a borderline thief and Jadu being a bookworm who constantly hungered for knowledge—the idea of being alone in a grand enchanter's abandoned tower that could be rife with strange and exotic oddities was more than likely overloading their fantasies at the moment.

Reza knew they didn't have time to argue over the matter, and she also knew she was on thin ground with even getting Fin to agree to follow through with the dangerous mission in the first place, so she decided to not contest the surveying location.

"Alright, the tower it is. Just be careful. An enchanter's den is a web of illusion and danger, let alone a renowned enchanter's private college. Be alert, and be quick to obtain the information we need, and then return. Do not linger."

Fin and Jadu were back in their fevered fantasies and didn't even acknowledge the word of warning with a reply.

Nomad, seeing that Reza waited on an answer she was not going to get from them, said, "So, when do we set out?"

"As soon as Bede strips down to a light load and as soon as Fin and Jadu find their way back to reality," Reza answered, shaking her head disappointedly at the two.

"What? We're ready," Fin said, suddenly more than attentive to the conversation.

"Yeah, let's get going!" Jadu excitedly agreed.

Without a second look back, the small, bouncy praven and man adorned in daggers turned and were off down the corridor that led to the city proper. All the while, the rest of the group stared concernedly at the happy couple who could be easily skipping straight to their doom.

20

THE EXPANSIVE GROUNDS

Fin was quite surprised to find that the small praven, when he wanted to be, was a natural at keeping hidden and moving silently through the streets.

The two had navigated their way down to the first story of the officer's building and out a side door, delivering them out into the city streets that they had been slinking through for the past hour without any opposition.

Though most of the buildings in the business end of the city were notably neglected and fire had scorched some streets they had passed, for the most part, the damage done to the city as a whole wasn't completely irreparable. If the arisen army was ever pushed out and the former residents of Brigganden were to move back in, Fin suspected life would return to normal within a short time—and that thought was heartening to him.

Fin, coming up to another street intersection, put a hand out to halt Jadu. Fin's hand landed on the short praven's face, just as he had subconsciously done twice before when calling for a stop, apparently forgetting that he was more than a foot and a half shorter than Fin was.

Swatting the large hand off of his face, Jadu gave a perturbed look up at Fin, who wasn't paying the least bit of attention to the miffed praven. He took a quick look at what had the tall man's attention so fixedly, and once he saw the tall tower that stood before him, his gaze also stuck like a fly to honey.

Darendul Tower stood before them, surrounded by a hedge of considerable height. A gate was opened down the street, leading into the property's garden. Standing close to three hundred feet, the base of the tower appeared to be constructed of granite stone blocks. The second tier of the tower looked to be small sandstone blocks, followed by the third and final tier constructed of tiny half-sized reddish-black bricks. The whole shaft of the tower was cylindrical in shape, and each section of the tower was adorned with various trimmings made from all three main stone types the core of the tower was constructed out of.

"Every time I see it, I can't help but take a moment to gawk," Fin said under his breath, almost already seeming as though he was under a spell just by looking at the structure.

Snapping out of his daze before Jadu had, Fin looked both ways down the street, then nudged the back of Jadu's head to get them moving towards the open gate. Both slipped silently like shadows across the street to enter the stone trail leading into the green gardens.

"Wow," Fin let out, the two taking in a view of vegetation that was so luscious and vibrant that it seemed impossible that such a sight in the desert could even exist.

"Yes, this is quite an oddity. I recognize some of these plants, and some only thrive in cooler climates. That such a span of botanical variation is not just surviving, but thriving here alone, would be incredible, let alone the fact that the city has been under siege for a year now and this garden would have been a year without gardeners," Jadu said, his head darting around excitedly as he spoke.

"Something's off about this garden size-wise," Fin suspiciously said, trying to judge the length and width of the garden as he spoke.

"The tower grounds from outside the gates looked much smaller than this."

Jadu quickly looked around to assess Fin's claim, agreeing by nodding his head and adding, "Looks like there's roughly twice the space than what appears to those from the outside—Oh! Look up!"

Fin, momentarily worried at Jadu's urgent tone, was quick to follow the praven's pointing finger heavenward to the span of the tower to find that the once three-hundred-foot tower now appeared to be closer to six hundred foot tall.

"Impressive…" Fin softly spoke, taking in the massive structure.

"It's twice as tall as it appeared from outside the gate!" Jadu added.

"That means twice as much to find," Fin said with a smile and a sideways glance.

"Very true!" Jadu chirped, then skipped ahead of Fin towards the front door, eager to begin his hunt for secret knowledge that he suspected the tower was brimming with.

21

UNDONE IN THE DARK

Gripping Bede's outstretched hand, Nomad helped Bede up over the balcony's stone railing overlooking what they believed to be the king's courtyard.

There had been regular activity in the area and it had taken them a few hours just to make it over into the next district. After scoping the main palace's courtyard out for thirty minutes, they had made their move to scale the twenty-foot wall at the first sign of no one in the court.

Just as Bede dropped over the railing, the two could hear the distinct sound of marching boots enter the court through the main gate headed towards the large stone palace.

Lying flat on their backs, hoping the small lip of the base of the railing adequately blocked them from the view of the approaching regiment, Nomad and Bede waited for the troops to pass, listening for the drudged footfall of the soldiers march off out of hearing.

Slinking to their feet, Nomad led Bede up past a fifteen-foot statue to the building's wall, sneaking a look in through the windowed doorway.

The room was dark, and it took a few moments for Nomad to

make out that the room was a conference room of some fashion. A massive marble, mahogany table stretched the majority of the room. Chairs, overturned and scattered, dotted its borders. He could also see that the room led into a great hallway, which was also dark—so much so that he couldn't determine how deep or long the hallway actually was.

Taking a moment to speak with Bede while they had the liberty to do so without the risk of being heard, Nomad cupped a hand to Bede's ear and whispered, "There has been enough traffic coming and going from this building that there has got to be something or someone of note inside.

"Once inside, whisper only if absolutely necessary, or if we are certain we are out of perception of any hostile ears.

"Also, we do not exactly know much about how these *things'* senses function, if they smell, hear, see, or have a spiritual attunement to detect the living. We stay out of sight, sound, and do our best to keep our distance from any threats we come across, and if we must, we take threats that get too close down fast and silent.

"Once we locate high-value targets, we will camp and obtain as much information as we can before heading out back to base camp. Sound like a plan?"

Bede nodded, ready to follow Nomad's lead. Nomad turned and twisted the door handle and slowly pressed on the windowed door leading into the conference room.

The door opened, to Nomad's relief. Without Fin's lock-picking tools or expertise with them, his only other option was to smash a windowpane to unlock the door from the other side, and that would have been a horrible way to begin their stealth mission.

The door opened without trouble or sound and the two entered the room silently before closing the door behind them.

Just as the door closed, they could hear another door in the hallway open, a few pairs of brisk footsteps sounding off down the hall on their way towards the conference room Nomad and Bede were hiding in.

Urgently motioning for Bede to follow his lead, Nomad quickly stepped over to a corner of the room, hiding behind a long, cushioned couch, Bede ducking behind it next to him.

The march was about to pass the conference door when the group suddenly came to a halt, the soft jingle of equipment on plate armor accentuating their otherwise silent presence.

A deadly hiss of a voice reached in the conference room, just audible enough for Nomad to hear.

"A presence looms near. A holy worshiper even."

Nomad nervously looked to Bede, who, by her look, seemed to be straining to understand the words from the soft voice that echoed in from out in the hallway. Nomad placed a hand on his sword hilt, readying himself for action, only *he* seemingly understanding that their presence was potentially blown.

Bede, though she hadn't been able to discern the words from the wicked voice, had taken note of Nomad's right hand sliding to his weapon. Placing a hand on her mace grip and the other over the strap that secured it to her hip, ready to loose it, Bede made ready to pounce from her hiding spot.

A few moments of stilled silence more and the voice came slithering back into the room.

"Perhaps I misjudged. Come. Our lord expects our prompt arrival. To leave him waiting would not bode well for us."

The march continued down the hall, past the conference room door as quickly as it had halted, and both Nomad and Bede let out a held breath in relief of the lucky break they had just been given.

"Bede," Nomad whispered as soon as the footfall was out of sound. "It said it could feel the presence of a holy worshiper. I worship no God. I wonder if they can detect our presence by your faith."

"It's possible. It's not uncommon for attuned priests to detect those rife with sin amongst a crowd. I don't doubt the same ability might be available to higher-ranking followers of the dark beliefs," Bede whispered back.

Nomad nodded, considering his suspicions to be validated. Looking to the door, then back to Bede, he softly spoke, "I might need to continue this mission without you, Bede. Can you make your way back to Reza on your own? I cannot let that group slip us by. They will lead me to the head of this unknown enemy, but if that lesser threat can detect you, their leader most certainly will."

Closing her eyes for a moment, considering Nomad's proposition and line of reasoning, she looked back up at him with a look of worry clearly on her face.

"I will never forgive myself if anything should happen to you," she said, placing a caring hand up to the side of Nomad's face.

"Thank you," Nomad said, holding Bede's hand as he helped her up, adding, "Careful heading back."

Bede made her way to the door, opening it without a sound, then headed out onto the balcony as Nomad watched her from the darkness of the room.

Seeing that she was to the balcony's stone railing, he turned to be on his way, sliding up to the side of the door leading out into the hallway.

Taking a strip of black cloth from around his neck, he threw back his hair and tied the head wrap tight to keep his hair from his face, having left his bulky helmet back at their headquarters.

Listening a moment for movement in the hallway, hearing nothing, not even the distant footfall of the group that had passed them by, Nomad popped a head out to look down the hallway the direction the group had gone.

The hallway was large. Large enough for Nomad to consider it more of an indoor causeway rather than just a hallway. Mosaic tiling stretched down the way with great stone pillars lining the walls.

Taking a quick glance back the other way, seeing nothing of importance, Nomad stepped out into the corridor.

Just as he took his first step into the hall, he heard a shuffle from behind.

Nomad's eyes opened wide, catching a glimpse of an armored figure, donned in similar fashion as the dark knight he had fought in the desert beside Reza, which now lunged towards him with a longsword held high.

Swinging the sword down at him, Nomad managed to roll out further into the corridor, avoiding being struck by the shadowy figure's blade.

Upon the missed attack, an ungodly shriek issued from the visored helm.

The shriek spurred Nomad to go from defensive to offensive, knowing full well that he could not let the foe continue to sound the alarm.

His curved blade was out and striking almost instantly, clanging off the heavy knight's armor twice before the thing could even begin to respond to the attack, its shriek being prematurely cut off, focusing now on defending itself.

In the dark corridor, Nomad was finding it difficult to hit the knight's joints with precision, and the knight would be able to take hits to the plate section of its armor all day long. With his position more than likely compromised, he knew he had little time to deal with the knight before backup came rushing their way.

A blade point thrusted in at Nomad, which he narrowly dodged in the dark, taking the chance to sidestep up to the knight.

Swiftly bringing his blade up to the thing's throat, Nomad gripped the tip of the blunt side of the blade, planting a foot around the back of the knight's legs, pulling the large armored foe over his shoulder.

The knight came slamming down to the ground, its visored helm and skull popping off of its body. It clattered down the hall, smoke issuing from a broken rune etched along its spinal column as it skidded to a stop.

The short engagement had taken only seconds, but the clatter had echoed off the long corridor's walls resoundingly. He knew he needed to move fast now.

Looking briefly over to the balcony that Bede had headed off from, he let out an exasperated sigh as he saw Bede rushing back into the conference room, apparently hearing the scuffle, coming to check on him.

Holding up a hand to wave her back, he was stopped short as a bolt of purple light shot over his shoulder, ripping angrily by him, dissipating into the rock pillar behind him.

Turning back up the hallway where the projectile had come from, Nomad saw three more knights and a hooded figure donned in half-plate holding a polished wand just as another bolt of purple light burst forth from the device, landing squarely upon Nomad's chest, sending him reeling backwards before being hit a second and then a third time in the shoulder and leg by two more bolts, dropping him to the ground.

Just as Bede was about to run out into the corridor, three large, dark knights ran past the doorway, seizing Nomad, who appeared more than just dazed from the magical assault, almost unconscious at that point.

"Up! Get him up!" the same snake-like voice they had heard earlier commanded, a hooded figure passing by the conference room, allowing Bede a view of the enemy.

"It seems I wasn't mistaken in sensing a presence nearby," the hooded figure hissed, throwing aside his cloak to reveal a skeletal hand as it gripped Nomad's jaw.

Considering the dazed man for a moment, the hooded arisen ordered, "Bring him. The master will be pleased with this find."

The large dark knights hefted Nomad, two knights grabbing both his arms with one coaxing him forward at swordpoint.

The hooded man lingered a moment longer, looking down the

dark, long hallway before turning to follow behind the knights, leaving Bede there alone in the dark.

"Elendium, help him," Bede choked out, dreadfully worried for Nomad, knowing for him, things just had taken a, quite possibly, fatal turn.

She knew that she, unlike Nomad, stood no chance against such numbers. That she was a seasoned adventurer, it was true, but against such an armored opponent, let alone three plus a—whatever the hooded one was—she knew a confrontation would not have turned out in her favor.

Her only hope currently was to follow wherever they took Nomad and attempt to rescue him when the opportunity showed itself to her.

With a prayer now in mind for herself, she rounded the corner and headed off as quietly as she could in the direction of the faint clank of armor up ahead of her.

22

THE OLD MAN IN THE PAINTING

"Forty flights of stairs and no magical traps of any kind. How odd," Jadu said, looking around up at the spiral staircase in the center of the tower that appeared to go up another twenty more flights.

"Yeah, and no sight of valuables either," Fin answered back, disappointment easily discernable in his voice.

"Not all valuable things come in the mold of metals," Jadu tritely said, looking through a tome almost as big as he was that he had picked up on the last floor Fin had randomly decided to take a detour to inspect.

Fin huffed, partly out of disdain of the notion, and partly due to the forty stairs they had just finished climbing. He was about to start up the stairwell once more when he thought he heard a sound in the room the stairwell led into.

"Keep talking," Fin said, slipping past Jadu, into the room he had heard the bump in.

Jadu needed no further word to launch into a long-winded explanation of the interesting book he had found. Taking a seat on the stairs, Jadu began flipping through page after page, explaining the strange incantations he had found, all the while chatting to no one in particular as Fin quietly made his way through the room, listening for whatever had made the sound he had heard earlier.

A jovial, hoary voice, very close to Fin, spooked him so badly that the experienced rogue nearly fell over.

"*Ooohehehe*! You don't seem to be with that boney fellow. Not at all! *Ooohehehe*!"

Fin, looking all around for the invisible entity, drew his dagger and backed up to the wall.

"Ooo, so, you think I am a danger to you, do you? Well, perhaps I am. It all depends on who you are and why you're here."

This time, the voice came from right behind him. Jumping out into the middle of the room, Fin turned to see a plain stone wall, decorated lightly with a few pictures of robed peoples of differing races.

Seeing how the source of the voice eluded him once more, Fin considered the old man's last response and answered, "Ah, yes. I'm nobody, you could say. Just found the doors open and the city surrounded by the dead and decided to have a look-see."

Looking around the room frantically now for the source of the old man's voice, the hidden speaker answered back, "An opportunist is it then? Well, I suppose the company of a thief is better company than the walking dead. Sense of humor with them is nonexistent!"

"Why is that painting talking?" Jadu asked, waddling into the room with his recently acquired massive tome. Fin, now totally unhinged, jumped and turned to find that it was Jadu who had walked past him, looking at the largest painting in the middle of the stone wall.

"Ooo, my spellbook! It has a way of finding its way into others' hands. Do me a favor if you would be so kind. There is a spell incantation in there. It only requires recitation to work. Could you find the animated painting enchantment—"

Jadu cut the old man off, excited to finish his thought for him. "Yes! The animated painting enchantment. Fascinating spell! I read up on it two flights ago when Fin was keeled over catching his breath from the climb.

"I must say, much of sorcery and alchemy seems to share quite a few of the same principles and rules at a basic level. It's too bad I didn't have access to proper magic training earlier in my life. It would have been a wonderful second emphasis.

"But I digress. The enchantment unlock incantation must be spoken by anyone, or thing, other than the caster themselves. Why one would willingly cast that spell on themselves is beyond my comprehension, but allow me to assist you by reading the enchantment unlock words for you."

Once Jadu pointed it out, Fin noticed that when the old man spoke, the voice *had* been coming from the painting, and upon further scrutiny, he could make out the figure's mouth slowly moving, the eyes turning from Fin to Jadu.

"Pon eht—" Jadu started, but was muted by Fin who abruptly slapped a hand over his mouth.

"Wait. You're telling me he can't get out of this painting unless we let him out?"

"Yeah," Jadu replied, quickly going back to reciting the unlock chant. "Pon eht—"

Again, Fin's hand covered Jadu's mouth, obtaining the answer he was looking for.

"Well, then think of this for a moment, Jadu. We're in an enchanter's tower, uninvited. We have the option to release an enchanter from entrapment without knowing how powerful or dangerous he is; *or*, there's also the option to leave him where he is, perfectly harmless and secured within that painting while we continue with our mission.

"Which of the two options sound smartest and with less risk to our health?"

Jadu held up a finger and mumbled something into Fin's hand, causing him to lift his hand from the muted praven's mouth. Jadu started again.

"Option one, please."

An entertained cackle sounded from the painting at Jadu's answer, and Fin looked up with a stern look to attempt to silence the humored old man.

"More risk—perhaps, but also more to gain! He seems like a decent fellow. From reading his book, *most* of the spells and notes don't include heavy occult influence or devilry. Besides that, consider having a powerful wizard on our side! Finding the motives of the arisen army would be made quite a bit easier with sorcery at our disposal. Plus," Jadu began to whisper, "there are some languages in this tome that I don't know and I desperately would love to have him interpret them for me."

Fin incredulously looked at Jadu, stooping down to the praven's level to make sure Jadu saw how astonished he was by his crazed logic.

Jadu stared Fin directly back in the eyes for a moment before blurting out, "Pon eht weya," a hand slapping over the little mouth a moment too late, the short incantation already echoing through the room, the painting now reverberating on the wall.

The old man's cackle could be heard well at first, but the cacophony of the painting rattling on the wall quickly overtook the man's crazed laughter.

The frame rattled so violently that it popped right off the wall, slamming picture first on the floor, the frame breaking into splintered bits, leaving Jadu and Fin staring wordlessly slack-jawed at the spectacle. A mound began to push up the back of the canvas, standing up tall, and a robed man that had grown out from underneath the painting feebly pitched the now-blank canvas off to the side.

"Ah! It's a cypher!" Jadu exclaimed, sounding quite pleased with himself, meriting only a very concerned look from Fin, who turned back to worriedly observe the freed enchanter's next move.

"*Ooohehehe*! My, my. This one's cleverer!" the bearded old man laughed, barely able to stand.

Encouraged, Jadu continued. "Yes, uh, the sequence. Pon eht weya. Invert every other letter and invert letter-to-word count. The original message is, 'Open the way.' I'm very good with patterns, you see. You need a sharp eye as an alchemist. Unstable elements are not long kind to those who can't see ten steps ahead in the process."

The old man stepped over the debris of his former prison and stood tall next to the small praven, inspecting him.

Smiling, he patted Jadu on the head and said in a sincere tone, "Thank you. I don't blame your companion's hesitation to release me, but it's a kind thing you've done for me."

Adjusting his robes and standing up straight, the old man introduced himself to the two.

"The name's Zaren. Zaren Zebulon. And who would be my liberators?"

Fin was about to answer, but Jadu, chomping at the bit to speak to the man, said, "I'm Jadu, and he's Fin. So Zaren, you're an enchanter, are you not? I'd very much like to pick your brain over some of the content in this spellbook of yours if you don't mind."

"No, not at all. Ask your questions. It's the least I can do after you released me from that dreadful painting."

The two struck up conversation as they aimlessly strolled towards the staircase.

The old enchanter was quick to ignore Fin's presence, and Fin figured it was all for the better as he desperately wanted to inspect the tower privately rather than have the old man's eyes on him during his perusing.

Fin easily outpaced them, making his way up the stairwell, finding at the top an opened hatch that led into a large and open room. The ceiling stood perhaps just over twelve feet high, and he could see in the wooden rafters at the vaulted ceiling that there was perhaps another small attic room above that.

Large, open archways leading out onto stubby balconies let in a refreshing cool breeze that blew thin, wispy curtains gently in and out of the threshold.

Tables, chairs, bookcases, shelves, and couches were placed comfortably around the room. An exorbitant amount of scrolls and books lay open across all surfaces, oddly unaffected by the breeze that could have easily carried them away.

Four light blue flames in black and gold braziers stood at the corners of the room, easily illuminating everything with a penetrating light that was noticeable even during the day.

Cluttered around the edges of the rooms were stands holding robes, armor, staves, and weapons. There were glass display cases, most empty, with some remaining filled with various items, be it jewelry, gloves, or fragments of different materials. On the floor were more than a few chests—some open and empty, some closed and locked—sending Fin's imagination into overdrive.

Fin rushed to the open stairwell and looked down it. Jadu and Zaren still seemed engrossed in conversation some fifteen floors down. He had plenty of time to search the room before their arrival.

Sprinting back up into the room, he looked around, almost like a madman, the possibility of the greatest haul in his life rattling his composure.

"Who's first, who's first…" Fin feverishly mumbled, looking around at the various objects that stood out to him, begging for him to stuff them in his pouches.

Picking a closed, glass display case at random, he rushed over to it, inspecting its contents.

"Hmm, a set of rings. Good risk there," Fin whispered to himself. He had no way of knowing what items were magically enchanted and which were not, but he did at least know monetarily how much the physical properties of the items would go for at market, and with any luck, he'd score and get the items that had not just a good street value, but also were powerful relics, enriched with hexweave.

About to touch the display case, he stopped last second, noticing a plaque at the base of the case that was engraved with a message in fine cursive.

Stooping and squinting his eyes to read the fancy writing, he read the message that was engraved aloud.

"Items still to be studied."

Scratching the stubble on his chin for a moment, he assessed each of the rings by worth and price point, trying to decide which to take first.

"Rubies. Those always sell well in Tarigannie," he said, gently lifting up the lid on the display case, apprehensively reaching his hand in to pluck the gold, twin-ruby ring.

Holding his breath, he felt his heart skip a beat as his hand froze involuntarily as he was pulling the ring out of the case.

Some unseen force tugged at the ring, and Fin felt the ring slipping from his trembling, moist fingers, but the faint sound of Jadu's voice from the stairwell spurred Fin to tug with all his might. He ripped the ring from the invisible grasp of the display case, which landed him on his back on the floor.

Fin sat up, looking unflinchingly at the defiant display case that had tried to rob him of his rightly earned treasure.

"Not keen on giving up those rings without a fight I see...," Fin mumbled at the display stand. In response, it opened its glass door like a mouth, hinge creaking loudly, sounding like a belch, before abruptly closing again.

Fin gave the animated display case an incredulous look a moment longer before tucking the ring in a pocket high on his pants—Jadu's little voice coming clearer into focus with every passing second.

The approaching duo spurred Fin to his feet, frantically sending him skittering about the room, looking for another shiny object to snatch before the enchanter's more than likely disapproving gaze entered the room. He was stealing from the enchanter's people after all, and he made no illusions to himself about that.

Halting at another display case, he found a bejeweled bracelet. A mixture of opals, alexandrite, onyx, and diamonds were socketed in a stunningly crafted white-gold bracelet.

"That's an odd mix of gems," Fin said, admiring the expensive, albeit clashing colors of gemstones that shone in the aqua-hued light.

Noticing another engraved plaque down at the base of the case, Fin let out an exasperated sigh before stooping to hurriedly read through the warning message.

"An opposition within our souls shall stir and reverse one's roles."

Tapping his chin in thought for a moment to consider the vague message, Fin threw his hands up in defeat and went to open the case.

He was met with no invisible resistance as he reached in, but his brow was furrowed and lightly perspiring. He clearly was not trusting the mysterious nature that seemed to linger amidst most of the room's trinkets.

Clenching the bracelet, he ripped it from its case as quickly and forcefully as he could.

It came out with no unseen opposition.

He held the band in the air, staring intently, waiting for a response from the stand that now stood bare of its charge.

No glass door opened and no squeaking burp sounded out.

"Well then," Fin said, loosening up, his confidence coming back to his voice. "That's that, I guess."

He could hear Jadu's voice easily now and knew the two only to be a flight or so away from the room.

Left with time enough to do not much other than make a gloating gesture to his good fortunes, he held the bracelet forward and took a bow at the empty stand, whispering a sincere *Thank you* to the display case.

Before Fin rose from his bow, the case's glass door swung open and jettisoned the cushioned interior that held the bracelet, nailing Fin right on the crown, causing him to startle so badly as to land him right on his rump.

The glass door abruptly shut itself once more, leaving a very bewildered Fin, sitting, wondering what had just happened.

With Jadu and Zaren only paces away from entering the room, Fin threw the case an ugly look, picked up the cushion, and tossed it over to the side of the room, out of the way, then tucked the bracelet into a satchel hanging from his side.

"Well, here we are, it seems," Zaren said, cutting Jadu off from his continuous, one-sided conversation he had been having with the enchanter.

"The Darendul's Highstudy. A place normally only the highest-ranking enchanters here at the tower are able to regularly visit. A great many mysteries and relics reside here."

Jadu, taking a moment to look around at his surroundings, exclaimed, "Oh! How interesting! I hadn't even heard of the Highstudy! Oh, do show us around a bit, Zaren. It's the least we might hope to indulge in after infiltrating an occupied hostile city and climbing so many stairs."

"Hmm, yes, indeed," Zaren thoughtfully replied, keeping an intrigued, steady eye on the eager little praven. "I suppose I could explain the room a bit.

"As I said, it's somewhat of a study, treasury, and meeting place for the uppers of my order. Most of the important relics, as you can see, were taken with my order into a rift realm created by powerful hexweave enchantment. This alternate plane of existence that they retreated into during the arisen army's occupation, however, does have its limits. It can only contain as much hexweave energy as was used to create it, so my order had to select with care what they took into the rift as they couldn't bring everything.

"This meant they had to leave either lesser enchanted items and relics or items that had the least potential to do the most harm to the public if looters happened to obtain them during our absence."

Zaren closed his statement by casting an eye on Fin for the first time since he had entered the room, looking the man up and down before continuing.

"Those that take from what is left up here may be—" Zaren paused to consider the most appropriate word. "—horribly vexed with what they thought would be a wonderful find."

After another suspicious glance at Fin, who sheepishly smiled at the old man, Zaren went on to ask, "Now, I've entertained your curious mind. Perhaps you could indulge me and answer me this. What are you two doing in this city and in this tower—honestly."

Jadu didn't hesitate to jump to answer, and Fin was too worried now about the two items he had pocketed to stop the praven from divulging the summary of their mission in whole.

Zaren listened to Jadu quietly, only interrupting to ask short, pointed questions occasionally, coming quickly to understand how they had gotten into the city, what they were trying to accomplish by doing so, and why the two had been headed for the top of the tower.

"So, you'd like a view of the city from up here? Well, there's no nicer view of it than from these balconies," Zaren said, waving towards one of the open doorways that Jadu excitedly skipped to, with Fin reluctantly following close behind under Zaren's stern eye.

"Wow!" Jadu couldn't help but let out in astonishment, piquing Fin's curiosity, shuffling over to get a good look out over the railing.

Below, the city seemed magnified wherever they looked. It was as though all sight from the balcony passed through some telescopic lens, showing them fine details of streets that were far below.

"Yes. It's a way we enchanters keep an eye on local happenings. No one knows about this feature of the tower, not even the city leaders, and I shall have to kill you if you ever speak of anything you witness here in the Highstudy," Zaren said with a chuckle, to which Jadu joined in, honestly humored by the joke, with Fin making an uneasy attempt at a laugh, still horribly uncomfortable around the old enchanter.

Zaren continued to speak as the two went back to viewing the many regiments marching or standing post throughout the city.

"As you can tell, there's quite a number of arisen occupying the city. Before I entered the painting, I counted an army just under a thousand. If they've raised more dead from that time, I have no idea of knowing, but the army seems to be ordered about by only a few sentient arisen—very dangerous and powerful, but it seems there's maybe three or so of them.

"The leader I only know as 'the master.' I haven't seen him, or her, whatever it may be, but the second-in-command has mentioned his master once in talking to himself."

"Second-in-command? You've talked with the enemy?" Fin questioned, curious as to how Zaren obtained so much information of the commanders of the army.

"Not talked to, but a few days ago, one named Lashik finally broke through this tower's incantations and began ascending the tower. Before entering the painting, I myself oversaw many of the traps in this structure to keep out all but the most adept arcanists, diviners, and enchanters. As Lashik broke through the main entrance, he's spent most of his time these last few days disassembling various enchantment traps throughout the tower. If he hadn't have done that, well, you two probably would have been dead before you had entered the outer gates."

Both Fin and Jadu looked with raised eyebrows at each other over the news of the fortunate timing of events.

"Through the painting, I was able to effectively slow time drastically for myself. The plan was for my order to enter the rift and wait out the invasion. Eventually, a liberating force would drive this army off, even if it took centuries to do so. Time in the rift is also slowed, so we could afford to wait out the occupation.

"I was to stay and observe and intervene if need be, as well as open the rift when all of this blew over; but, during Lashik's ascension of the tower, he came to the room I monitored through the painting and found interest in and snatched up the object that was endowed with the enchantment's unlock words that would release me from my spell. Without someone, or something, to say the unlock words, I was stuck until someone came along, like you two, whom I might be able to trust to say the unlock words for me.

"To your point, though, Fin, I came to know of Lashik a bit through observation as he cleared the room I was in. I have seen and heard another intelligent arisen pass by and report to Lashik. A cloaked skeleton that Lashik had called *Dubix*. He ordered him to organize troops and to send them to various areas of the city at the time, nothing important, but as far as I know, that's who is leading the army. It seems it's a relatively small chain of command. I have observed for many weeks the streets and city from this balcony before I hid away in the painting, and that's my assessment of the situation."

After gazing a while longer down into the shadowy, abandoned streets, the evening sunlight beginning to stretch long over most of the city now, Fin nudged Jadu and said, "Well, I guess there's our answer we came here looking for."

Turning to look back inside, walking past the drape-lined doorframe, he added, "The dead army's number seems to be upwards of two thousand according to Zaren. I loosely counted maybe four hundred or so at their posts or on patrol. Many more hundreds could easily be hidden away in garrisons down below, scattered through the city, or out in the countryside on patrol. I don't doubt Zaren's estimate to be pretty accurate."

"I know barely anything about military subjects, so if you say so, then that's good enough for me. Objective complete then. That wasn't so bad! I hope the others have fared well with their tasks," Jadu said, turning to follow Fin back inside, adding in a sanguine tone, "I just hope we still get the chance to examine one of those arisen specimen. I'm curious as to their animation origins."

Zaren, leading them out of the Highstudy, offered, "That is a subject I know a bit about. If you're interested, I could discuss it further with you on the way down."

"Oh, that would be lovely!" Jadu said, jumping with excitement, asking, "If you have insight into the nature of this army, I'm sure that

137

Reza would also be interested in learning more about these unnatural specimens. Would you mind visiting with others in our group to discuss the subject further?"

Fin was about to suggest otherwise, not comfortable around the enchanter they knew so little about, but he knew that Jadu had a point. Reza would kill them if they passed this kind of information asset up and went their way without grilling Zaren for everything he knew about the situation. Such an intel score would probably pay off any debts he owed Reza, and perhaps even Sultan Metus would increase the reward for such a detailed report upon their return.

The two waited for an answer as they started down the long flight of stairs. Zaren considered the invitation with a scrunched up brow before smiling wide, the exact kind of odd smile that caused Fin to worry, and said with a chuckle, "Ask for my help? The help of an enchanter always comes with an unseen price. I suppose I could visit with you and this Reza friend of yours to discuss what I know of the enemy you face. If it further aids a mounting resistance to expedite the purging of the city from this threat, then who am I to refuse to help? Lead the way, little one."

Thrilled that the learned enchanter had agreed to tarry with them a while longer, Jadu pinched Fin's elbow with an unsuppressed smile and followed after the strange, tall, robed figure.

Fin, holding back a moment to let what company he had allowed to jump aboard, let out a sigh and mumbled, "I'm going to regret this—I can already feel it."

Fin slowly started back down the stairs to catch up to the two who were already deep in conversation about enchantment, spells, and the living dead.

23

FADING LIGHT

The large hallway left few places to hide, and following Nomad's four captors had Bede on edge as she entered an adjoining corridor she had seen the ghastly group head down.

Hearing the hissing voice of the cloaked one far down the hallway, she halted to see if she could catch the rest of his conversation.

"No, stay here. I'll visit our lord alone. If there's one intruder, then there's likely more in the shadows," the hooded figure spoke.

Bede slowly peeked around the corner to get a glimpse of the group as the leader continued.

"It seems our little snitch was right about an invading group. Keep an eye out. The enemy is reported to possess some strength and a biting light. I'll be out after I see what our lord wants to do with this one."

The shrouded figure jerked Nomad from the grasp of the large, armored skeleton that was holding him, dragging a barely conscious Nomad towards the large doors at the end of the hallway.

One of the two doors opened, then slammed shut, leaving only the three dark sentinels standing idly outside of the room that

Nomad had been taken into.

Slinking back around the corner, resting for a moment to attempt to establish an actual plan of how she was going to break Nomad free, Bede pulled her talisman out from beneath her robe, noticing that the seal had begun to warm to uncomfortable levels.

Cupping it in her hand to shield its growing light, she stabled herself as the intense impressionable flash of impending danger assaulted her.

Regaining her balance after the ominous premonition, she stilled as she became aware of footsteps approaching from the guarded hallway.

She jumped up, her mace loudly popping off the marbled floor as she did so. She started to retreat back the way she had come, but she was too late. A wicked, bare skull weaved around the corner, spotting her instantly, and began following in pursuit, soundlessly lifting aloft its greatsword as it advanced.

Seeing that the knight would soon overtake her if she continued to run, Bede unloosed her mace just in time to ready a parry as the greatsword came down, striking with such unholy force that Bede barely held to the weapon, readjusting her grip on the wrapped handle as the knight brought up its weapon again, coming down in a chopping motion once more. This time, instead of attempting to deflect the blow, Bede jumped to the side, dodging the heavy swing.

Two jubilant shrieks sounded from behind the looming figure, and the attacker answered back, barking a horrible command in a foul language Bede knew to be Felmortum, a language that belonged to the wicked dead.

She had never heard the language spoken in its natural tongue, only through her academic studies at the monastery. The supernatural shrill inflections curdled her blood and blew an instant fear into her core.

The leading knight viciously thrust its sword's point back in at her, cutting in past her defenses, sticking deep into her chest, pushing her back, dropping her heavily down to the floor as the point was wrenched back out.

Cackles sounded from behind the looming knight as it brought up its sword into a downward thrusting position, coming down as Bede desperately attempted to keep her attention on the fight and not on the pain that shot through her chest with every movement.

The sword tip cut into her side, Bede not quite getting free from the knight's would-be deathblow.

The shock of the wound caused her to reflexively strike at the sword's flat with her mace, snapping the old blade in half.

The knight was quick to respond, though. Snaring Bede by the wrist with one boney hand, it pulled her close to its bleached skull until they were face to face.

Bede's free hand came around, slugging the knight in the skull, twisting its head around momentarily.

Attempting another strike, the knight hastily dropped its broken weapon to shield its face from another blow, cleanly catching the oncoming fist in its claw-like grip, penetrating her hand with its pointy fingers, drawing thick lines of blood as the boney tips gripped harder, securing his control over her.

A knee to the groin did little but hurt Bede's knee, and the knight swept her feet forcefully off to the side, dropping her to the ground. She was now completely pinned by what was quickly becoming her personal grim reaper.

She could feel blood issuing from her desperate struggle, and she knew she had little fight left to give against the demonic strength of the arisen knight.

Jerking slightly from actively constraining the still-fighting woman, the skeleton slowly lowered its skull till it rested beside Bede's cheek, its cold, abrasive bone roughly scraping along Bede's flesh, opening up small cuts along the right side of her face.

Bede couldn't see now what the thing was doing, it being too far beyond her periphery, but chills involuntarily went down her body as she felt the skeleton's champing teeth slowly grind down upon her hair and ear, gnashing through skin and cartilage, causing her to scream out in pain. She was completely helpless.

Tearing away, the knight ripped off part of Bede's ear, causing another cry from her as it came back to face her.

The last cry had dizzied her, and she began to feel distant from the whole scene, as if she was slowly being detached from her physical senses.

She knew vaguely that she should be resisting to the end, but the foggy feeling of physical detachment was a welcome relief and, at the same time, a guilty pleasure.

Her head dropped backwards, languishly rocking from side to side as she attempted to regain control of her body. Her neck was fully exposed to the knight, who was taking in the exquisite sight of pain and surrender, sensing its victim's end near. It slowly came in, its bloody teeth trembling with anticipation, lightly resting its shut, dripping fangs against Bede's bare neck before slowly opening its mouth for the kill.

Bede's vision had faded fast, darkness engulfing her whole being, as if all awareness was quickly being flushed down a drain.

Then, a hot flash pounded into her, flooding her system once again with the ability to feel.

Snapping her head up, looking down past her prone body, she saw her ravager was also prone on the floor, skull smashed and smoking, the other two knights quickly moving in towards her.

Light from her chest shone brightly, enough to cause the dark knight's pause, and Bede clutched her glowing talisman and instinctively held it aloft, standing up to face her backpedaling adversaries.

"Abominations!" she shouted in a forceful tone, one that seemed to have been reinforced by some otherworldly source.

The empowered word jolted the two skeletons, shaking their hollow frames, causing them to drop their weapons.

Seeing that they were about to retreat, Bede rushed the nearest foe and slammed the talisman against its skull, pushing it back against the wall, bone popping off angrily as the skeleton was quickly reduced to smoking dust.

Seeing the fate of its comrade, the other knight turned to retreat back down the hallway that led to the room Nomad was in.

"Halt!" Bede ordered, causing the knight to stop momentarily, seeming to struggle against unseen bindings.

Bede began walking towards the creature, it slowly inching its way towards the doorway of the next hall.

Holding high her radiant source, golden rays shone down over the bare skull of the arisen warrior, smoke forming on its crown, layers of bone peeling away as it frantically fought the unflinching, unseen bindings that held it in place.

In a blind rage, Bede let out a furious scream, drilling the light down into the skull of her foe, shattering it upon impact. Driving her hand through its spine, she dropped the puppet in armor to the floor, leaving her standing alone, trembling with fury.

With the fight now ended, she huffed for air as her muscles relaxed. Collapsing to the ground, she clutched the talisman so tightly that the metal threatened to bruise and cut her skin as its light began to fade.

Her features snapped, hot tears streaming down her cheeks. Slowly bringing her trembling hand up, she clutched the side of her head, feeling an ear that was there, that shouldn't be, and scratches along her face that were no longer there, but could still feel.

A sob shook her body once; then, a long, dreadful moan that transitioned into weeping.

Her grip on the talisman loosened and she dropped it to the floor where she was hunched over, raining tears down upon the indifferent metal symbol of her faith.

24
KNOCK AT THE DOOR

"That was quick. Where's Jadu?" Reza asked Fin in a hushed voice as Fin walked quietly into the room Reza and Cavok were holding out in.

Looking past Reza to find Cavok snoozing loudly in the corner of the room on one of the officer's beds, Fin nervously turned back to Reza and answered.

"He's not too far behind me," Fin started to explain as two distant voices began to become audible down the hallway.

Seeing Reza's concerned look, he quickly added, "And he's got company with him. We picked up a local, as odd as that sounds."

Down the hallway, a humored cackle echoed, filling the halls as Fin explained to a confused Reza, "He's an old kook. Not sure how far we can trust him, but he claims to have a great deal of information on our enemy. We figured it'd be worth the risk to bring him here for questioning."

As the enchanter and Jadu rounded the corner, Fin threw in one last word of warning to Reza, whispering, "Careful how hard you press him—he's an enchanter. Apparently pretty high ranking too. Can't trust their types."

Just then, a tall, frail man garbed in periwinkle robes, accompanied by Jadu, who only exaggerated the robed man's height, entered the room. Holding the doorframe for support, the old man rested a moment before making his way tiredly to the bed Cavok rested upon.

"Shoo! You'll have to excuse me. I haven't walked that far in months. Being cooped up in that painting does a number to an old fellow's joints, you know."

As he spoke, Cavok's snoring began to halt. He stretched a bit, waking from his slumber. Zaren made a brief, subtle movement with his hand, drawing a cross upon Cavok's forehead, which caused Cavok to settle immediately back in bed, where he began to snore loudly once more.

The act wasn't secretive enough to throw anyone off but Jadu, a pang of worry causing Reza and Fin to exchange concerned glances.

Reza, after a moment to consider how to approach the odd man, started with an introduction.

"Greetings. Glad to see you're doing well considering the place you choose to reside at. My name's Reza," she said, offering a hand to the old man.

Zaren gave her a wiry smile and stared calculatingly a moment before returning the gesture. Clasping his hand in hers, putting his other hand atop the handshake, he patted the back of her hand with his wrinkled palm as he answered back.

"Reza. Interesting name. And a face that belongs among the angels—surely garb that belongs to a heritage that shares a bloodline with the angels at least."

Fin smiled slightly, seeing the old man trying to put the moves on the least flatterable woman he knew, but Reza, more concerned at the old man's hints at knowing what race she belonged to, appeared quite displeased with the response.

"I'm Zaren," he continued, gently taking his hood off to reveal a wispy head of long, white hair.

"I understand you're the leader of this daring duo of scouts who wandered into my tower? Quite a mission you undertake. I know I suggested to your colleagues that I might be able to offer information in regards to the arisen army occupying this city, but it would be prudent for me to know a bit more about your motives and what you plan on doing with the information you might acquire from me before I give it. What brings you to this city under these hazardous circumstances?"

Reza, finding Zaren's request and reasoning understandable, whispered to Fin to keep an eye on the halls before pulling up a chair. She sat facing Zaren and started to summarize their mission.

"Sultan Metus, the sultan of the neighboring region, commissioned us to acquire a report of the enemy's numbers, leadership details, and motives. It's been a year since Brigganden was sacked, and Sultan Metus is concerned with this unknown, hostile force. It's our mission to report any obtainable data we can on this arisen army and report this information to the sultan. What he plans on doing with our report, I can't say, but I would guess it is to assess how, and if, an attack would be feasible. A main trade route has been disrupted, the Plainstate has taken in hundreds of refugees, and he worries the aggressive force that resides now in Brigganden might soon move to invade his lands next.

"That's why we're here and what we're attempting to accomplish, and any information you would be willing to provide us with in regards to this loathsome enemy we face would be most appreciative."

Zaren, nodding occasionally as he heard Reza's explanation, looked up, quietly pondering to himself before glancing over at Jadu, who seemed to be chomping at the bit to start up their conversation they had earlier. They'd been discussing the mystical properties of the hexweave, the ethereal element that makes enchantment possible.

After a small chuckle, seeing Jadu's eager expression and uncontainable excitement at just having the prospect of holding a conversation with him, Zaren sighed and said in a surrendering voice, "Alright, you seem like good enough company to trust you with some meaningless information."

Reza's relief was slight, but visibly noticeable, and she leaned in as Zaren began to elaborate on the details of the arisen army they were currently surrounded by.

"There are three types of magic in this realm as far as we know—arcane, enchantment, and divine. The creatures, for the majority of the army, are mindless puppets. Corpses that have been animated through the latter type of magic mentioned—divine.

"The leadership, which by my limited estimate to be few in numbers, have some degree of sentience, and are quite skilled in the divine currents of the hexweave…"

Seeing Reza's slightly confused features, Zaren huffed and attempted to simplify his last statement for her.

"They are very competent in ritualistic magics," then continued his train of thought.

"Their competence in the occult divine magic more than likely signifies that their leader holds high favor with whatever deity they worship and serve, and is more than likely of some high importance, maybe even renown—at least to the likes of your company."

Not overly happy with Zaren's supercilious tone, but still wanting to remain diplomatically humble enough to juice every bit of information she could on the occult, arisen army, she ignored the comment as best she could and continued to prod the man for more details.

"So of the leaders, what else do you know of them?"

Zaren easily slipped right back into describing them, casually conversing about the subject.

"Well, not too terribly much, I'm afraid. I know most about the second-in-command. He's the one I observed close up for the most amount of time. His name is Lashik—"

Immediately upon uttering the name, the room seemed to grow dim, the flame in the lantern on the table waning. Quiet, but biting utterances and whispers issued from Reza's back pouch.

Reza recalled the name Isis had warned her about. The one who was responsible for desecrating the bound soul's family's resting place and remains.

Until then, Reza had not known that Isis had the power to influence the material world, but seeing the brief, startled expression on Zaren's face told her that this time, it was not just her that the ring had reached out to.

As the voices faded, the enchanter's expression turned from surprise to pleasantly intrigued as he stroked his beard and softly said, "Interesting. Very interesting. Perhaps your little band holds more intrigue for one like me than just your extraordinarily acumenistic alchemist here. Where did those voices issue from? Surely not your behind. It'd be a strange magic trick and an odd amount of trouble to enchant one's own rump, no matter how fine it may be."

Reza, a swirl of emotions, both defensive of keeping the enchanted ring a secret while being indignant of the old man's odd humor, forced herself to stay on task, once again ignoring his offhanded comments, attempting to put the ring in her back belt pouch out of her mind for the time being.

"What about this 'Lashik?'" Reza demanded.

Leaning back on the bed a bit more, backing off of the subject, Zaren put his hands up momentarily as he said, "Alright, it's none of my business what one does with their own body," which garnered him a look so scathing from Reza as to cause him to clear his throat before responding to her original question.

"Lashik. He seems to be beholden to a master. I don't know the master's name or much else about him, but Lashik himself is also an arisen.

"Arisen, also known by countless other terms, are simply dead corpses that have been imbued with a spirit. Lashik, and Lashik's commander, Dubix, appear to be quite sentient, which is rare with the arisen. Both are comfortably powerful individuals as far as I can tell. Very dangerous to the likes of you.

"As to their motives, I don't know. As to their army size, their numbers likely range in a few thousand, if that. The vast majority of the army are order takers and, for the most part, are controlled mind and body by their masters. That is what I know about the enemy you face."

Before Reza could finish processing Zaren's words, Fin entered the room and shut the door quietly behind him. Everyone could tell instantly something was up by his hasty entrance.

"We've got visitors—a lot of them."

Even as Fin talked, they could hear the approach of numerous boots sounding in the hall.

25

THE LAST LIGHT OF DAY

The chamber door flew open as Bede stepped into the room where she had seen Nomad taken. Smoke still lingered in the room, incense appearing just lit in trays on either side of a large throne on the other end of the grandiose room. Gold and marble pillars lined the walls, and lavish crimson drapes covered most of the room.

Looking around hastily, Bede saw an open door to the left of the room. Guessing that to be the direction they had taken Nomad, she took off running through the threshold.

Finding added confidence in each stride from her newly found powers gifted to her through her talisman, she ran headlong now down the dark hallway which looped around, coming to a spiral stairwell, leading both up and down.

Pausing for a moment to listen for signs of Nomad and his captives, she thought for a moment she heard something up a few flights.

Without stopping to confirm it, she strode up the stairs, getting off on the second floor, hearing a serpentine voice echo in from somewhere on that floor.

The room let her out on an indoor balcony that ran along a large, open room with sweeping stairs leading down to numerous fountains and plant beds. At the end of the room was a large archway leading out to an outdoor veranda, upon which she could see figures in the moonlight hauling Nomad out into the last remaining hues of a sun that had set some time ago.

Jumping over the balustrade, Bede fell fifteen feet before touching down on the hard, sandstone floor, tucking into a roll to soften the landing. She grunted through what felt like a pulled hamstring, forcing herself to get back up to speed as she sprinted towards Nomad's captors, who seemed to take note of her as they rounded the archway.

As Bede approached the veranda, she could hear the snake-like voice command, "Take care of her," and just as she approached the threshold, a large skeletal knight came back around the pillar swinging its long bastard sword at Bede's head.

She didn't have enough time to stop her momentum, so she leapt in at the knight, plowing into it before its sword could make contact with her, sending the two barreling out onto the veranda.

The knight's heavy armor made it difficult for the arisen to right itself. Bede sprung back up and dodged a weak sword swipe from the prone foe before clutching her brightly glowing talisman, shooting it towards the abomination's bleached skull.

Its teeth violently rattled out of its skull before its face began to disintegrate, bone flecking off under the presence of the bright light.

Sword clanged to the stone floor as the thing ceased moving, meriting the attention of the hooded one holding Nomad along a flight of stairs that led down off the veranda.

Bede turned around, looking straight at the one in shrouds. Out of its robe folds came a polished wand. Quick as a blink, the skeleton snapped out an undiscernible bark as a bolt of purple light shot directly at Bede's hand that was holding the white, glowing light.

The purple bolt evaporated upon striking the talisman, and Bede, not fazed in the least by the attack, began to raise the symbol up over her head and started to walk towards the evil being.

It shot an another bolt, this time at Bede's legs. Bede stumbled as the purple energy chiseled into her flesh, bringing her to one knee.

She could feel her whole leg go numb by the energy-draining blast. She worked to stabilize herself when she realized the skeleton had the wand pointed at her head, already speaking the command word to fire off another bolt.

Nomad, coming to, shoved the wand wielder, causing the shot to fire slightly off target, hitting Bede in the right shoulder, sending her down to the ground as the skeleton stumbled on the stairs with a still discombobulated Nomad.

The skeleton seemed to stable itself for a moment, but Nomad snagged the skeleton's hood before falling backwards down the stairs, a purple ray shooting off into the night sky as the two tumbled head-over-heals down a flight and a half of stairs before landing in the courtyard, neither moving once they came to a stop.

Bede, grunting through a short prayer, held aloft her talisman. It burst forth with light, instantly restoring to her control over her limbs.

Struggling to her feet, the previous encounter taking a toll on her now, Bede hurried over to the balustrade of the veranda, leaning over it to spot Nomad lying very still with the cloaked figure rolling over, attempting to get to its feet.

Bede ran over to the stairs and started down them, stumbling a few times before shakily making it to Nomad, who was unconscious, a stream of blood running down from his soaked, black bandana.

"Nomad!" Bede sobbed out, taking off his head wrap to find a very serious head wound from the fall, paying no attention to the retreating cloaked skeleton.

Nomad lay limp, head now cradled on Bede's lap, the darkening night sky casting a soft periwinkle tone over his pale skin. Whispering through a frantic prayer, Bede kissed her talisman and held it over Nomad's head wound, holding it there for a moment, continuing to pray as sinew began knitting itself back together, blood multiplying at a super-accelerated rate to renew what blood he had loss.

A sudden gasp of breath and a fluttering of eyelids later and Nomad sat up to find Bede slumped against the wall, completely exhausted now, finding that perhaps what had been draining her wasn't just the physical exertion of the chase she had been engaged in, but the repeated use of the holy power she had been endowed with.

"Bede!" Nomad shouted out, helping her to stay sitting upright. Looking around, Nomad could see at the far end of the courtyard troops beginning to enter through the high arches, the hooded figure conversing with another robed figure who turned to look at the two lying at the foot of the stairs.

"We need to move, Bede. That is a whole regiment, and they are headed right for us."

Bede knew she didn't have enough energy in her to flee. She'd just slow Nomad down. She also knew Nomad wouldn't leave her, even if she commanded him to.

Gripping on to Nomad's shoulder to help her get to her feet, she spoke in a solemn tone.

"Stay, and witness the unmatched power of Elendium."

Stepping out to meet the approaching band of arisen, Bede clenched the talisman to her chest, its glow radiating brightly.

She could now feel the energy it so subtly sapped from her, taking more as the light grew brighter in her hand. She knew she didn't have much more to give, but she at least had one last fight left in her.

She'd use everything she had now. She had to level the enemy with this attack, and she'd have to spend her life to do it. If she didn't, she knew Nomad would linger, attempt a rescue, and be overwhelmed.

The robed figure came closer, walking past the slowly approaching horde, coming into clearer view. Moonlight momentarily shone down through broken clouds, soaking into the arisen's deep-violet robes, glinting off the multiple gold adornments it wore, including a crown that sat upon its tattered and torn ashen face, flesh still desperately hanging onto its skull. Gaping holes where its eyes should have been shone with a faint crimson glow that emanated from two suspended beads within its skull.

It halted its advance, the rest of the regiment stopping behind their leader. It stood there as the moonbeam retreated from the courtyard behind a cloud, enhancing the glow from the arisen's piercing eyes.

It opened its awful maw, breathing out, "A maiden of Elendium. Most...pleasing. I've felt the power of your presence since the moment you entered this city. You are favored among your righteous god. You will be my companion, fair one. This night I prophesize it!"

As the profane voice of the robed one spoke, and as she faced a small army of the most abominable creatures she had ever faced in battle, she couldn't help but tremble at the awful evil that stood against her.

Her hand fell to her side, despair and exhaustion seeping into her flesh, when a warm, strong hand gripped it from behind.

Looking over, Nomad unlooped her mace and placed it in her open hand, smiling at her as he drew his sword, flourishing it once before looking forward to the impossible enemy they faced.

Heartened by her comrade who had become so dear to her so quickly, coming to some level of peace with this, their last stand

152

against an evil that needed to be confronted, she looked over to Nomad and said in a voice only he could hear, "This day you have found an irrevocable place in Elendium favor, and in mine. As a saint and a light bearer of his, I seal this blessing upon you for all eternity."

As she placed a hand on his sword arm, a portion of light transferred from her talisman, through their touch, to his blade, which faintly glowed as he held it in front of him.

Bede took a deep breath to steady herself and looked up with a newly determined gaze, along with Nomad, at the robed figure. It now raised its withered fleshy arm, bringing it down to point at the two, causing the regiment of death to start its march towards the horribly outnumbered duo.

26
JAWS AT THE DOOR

Boots sounded outside the five's hideaway door as a troop marched down the hall that led to the hidden underground city entrance the group had entered by.

For a good minute, boots continued to pass by the door, it sounding as though a whole regiment was passing them by.

A sudden sharp snort from a now rousing Cavok caused everyone in the room to turn an eye to him. He smacked his sleepy lips, coming out of his long nap.

A yawn, followed by a slurred "What?" caused Reza to leap over to the bed he had been sleeping on to slap a hand over his mouth.

Guttural moans in the hallway issued in response to the large man's voice, causing a wave of anxiety to sweep through the room, Cavok slowly becoming aware of the dangerous situation they were in.

The room was silent as more moans joined in, the group hearing the soldiers outside opening and inspecting the room down from them.

"Get your things. Get ready for a fight," Reza whispered as quietly as she could.

Cavok stood up and grabbed his large greatsword. Everyone else was still and quiet as death, waiting to hear what the troops outside would do next.

The door handle began to rattle. Fin flipped the lock to secure the door and looked around at everyone as the door handle started to rattle violently; then, the awful pounding of arms against the wooden door began.

For a moment, the group remained still, perhaps hoping desperately that the troop would give up their witch hunt and leave their room uninspected, or perhaps still processing their best, next move. Whatever had the group in a stupor, the spell was broken as Cavok brushed aside Fin from the door and launched a heavy kick, slamming it open while knocking multiple arisen soldiers down across the hallway.

Stepping out into the horde-infested hall, Cavok brought up his greatsword and skewered the first victim that came within reach of him, shoving him off his blade tip afterwards. He sprinted off, disappearing from the group's sight as he charged off down the hall shouting battle cries, dismembering anything that got in his path.

With a rustle of chains and hefting her shield, Reza was the first to respond to Cavok's surprise hallway entrance.

Leading the rest of the group out into the carnage, Reza could instantly tell that Cavok hadn't just leapt into the enemy aimlessly. He had cleared a path towards the hall that led to the courtyard, there being only ten or so bodies standing between him and the stairs that led down and out of the building.

"Go!" Reza shouted at Fin, Jadu, and Zaren. They quickly ran out after Cavok towards the exit. Reza bolted towards the horrors, slamming two of the walking corpses that managed to stumble past the bodies that were still prone in the middle of the hall from the door slamming open.

Reza could see that most of the hall towards the tunnel was packed with arisen, all turning around now to charge back the way they had come to rush her.

Slamming another rotten body aside with her shield, she took one last assessment of the thirty or so bodies that now wholly focused on her, their dead eyes locked on her, a tinge of demonic hunger seemingly resting just below their emotionless expressions.

The body jam in the hallway was quickly working itself out, and Reza, noticing her comrades already around the corner out of her sight, took off to follow suit.

Some of the bodies on the floor that she passed were not motionless, but they were in no state to impede her flight. Turning down the hallway, sprinting down a flight of stairs, brought her through the open doorway and into the courtyard where her comrades stood.

The group looked into the strangely lit purple night sky, illuminated by a purple bolt of light shooting higher and higher until it disappeared into the low-hanging clouds, defusing until the night was once again gently awash in only pale moonlight.

"What do you suppose that was?" Fin asked, only receiving a cacophony of moans from inside the building as an answer.

"We need to get Bede and Nomad and get out before we have the whole city bearing down on us. That direction was where they were headed. It's our best bet to finding them. Fin, you get a good look at where that flare originated from?"

Fin nodded as he pulled out two throwing daggers from sheaths along his hip.

"You lead the way then," Reza said, pushing the group forward as the first arisen corpse stumbled out of the building behind them, being met with a shield slam so powerful that it split open the rotten thing's cranium, brain matter spilling all across the ground as the small group sprinted off across the open courtyard.

27
INTO THE PRESS OF WAR

Even the thoughtless dead hesitated to rush the two glowing figures ready to welcome them. They shuffled to the side to surround the duo, moans and scathing hisses issuing from the horde of one hundred arisen at various states of decay.

The robed leader behind the horde stretched out its hand, materializing in a wisp of black and purple smoke a staff—twisted, gray, and grooved with a knot at its head. As the leader brought it down forcibly to the stone court floor, the hollow sound marked the signal for the troops to make their advance.

Bede was already channeling power through the talisman, transforming it into a floating sphere above her. She collapsed to her knees as the glowing, white orb became complete.

Bede held up a trembling finger and pointed towards the advancing horde, directing the orb to begin floating to the closest enemies. It flared brightly as it came closer to the decayed warriors, peeling flesh and bone from their frame. Those closest to it were being completely disassembled by the ball of holy light. They fell to pieces on the ground—swords, armor, and body parts collapsing in piles in the wake of the orb of pearlescent light.

Nomad charged the line to their left, knocking a spear out of his way as he came in on the front line, spinning around, slashing the upper torso of the unarmored standing corpse that had been clumsily holding the spear. The cut split the arisen's chest almost in half as it fell back on its arisen comrades.

Reversing his spin, Nomad hastily swept his sword around again, slashing through and knocking back three enemies that pressed fast in from his right, attempting to take advantage of his open side.

Circling his sword over his head, keeping his momentum, he brought the end of his blade down across the arms of a lightly armored skeleton to his left who was raising its sword to strike him. His dimly illuminated sword broke through bones like they were twigs, leaving the skeleton with nothing but stumps to defend itself with.

He was about to follow through and kick the disarmed skeleton when another one came in from his other side, slicing a falchion down towards Nomad.

Quickly repositioning his blade over his shoulder to catch the sword blade that had almost struck along his back, Nomad thrusted upwards, the skeleton's blade flinging skyward with the force. Nomad spun around to face his enemy, slashing the arisen cleanly across the spine, severing its two halves—its torso and sword landing simultaneously well behind him.

Two arrows flew in, one skipping off the stone floor beside him, giving him just enough warning to dodge the second one, purely due to luck, the dimness of the night not helping at all with seeing the projectile's path.

Another arrow came in at him, this time embedding into his thick leather pauldron, sinking into his flesh enough to cause pain, but not enough to disable the use of his arm.

Looking at the direction the shaft had come from, he spotted the three archers at the back of the ranks, notching their bows for a second volley.

A longsword slammed him from the side, luckily across his steel side plate along his hip. The blade slid off without doing any real damage but turned his attention forcibly back to the fight directly in front of him.

Bringing his sword up and sweeping it back down across the shoulder of the rotted corpse that assaulted him, Nomad sunk his blade deep into the chest cavity of the walking body.

His blade stuck in his newest victim, and the nearest arisen that surrounded him all went in, hoping to overwhelm Nomad with a rush of sheer numbers.

Gripping his sword hilt, he powered the blade through the rest of the corpse's torso, it bursting forth through the other side. Entrails spilled out of the hollow half of the fallen enemy, his blade creating a stark, contrasting glow amidst the gore as it pulsed now brighter than ever.

Nomad noticed his blade had glowed brightly when he focused his energy on the last draw. The cut, a massive eight inches of bone and flesh from a dead press, had been relatively easy for him to accomplish.

Eleven armed warriors rushed in at him. He held his sword out to his side, awaiting his attackers to get within striking distance, focusing his energy into his blade.

Rising his brilliantly glowing blade up beside him, crouching in a defensive stance, he swept the first attacker's longsword over and across before cutting back in, dropping the attacker's arm and sword. Deftly stepping past the disarmed foe, he snatched the falling longsword with his other hand as he passed, slashing into the unprepared corpse behind him, stepping out of the circle of death and into a more sparsely occupied section of the regiment.

Down slashing with both blades, Nomad blurred in and out of the confused inner ranks, dropping any that came under attack from his glowing curved sword, the longsword easily parrying clumsy attacks made at him.

He dropped two more, then leaped across the pile of fallen bones. He landed outside of the left flank of the regiment, giving him space and time to breathe.

In a wide stance, curved sword threatening any who dared to come in at him, he held his longsword back and to the side, warding off another flanking formation, nostrils flaring, slanted pursed lips hissing air violently in and out.

Looking over the battlefield, he could see Bede was still on her knees, attempting to stand. A wide swath of arisen, twenty or thirty, lay fallen close to Bede, with more disintegrating that dared to advance towards Bede, her glowing sphere burning down any that wandered too close.

A sharp pain dug into his arm, causing him to drop his longsword, two more arrows bouncing off harmlessly along his breastplate.

The soldiers who had been waiting just out of attacking distance piled in, rushing him, and this time, he had to retreat, the press of dozens of flailing weapons quickly threatening to overtake him.

―――――――――――◆―――――――――――

Her conjured holy manifestation continued to ward off any advancing group of dead that came in at her. She was supremely thankful that the killing light that hovered in her proximity was there to shield her as there was no way she had enough strength left now to even attempt to wield her mace in defense if an attacker did make it through.

She had glanced over at Nomad a few times to see how he fared, and could see that though he had cut down a good fifteen or so troops, he was dangerously digging deep into the ranks of the enemy and was too far in for her to even consider trying to help him.

The robed leader pounded the butt of his staff down on the ground once more, the sound resounding louder through the court than it naturally should have.

Bede looked up to see that the horde, all in unison, began moving in on her, slow at first, picking up speed as the front line began to fall to the ball of light, which now began to fade.

Flickering, the orb flashed one last time, blowing down the arisen that were closest to it, reducing ten rushing corpses to dust instantly.

With Bede's light now gone out, darkness instantly swept the battlefield. The front line now sprinted headlong with nothing standing between them and their target—now only a few strides away from Bede.

Bede got to her feet, having no time to summon a defense, bracing for the imminent impact of metal, rotten flesh, and gnashing teeth.

A light, shining fervently, swept in front of her, cutting through corpse after corpse on the front line, then came back around, felling the next five that rushed madly into the light, which cut like white-hot steel through straw.

Nomad moved almost too quickly for Bede to track his movements, realizing it was him only after taking a moment to assess what had leapt in front of her to save her from her impending demise.

His one good arm kept his blade in constant motion. He expended everything he had, knowing that to slow now would mean the death of both him and his battle companion.

Parry, attack, parry, attack became his sequence of death dealing as he made his way back around to their flank where the troops that had followed him began to file in, closing off any options for their escape.

Emboldened by the effective encirclement, the hoard became increasingly aggressive with their press, jabbing at the two who were quickly becoming targeted by multiple weapon points.

His armor had deflected a few blows, allowing him to switch stance to counter-attack, but he was taking a dangerous risk with every weapon that slipped through his defenses.

A spear came in at his back while he fended off three attackers from his front and two from his side, and this time the attack gouged straight through his chainmail that lined his back, the spear point piercing with enough force to split links and dig deep through his ribs.

The sharp pain caused Nomad to stagger forward, gasping in shock of the potentially fatal wound.

Three whistling arrows announced their presence a fraction before splitting into the skulls of two of his closest foes, the third arrow sinking into the base of Nomad's neck, close to his shoulder, pitching him back, strength instantly failing his already spent legs and arms. He collapsed on his back in front of Bede.

There was a momentary hush amidst the horde as the candle of intelligence inside the arisen horde's wicked souls took in their accomplishment before all hollow and dead eyes turned to lock on the remaining victim, who was barely standing.

Feebly lifting her talisman, etched with worshiping symbols to her God, she closed her eyes, transferring reserves of energy to the holy symbol, years of her life, entering a fatal bargain of *her* life for *their* death.

The talisman, glowing just as brightly as the sun at noonday, sent a burst of energy rolling through the ranks of the dead, violently blowing apart those closest to her, with a soft lightning storm rippling out to the far reaches of the vast host, rattling every last standing foe to its core, laying low the rest of the troop.

All foes—except for one.

Slowly lowering its half-bare skeletal hand, a dark-purple energy bubble slowly fading as the dust and white, glowing clouds dispersed, the leader began to walk slowly towards the two that had leveled his troop.

Nomad gasped for air, sitting up as Bede's dimly glowing hand slipped from his chest. Looking down, he could tell the arrow that had been in his neck was no longer there, and though the wound wasn't quite healed, he knew it had penetrated further than it was now—the same with his other wounds.

A quick glance around showed him a devastated enemy force, all reduced to dust or not moving on the ground except for the robed leader, which was taking its time to make its way to their location.

A commotion behind him whipped him around to find Bede collapsed on the ground next to him, all light now faded from her talisman.

"Bede!" Nomad shouted, reaching over to hold her head, looking for signs of life.

Her lips twitched and let out a breath so belabored, Nomad instinctively knew that she was on her way out of her body.

Slowly opening one eye, then the other, she looked around, confused at first. She locked eyes with Nomad, seeming to come around to where they were.

She started to speak, whispering in a voice so quiet, Nomad had to lower his ear to her lips to hear her message.

"That was all I had. I gave it all."

A gentle hand idly stroked her hair out of her eyes as Nomad looked off to the side at the ground, tears welling up in his squinting eyes. He trembled as he held her limp frame, refusing to let her let go.

"It's been an honor to have you in our lives, Kazuhiro. Keep strong…live."

"Don't leave, Bede," Nomad said in a broken voice, tears beginning to fall freely now.

Bede's eyes wandered aimlessly momentarily before closing. She parted her lips one last time to breathe out, "The doors are open…Elendium awaits my return, child—"

All tension that was left in her face relaxed as a last hollow gust of breath fled from her open lips, her hand letting go of Nomad's clutch.

Nomad couldn't see through the tears in his eyes, but he knew life had just passed from his companion.

Looking heavenward, he let out a soul-tearing scream—a primordial dirge of loss.

Hunching back over her body, sobbing, he began to notice a

shadow form over him and his fallen ally. Metallic scratching of metal footwear on stone sounded directly behind him; then, a staff landed hollowly a foot from him.

A bemused croak, then a cackle from the robed leader instantly sent Nomad's blood into a boil, evaporating the moisture from his eyes.

"She will make a wonderful maidservant," the skeletal corpse rasped out through a half smile, only some of its lips remaining to show a grin.

Nomad clutched his sword's hilt, the blade instantly lighting, white flames licking the air around it.

"I will hunt you and your evil kind to the ends of time," Nomad spat. He jolted to a low stance, yelling as he turned and swung his blade towards the robed abomination.

"Beyond death you will fear me!"

28
AT A DAGGER'S DISTANCE

Entering the shadow of the gated wall at the edge of the courtyard, Fin looked back to find the group had greatly outdistanced the pursuing arisen troops. Rushing under the raised iron gate, he stumbled onto stone flooring, passing through the large archway into a walled causeway that led towards where the purple flare had shot off from.

Coming around a sharp corner, he dodged out of the way as a long, pointed kris deftly cut in at him, the blade raking his side, luckily not finding purchase against his leather armor, but cutting loose a few belts and loose-hanging pouches.

A hooded figure, visage obscured with the shadows of a midnight cloth, stood ready for another strike, the kris held reversed in its right hand with a curved stick held outward in his left.

Fin, upon seeing the weapon his foe had chosen to confront him with, smiled.

Getting to his feet, he yanked two daggers free from their sheaths along his legs.

"You want to take me on with a dagger and a stick? That's rich," Fin chuckled, sidestepping to line his new playmate up for an attack.

A hissing whisper sounded from the shrouded figure, and a purple light emanated from the tip of the skeleton's wand. A bolt blasted forth, and Fin sprung out of the way a moment too late, the numbing energy bolt zapping into his thigh.

Fin stumbled and laboriously stood back up, his whole left leg now completely numb.

His eyes widened as the hooded figure began to hiss forth another command, wand tip glowing once more.

This time Fin was able to dodge the shot in time, knowing what was coming. As the purple bolt hit the wall behind him where he had been before his leap, Fin threw end-over-end the dagger he held in his right hand, knife knocking into the skeleton's wand hand, knocking the wand free of its grasp. The stick went flying backwards, bouncing with the knife a good distance behind the devilish attacker.

Fin landed prone on the ground, struggling to get back up, settling with a kneeling position as he studied what his foe's next move was going to be.

"Fin!" Cavok bellowed from behind, just passing under the iron gate, putting Fin in his view.

Fin turned at the call, only for a moment, but the momentary distraction was enough for the hooded skeleton to stoop down and snatch two satchels that it had sheared off of Fin earlier.

Fin, seeing the movement from the corner of his eye, cocked back his other dagger and tossed it at the figure, a skeletal hand intercepting it just before hitting its center.

A wicked laugh slowly sounded from the faceless victor of the scuffle as it backpedaled with Fin's dagger in hand, snatching up his dropped wand, rushing off through an archway in the wall into a small garden.

Feeling the remainder of his side pouches, checking what two pouches the hooded one had made off with, he pounded the ground in frustration as he realized one of the pouches held the bejeweled white-gold bracelet he had found in the enchanter's tower, the other pouch being filled to the brim with gold.

"Damn it!" Fin hissed out as Cavok and the others sprinted up to him.

Reza and the rest met him with concerned looks as Cavok patrolled the area for threats as they waited on Fin.

"Had a run-in with a particularly nasty cloaked skeleton," Fin mumbled, trying to explain off his exhausted state,

"Cloaked skeleton you say? Did he speak?" Zaren asked in a curious tone.

Fin got to his feet, Cavok helping him, seeing that Fin was having trouble with his left leg.

"Yeah, it did. Though it spoke in a tongue I've never heard," Fin answered, adding, "Hit me with a blast from its wand, numbed my whole leg."

"That was Dubix, more than likely. Sentient dead are quite powerful. Lucky you came out of that with just a numbing spell. Here, I'll take a look and see if I can undo at least some of the spell's effect," Zaren said, slipping an amethyst monocle over his eye, looking Fin's leg up and down before pulling a small, stone cube out of his robes, pressing it onto Fin's thigh and whispering a few words in a language no one in the group understood.

"Ooo! Ah!" Fin yelped and squirmed in discomfort as a popping sound issued from his hip as he skipped away from the old enchanter's painful little stone.

"There," Zaren said, a pleased grin across his upheld face.

Rubbing his sore, but once again working, leg, Fin gave a dirty look in Zaren's direction before Reza slapped Fin on the back to get him moving forward again.

"No time for antics," she said, looking back the way they came, Fin following suit, seeing that the scattered band of pursuing arisen were passing through the raised iron gate.

"Come, everyone. Together this time," Reza ordered, leading the charge forward down the enclosed causeway, covering the remaining fifty feet of street before passing through a large, stone archway that led out into another courtyard, the one that they guessed had been where the flare had been shot off from.

A soft, white glow lingered in the large courtyard, not quite covering the scores of bodies that were scattered all through the enclosed area.

One figure stood standing, and Reza pointed it out to the rest. Voices hissed forth from Reza's ring, Isis biting, scathing from her back pouch. Reza placed her flail in her shield hand and reached back to take out the enchanted ring, drawing special attention from Zaren as she placed the ring on her finger.

Zaren had felt a ripple in the hexweave, noting Reza's pupils widen and her breath halt. He suspected that she was under the influence of an enchantment from the ring. None but Reza, however, saw Isis step up to her, facial features twisted in anger and vengeance, pointing to the robed figure across the court as she seethed.

"He is Lashik, the one that ravaged my little ones. Give him no quarter. Spare him no pain. He is powerful, but you will not fight alone. I will be your strength."

Through the white mist that hung in the air and the blood-red swirl given off by the ring she wore, she could see another figure stand up out of the dispersing white mist, screaming a phrase. Though she couldn't make out the message, she could discern the speaker's voice and was instantly filled with dread. She had never heard Nomad so distraught, or even imagined him capable of such passion.

"To arms!" Reza quickly called to her companions, seeing Nomad alone next to an entity she doubted any of them were prepared to take on alone.

Readying her shield and flail, she began the charge towards the distant, robed foe Nomad now lunged at; and, though she no longer could see Isis, she could feel her incorporeal companion's bloodlust for the being they all now charged.

29

HELL'S CRUCIBLE

Nomad put everything he had into his initial strike at the oppressive, robed figure, his blade flashing a bright white through the whole arc.

The strike halted right before cleaving the arisen in half, snagging against a dark-purple net of energy that materialized. The blade hissed against the barrier, which gave in slightly as Nomad pressed in harder upon the hexweave-spawned substance.

A skeletal hand, adorned with a set of illuminated rings, emerged from folds of robes, latching its claw upon Nomad's skull. A dark ember formed, penetrating through skin, beginning to drain the life from the mortal man at a frighteningly rapid rate, forcing Nomad to relent his attack. He pushed the arisen back and away from him.

The arisen readily gave a generous amount of ground to the hunched-over warrior, laughing, waiting for his raging, but fatigued, opponent to come in at him again.

Nomad paused a moment to snort through the waves of pain and exhaustion that had just come over him. The strange magic that the being had assaulted his head with drew instant pain, but even before the attack, he had felt energy leaving him the brighter his sword had gotten.

He was still attempting to comprehend the new endowment of power Bede had bestowed upon his weapon, but with a lens of rage over his vision now, the idea to temper his usage of the sword's power was only a fleeting thought as he rushed in with a thrust to the corpse's throat.

The strike landed right over its intended target, but jerked to a halt as the purple weave guarded the arisen against the blade. A faint, crimson glow emanated now from the corpse's eye sockets, the two beads of unlife meeting Nomad's gaze, its intense stare penetrating to his core.

Nomad jolted back as he felt all wounds that Bede had healed start to open up again, a sharp pain in his neck and back cutting back into existence, blood seeping from the reopening wounds.

The grinning robed cadaver took a step towards Nomad, who now clutched at serious wounds, the white glow of the sword's light quickly fading. It raised a hand, robes falling down to display a bloody skeletal hand, rotten flesh at the arm joint and above, glowing with an agitated, scarlet swirl of distortion.

Just as it thrust its empowered hand down towards Nomad, a huge blur slammed Lashik far to the side, easily toppling him, rolling him off into the white fog that still hung amidst the battlefield.

Cavok was quick to Nomad's side. He hefted him up like he weighed as much as a small child. Nomad wobbly kept his footing once up. He was heavily dazed, but very appreciative of the large man's presence and entrance.

As Nomad looked back to see Reza and the others parting the fog, rushing to their location, Cavok asked a very pointed question that brought Nomad's exhausted gaze back to him.

"Where's Bede?"

Nomad slowly pointed over to Bede's resting body lying on the stone ground, the white fog settling around her, still ever so faintly aglow in a white luminescence.

"No," Cavok involuntarily let out, and Nomad could see the strength give slightly at the sight of his downed friend—a woman that he had felt closer to than his own mother.

Stepping, almost falling towards her, Cavok started to make his way to her body.

Fire licked away the fog as gouts of flames poured across Cavok's path, blocking him from his cherished companion. With flames rising high into the night's sky, forcing him reflexively back from the searing heat, Cavok's face turned from desolate slackness to an instant unstrung mask of wrath, his attention now fully focused on the robed figure that had conjured the flames.

Nomad clutched his sword, it glowing faintly as he saw Cavok heft his greatsword up, ready to charge and decimate the half-grinning corpse.

Cavok rushed in first, releasing a bellow of palpable fury, but Nomad was quicker, sprinting to Cavok's side, lunging in at the dark cleric, sword still glowing, though dimly now.

Striking at the cleric's chest, bending into a more pliable protective weave of energy, Nomad pressed once more the attack, almost breaking through when a greatsword came in over Nomad's head, slamming down on the cleric's outstretched, awaiting hand, stopping the blade in its skeletal clutch.

The energy shield waned greatly now, but the cleric brought its staff high, shouting a command in a demonic tongue.

Both Nomad and Cavok shouted as their bodies began to heat up, their blood seeming to boil, cooking them from the inside. Their veins began to bulge, skin turning pink red, and blood began to bleed from their ears, eyes, and nose.

Nomad's sword tip was through the magical impediment, slowly entering the side of the evil corpse, but at tremendous cost.

Just as he felt his eyes were about to burst out of his skull, he withdrew, sword clattering to the ground as he half rolled, half crawled away from the wicked cleric, attempting to retreat from the flaring pain that squeezed agony from every receptor in his body.

Cavok stood his ground, gripping with one hand on the corpse's neck, lunging in like a feral animal to bite at the decaying thing's face, being slowed by the still lingering shielding weave of purple energy that wrapped itself around the rotting cleric.

Cavok, in a crazed state, seeming on the verge of self-immolation, was blasted to the ground as a chain of lightning struck the arisen's side, blasting the thing's robes apart, leaving the right side of its rotten torso exposed as it stumbled back.

Looking for the source of the last attack, the dark cleric looked around, waving away black smoke issuing from an area of charred flesh on his side. Spotting an oddly familiar-looking, old man wearing pale-purple robes, the arisen narrowed his eyes and saw smoke dispersing from the old man's contorted, upheld hand.

The dark cleric's visage now a wicked scowl, obviously not pleased to have a fellow hexweave adept enter the fray, raised its staff while chanting a long line in a foul tongue.

Zaren was quick to reply in kind, adeptly taking out his spellbook. He found the page he was looking for in one flip and began reciting the ancient command words from the page as quickly as he could.

The drone of the two voices crescendoed as the dark cleric thrusted forth his staff, launching a whirling sphere of embers as large as a man hurling towards Zaren.

Zaren had just finished reciting his spell. The page he had been reading from flashed bright before dissolving into a spray of water, ice, and hail, colliding with the ember sphere almost instantly after being conjured.

The two elements swirled together, exploding in a bang of steam and cinder, causing such a blast that the two hexweavers staggered backwards a step as it went off, completely knocking out the already dazed Cavok and Nomad, rolling them over to the side.

"We must retreat. I am in no condition from just being released from my enchanted prison to be channeling hexweave. You will most certainly lose this fight if we stay for a few more spells," Zaren shouted above the tumult.

Reza, who had along with Fin and Jadu, been readying for the approaching gaggle of arisen troops flanking them from behind, turned to consider their options and Zaren's advisement.

She could see Cavok and Nomad's limp bodies halfway between them and the cleric, who appeared to be gesticulating, speaking in a low, sinister tone, waving his glowing blood-red ring hand in jagged motions. With the chaos on the battlefield, she wasn't quite sure what had happened to her two comrades to take them down. She didn't even know if they were dead or just unconscious, and where Bede was, but she knew Zaren's advice was sound. With explosions sounding off along the battlefield, with Nomad and Cavok out of the fight, Zaren admitting his sorcery was no match against their foe, along with being flanked by a growing number of dead behind them, she knew their only option at that point, for the safety of the group, was to retreat.

The cleric finished his chant and held the glowing ring towards Zaren, unleashing three white, phantasmal orbs of wisp, which formed into open-mouthed skulls as they made their way to the old man.

Reaching in a pouch to his side, Zaren grabbed a hand of prismatic dust. He cast it into the air right as the skulls approached him, the skulls dispersing, the disbanding animated mist filtering around him.

Multicolored flames spouted up as Jadu shattered vial after vial on the ground between them and the approaching dead ranks still filing out of the causeway corridor they had entered through. The flames roaring up from the flammable vials seemed to deter the dead for the moment, but the flames, just after being lit, already died down by a degree or two. Reza could see that the ranks were piling up, starting to push the hesitant front line into their fiery doom.

"Fin," Reza called as Fin chucked his fourth dagger into the crowd as they started to make their way through the flame wall.

"Yeah?" he answered, turning to huddle near Reza, cocking his head to hear her better over the noise on either side of them.

"We need to get Cavok and Nomad and get out. You take care of Cavok. I'll get Nomad. We break for that corridor off to the left of the courtyard. See it?" Reza said, pointing to their planned escape route.

"Yeah, but what about Bede? If Nomad is here, she's got to be close!" he shouted, having to raise his voice considerably due to another blast of flame plowing into Zaren's defenses.

"Nomad looks unconscious and I don't see her. We're all dead if we stay here any longer. We need to pull out. The city is mobilized and alerted. We're going to find no refuge within the city walls now. Pick Cavok up and head for the exit. Once that cleric realizes we plan to retreat, all hell will be bearing down on us. No looking back, got it? You lead Zaren and Jadu, who I'll hand Nomad over to. I'll be right behind everyone, watching our backs—understood?" Reza yelled back, her tone not leaving any room for debate.

Fin didn't answer, but his gaze lingered a painful moment longer before he turned to look towards Cavok's fallen body. He realized Reza was ordering a full retreat out of the whole city, not just a relocation to formulate an immediate plan to extract Bede, who was missing in action.

"Jadu, Zaren! I'm going to retrieve Nomad's body and hand him off to you two. Get ready to run for the far-left corridor and follow Fin. Don't stop, and don't look back."

The commotion of torrents of flames on both sides of them, mixed with the moans of dozens of arisen approaching behind them, parting through the flames now, made it impossible for either of the two to catch Reza's whole message, but they both nodded, showing that they understood the gist of the order just as another spray of flame came in at Zaren.

Zaren held up the pouch of prismatic dust, which exploded in front of him just as the flame tunnel crashed into him, singeing the hems of his robes as the dust broke down the incoming cinders.

"Now!" Reza shouted across the chaos to Fin, the two leaping in towards where their comrades lay on the ground halfway between Zaren and the cleric.

Zaren, opening his book instantly to the page he sought, barked out in a raspy voice, which seemed more worn and old than moments before, a quick incantation.

The page lit aglow and drifted off into nothingness as the once pale clouds above them sagged now in darkness, coalescing over them.

A thin bolt of lightning struck down along the cleric's staff, shattering it into a thousand splinters, knocking the cleric over as the clouds immediately began to let up.

Two daggers came whizzing in, thwacking into the skull of the fallen cleric, the hilts protruding from his forehead like two metal, leather-wrapped horns.

Reza snatched Nomad's sword up and sheathed it, then grabbed Nomad by his chest piece, hefting him up with a grunt, rushing back to Zaren, who now looked a picture of age, bent over and wheezing, wrinkles and sagging skin suddenly extremely exaggerated.

"We leave now. I am of no more use in this fight in my current state," Zaren hoarsely called as Reza approached with Nomad across her shoulder.

Tossing the square stone he had used on Fin earlier to the ground, it floated up and expanded under Nomad as Reza lowered him to the disk, lifting him two feet off the ground, levitating him along as Reza let go of him.

Calling Jadu over, Reza ordered the little praven to push the floating stretcher and to follow Zaren out of the far-left corridor.

Fin was no twig of a man, but he grunted as he propped the large man up, positioning the bulk of Cavok over his back, struggling his way back to the rest of the group.

The cleric staggered to his feet as Fin rejoined the group, exchanging Cavok for Nomad on the floating stretcher.

Countless splinters stuck to the rotten flesh of the cleric where it still possessed flesh, pinning its blasted violet robes to its smoking skin, the surrounding air wreaking of burnt hair, fabric, and flesh.

Steadying itself, raising a hand with both rings on its boney hand aglow in an unholy blood aura, it began chanting and walking towards the now retreating group.

Reza looked to Zaren to see if he was going to retort the spell, but Zaren, who caught Reza's questioning look, just shook his head and rushed along towards the exit threshold out of the courtyard.

"Do not fear his magic," a ghostly female voice hissed. Reza looked down to Isis' ring, then back up to the dark cleric, who had just finished his incantation, hand awhirl in incorporeal black and red tendrils that were now reaching out to the retreating group.

Reza had no time to think, she simply reacted, rushing in front of the ragged band, placing herself between the tendrils and everyone else.

Fearing the worst, seeing already how competent the cleric was in weaving the hex, she braced for a nasty, burning, soul-sucking impact, but squinting one eye open, she looked around at the honey glow that now surrounded her like an orb of opposition to the dark magics the cleric lashed out at her with.

"Go! Destroy that wretch!" Isis shouted at Reza from the ring, almost overpowering Reza with the strong telepathic command.

Reza let down her flail, sprinting in towards the cleric with shield leading, flail hanging back, cocked and ready for a blow upon arrival.

Not sure what had happened with his spell, but knowing his spell was being heavily contested by something, the cleric pumped more energy into his conduit, the ring spewing forth more lashing tendrils that were being sucked into the amber orb surrounding Reza.

Leaping the last few feet, Reza brought around her flail, slamming the chained, spiked balls down on Lashik's upper chest with bone-crushing force, pressing her shield against his body to launch Lashik to the ground as she finished out her attack with a flip, rebounding off Lashik's body to land her on her feet behind her foe.

Bones jabbing through what was left of Lashik's robes and flesh, the dark cleric began raggedly to stand back up, for the first time in the fight showing signs that the battle was taking a toll on him.

"Again!" Isis screamed into Reza's mind, spurring her on, driving her back in at the downed cleric.

Clumsily fishing through his folds, Lashik barely pulled out a small obsidian marble with ruby tendrils etched all around it before being slammed again by Reza's flail, sending him rolling to the side.

"Don't let up, Reza! *Rip* the perverted life from him! Snuff him out!" Isis screamed, the constant hounding adrift now in Reza's battle-focused gaze. She locked onto Lashik and lifted her flail again, ready to bring it down on his head.

With fractured fingers, Lashik managed to toss the stone to the ground, a purple weave of energy building up over him, hissing promises of protection from Reza's attacks as Reza brought her flail down on the crumpled lump of robes.

Her attack smashed through the underdeveloped evil shield, slamming the arisen's half-raw skull, producing a sickening crack.

"Don't stop now!" Isis continued, her voice trembling in desperation.

After raising up her flail again, with no remaining magical impediment between her and the thing's head, Reza brought down her flail with all her strength for the killing blow, but the next thing she knew, she was on the ground, air knocked out of her, head crooked against something soft.

Gasping now for air, getting to her knees, she was faintly aware of Isis wailing uncontrollably, unstable in her profanities as Reza attempted to stop the world from spinning.

She looked around, trying to figure out where she was and how she had gotten there. The first thing that came into focus was the object that had cushioned her head upon impact with the ground— and the sight she saw stilled her other, relatively unimportant, concerns.

Bede lay before her, very still, very white, not breathing.

"No," Reza shakily let out, still trying to keep her eyes in focus, recovering from whatever had landed her where she lay.

Holding Bede's head up, Reza immediately rested it back down, feeling that every muscle in Bede's neck was completely lax, seeing clearly that Bede was not simply unconscious but departed from their realm.

White hair cushioned Bede's head as it rolled to the side, quiet sobs coming from Reza as she hunched over Bede's body.

She didn't know how long she wept there, but the battlefield, in her perception of it, was still. Even the constant torrents of fire that had once scattered the courtyard died down in reverence to her mourning.

Brushing aside tears and stray hair, Reza attempted to stand back up, noticing for the first time a huge depression in her chest plate armor, the metal pinching against her body uncomfortably tight.

She limped to the side and stood for a moment, a sharp pinch along her side caused her to clutch at her armor. She realized that some ribs had been either horribly bruised or broken from the impact of whatever had hit her.

She looked out, spinning around to find where Lashik still lay, twitching from time to time. Next to him she saw a hulk of an armored figure, white hemmed, black cloak covering its head, its attention turning from tending to Lashik to consider Reza.

As it stood up to its full height of seven feet, it brought two large, angled gauntlets up to pull back the hood covering its bannered helm, strips of inscribed cloth flowing down from bands and waxed stamps adorning its exterior.

Reza stood, not sure what to do next, realizing Isis' silence for the first time since her attack on Lashik.

The figure stood silently, the night breeze rustling through its loose cloth and straps, tinkling hollowly against its impossibly thick plate mail.

Reza could see now that they were alone in the courtyard, all the other mindless arisen departed from the scene, and Reza wondered if they had passed through to chase after her comrades or retreated from their master out of respect or fear. She hoped it was the latter, if indeed this was the whispered master of Lashik.

"Isis," Reza whispered, realizing that she was not seeing the night through the ring's usual spectral lens, the enchantment either greatly diminished or completely inactive.

Whatever the case, Reza had no time to call for help from her spectral protector now as the large knight began walking towards her, dragging a warhammer by its side, the four-pronged head of the weapon being as large as a maul, with the pick curving out extensively, almost as if it were a scythe. The massive weapon must have stood almost Reza's whole height, and now she understood how her chest plate had come to harbor a massive dent in its center.

Bringing her shield up, attempting to present a defensive front against the looming figure, she looked back at Bede quickly to consider if she should hold her ground or attempt to retreat, knowing full well she wasn't going to be able to heft Bede's body and outrun her opponent with her possibly cracked ribs and armor that was crushing her with every wrong move.

The oppressive knight was deceptively fast, switching his stance last second to throw all its weight into a sweeping attack. The warhammer's pick end latched behind Reza's shield, easily ripping it from her arm, flinging it off to the side, it clattering end over end along the stone floor.

Reza toppled, the force of the yank easily pulling her down in front of the large knight. She scrambled to get back up, fighting through the pain as she stood back up to find the knight simply standing there before her, waiting on her to stand.

Resting its warhammer downward in one hand, the knight tauntingly puffed out its chest, presenting Reza with a clear blow anywhere along its body.

She staggered a moment, shaking off the torsion pain from having her latched shield so violently ripped from her arm.

Leaping up, she slammed the knight right across the neck and side of its head—the spiked, chained balls seeming like little marbles plinking against the massive figure's armor.

The knight stood standing, only the armor it wore moving with the blow that Reza gave. Reza seemed more hurt from the attack than the knight was, stumbling against her foe as her chest exploded in pain from the dynamic movement.

A large gauntleted hand gripped Reza by the head, throwing her off the mountain of armor she rested against, flinging her like a ragdoll across the court.

She tumbled to a stop, pushing up quickly to spot her opponent, jumping to her feet, fighting through the pain in her chest that was telling her to stay still.

She had to move now, or die. She knew she had to retreat, but looking for Bede's body kept her attention back towards her foe instead of to the exit.

"You would make a determined champion," a voice spoke, seeming to come from beyond the walking wall of armor that strode towards her, springing forth from the very bowels of hell.

"And only days before we walk upon the Plainstate. Such convenient timing. The countryside villages stand no chance against our forces and will only add to our numbers. The Capital will fall effortlessly, and you will be there not only to witness it, but to partake in its decimation."

Frantically looking to the approaching knight and the surrounding battlefield, Reza finally spotted Bede's body again, but it was far behind the brute that stood in her way.

She leapt to the side, attempting to get around the knight, but its massive warhammer came up just in time to bat Reza down once more. Reza managed to scurry out of the way just before the hammer side of its weapon came down, shattering the stone floor that had been beneath her.

A rune-inscribed banner burned off from the thing's helmet, wax that once held it in place melting like blood, dripping down over its face slits.

177

Dark energy tentacles burst forth from the arisen's hand. The tendrils licked out at Reza, latching on to her limbs as she struggled, gasping through the pain as she attempted to get to her feet again, holding her in place.

Stepping up to Reza's bound body, the thing reached out slowly with an open hand, gathering a swirl of darkness in its clutch. Reza began to feel her heat and life starting to drift away into the palm of the death bringer that stood before her.

The blackness within the knight's helmet echoed out its hollow voice once more.

"Have you ever felt the pleasure of slaughtering innocents—torturing those that know love—or will I be the first to show you the resounding sedation of suffering?"

Reza's jaw went slack. Her eyes wandered up into her lids as she started losing her hold on her mortal body, her soul being whisked away as the hellspawn spoke.

Amber light coruscated out from the ring Reza still wore, disintegrating the tendrils that bound her, shielding her from the whirl of death along the knight's hand.

Landing on her feet, her muscles once again responding to her command, though greatly weakened from the life-sucking assault she had been subjugated to, Reza heard Isis' faint voice.

"Go—"

Reza ran, the tendrils licking at the fast-fading golden aura that encircled her, the warding effect wearing off just as Reza passed through the threshold she had sent her comrades through, delivering her out of the reach of the molesting tendrils.

As she perfunctorily staggered down dark corridors searching for the city's exit, an empty sob escaping her from time to time, she could think of nothing other than her fallen friend she was leaving farther behind with every step she took in fleeing that damned city.

Part Three: The Vise of Vengeance

30
THE BROKEN BAND

Reza stumbled down a windswept street just outside of the city's gates. She had made it past the gates with little resistance, bolting past fifteen sentries before the troop could mobilize to stop her from leaving.

The warning call had been sounded, though, by the gate guard at the top of the watchtower, which now stood lit by the morning sun, and the distant clopping of hooves could be heard within the city walls, rushing towards her.

Just as she was about to turn down a side street to attempt to lose her pursuers, when around the sun-basked street ahead of her appeared four horses: Fin, with an unconscious Nomad tied to his back, Zaren and Jadu on another horse, and Cavok lashed like luggage across his own horse.

Rushing now towards her mounted comrades, she could tell by their expressions that not too far behind her approached mounted pursuers.

Risking being speared in the back by a charging lance, she kept looking ahead, sprinting, making it to the vacant horse that Fin held the bridle to, jumping up onto the saddle just as Fin began tossing dagger after dagger behind her at the thundering sound of hooves.

Turning around in her saddle, she could see Fin had taken the closest foe down with two well-placed daggers now stuck into the skeletal knight's head.

The blow from the daggers tipped the knight off the mount. It spilled out onto the causeway, rattling apart as it was trampled under hoof as the other mounted skeletal knight came rushing in, charging Fin, lance leading the way.

Fin held out his hands, maneuvering his horse with his knees to trot to face the oncoming attack. As Fin kicked his horse to sidestep, the horse moved him and Nomad out of the way of the spear point at the last second. He snatched the spear shaft as the knight dashed by, forcing it to the stone street. The spear point caught along a crack in the road, jolting the rider enough to become unseated from its skeletal mount, the knight landing on the ground in a heap of steel with a clatter.

Fin clapped his hands together, a puff of dust showing in the morning light, then called to Reza, "Two down, but looks like there's more on their way. They're not too fast or nimble on those wretched mounts, but we had better be going now if we don't want to get overrun. You lead the way, Reza."

Reza, trying to catch her breath after the lengthy sprint through the city with injured ribs, nodded to Fin. She kicked her horse hard, bolting it forward, turning the group down a side street that led around the city towards the highway to the Plainstate.

The road did not favor them that day. Luckily, they had not been trailed far by the arisen riders, but Cavok had been unconscious the bulk of the day, causing Fin to have to stop multiple times to adjust him on his horse's back before continuing on. Even when he awoke in the afternoon, he was unresponsive for hours later. Nomad too remained unconscious, but did not awaken until they stopped that evening to give the lathered horses a rest, some of the mounts' gasps for air starting to sound dire.

As the night drew near, the oppressive desert sun began to set on the group perched on the side of a knoll surrounded by low-hanging, scraggly ironwood trees. Fin handled the horses, giving them what little water they had brought with them from the farmhouse they had quickly raided before snatching up the steeds and rushing off to pick

Reza up in the streets.

Reza helped situate Nomad, who was just now coming around for the first time since the previous night's battle, while Jadu helped as best he could to dress the camp, getting bedrolls set up, rummaging through the group's remaining dry victuals for everyone to snack on before bed.

The group silently worried over Cavok and Zaren, both out of camp though still within sight.

Cavok stood, looking blankly in the direction of Brigganden, and Zaren sat on a large rock, looking unbelievably old and drained, shivering, mumbling to himself almost in a hysteria, turning over an odd, oblong marbled stone in his hands.

Reza and Fin, the only two in the group who had the awareness to notice, exchanged worried expressions as Cavok lumbered out of the camp and into the low mountains rising up behind their camp.

"He'll be back," Fin mused, going back to patting down the horses, sounding as though he was trying to convince himself of that more so than he was to Reza, adding, "Just needs to sort some stuff out alone."

Behind them, Nomad's voice brought their attention back to the camp. Sitting up, Nomad thanked Jadu for his offering of water.

Looking as if every muscle or bone in his body was either bruised or broken, Nomad attempted to take off his armor, not getting very far before Reza started to assist him, taking over the process while Nomad simply attempted to not cry out in pain as she peeled off battered and abused sections of armor.

"Wow," Reza murmured, taking note of the multiple complete breaches along almost every piece of equipment she took off.

"You'll more than likely need to acquire new gear after that beating you took."

Nomad just grunted, suppressing as best he could the urge to shout the pain off as Reza ripped out a side plate in which punctured metal had stapled the plate to his torso.

"Fin, where's that high-proof liquor you said might be suitable for treating wounds?"

Fin turned to consider the question and hesitantly answered, "Gave that…to Bede."

Reza looked down for a moment, having put off the thought of her fallen friend the whole day, then looked back up, putting the subject aside again, ordering, "Give me the best stuff you've got for cleaning wounds."

Fin slowly got up, rummaged through his horse's side pouch, uncorked the dark-brown bottle, and whiffed it.

"Rum's best we got. It's no pure grain, but it'll work. Hurt like the dickens and probably won't completely disinfect, but Nomad can take the pain, and it's better than not treating it at all," Fin said, replugging the bottle and tossing it to Reza.

Ripping off a strand of her tabard, Reza soaked the make-do cleaning rag in rum, asking Nomad where his wounds were that he needed her to treat.

Flinging off his whole blood-soaked top smock, Nomad exposed a myriad of wounds. Most were sizable cuts and scrapes mingled with deep-colored bruises, but there were more than a few serious gouges.

Eyes widening in surprise, not thinking he harbored so many injuries beneath his broken armor, she took in a deep breath and handed the rum over to him to swig as she got ready to start in cleaning the superficial abrasions first.

Taking a few swigs of the potent rum, Nomad nodded for Reza to start in on his back. He choked on some rum as Reza began smearing the liquor along his cuts.

"Better keep that stuff down—you'll need every last drop of it," Fin said, slightly losing interest as Zaren's rock began to glow, then flash.

A sudden laugh turned everyone's attention back towards Zaren, who seemed to look back to his former age, seeming more of his slightly unhinged self.

Giving Zaren a confused look, Fin was in the middle of asking what had just happened when Zaren explained, "Weaving so much hexweave in my weakened state began to unravel my aging spell, and a lot of other essential spells might I add. Rarely will you see me risk so much for strangers, but I did, and I paid dearly for it. But I'm at least at a maintained state now. Won't be able to weave even small spells for a while, but at least I'm out of the woods, so to speak."

Zaren smacked his lips, adding that he was hungry, offhandedly mentioning to a still dumbfounded group of onlookers, "Where's Jadu?"

Fin, Reza, and Nomad looked around, noticing for the first time the little praven's absence.

⁓

It had not taken Jadu much effort to follow Cavok's trail, his lumbering footsteps easily leaving prints in the thin crust of the high desert sandy loam.

Hopping up the last boulder, leading up to an overwatch across the steppe they had been traveling through, the last light of dusk casting its remaining light along the stretch of desert brush before them, Jadu quietly took a seat beside Cavok, who sat on a downed tree, looking out over the beautiful scene.

Jadu hadn't actually seen Bede or knew of her fate, and since no one had spoken of her that whole day, he was only able to guess why they had left the city without her.

He guessed the truth of it; that she had probably died somewhere along that terrible battle the night before and that some in the group somehow knew the details of her demise, even though he and Zaren had been kept out of the loop, more than likely not purposefully, but rather due to the tenderness of the subject.

He had never been one to truly value personal connections, prizing his research and study more than his acquaintances. He admitted to himself that to truly sympathize with any of the group that knew Bede on a deep level was more than likely out of his ability; but, for Cavok, who he had, for the first time in a long time, felt something of a connection with, perhaps along with Nomad as well, he wanted to attempt to console the man that he considered to be a friend.

Pulling out a familiar bottle, offering it to Cavok, who after a moment looked down to acknowledge Jadu's special liquor flask, Cavok let out a small chuckle before saying in an unusually soft tone for the large man, "No, little one. Some losses and pains deserve a clear head to remember."

Jadu lowered his offering, tracing the rim of the bottle idly as he silently considered Cavok's words, tucking the drink back into his pouch as he looked back out into the, now dark, landscape, the stars coming out in full bloom.

"She was a mighty woman," Cavok said, looking out into the heavens.

"More a mother to me than even my own ma. Fearless, kind, accepting, but exacting at the same time. Always expected more of you than you were, and helped to guide you to that better place. She will forever be with me in memory."

Wrapping his arms around his knees, Jadu let out a soft sigh as he sat in silence next to his reflecting friend, both observing the flickering stars long into the night.

31
A RENEWED PURPOSE

The morning sun woke the group from their uneasy sleep, Jadu being the only one to chipperly greet the new day.

Offering everyone a bit of worm jerky and the last of their water, he added that they should savor the meal as that was the last of their rations.

Reza had finished dressing Nomad's wounds the night before as best she could, and Fin had helped Reza with hers, Reza having horrible abrasions along her sternum from her inwardly dented breastplate. Not much could be done about the broken bones and bruising for either of them, most of the damage being located along their torso, but neither of them murmured over the pain as they helped pack up camp.

After having some time to mourn, rest, treat wounds, and have a bit to eat and drink, the group was ready to head out, but as to where they were headed, they hadn't discussed yet.

Reza, knowing tension on the subject of their next move was heavy in the air, called everyone in for a huddle, and the group congregated in a circle in the middle of their camp.

Reza hesitated, looking out across the warming sagebrush. Those in the group who knew her well knew that whatever the subject was, it was going to be a tough one for her to broach.

"Bede is dead. I don't know how. Nomad, I would like to know the details of her passing and how you two came to be there later, but there is an even more important matter to bring up with the group—more important even than the passing of our comrade and friend."

Her voice wavered on the last words. Clearing her throat, she pressed on.

"We got more than what we came for. Lashik's overlord showed his face once everyone left. We cannot match them by ourselves. Though my heart begs me to rush back in to avenge Bede's death and recover her body to put her at peace, we all know that would be suicide, especially with us in our current condition—so don't plead that case. I will not hear it. Bede would not want us to throw ourselves away at her expense and over remains alone at that."

Watching everyone's expression as she preemptively closed the conversation on any rescue attempts others might suggest, paying close attention to the disappointed looks she garnered from Cavok and Fin, she continued.

"That doesn't mean we won't soon be back to rip those necromantic bastards to shreds. Lashik's master let me in on their plans over the next few days. They will be marching on the Plainstate countryside, burning a path through smaller villages, gathering more to their arisen army until they assault Plainstate's capital.

"Our mission has more urgency to it now than ever. Sultan Metus must be informed of this imminent threat or the people of the Plainstate will begin to pay a hefty toll.

"We'll need to travel fast and light. No stops for rest until we're in Sultan Metus' hall—we're out of food and drink anyways.

"We've been heading northeast, off the trail to make sure we evade any potential trackers sent out after us. We made great ground yesterday, so I'm assuming we're just northwest of the town Warwick, and a good deal west of the trade city Viccarwood, which is a few hours south of the capital.

"We'll run the horses all day until we hopefully hit Viccarwood. Without a map, and none here as to my knowledge knowing this wilderness well enough to act as guide, it's going to be luck that we hit Viccarwood by nightfall, but that's the plan. If we make it there in the night, we'll pick up fresh mounts and head out to the capital and report immediately to Metus. Is everyone on board with this plan?"

Usually the quiet observer, Nomad now spoke up. "And then

what? You said we would soon return for Bede, but you would lead us away from her—a great distance away. Retrieving her body is perhaps more important than you know. Lashik promised awful things—things I wish not to speak of. Even in death, he holds great sway over the fate of a soul. It is vital that we recover her remains."

Fin and Cavok didn't need to say it, but Reza knew from their unwavering glares that they felt the same way and demanded a good answer from Reza explaining how reporting to Metus was going to help them recover Bede's body from the arisen city.

Reza doubled down on her authoritative tone, strongly replying, "You think I don't know the risks that come with leaving Bede's corpse to those beasts? We will return for her directly after informing Metus, and with his finest troops, but rushing back in now would be throwing ourselves to the afterlife.

"Perhaps we could take Lashik, though I doubt it, but you haven't witnessed the power of his master. We stand no chance. We need reinforcements. We need a whole army because we're up against the same. This is no task for a ragged group of scouts. Once we inform Metus of the danger and the threat of imminent march by the arisen on his lands, he'll have to respond, sending forces to his borders, and I'll plead the case to siege Brigganden before the army is mobile. We can lead a special unit and lead the attack since we best know the enemy. I know Metus. He'll comply, and we'll be back here within days to reclaim the city and Bede, and we'll prevent a mass slaughter of countryside villages on top of that. It's the only sensible solution."

Though she was speaking for a sultan, and perhaps oversold her relationship with him at that, she knew she needed to convince the others of her plan of action, knowing full well that if she didn't convince Nomad, Fin, and Cavok that her plan was better, they'd be rushing back into that city to their deaths, none of them standing any chance against the dominating knight of death that she had faced and was helpless next to. Even without the arisen master's anomalous and formidable command over the hexweave, she doubted that Cavok, in all his strength and determination, stood much of a chance against the arisen king's raw power.

The three were silent, each brooding over the sensible plan that Reza laid out that ultimately pulled them away from immediately doing what all three yearned desperately to do—put Bede to rest and destroy those responsible for her passing.

Nomad was the first to speak, saying, "I promised to follow and aid where I could in this mission, and I now keep that promise to you, Reza. I will go with you on the path you think best for the group—but, if we are not back to Brigganden's gates within three moons, I will come back for Bede, and I will avenge her—alone if I must. I cannot long forsake her to the cruelty of Lashik's domination in death."

Reza, noticing Fin and Cavok's approving nod, saw that she had just been given a deadline to make her plan work.

"Agreed. Three nights and we'll be back, returning to take care of Lashik, his master, and the city of dead, with or without Sultan Metus' help."

32
THE DESOLATE RIFT

The high steppe offered little for the eye to wonder about. They traveled east the whole morning, passing a lone mountain to their north, bringing a drop-off into their view on the horizon.

The horses had gotten one break the whole day. The group had unmounted to allow the mounts to completely lap up a shallow basin of water that sat in the depression of some exposed bedrock.

The pack, even the riders, now rank of horse sweat, the horses having been coated in white frothy lather from midmorning on.

An hour later, Reza called for a halt at the edge of a large ravine that stretched as far north and south as the eye could see, impeding them from continuing east.

Fin trotted up, the horse's knees buckling dangerously close to the cliff's edge due to fatigue, forcing him to back away.

Fin, jumping down off of his horse, said, "Maybe another day's worth of travel just to get around this canyon on horse—who knows, maybe more. The horses are spent. They haven't had a good ride in years. I doubt they've even got a few more hours left in 'em before they collapse. What do you say about crossing that ravine on foot and turning the horses loose?"

Reza was thinking quietly to herself as Jadu piped in, "That cliff is no less than three hundred feet sheer! For a praven, that's more like six hundred feet! How on earth do you propose us descending that height without the solution ending in a splat?"

Wanting to see if Fin had an answer, Reza allowed him to answer before jumping in.

"Well, take a look," Fin said, jumping up dangerously close to the cliff's edge, hovering over the three hundred-foot drop without even a second thought to the danger he was standing over.

"It's only this side of the canyon that'll give us trouble. The other side, and the canyons beyond, look quite graded. Slopes will slow us down, but won't be tricky like this cliff face."

"How does that answer Jadu's concern?" Reza scoffed.

Fin looked back and then pointed to a broken section of cliff face out of everyone's sight but his.

"I was getting to it. Look there. A few hundred feet down is a section of cliff wall that seems manageable. Really manageable with rope, which we don't have, but maybe doable with my supply line."

Fin, stepping back to the group, pulled something out of the leather bag that hung along his back, producing a long cord of thin, braided cable.

"It's only seventy-five feet, but it's probably enough to get us through the difficult parts."

Reza gave him a hard look, internally considering their options. Dismounting, she crept over to the edge of the cliff, taking a closer look at the broken section of wall Fin was suggesting they descend at.

It looked rough, and though she knew Fin would have no problem downclimbing the treacherous heights, she had no idea how some of them would make the feat, Jadu and Zaren in particular, or her with her bruised ribs, or Nomad for that matter with his many injuries.

Backing away from the edge, she turned Fin's proposal down.

"It's too dangerous. How can you expect Zaren or Jadu to make that descent?"

"*Ahem*," Zaren mumbled, clearing his throat to enter the conversation.

"We would be the least of your concerns. I've been talking with Jadu here about teaching him a bit of my craft, and a levitation spell would be a great first trial for him! He could attempt to levitate him and myself down the cliff wall. I'm still much too weak to channel that amount of hexweave, but I've got one more page for that spell prepared and he could do it for a party of two. You all would still need to make your way down somehow, but we'd be fine."

Somewhat taken aback by the twist in the conversation, Nomad asked, genuinely concerned for their safety, "What if Jadu can't hold the spell and you two fall?"

"*Ooohehehe!*" Zaren laughed, causing even Cavok to look over in concern at the odd old man.

"Well, then we'd fall to our deaths!"

All eyes turned to Jadu, who only just shrugged his shoulders and said, "Best way to learn how to fly is to jump and try, right?"

Reza turned away to look at the vast expanse again, muttering, "This is crazy," while Zaren continued to cackle, patting Jadu on the back, laughing longer than he should have at any joke, let alone a statement where no one but he found the humor in it.

Sighing heavily, frustrated at the hand they had been played, Reza turned and asked Nomad and Cavok, "What do you two think? Could you handle that climb? We'll stick to the horses and head north if not. Viccarwood has got to be somewhere just beyond that line of canyons. If we travel through the night, we might reach it by morning. Once we make it past this cliff, we should be able to handle the rest of the terrain without too much trouble—I agree with Fin on that."

"Yup" was all Cavok had to say, not even taking the initiative to look at the cliff wall Reza was asking about. Nomad, however, took a peek over the edge before nodding his affirmation to that route.

Looking hard at the horses, Reza took off a pouch she had looped around the saddle before slapping the horse's rump hard, sending it off into the desert prairie.

"Hope they can find some water. There's plenty of edible grass for them out there," she said while watching the horse gallop away.

She let out another sigh as she started over towards the cliff's edge where they were to make their way down a sketchy, three hundred-foot stretch of rock and narrow ledges with nothing but a seventy-five-foot cord between the four of them.

33
THE CLIMB

The rest of the horses were unloaded and sent off. Reza and Nomad shed the remaining armor they wore, seeing that they'd need all the mobility they could get, along with a streamlined load, in order to make the climb.

Cavok took off some heavy plates of armor from his side and lower body too, but instead of placing them in a pile up top, he tossed them into the canyon to retrieve them after the descent, the plates falling for many seconds before clanking off rock and dirt at the bottom.

Looking over the edge where they were to begin their descent, Fin started talking his way through the planned path to the canyon floor so far below them.

"See that first ledge maybe a hundred feet below us?" he asked Reza, pointing to a narrow, sloped section of dirt that shot out from the side of the cliff wall.

"We'll use my cord for this first section. I'll go last to recover the cord and down-climb this without the assistance of the line. After that, I don't know if you can see it from here, but I saw a chimney from the other vantage point over there. We'll shimmy down that as far as we can and then use the cord again to rappel down the seventy-five feet that cord will give us, and then climb down to the second shelf, which again, you can't see from where we're at, but it's down there, believe me. After that, it's pretty simple bouldering down a steep, but not vertical, hundred feet or so."

Reza, looking very much as though she wished she had not sent the horses off so early, got up without responding to Fin's plan and walked over to Jadu and Zaren, who were sitting down and poring over a book together.

"Odd time to read," she said, getting Jadu's attention, his smiling face looking up immediately as soon as he realized someone was talking to him.

"Oh, not at all! This is Zaren's spellbook. He said it's been with him for longer than any of us, together, have been alive—can you believe that? He's going over the fine details of the lesser levitation spell he wants me to perform. Very complex matter it is, much closer to a science than anything. Which is good, since I'd hardly be able to master it if it were an art," adding in randomly, "Apparently casting an enchantment without a focus to draw the energy from will drain some of one's own life essence! Isn't that amazing!"

Reza looked worriedly to Zaren, knowing how seriously wrong spells could go in the hands of even learned apprentices, let alone first-time enchanters.

"You have a focus for him to use in casting this spell, don't you?"

Zaren looked up, smiling, but still seeming quite tired, as if not fully recovered from the rough time they all had over the last few days. "Yes, yes. I have something that'll do for this spell. The page the spell is inscribed upon alone will cover most of the spell's required hexweave resources. We'll be fine."

Jadu began asking a string of questions Reza didn't understand, the two conversing once again, ignoring the rest of the group.

"Good luck," she offered to the involved pair as she went back over to the rest of the group.

"Done. The anchor is set," Fin proclaimed, finishing off hooking the cable around a large shrub a few feet back from the edge of the cliff.

"That's going to hold Cavok?" Reza asked, worried at the prospect of their lives literally hanging from a bush on a cliffside.

"Yeah, that stuff's copper oak. Roots are supposed to go down pretty deep and wide."

"Ready, Nomad?" Fin asked, handing him the cord, Nomad

nodding in affirmation, slinking over to the edge and dropping over before Reza could object to demand she be the first one over.

"Guy's not afraid of anything," Fin said with a grin, watching the foreign man gingerly maneuver down the cord in a strange method, facing down while walking downwards, gripping securely the cord by his hip.

Nomad was at the end of the cord within only a minute or two, halting at the end of the cord to inspect the best method of getting the rest of the way down the twenty-five to thirty feet of wall.

The wall wasn't featureless. There did seem to be quite a few nooks and crags to cling to, but the only line that he could see that would get him all the way to the ledge below him was a small, vertical crack in the wall to his left below him. If he could get to it, the broken line of rockface would more than likely be able to offer him enough handholds to work with.

Swinging over gently on the cord, Nomad had to painfully stretch, reopening freshly healing wounds, to plant two feet along a ridge just about where the crack started. He came to the end of the cord and his hands became slightly moist, forcing him to work fast on the task at hand. He did not know how long he could continue to hold the thin cord at its very end with a moist grip.

Slapping to the wall, releasing the cord, he immediately began to work his way down to get his hands where his feet initially landed, giving him a great hold on the wall.

The screech of a hawk overhead and a gentle breeze were the only sounds to accompany his descent, the rest of the group watching silently as the man dangled from the rockface far below them.

Reaching down, he latched on to the lip of the crack, leaning on it tentatively at first, then placing all of his weight on his fingers as he clung to the side of it.

Splitting his legs slightly outward, bracing himself and walking down as he hung off to the left of the crack, hanging from his frame, Nomad began working his way down the crack.

It took Nomad twice the amount of time to climb down along the rock wall than it had taken him with the cord, but as he touched down along the large, sloped ledge, the group up top cheered, excluding Reza, who wiped a few beads of sweat off her brow. She exhaled and looked away for a moment.

"How was she?" Fin yelled, referring to the climb.

Nomad clapped his hands together in victory, taking note of his audience. The bandages across his chest and stomach were noticeably bleeding through in spots, but as he looked up, he smiled and called out, "Not too bad! Hands got a little sweaty towards the end of the cord, and you will want to watch out for that. There is not much to grip with that line. There is a crack that runs all the way to the ledge and that worked well for me."

"Can't wait to try it!" Fin yelled back down, looking over to Reza, asking, "You next, milady?"

Looking to Fin with a blank expression, she looked down the wall, spat out a swear, and snatched the cord from Fin's offering hand, then slowly made her way over the edge of the cliff.

Reza clung to the cord, holding it close to her chest. She walked her way down the cliff, slipping once or twice a few jerky inches before catching herself, putting the onlookers on edge as she made her way to the end of the cord.

Wrapping her hand around the cord's end held her up short a few inches from making it to the ledge Nomad had pointed out.

Looking for another option to make her way to the ledge, she spotted a potential hold she could reach.

Knowing she had little time to dally on the end of the line, she swung herself over to the large hole in the wall, far to the left of the ledge, reaching out to throw a hand in the hole, supremely relieved as her four fingers latched on to a nice lip in the hole just as her grip on the cord unexpectedly slipped from her.

She wasn't looking up at Cavok and Fin, but their worried expressions, especially that of Fin, who had his palm pressed firmly to his forehead, did not bespeak confidence in Reza's climbing abilities.

Reaching over to the ledge Nomad had used, she leaned over and made her way to hang along it, getting a bit more comfortable with the flow and rhythm of the climb, seeing that there was a clear path down to where Nomad stood looking up at her.

"You are doing great, Reza!" Nomad offered, hoping to help encourage her along down the crack.

Wedging her fingers in along the black depth of the crack, she started to attempt to position herself just as she saw Nomad had done. Her technique looked shabby compared to his, but it proved an effective method for traversing that stretch of wall and was working for her.

She slowly worked her way down along the crack into Nomad's helping arms, Nomad making sure that she landed on the sloped ground without issue.

"Nice job—we're proud of you!" Reza could hear from above.

Putting on a half-crooked smile, Reza checked her placement on the sloped cliffside, looking back up with a once-again serious face, waiting for the group's attention to be off of her and for Cavok to start his descent.

Reza and Nomad waited a good minute or two, both starting to wonder what the holdup was when Fin, not Cavok, came over the edge of the cliff. Wearing Reza's discarded gauntlet, steel cord wrapped around it, Fin easily managed just the right amount of slack and speed to lower himself quickly to the end of the cord.

Without coming to a complete stop, Fin hopped onto the ledge that rested just above the vertical crack that led down to Nomad and Reza.

Crossing his weight with every downward movement, Fin walked his way down to land between Reza and Nomad, tossing Reza her gauntlet, saying, "Rappelling down that tiny cord might work out to be a lot more manageable if you use this. I'll show you how to work it while we wait for Cavok."

Though Reza didn't seem too concerned about Cavok being the one to free-climb down the hundred feet of rockface without the aid of the seventy-five-foot cord instead of Fin, Nomad looked up, an uneasy expression clearly visible as the large man crested the edge of the cliff and started his way down the cliff wall, meticulously at first.

"Don't worry about that one. I probably should have suggested to have him do the bulk of the heavy lifting on this climb from the start. He's a much better climber than I, though he may not look it," Fin said to Nomad, seeing the worry on the man's face at a glance.

Cavok was picking up speed now, becoming more limber as he stretched out his massive muscles, his legs bulging with every step down, arms supporting him during key transitions of his hefty weight.

"He used to climb nonstop with his brother growing up. Though they've been separated for years now, he still wanders off as he's been with us to go climb mountains we rest near. I say he's crazy, but he is very good at it. Has to be, or he'd be long dead. Can't take many long falls and get away with it, right?" Fin added, softly talking sideways to Nomad as all three looked up at the spectacle that was Cavok, his back a constant motion of corded tissue as he worked his way down the cliff at his own, leisurely pace.

Cavok slung down to the nice-sized ledge that the rest had all started their climb on, easily passing it by, going to the crack, using the same back-and-forth method of down-climbing that Fin had used to walk down to where everyone now stood, the sloped edge starting to get uncomfortably crowded with the addition of Cavok's large frame.

The rest of the group attempted to gingerly spread out to give Cavok some room to stand on the slope. Reza went rigid as she attempted to plant her heels in the shifting dirt, her footing slowly giving way, promising to slough her off the angled cliff edge within a few feet.

A large hand snatched Reza by the scruff of her shirt. Cavok acted as an anchor, the group watching as dislodged rocks continued to slide along the path Reza had been on towards the cliff's edge, rolling off out of their sight. The only sound was that of trickling sand being carried up in the wind as it was whipped back up to the slope's edge. The group listened as the rocks a few seconds later exploded hundreds of feet below them.

The whipping sand flow died down and the group stood still as their attention turned from the grim close call to the odd image of Jadu and a displeased-looking Zaren dropping quickly past them, seeming to be falling slightly slower than they should, but not by much.

The group on the ledge could make out Jadu saying, as he zipped past them, "Let me try that again," the two then disappearing out of their sight a moment later.

Reza, along with the rest of the group on the ledge, held perfectly still, listening for word from the oddball couple, hoping to not hear the same explosive ending as they had with the rocks a moment earlier.

Gut-churning moments passed by, and after a few seconds of supreme stillness, they could just make out a tiny voice loudly exclaim, "Told you, I always get it right on the second try!"

With everyone letting out a collective sigh of relief, Cavok began looking around for the rock chimney Fin had mentioned earlier.

"Thought that was our best route, Fin?" Cavok asked. Fin turned to consider the section of wall.

"Yeah, it goes down maybe twenty feet before it lets out to more cliff. There seemed to be enough cracks and spires that we'd be able to anchor the cord at the end of the chimney, which should give us enough length from the cord to descend most of the sheer wall before touching down on the next ledge."

Cavok pulled the cord from around his waist, looping it up once more, checking to make sure everything was in order for him to utilize it while under pressure on the wall.

Setting an anchor while climbing was no small feat, even for him, and he took two deep breaths before starting down the slope to the right to start the climb, calling back as he began testing his footing along the rock pillar opposing him, "I'll call up when it's safe to start climbing down."

Bracing his back along one side of the large break in the rock, feet holding him up while he pressed against the other side of the rock slab, Cavok began sliding down the gash in the mountain face easily, disappearing from the view of the rest of the group, switching sides as the chimney became more pocketed on the other side the farther down he traveled.

Switching off to just one side of the wall as the gap widened, Cavok unlooped the cord from around him and looked for a good place to anchor it.

Looking around, poking at holes and protruding rocks in the cliffside, Cavok let out a frustrated sigh, hanging on to the rockface that, just below him, let out over a seventy-foot drop before hitting a ledge over a steep hundred-foot slope to the canyon floor.

The tip of the cord was clipped into a loop, which fastened to a steel ring. The best he could see to do with what the cliff face offered him was to wedge the ring into a crack in the wall. It wasn't how he preferred to anchor the cord, but it was all he was seeing available to him at the moment.

Finding the best slot within his grasp to wedge the ring into, Cavok slipped the end of the cord into the crack, fidgeting with it for a moment before it wedged into place, not giving any as he tugged the cord downwards.

Working with it a bit more, tentatively putting his whole weight on it once for good measure, Cavok called up the chimney.

"Alright, come on down!"

Hearing some scrambling up top, figuring that the group was getting ready to send someone down, Cavok carefully put his weight on the line, slipping down over the edge of the overhanging rock channel.

The overhang left him a few feet from the rockface, leaving him hanging in midair over a huge drop to the bottom of the climb, causing him to be hyperaware of the thin braided-steel cord he hung his full weight on.

Reaching up to the rock roof of the overhanging slab by his head, he sought for a place to hang on to, wanting to get back onto the wall, trusting his own hold on the wall much more than he trusted the thin cable.

He knew that since the cable had supported his weight so far, it was more than stable for the rest of the lightweights in the group soon to follow, but even still, depending on the cable put him on edge.

He and his brother had never used rope or other climbing gear for a number of reasons, and among those reasons was that they didn't trust their lives to the sturdiness of a single device. They much preferred to place their trust in their own skill and strength.

"There you are," he said, smiling as he spotted a huge cavity in the side of the rock just below the roof of the overhang. The lip of the cavity would provide for a nice hold to hang and rest out on, which came as a relief since the cord now cut into his fingers, naggingly so.

The hole was just out of reach, even for his long arm span. He looked up to the tip of the cord, knowing he was going to have to swing lightly on the cord to get over to the wall.

Pushing off of the roof gently, swinging his legs to get the momentum he needed to rock himself back, he swung on the cord once, building up enough movement to get himself close to the rock lip he was shooting for.

As he swung out one more time from the wall, a sudden jolt in the cord set his nerves firing, his mind for a split second in shock as he thought the cord had given out on him. The cord caught and held him a moment longer, swinging him back to the rock wall. His wavering faith on the line had been completely depleted with the sudden, inexplicable slack in the line.

As he swung in, his momentum bringing him within reach of the hold he was going for, the line completely gave out, dropping him, forcing him to leverage every bit of forward momentum he had built up to thrust him to the hole in the rock that held his last chance at recovering from a fall that could easily kill him.

Every nerve in his body was screaming—every muscle exploding beyond normal functioning limits. The moment passed in a blur as his hand slapped against stone.

34
TRUST AND SACRIFICE

Thrusting three fingers into the hole, slapping over the lip of the large pocket in the rock, Cavok clenched his fingers over the slope of the lip, locking his thumb over for support as his body rebounded off the rockface, luckily—very luckily he knew—sticking onto the wall after the initial slam and jostle of the impact, his vise-like grip holding steady through the tumult.

Gasping for air, wide-eyed, looking down over the vast expanse that he had just barely managed to avoid falling to, he took his free hand and wiped massive beads of sweat that had formed over his brow from the intensive movement and stressful few seconds.

Readjusting his weight, getting a more secure hold from the pocket hold, he looked down, seeing the cord finally touching down at the bottom of the climb. Jadu and Zaren were there looking up at him, spectating the almost disastrous moment on the rock wall.

Looking down below him, Cavok started to look for a route the rest of the way down, knowing that he wasn't going to be able to hang on to his spot on the wall forever. Luckily, it seemed like the rockface was very diverse, with rock formations leading all the way to the next ledge.

The climb down he wasn't worried about now, but the rest of the group now would have to make the climb with him, and on top of that, they also needed to traverse a difficult overhang.

Cavok knew that normally, just the prospect and sight of an overhang feature in a climb was usually enough to demoralize novice climbers and put expert climbers on edge. The very strange sensation of hanging over nothing was the hallmark and pinnacle of the most difficult technical features of climbing.

Cavok would have just talked the group through what they needed to do to traverse the juncture, but as he already knew from attempting that earlier, he saw nothing along the roof that offered much option for safely making it to the handhold he now latched onto.

"Cavok, where's the rope?" Reza called out from just above the overhang, a bit of concern discernable in her voice.

Looking around frantically for options to scream out to him, Cavok took a deep breath, steadying himself, thinking through briefly their only options.

He could tell Reza to attempt to climb back up the way she had come, a feat that wouldn't be very doable, he knew from the last ten feet of the chimney being the most difficult to not just down-climb, but would be that much harder to climb back up. If she did happen to make it back up to the ledge, the rest of the group would have to reclimb the hundred feet of wall to make it back to the top of the canyon's rim. If he had to guess, judging by everyone's performance thus far, Fin would be the only one he'd bet on to make it, with risky odds placed on an injured Nomad—but he knew Reza stood little to no chance at successfully rescaling the route, knowing her skill on a wall to be little better than a novice.

The other option they had was to continue down the wall. This was the crux of the climb, the most dangerous, technical, and difficult part of what the wall would be asking of them. If he could assist Reza and the rest past this point, they could more than likely handle the rest of the climb without issue. He just needed to figure out how to get them all past that barren gap that separated them from where he clung, latched to the wall some six feet away.

"Cavok! You down there?" Reza said, notably more worried now.

Deciding what he was going to have Reza do, a solution came to him, and he called up in a sure tone.

"I'm here—come on down over the lip. Don't worry, I've got you from there."

He listened—stillness answering him back as he knew Reza worriedly considered what Cavok was asking her to do. There was no rope where there should have been, and now Cavok was asking her to let herself down over a complete drop-off—suspended over thin air. He was asking her to trust him wholly that he did, indeed, have her from there.

"Reza. Trust me," Cavok called up, an underlying calming cadence clearly coming through to Reza up above, neither being able to see each other but understanding one another through tone better than if they had been face to face.

Cavok could hear shuffling up above, then two legs hung over the cliff's edge, lowering the rest of her body over until she hung freely over the edge of the cliff. She assessed the situation, her limbs going close to numb with fear, a terrible sinking feeling in her loins, the feeling of terror sinking down through her core to her pelvis. She gave a look of incredulity, and then of fear, to Cavok.

He knew she felt as though he had just betrayed her and sentenced her to death, but if he didn't get her to move fast, the chances of her falling would rapidly become more a likelihood, as he knew her muscles weren't trained for the wall and would give out much, much quicker than his, seeing that the pang of fear already was sapping her of her courage and energy.

"That hold you have is solid," Cavok started, trying to inspire a bit of confidence in her as he continued. "You need to swing on that hold. Swing to me. It's only a few feet. I'm here. You jump to me and I've got you. I'm ready for you."

Reza, turning her gaze from Cavok to below her, revealing a hundred and seventy foot space between her and the canyon floor below, froze up. She looked up the way she had climbed down, considering if she would be capable of rising up to the necessary challenge of reclimbing the route she had been led down.

"Nope," Cavok forcefully said. "You can do this. We're here already. You have to make this jump. Don't look down. Clear your mind. Focus on this one move. Think only of this leap. Focus. I have you—trust me."

"Bastard," Reza spat out at Cavok while making a nervous attempt to reposition her sweaty palms on the rock ledge she clung to.

A tremble in her left arm showing, she eyed Cavok again, knowing now that there was no other option. She didn't have the strength to pull herself back up over the ledge. She had to do as

Cavok had commanded—focus, leap, and trust that he would catch her. That was the only choice she had now.

Rocking her body forward, then back, once, twice, she decided that on her third lunge, she was going to launch herself at Cavok, who clung to the wall with one arm, leaning as far out as he could, ready to catch her.

Letting slip the ledged section of rock that she held to, sand sprinkling down from the cracks in the rock above, Reza shot forward, her trajectory quickly sagging, gravity pulling her down, out of reach of Cavok's outstretched hand.

As he lunged out his arm, a distance that she didn't know Cavok was capable of, his hand gripped her wrist crushingly so. They both swung up against the rock wall, crashing hard, but with Cavok still holding to both the wall and to Reza, a desperate gasp for air issuing from her once she realized she wasn't falling any longer.

"Told ya," Cavok smiled, hefting Reza up to cling to the wall alongside him. "I'll always have you."

Reza laughed in nervous relief. Cavok knew he was probably going to get a wicked earful from Reza later about tricking her into the difficult situation, but for now at least, she was alive, and that's all that mattered to the both of them.

"Rest a bit with me here and regain your strength for the rest of the climb. Looks simple enough. Think you can handle it. Soon as Fin or Nomad gets here, though, you'll have to be on your way. I'm going to need to do the same for them."

Reza nodded, catching her breath while inspecting what was still below her to downscale. Spending a few moments to confirm that the climb below did seem a lot more manageable than previous wall sections, she looked back to Cavok with a smile.

"Thanks for catching me."

Never had Cavok heard a more sincere, simple statement before from Reza, and he could only think to respond with, "Next time you can catch me—deal?"

Reza let out a tension-relieving laugh. She looked below for the first time to notice that they had an audience who Reza could barely make out, Jadu and Zaren, watching them from a couple hundred feet below them along the canyon floor.

"I think Jadu and Zaren are pointing above us. What do you think, Cavok?"

Squinting down below, Cavok nodded in agreement just as Fin called out, up and over the overhang, "Cavok—Reza."

"That's your cue," Cavok said to Reza, calling out loudly to Fin, "Yeah, I'm here. Reza's on her way down now. You need to come down off the overhang's lip. I'll fill you in with the rest once you're there."

Reza, shaking out the tension in her forearms, started to climb down to the first clear line of foot and hand holds, leaving Cavok up under the lip of the overhang alone again.

The two could faintly hear Fin mumble, "Fill me in with the rest as I dangle in midair? He's gonna hear it from me once we're down off this rock, that's for sure."

"Reza," Cavok called as he waited for Fin to make his way over the lip of the overhang. "Make sure if you start getting fatigued and need a break to stop sooner than later to do that. Never know when you'll find a good hold to shake out on."

"Got it," Reza called up as Fin popped down from the ledge, hanging on the same lip that Reza had clung to for dear life.

Looking down, seeing that Reza was safe and climbing down a well-featured route, Fin looked over at Cavok and said, "Well, you're a good six feet away from me and I don't see a nice way to get to where you're at. What's the plan, and more importantly, what did you do with my cord?"

"Your cord was garbage. Almost cost me my life," Cavok stated, moving on to answer Fin's first question.

"You're going to swing and jump to me and I'm going to catch you."

"That's the plan?" Fin asked, a bit uneasy.

"That's the plan," Cavok said evenly.

"Alright..." Fin murmured, pointing a demanding finger at Cavok and adding, "Better catch me."

"Better jump far enough," Cavok shot back, leaning out, getting into position, reserving his stretch slightly to force Fin, just as he had done with Reza, to jump farther than they thought they would need to so that he could make up the difference if he needed to.

"Here we go," Fin grunted as he started to swing his body forward and back, a bit of grit pouring down from above as he swung.

Leaping forward, letting go of the ledge, Fin launched forward with such force that he practically slammed right into Cavok's mass. He clung to the man with all his limbs, so wrapped up around him that Cavok didn't even need to hold on to the cat-like object that clung around his chest and legs.

Gripping Fin by the scruff of his clothes, Cavok lifted him from around him and placed the man on the wall, saying with a smile, "Here you go, little one. Your own spot on the wall."

Now clinging to the wall, his breathing noticeably heavy, Fin gave Cavok a glare before starting to climb down, mumbling under his breath, "Don't you call me *little one* or you'll be drinking alone for the next month…."

Giving him a few moments to vent, Cavok called down after Fin managed ten or so feet of cliff, "Hey, Fin. How soon do you think Nomad will be along? My arms are starting to get a little pumped."

Showing the slightest concern for his friend's tough role of having to stay on the wall longer than all of them and taking into his own hands the personal safety of each of them, Fin obliged Cavok with a reply.

"Should be down in just a few minutes. He knew I was going to be climbing fast so he started even before I made it to the end of the chimney."

Cavok traded off hands and rested the arm that had born him up for the last ten minutes, stretching out his stressed arm.

Without warning, Nomad's legs slipped over the ledge into sight, followed by his increasingly bloody torso, and finally his head. He looked quite relieved to see Cavok close by.

"Change of plans? Where's the rope?" Nomad asked, seeming more curious than concerned about the unexpected change in the route.

"The rope didn't hold my weight, so you're going to have to swing and jump to me. I'll catch you."

Looking down, Nomad could see Fin and Reza descending along an easy route, with Reza almost to the bottom already.

"Alright. Ready for me now?" Nomad asked, squinting to look at Cavok through a curtain of sand from above as Cavok again switched hands so that he had his predominant hand open to snatch Nomad once he jumped.

"Ready," Cavok answered, leaning out to catch the man.

Nomad swung back on the ledge to get some momentum for the leap when the slab of rock he hung on shifted, pouring more sand down on him, blinding him as he swung in and then back again, Cavok yelling to him to jump through the swirl of sand—but it was too late.

The rock slab that each member had swung on had had enough, and as it broke off from the rest of the ledge, it swung Nomad out away from the cliff face, leaving Cavok hopelessly reaching for him.

Nomad fell alongside the slab, a sick feeling of fear instantly pounding into his gut.

Gripping to the falling slab and launching off of it midair, he attempted to make his way back to the wall, but his spring just sent the slab slightly farther outward, and by the time he had performed the quick midair feat, the fall was over.

Blackness, then a sickening commotion, then pain, then blackness again assaulted him before he realized he was spinning—tumbling uncontrollably—on and on until he came to a sudden stop, his face cracking against a rock.

He had no notion as to how much time had passed—it seemed like only moments—but soon he was partially aware of a voice calling to him, yelling at him.

His mind was a swirl of impending unconsciousness and agony, but through the midst of it all, he was distantly aware of his thoughts.

The voice screamed to him again and his head was lifted up.

Was it Reza? *Gods, the pain!* A hundred points on his body stung, each vying for his attention.

A crippling crunch snapped through his chest, as his head was raised. His lungs exploded in pain, his breathing immediately becoming more laborious, feeling now like he was drowning, though he knew that they were nowhere near water.

The darkness that had been ebbing and flowing now washed over him in full force, threatening to snuff his consciousness out, washing away the pain with it.

Only gingerly fighting it off, he let go as a torpor blanket fell atop his mind, shutting all stimuli out.

35
NIGHT COACH

He had had visions of an angel visiting him in his unconsciousness. A holy figure administering to his wounds, coaxing him back to a more lucid state, rejuvenating his body, nursing it back from the brink of destruction.

He saw through a haze, devoid of time, and as he opened his eyes, he realized that he was waking back to the physical realm. He wondered if he had slept his whole life away, having no reference of how much time had passed.

"Nomad." A voice cut through the dim of the night, stirring him out of his half slumber.

A hand gently grasped the side of his face, and the same voice, a voice he recognized to be Reza's, spoke his name again.

"Nomad. How do you feel?"

Looking up at Reza through the dim light, Nomad attempted to sit up, wincing only slightly as he felt soreness along his sternum and ribs.

Looking around, he saw that they were in a moving carriage, the faint starlight of the desert night sky twinkling outside, accompanied by the paced *clip-clop* drone of horses' hooves in the background.

"We just left Viccarwood—now we're headed to Plainstate's capital, Sheaf. Going to be morning soon."

Nomad could tell that Reza was more subdued than normal, her voice more soft than even he thought it could be.

"What's wrong?" Nomad asked, looking into Reza's sleepy eyes, seeing now that she was barely sitting herself.

Slowly blinking, seeming to strain to stay awake, Reza began, "You were dying."

Sitting back, resting against the wall of the carriage, she continued, "I got to you just in time, I think. You seemed to be slipping from us fast. I had to heal you or you weren't going to make it."

"The touch of a saren," Nomad whispered, realizing that she had used her innate healing ability to revive him.

She nodded. "Yes, and the greater the healing, the greater the toll it takes upon me. I almost passed away from that one. You were upon death's door. So many injuries. So much pain…"

Nomad looked off into the passing landscape, the weight of Reza's sacrifice slowly sinking in

"Thank you, Reza," Nomad said, placing a hand over hers. Reza answered with a smile of acknowledgment as she rested her eyes, falling asleep quietly in the dark, rhythmic drum of the carriage.

36
A ROYAL AUDIENCE

"You two, we're here," Fin said, nudging both Reza and Nomad, waking them from their deep slumber.

Nomad sat up, still feeling the soreness along his chest, but moving quickly to help Reza lean forward, allowing Fin to assist her out of the carriage, Nomad stepping out afterwards.

"Daren, see to their carriage and horses," ordered a smartly dressed female Nomad knew to be haltia, an elegant race whose bloodline and history traced far back into the world's past.

"Guard. With us," the haltia crisply said, ordering one of the gate guards to follow behind the group as she led them through a small garden towards a mansion the size of which Nomad had not often seen.

Looking back at the guard, still a bit befuddled as to where they were and who their new company was, he looked ahead at the haltia once more, looking her over more carefully to try and piece together what was going on.

She stood high, perhaps a foot over him, more on par with Cavok's height, and her elegant gait was fluid, effortless. Her hair shone a bright white, the noonday sun shimmering along her long, breezy hair as she walked. Her physique, as with most of her kin, was trim and delicate, though from the stories he had heard, their size was no gauge to measure their strength by.

He had also glanced at her face upon exiting the carriage and knew she bore the trademark sign of her race—large, metallic silver irises and frosted lashes and lips. Their stunning visage was a sight few, other than haltia themselves, ever got over.

"Do you need assistance, sir?" the guard behind Nomad discreetly asked, apparently noticing that Nomad was favoring a leg and unwittingly clutching at his side.

"No, thank you," Nomad said, waving off the man's concerns, clearing his thoughts of the striking haltia as the group entered a great greeting room, two balconies lining the tall walls up above them, a grand flight of stairs stretching out before them.

The group was led up the stairs, the sweeping banister that ran along it a welcome sight for Nomad, who leaned on it liberally as they made their way to the third floor.

The haltia turned left at the top and raised a hand, landing three brief knocks on a door that was framed with gold inlaid rosewood.

"Yes, Leith. Come in," a man's voice within the room spoke.

Turning the gold handle, the haltia opened the door and entered, announcing, "Lady Reza and her company just arrived. I brought them straight in. You mentioned that you wanted to see them as soon as they returned."

Everyone entered the room with Reza at the front, standing steady on her own now, having shrugged off Fin's support as they entered.

A man whose age evaded Nomad, looking rather young, but with the occasional slight sign of time to his features, stood up.

He was robed in royal-purple, loose-fitting open robes that cut in a V line all the way down to his navel, showing a slit of his well-toned torso. His garb was lined with tiger's fur, and his whole ensemble easily bespoke extravagance and a culturally rich local, which Nomad comfortably assumed to be the sultan the rest of the group had spoken of. The turban on the man's head, topped with a red, large feather up the front, caused a raised eyebrow from Nomad, impressed with the strange new sights that the sultan's establishment provided.

With the rest of the group dropping to a knee in respect, Nomad followed suit, not knowing the customs in the presence of royalty in this region, completely relying upon the others' actions to guide him through the meeting.

"Arise," the man said with a smile, walking over to Reza, offering her a hug just as she struggled back to her feet.

"Good to have you back. I was beginning to worry for you, Reza," the man spoke in an easy tone, and added, "as I also worried for you, Fin and Cavok!"

Nomad sensed an uneasiness in the room by most present, and he was beginning to wonder if perhaps the personable display the sultan was showing was too informal for Reza and the rest of the group to feel comfortable with. Not knowing the culture, he could only guess, but as Sultan Metus brought up his next question, Nomad reconsidered his assessment of the uneasy tension in the room.

"Where is Bede?"

"We need to discuss our mission with you, your highness," Reza said in a controlled voice, her staunch soberness erasing Metus' cheerful demeanor.

"Yes," Metus said gravely, then called for his steward to retrieve a few more chairs for everyone to have a seat.

The haltia returned with two more chairs, one for Zaren and the other made for a praven, which Jadu hopped up on almost as soon as the haltia had placed it down.

"Thank you, Leith," Metus said softly, adding, "Stay if you would," halting Leith as she was heading out the door.

Closing the door, she came to stand by her liege, the room quieting before Metus asked, handing a pad of paper and a wetted quill to Leith, "Now, your mission. If you are ready to give a report, I will listen, and Leith will record. It seems urgent, whatever you have discovered. Take all the time you need."

Taking a deep breath, gathering her thoughts, Reza began.

"After we set out for Brigganden, which we had decided to approach from the north, we came upon an odd caravan. They were far off, but seemed heavily armored and dark, not seeming to be any local militia that any of us could recognize.

"We tracked them through the day when a sandstorm hit, and shortly after, we were attacked. I got separated from my companions in the fray, and this man," she said, motioning to Nomad, "came to my aid. I would not have survived without his care as I was poisoned during the battle and would have surely died without the medical help of *this* skilled praven," she followed up, now motioning to Jadu.

Being mentioned, Jadu hopped up from his chair and walked over to Metus' study desk and held out his hand, saying, "Jadu, at your service, my lord!"

Metus smiled and gladly accepted the offer, shaking Jadu's small hand, looking up to Nomad to ask his name as well.

"Nomad, also at your service," Nomad added, leaning forward, offering a bow instead of a handshake, Metus returning the gesture with a nod of his head.

"As you have saved the life of a servicewoman and a dear friend of mine, I thank you. If I can ever repay you for your kindness, you simply may ask it and I will do what I can to assist."

"We are grateful," Nomad said, bowing his head once more in appreciation, Metus again returning the gesture with a smile, asking Reza to continue the report afterwards.

"Recovery, travel, and regrouping back up put us a few days behind schedule, and once I was reunited with Fin, Cavok, and Bede at the Gravine Ruins, Jadu and Nomad here wished to travel with us. I allowed them to join our company as both had already proved their worth and knew of the risks involved with traveling with us.

"The six of us then headed south to Brigganden. We arrived there without too much trouble. We spent the night in the residential district outside of the city walls. The houses and land seemed to be partially destroyed, mostly by fires, and as far as we could tell, completely abandoned. Looted caravans line the main highway.

"We came to be aware of scouting regiments of twenty or so armored soldiers—enough to determine that there was an occupying army within the city walls. The soldiers consisted of, as earlier reports had said, arisen. We can now confirm those outstanding claims that were in question."

At the news, Metus' demeanor darkened noticeably. He looked off to the side to consider the confirmed malicious presence at the borders of his lands.

Reza only halted for a moment to allow Metus to take in all she had reported on thus far, which also allowed Leith time to catch up with her record-keeping.

"We gained access to the city by route of a hidden, underground military access tunnel. Its location, if you don't already have records of, I can later show you on a map.

"Once inside, we set up camp in an officer's quarter, deploying Fin and Jadu to gain access to Darendul Tower, which is the highest point in the city, to survey the enemy force's numbers and activity.

"We also deployed Bede and Nomad to investigate the royal court district, assuming any leaders present in the city might naturally establish themselves in the preexisting locations of power and luxury.

"Fin and Jadu successfully gained entrance to Darendul Tower and happened upon this enchanter, Zaren," Reza said, finally motioning somewhat reluctantly to the old man, who, up until that point, hadn't seemed interested in the least to the report Reza was giving.

"Zaren Zebulon, Seal Keeper of Darendul, High Arbiter of the Order of the Bolt."

Though Metus seemed to keep his composure better than his steward, it was obvious to the group that both Leith and Metus had heard of their aloof companion.

"It is an honor to welcome a Seal Keeper *and* a High Arbiter under our humble roof. What a pleasure," Metus said, bowing his head, clasping his hands together, Leith following suit.

"Rarely do Seal Keepers leave their places of power. Many years ago, as I understand it, the Darendul order considered settling here, but chose to settle in Brigganden instead for social-political reasons. We've always attempted to maintain a positive relationship with the Darendul, even though we've had our, sometimes extreme, differences with Brigganden. It's good to welcome even a servant of the order, let alone the Seal Keeper to our capital. You are always welcome here."

Reza at least attempted to conceal a confused glance back at Zaren, but the rest of the group openly showed their surprise.

Zaren, holding up a hand, waved off the usual display of generous hospitalities shown to him from rulers and magistrates who knew the importance of his station and bade Reza to continue with her report, interested even less in Metus' offers and praise than he was in Reza's report.

Gladly getting back to her report, Reza continued.

"Fin and Jadu came to learn that Zaren had a great deal of information on the occupying enemy force and they convinced him to return to the officer's quarters to relay that information to me.

"He did so, but during the meeting, our location was compromised. Arisen swarmed the wing we were in and we fought our way out to link up with Bede and Nomad."

Reza paused a moment, deciding how best to phrase the next part of the report so that she would be able to get through the emotionally heavy details without compromising her composure. She was already completely exhausted, and with the added task of having to detail the fall of her friend before everyone was going to be difficult, she knew.

"We came upon Nomad, who was engaged in combat with an evil cleric, and Bede…was dead by the time we arrived. I still don't know the full details of what transpired with Nomad and Bede's mission. Perhaps he can tell us himself, but we were forced to retreat. The cleric was too powerful for us to effectively combat in our wounded state, and the cleric's master showed up then, preventing me from retrieving Bede's body.

"We traveled as quickly as we could to come here. It's only been two nights since we left Brigganden, and we came in a hurry, risking a great deal to deliver vital information regarding the enemy's size and their motives, but most importantly, their imminent plans to march upon the Plainstate."

Metus, though he seemed crestfallen after the news of Bede's demise, continued to pay attention intently to Reza's report till the end, sitting back in his grand chair, taking a steadying breath before speaking.

"Though I have known you, Reza, and Fin and Cavok, for a few wonderful years, Bede, as you know, was the one that introduced all of us to each other. She had served as my advisor to the small number of Elendium followers we have in the Plainstate since I have been in power. There's only a few flagging congregations within all the Plainstate, and her role wasn't of great import in a regional sense, but she, out of all my religious council, I could relate with. A wonderful sister of the faith, and a brave, strong woman. Never once did she let her years show, and I'm grieved to hear that she's left us.

"You may know better than I of what type of proceedings would be appropriate to pay respects to her. Let's discuss them together after we discuss the details of the imminent threat you mentioned from this arisen army."

Reza nodded, agreeing to get through the rest of the threat of invasion she had hinted at first before discussing what he could do for Bede further.

"By our estimation, and Zaren's count, the arisen force consists of a few thousand soldiers. We had encounters with all three of their leaders and know two of them by name.

"Dubix, who seems to be the underling of the other two, but still formidable, seems to command the army under the orders of the other two arisen leaders.

"Lashik is second-in-command, and he's a very experienced cleric. He is extremely dangerous. I would not face him without the aid of divine holy aid.

"The last, and the biggest threat of the three, is their master. We don't have a name for him, but when I faced him, he told me they were about to move upon the Plainstate within days, decimating the smaller settlements before coming here to sack the capital before looking beyond the Plainstate to war and expand their foothold in the region.

"I managed to slip away, but I can say, his power is evil on a level I've never experienced. Such a vile creature of darkness, I've never faced in this life."

Bringing a hand up to his chin, considering silently Reza's report for a long while, Metus said, more speaking aloud his thoughts than asking Reza a question, "They are to march upon our lands within a day or so. That's assuming he wasn't goading you, feeding you information and then letting you go, or that he hasn't changed his plans due to your escape—"

Reza cut into Metus' verbal musings, firmly stating, "Of changed plans, I cannot say, but of him purposefully feeding me misinformation, I know it was not his intention to let me slip from his grasp. He fully meant what he told me."

Though Leith seemed displeased with Reza's interruption, Metus took Reza at her word, seeing how convinced she was on the matter, surmising, "Then we must make all preparations for war. Either this arisen lord intends to march upon our people immediately, or he has the lingering motive to do so eventually when convenient. We will be there when that move comes, and if it doesn't soon, then we shall use your advisement on where and when to strike the city to break up that lingering threat. It's been a year too long already, and now that we know our foe and their motives, it is time to dispel them from our borders."

"How swift will be your march?" Reza asked directly after Metus had finished his statement.

Metus considered Reza's heightened concern over the matter for a moment before replying with more details regarding the assault timeline.

"As quickly as we can. We have reserve soldiers barracked here in the capital along with a missionary force of priests, but they only number near a thousand. We'll need to send for militia in the two northward towns of Ashfield and Dover and draft from Viccarwood, Warwick, and Barre to have a sufficient army to contend with roughly two thousand arisen.

216

"To send word to and organize that many men, we should have the main force down in Warwick within a week.

"We'll send word to Viccarwood, Warwick, and Barre to mobilize within a day or two in case we don't show up with the rest of the army before the Arisen force begins their march since their first target will likely be the closest village to Brigganden, which is Warwick.

"If, after that point they haven't attacked, I'll send scouting parties out to provide reports of Brigganden. If it does appear the army is there, we'll surround Brigganden, rout out the enemy, and reclaim it."

Metus could easily discern that Reza was disappointed with his answer. Looking back at her comrades, she could see that the group now exchanged clued-in glances between one another.

Metus called to Reza, directing her attention back at him.

"Reza, what is this about? What concerns you?"

Reza turned to see that Fin, Cavok, and even Nomad looked as though they were about to speak in her place if she didn't come forward with their concerns for the timeline Metus had just laid out. She replied, "Is there no way to make it to Brigganden sooner than that? We made it here in two days, partly on foot. Surely you could summon enough troops and move on the city sooner than a week or more."

"Reza," Metus replied, showing the slightest sign of strain, "you know full well that I can't just throw men haphazardly into enemy territory. These are lives, not just numbers, we speak of. To not ensure we have an adequate force and intel before going to war would be a horrible malversation on my part. A week is as soon as I can promise to have a force strong enough in number to confront this enemy at their own gates if they are still within their city walls."

A quiet voice behind Reza responded with, "Not good enough."

Leith, standing next to Metus, stiffened, giving a look so deadly at Nomad for his disrespectful words that it made Reza uncomfortable, even though the look wasn't directed at her.

"Bede will be lost to the perverted clerk long before then. It has been two whole days since her passing. Perhaps she has been puppeted by Lashik already. We cannot allow her to remain in his hands a whole week longer."

As Nomad talked, Metus and Leith realized he spoke not to Metus, but to Reza, who, instead of turning to face him, pinched the bridge of her nose, closing her eyes, facing the floor.

Metus, finally beginning to understand the strange time requirements Reza was pushing on him, asked, "Bede's body remains in the arisen's possession?"

Reza opened her eyes, looking up at Metus, but could not speak, a powerful wave of grief and guilt sweeping over her. The kindled understanding of Lashik's and his master's dark intentions and powers, having their way with Bede's body, and possibly her soul, easily painted a bleak, likely picture of what might have already become of her dear friend.

The silence prompted another question from Metus.

"This Lashik. You believe he will attempt to corrupt and raise Bede as one of his own?"

Reza's continued silence moved Nomad to answer for her.

"Yes. Lashik made many threats to Bede during our encounter of that nature. And judging from the powerful understanding of the hexweave, I do not doubt he can make good on his threats. I have sworn to avenge her and do what I can to make sure Lashik does not enslave her body under his dark influence—just as Fin and Cavok have sworn to. This is why we must return as soon as possible. Bede's body, and perhaps her soul, are at stake."

"Ah," Metus said, sitting back in his chair, considering the group's uncovered motives. "That makes more sense."

Letting out a sigh, care for Bede's predicament obvious in his demeanor, Metus looked to Reza and said after a moment of consideration, "I cannot push the timeline earlier than a week to move on Brigganden. I will not endanger a great many lives for Bede—but if you are set on moving in to recover her body, then I can provide support for your recovery mission.

"Any supplies you need, they will be freely given to you. The fastest mounts, a guide to lead you quickly back, rations, weapons, armor, I can even offer you the aid of a few of my elite guard if desired. We will push as fast as we can to siege the city, but no doubt if you depart for Brigganden today, you will arrive many days before we are ready to attack, and you won't be able to rely upon the support of the military of the Plainstate in any of your schemes."

Reza now spoke, pushing past the sorrow attached to the subject of Bede.

"We will not endanger the lives of your troops. This is a mission we take on ourselves. The aid of supplies and a guide would be greatly appreciated, though. We lost almost everything we had getting here."

Nodding his head, Metus said, "Very well. Leith will see to supplying you for your venture. I will assemble my council and set forth preparations for war immediately."

Standing up, Metus came around the desk to offer a hand to Reza, clasping her arm reassuringly as he said in a softer tone, "I most likely will not see you again until after this soon-to-be war has ended. I surely hope I do not send you and your crew off to your deaths. It is an awfully risky task you have set out for yourselves, but I wish you all safety and luck. May you accomplish what you set out to do."

"Thank you," Reza whispered, clasping Metus' hand firmly before he smiled and moved over to Fin and Cavok.

"Good luck, you two. Keep an eye on each other," Metus offered to the duo, who were more sober than usual.

With that, Metus beckoned for Leith to follow him out of the study room, taking her aside to whisper something to her out of earshot of the group before departing, leaving Leith there with the group.

"Reza, when do you wish to depart for Brigganden?" Leith asked from the hallway.

"Immediately," Reza answered, getting up to leave the room, the rest of the group following her lead, leaving the sun-warmed comfort of the study, heading off to the steel-lined palace armory.

37
REARM

A bladed tail whipped threateningly by Nomad, the four-foot-tall wolf-like creature staring calmly and unblinkingly at him. Thick, black plates of natural armor ran along its back and underside—sharp, protruded claws showing, even in rest.

"They really are tame beasts," Leith mentioned to Nomad, who wore his reservations for the beast on his sleeve.

"I know they look a bit—disagreeable—but they'll follow the stable master's commands, and if that means to follow your command, then that is what they'll do. Much faster than a horse off trail, and much more intimidating to hostiles."

"Yes, I am sure they are," Nomad nervously replied, slowly offering a hand face down to the beast as a peace offering for it to sniff him. The beast just stood there, gaze still fixed on Nomad, not appearing interested in smelling the strange man in the least.

"Don't worry, the trailblazer we're sending with you knows each of these dolingers. If there are any problems along the trail, she can handle it."

Giving up on making kind with his soon-to-be ride, Nomad turned to see what Jadu and Zaren were up to, seeing that Leith was now off to discuss something with Reza, who had just come into the stables from the armory, outfitted with the same garb they all wore now, save for Zaren and Jadu, who both insisted on only wearing their robes.

The outfit seemed to be of high quality. It was a light militia suit of thin plate mixed with a very light coat of mail. The patterning was one he had never seen in a mail weave before, and the alloy was unknown to him. The cloth and embroidery was some of the finest he had ever worn, and the sandy brown silk satin conformed and flowed with his every movement without much noticeable restriction or noise.

He had lost much of his previous attire in the battle with the hundred arisen, his armor taking so much abuse that it rendered it unusable. Though he had had that suit of armor for years now, it being one of the few ties he still had to his culture and people, the gear was beyond repair as it was already on its last leg even before being so brutalized in Brigganden. He had to admit, though he missed his old outfit, the new clothes and gear felt cool and comfortable on him now.

Nomad moved over to Jadu and Zaren, who were in the shadows of the corner of the stables.

"Jadu, seems you intend to return to the city with us? It will be dangerous, and I don't believe Fin, Cavok, or Reza expect this of you. Will you not stay here in Sheaf?"

Nomad's words cut through the ongoing conversation between Jadu and Zaren, but the praven looked up instantly, leaving Zaren frustrated with the interruption. Jadu squinted his face together, seeming almost offended by the question.

"Well of course I'm coming with you! Zaren's headed back to reclaim his tower, and I must help! He's offered that I could be his understudy if I help him around the place as he prepares the rites necessary to usher the other enchanters back in from the dimensional rift they currently reside in. What an exciting offer, is it not?"

Nomad crooked his head, not sure how he felt of his strange friend's motives for continuing on with them. He supposed Jadu and Zaren had little interaction with Bede, and to expect his, or the others in the group's, level of dedication to her cause from them was slightly unfair, but he guessed he was more taken aback by the straight honesty from Jadu's open motivation for tagging along than anything. Thinking of it then, Jadu had always been very open with why he desired to tag along, and never once had it to do with anything other than personal gain and scientific understanding.

"Then Zaren, you plan on heading back with us to the arisen city. Are you and Jadu to head straight to the tower, or do you plan to tarry with us until our mission is seen through?"

Nomad's question to the old enchanter seemed to increase his displeasurable demeanor. Scrunching up his lips as though he suddenly had a bad taste in his mouth, Zaren looked sideways at Nomad and reluctantly answered

"Help your little, clueless band which I have already helped enough? Finding Jadu here was a good trade for the information I gave you of your foe, but overexerting myself in a weakened state, forcing Jadu's first spell upon him so hastily on the cliffs, and now being asked to return and help you fight a foe who is so far above your understanding and ability that he'd sweep the floor with your corpses within a blink of confronting him without my aid is not worth any talent you could present to me for a pupil—"

Zaren paused, drilling a crusty look at Nomad doggedly as he stalled before finishing his statement.

Nomad smiled smugly in return. He knew Zaren's kind. Not enchanters, but he knew elders back home who on the outside showed an odd, and sometimes seemingly pointless, mulishness, but on the inside exhibited a betraying softness upon important matters.

Zaren's crinkled lips scrunched even more so as he spat out hurriedly, "I'll aid you where I can to retrieve your friend's body from that arisen. After that, though, I am done helping in your little adventures. To the tower it is for me and Jadu. You'll be able to rely upon our talents no longer!"

"You honor us, and Bede. Thank you both for returning with us," Nomad said with a small bow, getting an unpleasant grunt out of Zaren from the gesture.

Noticing a commotion over by Reza and Leith, Nomad watched curiously as a woman, the likes of which he had never seen before, entered the room.

She was tall, as to average female human height, but still a good six inches beneath Leith. She moved with the same grace present in Leith's heritage, the haltia, but with an added swagger. Her hair was long, streaks of stark white running through her hazel braids, her highlights shimmering even in the shade cast by the roof of the stables. Her clothes showed openly her smooth, toned physique— skin a sun-kissed tan.

Her face was the most striking of all. Though most of her

features were of a more average, but lovely, sandy-colored silken tone, her eyes speckled with light traces of metallic sheen—green irises frosted with silver flecks.

He had seen wonderfully exotic races in his time, like that of Leith's people, the haltia, and he had seen stunning, lusty beauty, like that in Reza and her people, the saren, but never had he seen the two so strikingly intermixed. He couldn't help but to stare at her, taking in her presence.

"Reza, this is Arieoneth. Sultan Metus' favored trailblazer and guide of the Plainstate—she's also my little sister. She knows every brush trail and indigenous creature within our borders. A better guide you'll not find within the Plainstate."

The woman offered a slight bow to Reza, holding an arm over her chest as she did.

"Call me Arie. I'll guide you to Brigganden. If we leave now, you and your company will be at its walls by tomorrow night."

After Arie's greeting, Reza replied with gratitude, exchanging names and pleasantries.

With hearing her smooth voice, one that seemed deceptively soft, but holding authority with every note, Nomad's fixation only tightened, and Arie seemed to notice, making a side glance at him.

Reza noticed the direction of Arie's gaze and offered, "This is Nomad," then walked the group over to him; he was still fixed on Arie. She smiled amusedly at the enchanted man, seeming to be quite used to the response.

"He's saved my life more than once and has shown his devotion and bravery in battle by our side. He owes us little and we owe him much. He's quickly become a good friend of mine."

Reza's last statement, though she spoke it tersely, snapped him out of his bewitchment. He looked to Reza, who seemed to be overcompensating her unusually sentimental words with a cold look on her face. An easy smile came to Nomad as he considered her.

"Fin and Cavok are over there," Reza said abruptly, obviously uncomfortable with the situation she had put herself in.

Expressing appreciation had never been a strong point for Reza, which Nomad had quickly picked up on about her. Working to contain his amusement, he watched as she now motioned for Arie and Leith to follow her over to her longtime companions.

As Leith turned to follow Reza, Arie turned to give Nomad one last glance, a smirk returning as she turned to follow Reza and her sister over to Fin and Cavok, who were busying themselves with going through the new provisions they had been given.

Catching his gaze sinking down her lower back as she walked away from him, Nomad shook his head, not having to forcibly temper his will with women in a long time. He did not need such a distraction now, and he knew while he stood there, goggling like a youth, so easily taken by a pleasing body and pretty face, Bede's immortal soul screamed out for his return and attention.

The sooner they were on the road, the better.

38

THE TRAIL BACK

The game trails had changed ever so slightly since the last time she had passed through the canyon's rough terrain. The quadspire boars that inhabited the area had trampled old trails and created new ones through the shrub brush—but it was not enough to throw her off.

Finding the narrow shelf along the Desolate Rift's canyon wall, the one that had given the group she now led so much trouble, the dolingers made quick work of scaling the narrow sloped shelf leading to the top of the cliff.

Just as the last dolinger that carried Jadu and Zaren crested the ledge, the deep-orange sun caressed the horizon, resting next to Desolate Peak, casting a purplish-red light all across the plains that seemed to stretch out forever.

"Sun is setting. Dolingers are fast, but their stamina isn't quite what a horse's is. We should set up camp here for the night to give them rest before tomorrow's long run," Arie said to Reza, who readily agreed, trusting Arie completely with the strange mounts that had borne them so quickly across the Plainstate wilderness that day.

Both women turned to look to Cavok as he spoke his first words that day on the trail.

"There's a smell on the air. I smelled it in the canyon too, but it was old. This is fresh. Some kind of large beast. Its musk is strong."

Fin and Nomad now also turned to Cavok, both very well aware of how accurate Cavok's ability to sense danger on the air was.

"You have a good nose," Arie said, giving the large man a look of praise, adding, "You smell the scent of a quadspire boar, probably more than one. They tend to wander in a drift. Not a large one by most species of pig, usually ten or so, but quadspires grow to the height of a dolinger."

Pausing, Arie waited for a response from Cavok, curious to see what the man's reaction would be from the announcement.

Cavok nodded, saying in a low, reverent voice, "Honorable beasts. I've heard tale of quadspires. Ferocious and magnificent to hunt. There is a people I have visited that require their youth to hunt quadspires alone. If they live through the hunt, they become an adult. If not, they're considered dead or banished from the tribe. That is the only time they are allowed to kill a quadspire in their life. The beasts are said to be a challenge to take down, even for fully matured adults, and in that tribe, I *just* qualify physically for a matured adult."

The quiet talk of the beast that was more than likely in the area caused Fin, Reza, and Nomad to shift uneasily in their saddle, not realizing what dangerous territory they had previously unknowingly wandered through.

Arie was impressed with the strapping man's knowledge and appreciation of the boar that had been the end of more than a few caravans and nomads in their lands. Outsiders rarely respected how harsh the wild in the region could be, and they often paid with their lives.

"Good. You know a thing or two of the wild. Rarely do I guide those who appreciate the danger I risk my life to keep them from," Arie said, giving Cavok the slightest smirk before Reza asked a question that the others wondered about as well.

"Will we be safe tonight then? Perhaps we should continue on."

Looking back to Reza, Arie said confidently, "No, we will be safe tonight. Quadspires *hate* the scent of dolingers. Their meat spoils horribly quickly after they die, and even a boar's gut isn't strong enough to stomach the various diseases inflicted upon those who attempt to eat dolinger flesh. Since they're not good for eating, and dangerous to confront, quadspires don't snoop where dolingers wander."

"Right," Reza said, and then called back to the rest of the group,

"Let's pitch camp here."

While Arie took care of the dolingers, the rest of the group laid out bedrolls and made a small fire, just enough to cook dinner on, which Nomad did.

Jadu served everyone a full portion, the group chatting a little with each other till the sun was completely down over the horizon and the sky turned from deep red to a dark blue, the stars casting a faint light across the ground, which still radiated heat from the baking it had taken all day.

Most headed to their spots in the campgrounds, bedding down for the night, but Arie stayed up, letting the group know that she'd keep watch that night so that all could get a good night's rest.

Busying herself with tending the fire and the dolingers from time to time, after coming back in the camp from checking on their mounts the second time, she noticed that everyone, but Nomad, was fast asleep.

She had heard that the group had come in after doggedly working their way across untamed country with little rest or supplies. She figured that the lack of any polite objections to her staying up alone on watch, and them falling asleep so easily, was probably due to the exhaustion each of them carried from pushing their bodies so hard the last however many days they had been on the trail.

But this Nomad, the one who had coyishly gazed upon her at their first meeting, refused sleep, and using the talent so naturally gifted to her by her heritage, she stalked quietly into the camp, watching the man, curious as to what was so important as to resist precious sleep.

His armor and upper garments were neatly placed on a cloth by his bedroll, exposing the man's lightly scarred, olive skin.

He was a specimen of a healthy, male figure, she would admit to that, and as he seemed to appreciate her earlier that day in the stables, she, under the secrecy of the night, did the same to him now.

Seeing the glint of steel, Arie paused, seeing that the foreign man held his sword out in front of him, either meditating, training, or perhaps up to something more sinister in nature.

Holding back, she decided to continue her surveillance, slipping a hand to her dagger's hilt at her side.

Nomad's forearms and bare chest heaved as he seemed to struggle with the blade, trembling slightly as the sword began to glow a faint, pearly white, striking a brilliant contrast to the dark blue of the night.

The white glow didn't hold long, and the blade's luminosity quickly faded back to its standard sheen, leaving Nomad heaving as quietly as he could, obviously exerted over the display.

"I wonder," Arie softly said, as not to wake the others. Nomad looked up slightly startled, realizing he was not alone.

"Did that glow come from the weapon, the wielder—or perhaps a little of both?"

Meeting eyes with her, Nomad retrieved his scabbard, nocked the tip of his sword along the lip, and crisply slid the blade in, setting the weapon gently down atop his clothes beside his bedroll.

"If I am to be honest, I could not say for certain myself," Nomad replied, going from a kneeling position to sitting cross-legged, looking up to Arie.

"You—" Arie started, lingering on the word, considering her next, "are a stranger to this land, but I can't place from where."

As she hovered by his bedroll, Nomad could see that her intention was to idly converse, and he offered her a seat at the end of his bedroll.

Arie gratefully accepted his offer, sitting directly across from Nomad, leaning in slightly.

"Far to the east is my home. Years has it been since I have seen the face of my people. It is rare that those I meet now have even heard of the land I hail from."

Arie knew of civilizations and cultures to the east of the Plainstate, but none that fit Nomad's appearance. He was surely human, but his olive-toned, tanned skin seemed a shade more light and yellow than that of the Tarigannie or Plainstate people, and his jet black hair, wispy facial hair, and narrow, slanted eyes spoke of distant origins, ones that she had never come across.

"Though," Nomad began to say, still thinking on her question, or his response to her question, "there are two faces from my kind I have been cursed to confront, time and time again. Lingering shadows from my past, determined to haunt me, across the lands, endlessly."

Looking up, noticing that he had perhaps delved too deeply into allusions of his past to a complete stranger, Nomad looked to Arie and asked, "What about your heritage? You seem different than most haltia I have met."

"That is because I am not *only* haltia," Arie stated, causing Nomad to look a bit abashed for intentionally bringing into question her mixed heritage, a subject that he realized easily could be sensitive.

Holding a hand up to reassure him she had no issue openly discussing the matter, she offered, "I do not hold any ill will to either of the races I was born of. It makes no difference to me if I were born full haltia, or full human. What matters is that I was born at all and that I am still alive to enjoy that life."

Nomad smiled at her reply, agreeing, "There is much wisdom in that. There is a word in my language, *naruofuro*. It means to become one with the flow of all things living. It is a cherished trait that my people generally seek after. You seem to possess it."

Now Arie returned Nomad's smile. She was fascinated by his unique, humble point of view. Though they had barely met, she seemed to get the feeling, and she was not often wrong about her discernment of others, that he was a good man, one that she could trust. There were very few of those kinds of men in the city.

"Thank you. I've had to have this *naruofuro* you call it. It's almost a necessity to my survival, I feel. From a very young age, I learned that life will have its way with you, regardless of whether you choose to curse fate and do nothing, or move with it and coax it in your favor as best you can. The fates were not kind to either Leith or I, and we had to make do with what lot we were given in life.

"Our father cared little for us, and when his attention *did* turn to either Leith or myself, it was in anger and frustration. We had only each other growing up, and we left home as soon as we were able. We've been together ever since. We're quite close, though being the sultan's steward has made our relationship more formal of late."

Nomad grunted his understanding, looking up to the star-filled night sky as he reflected on Arie's story, adding, "I have known friends that grew up in similar circumstances, and it was a very difficult thing for them to detach themselves from those abusers who were supposed to be close. However, each has mentioned to me in the end, that single decision to leave those hurtful relationships was later considered to be one of the best decisions they ever made.

"It hurts to give up on a relationship that *should* be one of our most cherished connections—that of a parent, sibling, spouse—but it takes those with special courage, and often wisdom, to leave those who do not return our love—in times past or in the foreseeable future."

Following his gaze up into the eternal expanse, taking in all the familiar constellations she knew and depended on nightly for guidance along her trail, she sat back at the end of Nomad's bed mat, not having a pleasant conversation like the one she was having with one as interesting as he for a long time. Rarely did she share her past so willingly with a stranger.

This one was different, though. She had felt a connection and a trust the moment their eyes first met. She was not one to generally be impressed by others, spending most of her time in the wild because she preferred the company of nature over that of people, but with Nomad, she preferred his company over seclusion—and other than her sister, she held none other over the comfort of her privacy. She was considering making an exception for this one.

At the very least, she could allow herself to indulge in his presence, if just for this one night.

39
AT THE GATES

"Reza," a weak voice whispered urgently, prompting Reza to lazily flutter her eyes open to see the dawn sunlight warming up the horizon, confirming her suspicions that she was waking up slightly prematurely.

"Reza," the voice persisted, calling louder now.

Opening her eyes all the way this time, she became aware of a wispy luminescence spreading around her, a ghostly familiar face appearing in front of her, seeming to threaten to disperse at the slightest of winds due to how faint the form was.

"Isis!" Reza hoarsely whispered, surprised at seeing the almost forgotten companion she had kept with her for what seemed like so long now.

"Good, I can still get through to you," Isis said, her voice waning, Reza straining to make out her words.

"I expended a great deal of energy toward you from the arisen's attacks. This enchantment that keeps my soul bound to this ring was at dire risk of breaking, but I saw your need and—"

Isis' voice cut out, her image fading, Reza watching the mist that usually stretched out for yards, now ebbed and flowed within inches of the ring she wore that held the enchantment.

Seeming to force her way back to audible clarity, Isis continued in a determined voice.

"The effort I made to protect you the other day may have had a permanent effect on the strength of the ring's enchantment."

Her words starting to break up once more, Isis desperately jumped subjects.

"I don't have much time, but I wanted to let you know, I will do my best to aid you again if you face Lashik. Do not fear him. I will give everything to help you defeat him."

With that, Isis' image broke completely, fading into the mist that seeped back into the diamond ring, the dawn sunlight becoming brighter, and she slowly became aware of a shadow that was cast upon her in the form of a woman who now stood near her.

Looking up, she could see Arie looking down suspiciously at her, asking, "Is everything alright?"

"Yes, I'm fine," Reza answered, getting up, looking around the camp, finding everyone else to still be sleeping. Arie's voice turned her back around.

"Day will be upon us soon. It'll be best if we push the trail hard before the day grows too hot. The earlier the start, the better."

She figured Arie's suggestion probably wise, knowing how hot the Plainstate sun could get at noonday and after.

"I'll wake the others. We'll eat and be on our way," Reza said. Arie nodded and headed off to the dolingers to prep them for the day.

Fin woke the easiest, and after a quick command from Reza, he was up getting to work on gathering breakfast. The rest, Reza had to jab sharply before they realized she was being serious about getting up, Nomad included—which surprised her considering his general tendency to sleep light and rise early.

Arie, having saddled all the dolingers, came back to join the group, snatching a handful of assorted indigenous nuts and a small bread loaf out of the ration pouch to join the group for breakfast.

"Eat your fill. We'll probably not stop for lunch; we'll slow to a gait for a bite on the go instead. We have a lot of distance to cover today to get you to Brigganden by nightfall."

Both Jadu and Zaren at the news let out a long sigh. Cavok handed Jadu an apple and cheese, patting the little praven on the back in an attempt to cheer him up, knowing that to the infrequent traveler, long stretches on the trail could be very tough.

Reza, at the news of travel the whole day through, asked, "Will the dolingers be able to handle an all-day run?"

"Oh yes," Arie answered, looking up from peeling an orange. "They do it quite often. That's why we use them in times of urgency. They're fast in quick bursts, maybe a few hours at most, then you trot them for an hour or so. They can go like that all day as long as you allow them to rest between runs. They don't have as much endurance as horses, but if you run them right, they can add ten or twenty extra miles a day onto the distance horses could get you."

The group now were all looking over to the pack of dolingers, quietly observing them as Arie talked.

"Terribly unapproachable things, though. Mostly reserved for high-ranking military, at least locally—and military animals generally are trained for one purpose," Fin added in after Arie was done addressing the group.

Fin's ominous assessment of the hairless wolf-like mount hung in the air momentarily before Arie admitted, "True. They don't look friendly or smell pleasant, and they often are used not just for their ability to outdistance horses, but because of their aggressive traits. Their claws and maw can make short work of, say, an unarmored attacker. But considering that they used to harass these lands, driving away early settlers of many of the more recent towns and cities when the Plainstate was still somewhat of a frontier, they're a much gentler, useful beast than they were back then.

"Centuries ago, they were known as Daruks—still are elsewhere, I've heard. It's an old name, and an old species. Primal and relatively unchanged by time. Somewhat of a miracle that they heel before us today after only a few short centuries of domestication."

"Comforting, to know that they are so freshly trained," Fin mumbled sarcastically, the whole group now staring at the pack of dolingers that stood gazing back hungrily at them.

"Fascinating specimens," Jadu said, oblivious to the fact that he could fit in one of the larger dolinger's mouth easily. Skipping up to the pack to get a better look at them, Jadu eyed the large beasts with a newfound appreciation.

"Did you, uhh…" Fin started, nervously giggling as Jadu approached the hungry-looking pack who all sat staring at the little approaching praven, Reza finishing Fin's sentence for him.

"Feed them yet?"

Arie, not so reassuringly answered, eyeing Jadu, "Yes, a little bit before you all woke up—but it's almost impossible to keep those

233

things completely satisfied."

Everyone watched a very pleased Jadu pointing to prominent unique features on the beasts, presumably making notes to himself of the strange anatomy of the creatures for possible future reference.

Reza got up, absently calling for everyone to finish their meal and get ready to head out, everyone mumbling their agreeance, all heading over to snag Jadu just before his little hand reached up to stroke the leg of one of the dolingers that eyed him intensely.

Everyone packed their things, and Zaren, making doubly sure to watch his investment pupil, Jadu, carefully loaded him onto the back of their shared mount. The dolinger's head arched back around to eye the little bitesize rider on his back through the whole mounting process, causing Zaren to tentatively swat away the creature's gaze.

The group headed off fast towards Desolate Peak across the plains just as the sun began to crest the horizon.

Just as the day before, the dolingers made good on any boasting the group had heard of in regards to their speed. Within a few hours, they had passed by Desolate Peak, and within two hours after that, they were leaving the high plains, descending down plateau after plateau into the scrub brush wilderness northeast of Brigganden.

Taking a two-hour trot to cool the dolingers off, the blazing sun rising higher and higher in the sky as the day wore on, Fin handed out their lunch sacks, filled with oat cakes and a local fruit, each generously accepting the reprieve from the full-on gallop they had been sustaining all day.

By the time the sun had peaked in the sky, starting its slow descent, the group had begun their second sprint, trudging through canyons, rushing through the off-trail brush, and finally traversing along a mixture of hills and dunes before the late afternoon was coming to a close.

Cresting a dune to put Brigganden into view after a grueling day of pushing their mounts to their limits, Reza called a halt, seeing a concerning sight in the distance along the highway leading away from the city.

From their vantage point on the dune, they could make out a long line of glinting armored troops marching forth from the city's tall gates clearly visible due to the sizable numbers of the army.

Dismounting and sending the dolingers down into the dip of the dunes, the group crept up to the crest of the dunes again, laying prone to keep out of sight and to get a good, long look at the formidable sight before them.

"So it's true. The dead march to the Plainstate," Arie whispered, the whole group in awe at the large army slowly making its way into the distance.

"A few thousand troops at least," Fin murmured, clearly impressed by the scale of the army on the highway.

"Look," Reza called out, pointing to the head of the march.

Miles down the highway leading to Warwick stood a figure, from their distant perspective, just slightly taller than the rest of the troop. Though it was a bump amidst many, Reza knew instantly who the large figure was.

A dark cloud, a depression of light, seemed to hang over the figure. And though Reza didn't often get a sense of evil, she did if the presence was strong enough, and she had never felt a presence that reeked of evil so profoundly as the one she had faced in the court that had almost taken her life.

"That one—the one at the head of the army with the shadow around him. He's Lashik's master—the arisen lord."

Everyone but Arie looked to Reza, considering her words.

Arie added after a moment, squinting, still set on the figure, "I think you're right. He's the only one mounted. And his mount looks terrifying at that. It doesn't look living, or if it is, it's an unnatural abomination."

"You can see that far?" Fin asked, squinting to try and make out details of the blurry bump in the distance. "*I* can't even see that far, and I can see eight of the stars in the Videnstride star cluster."

Smiling, looking to Fin now, Arie smugly said, "Eight? Most men can only see six. Eight is impressive for your kind. Most haltia can see fifteen. I'm only half haltia but I can still see twelve."

"Twelve—" Fin mouthed in disbelief, looking to Cavok, who simply shrugged at Fin's bewildered gaze.

Reza backed down from the dunes and remounted, everyone else following suit while Fin shook his head, mumbling, "*Twelve?* I didn't even know there were twelve stars in the Videnstride cluster, let alone fifteen," with an incredulous look still on his face.

"Come on, Fin," Reza called, turning her mount towards Brigganden. "We'll ride around, out of sight, and approach from the west wall. In a few hours, it'll be getting dark. That'll give us enough time to stealthily make our way back to that farmhouse we stayed at last time and bed down for the night."

Nomad disapprovingly jumped in.

"Time is in short supply now that the bulk of the army has left the city. If we infiltrate tonight, we may catch whoever's left in the city off guard. We have spent many days away from this place, allowing ample time for the wicked ones to have their way with Bede's body. I cannot willingly allow another cycle to pass while being so close to her. I vowed to avenge her."

Nomad's unusually hard eyes bore down on Reza, emphasizing his commitment to his proposed line of action.

Reza turned around, fully ready to argue the point, when Arie calmly interrupted.

"It probably would be wise to rest before entering. You all need to be at full strength for the task before you, and you'll only get one chance at executing it," adding, looking Nomad directly in the eyes, "If you fail, Nomad, due to fatigue, the group's failure and deaths are on you."

Nomad, looking back at the rest of the group, seeing for the first time how exhausted Zaren and Jadu looked, and even how subdued by the long day Cavok and Fin seemed, relinquished his press for the notion to move in on the city that night.

He let out a displeased grunt as Reza continued to study his reaction to Arie's reasoning.

"Then it is agreed," Reza confirmed. "We will rest at the farmhouse tonight. Arie, perhaps you can stable the dolingers there and wait for us to complete our mission. You should only have to wait a day or so. If we succeed, we'll meet back up with you at the farmhouse and ride back to Metus to assist in the war that's headed for them.

"Metus already knows of their advance. I'm not sure how much Leith told you, but they are already preparing to receive the arisen army at Warwick."

With no opposition from either Arie, Nomad, or the rest of the group, Reza curtly turned and led on, running the dolingers through dune troughs, skirting around the plains that separated them from the outer shanties of the large desert city—the sun staining the evening sky blood red earlier than usual that night.

40
ACID IN THE DARK

Reza peered inside the dark military building amidst the slums just outside of the city wall.

Looking behind her, seeing Fin, Nomad, Cavok, Jadu, and Zaren all waiting for her to signal it safe to enter, she pushed the door wide open, ushering the group in before closing the heavy door behind them quietly.

She turned to whisper for Fin and Jadu to light a torch, both doing so after fumbling a bit in the dark.

"Looks unchanged," Reza said, looking around with the aid of the fresh torchlight illuminating the dusty room.

"Shall I or Nomad lead?" Fin asked, bringing Reza's attention back to the task at hand, issuing Nomad to lead, with Fin following him with the torch to light the way.

She hesitated to admit it to herself, but now that they were so close to the dead city once again, she realized that since their departure from Arie early that morning at the abandoned farmhouse, she was becoming more apprehensive about their mission the closer they got to the cursed city. She had lost a friend the first time they had visited the unholy city owned by the arisen, and now she couldn't help but wonder how many it would claim this time around.

Though the defenses and number of those on watch had diminished significantly, she still feared the odds were not in their favor. With that thought lingering with her the whole morning, her level of trepidation only intensified the further along they were.

They walked single file down the hallway leading to the very back of the building, which descended into the stone-chiseled tunnel. On the other side of the tunnel was the officers' quarters wing, where they hoped no guards to be stationed.

Passing the iron-barred gate at the entrance of the cave, Nomad unsheathed his sword, the quiet sound of metal sliding against hollow wood, reminding Fin and Reza to do the same.

"I feel eyes upon us," Nomad said in a low voice as he slowly led the group down the dark tunnel, the perverse web of hair and putrid fingers and toes coming into the reach of the firelight, showing that some of the alarm web had been reassembled since their previous passing.

"Nomad, keep an eye ahead. Everyone else, watch the sides," Reza ordered.

Nomad swiped through the first wall of hair and fingers in their path, dropping a whole person's worth of digits, the *plip plop* sound of the chunks of meat hitting the floor causing an involuntary shiver to run up Fin's spine as he ducked the flame below the hanging hair so that he didn't have to deal with the smell of burnt hair on top of the sickening tunnel of human remains they were traveling through.

"I believe it was the greyoldor that told Dubix of our presence last time we came through here. He got away, and when Bede and I were spying on Dubix, he spoke of intruders. Other than this greyoldor, I do not know of any others seeing us before that point."

Reza considered Nomad's commentary as he continued to slash a path open for the group. After some thought, she replied, "If we see him again—kill on sight. Capturing and binding him I fear would prove too dangerous. It's a thing twisted beyond redemption or reason anyways."

"As you command," Nomad answered back, a bit too readily. Reza gave Nomad a look of understanding towards his extreme disgust regarding the little, wicked creature.

Fin shivered again after a few moments of the persistent, morbid tapping of the tips hitting the stone floor. Reza, and she suspected the rest of the group, felt increasingly uncomfortable as creeping shadows twisted and squirmed along the distant walls of the cave as the torchlight struggled to cut through the wall of hair.

Everyone was keenly aware that a creature lurked in the dark, watching them as they passed through its territory, while they stood oblivious to its location. The atmosphere of the tunnel was demoralizing, and Reza tried to keep panic out of her voice as she told Nomad to hurry.

Reza almost jumped as Cavok's booming voice thundered through the silence, the large man commanding, "Hold."

Everyone did so instantly, Nomad halting mid-swing, everyone watching, only moving their heads to see Cavok snatch Jadu's torch, holding it up to the wall of hair next to him, burning a window in it, a black, pungent cloud of smoke erupting from it. Cavok held the torch back to the side to get a better look into the dark window.

His eyes widened as he took note of something no one else had a vantage point to see, but no one had time to guess or ask what it was as a hiss and a plume of ash and soot exploded directly in Cavok's face, completely coating his head.

All now rushing to Cavok's aid, Cavok dove blindly into the net of hair, shaking the whole hair tunnel around, ripping down a good portion of it as he rushed out into the darkness of the cave.

Rushing in first, Reza could see briefly Cavok clutching something, slamming the thing violently with his torch, the light spitting all around with the rise and fall of Cavok's blows before the torch went out.

Fin, tearing through the wall of hair between him and Reza, re-illuminated the scene. Everyone got their first good glance at Cavok and the thing he grappled with.

Cavok's face was split open in hairline wounds, ash mixing with blood to produce a horrible sight. Cuts sizzling, his face was an emotionless expression of stoic determination to complete whatever beating he was giving.

The extinguished torch came down, handle point first, cracking through the skull of a barely discernable figure whose skin tone was the same as the rock it was crumpled on. Reza now recognized it to be the greyoldor they had encountered before in the cave.

All fight instantly stopped, the little figure dropping, a hole in its head with a torch sticking out of it. The greyoldor slumped over as Cavok let go of the torch and tiny figure, blood still boiling along his surface cuts across his face.

"Oh dear," Zaren exclaimed, pulling forth a little blue marble, holding it to Cavok's face and uttering words no one else could understand.

A fountain of water spat forth from the marble, splashing Cavok in the face, all ash washing way as it hissed upon contact.

"Here, help him to the end of this nasty tunnel. We need to cleanse his eyes as soon as we're away from this place," Zaren said, waving for Reza and Fin to shoulder the man's weight to guide him along the tunnel.

Cavok readily complied, keeping his eyes closed tightly, a look of pain hidden directly under his façade of composure.

As they moved, now rushing directly through the web of hair without bothering to cut a path through it, the group charged forward, making it to the end of the tunnel as Zaren talked.

"That little thing was a greyoldor. Very interesting to find a servant of ol' ash eye himself here. They have strange abilities granted to them by their master. A *perk* of being a follower, I guess you could call it. They can spew a very acidic ash from their mouth. I washed it from him in time to prevent further damage, but his eyes—I'm sure he took some in his eyes. That's not good."

Kicking open the barred door at the end of the tunnel, Nomad rushed up ahead to scout out a room to put Cavok down in, Fin and Reza leading him along with Jadu and Zaren close behind.

"In here," Nomad whispered loudly, ushering the group into an officer's quarters with two beds in it. Fin and Reza laid him down on the bed closest to the door, Cavok still squinting badly, tears streaming from his closed eyes.

"Move, move," Zaren ordered, pushing his way to hover over Cavok, holding his blue marble as he talked Cavok through what he was doing.

"Let's flush that ash out, Cavok. I'm going to hold open your eyes and spray some water in. Ready?"

Nomad closed the door just in time as Cavok let out an angry yell, Zaren taking it as a *yes*.

Zaren forced open Cavok's lids, and everyone could see that the man's eyes were filled with granules, fizzing, eating away at his fleshy orbs.

Zaren's words were quick and indiscernible, and a jet of water came forth, spraying forcefully the man's disintegrating eyes, clearing them of the caustic dust.

Cavok roared, back arched, then went limp, eyes closed once again, watering profusely, his body desperately attempting to expel any remains of whatever it was that had infiltrated it.

"Blind," Cavok moaned, crying out again with more anger this time. "I'm blind!"

"Cavok," Reza said in a hushed voice, gripping the large man's hand, "calm yourself. Any louder and you'll give us away."

Reza, looking to Zaren, knowing that he was the most knowledgeable about the harmful substance that had blinded Cavok, asked, "Is the blindness permanent? Is there anything you can do for him?"

The whole room turned to Zaren as he shrugged and answered reluctantly, "It's a natural chemical mixture, not magical. Natural injuries are much harder to heal magically than those performed by magic. There's often a strong leftover hexweave residue to work with in the case of magical wounds. If I were stronger, with access to more hexweave relics, yes, but I'm still weak from returning from the painting hex and from constantly being shuffled about by you lot, and most of my store of relics remains in the rift along with my associates. I can do nothing for him till we've opened the rift and I've had a chance to recuperate."

Cavok's head, which had been lifted up, listening intently to Zaren's answer, slumped back to the pillow. Reza now began to seriously worry for Cavok.

"I could help," Jadu piped in, rummaging through his assortment of pouches, pulling out materials only he knew the properties of.

Pouring a splotch of a liquid on a cloth, smearing a cream along it as well, Jadu hopped up to Cavok's bedside, gently pressing the moistened cloth over Cavok's eyes, wrapping it around his head, tying it in the back.

"This treats burns and is a drawing agent. Also helps aid the body's natural healing process. Should help your eyes recover faster—if they are to recover at least—" Jadu left off, clearly showing his hopelessness for the man's state.

"Well," Fin cut in, looking to Reza, "what now?"

41

DARK REUNION

"One of us will have to stay with you while the rest search for Bede's body," Reza said to Cavok, who had calmed considerably since Jadu's treatment.

Shaking his head, Cavok demanded, "I'm coming. Have Jadu lead me if you have to, but I can't just sit here and wait not knowing what danger you all face and are walking into. Even blinded, I can fight."

Fin held a hand up to halt Reza, who was about to reply, and said, "You can't come with us, big guy. You know you'd be more trouble to us than help without sight. Maybe if you were Blind Bat Matt," Fin said with a chuckle, referencing a quirky old acquaintance of theirs, trying to lighten the devastating decision of ruling him out of the mission.

Cavok didn't take the bait, his expression clearly frustrated, more so than Nomad had ever seen him be, but he could understand the man's frustration. He knew that being powerless in a time of your friends' greatest need was one of the most infuriating trials one could bear, and to willingly give up the mission that was so personal to him, putting Bede's body at rest and seeking revenge on those who had done it, was a struggle for which Nomad honestly didn't expect

Cavok to have enough willpower to choose the sensible path.

Cavok's angry features held for a moment longer, then softened, yielding to Reza's and Fin's arguments.

"Then go—everyone. I'll be fine here alone. Just bring Bede back—and kill that son of a bitch Lashik."

"Leave you alone here? Cavok—" Reza started, but again, Fin held a hand up, stopping Reza's would-be argument against leaving him alone.

Putting his hands behind his head, looking as though he was ready for the long wait of their return, Cavok took a deep breath, seeming quite done with the conversation, not willing to budge on the issue.

"Alright, Cavok, have it your way," Reza said, exasperation showing through slightly.

"Fin, mind leaving him with an extra supply of rations?" she asked, going over to Cavok, patting him on the shoulder, adding, "We won't be long. If night falls and we still haven't found her, we'll return."

Cavok's expressionless face held firm as Fin placed a pouch of food beside him, nudging him lightly while saying, "Heal up quick, all right? We'll be back before you know it and we'll be rid of this wretched place for good."

The rest of the group passed him by, saying a word or two before heading out into the hallway, leaving Nomad to close the door, leaving their wounded comrade alone and blind in the officers' quarters, still looking blankly at the food on the bed.

<hr />

"The courtyard and the whole military and royal court districts seem completely deserted. No sign of Bede or even arisen over there," Fin said, trotting back to the group that stood huddled under the siding of the officers' housing building, waiting for Fin to return from his quick scouting task.

"Not a single arisen?" Reza asked in disbelief.

"Nope. No clue where Bede or whoever's in charge here now might be residing. Maybe Lashik was left to guard the city in his master's absence, maybe it's Dubix, or neither, but whoever's in command isn't staying over there."

"*Oh*," Fin added, something coming to mind after his report, Reza giving him a questioning look.

243

"You going to share that thought with us?" she asked, prompting Fin to elaborate.

"Jadu, Zaren. You remember how Lashik had taken an interest in Zaren's tower? If Lashik was left in command here, that's probably where we'll find him."

Zaren lifted a finger, eyes lighting up, agreeing with Fin.

"You don't go through the trouble of breaking down highly complex protection enchantments unless you have plans for that place. Yes. Being one who weaves hex himself, he probably is naturally drawn to a place with hexweave significance rather than a place of bureaucratic authority like the king's courtyard like his master was. Weavers often prize knowledge over power—I doubt it's much different for arisen. Their minds are quite simple after all."

"Darendul Tower it is then," Reza said, having no other ideas of where to begin scouring the city for Bede's remains, adding, "Fin, you know the way. Lead us there."

The streets were empty, and Fin didn't have to halt the party once on the way to the tower. Other than spotting a far-off guard walking a route along the city wall, they saw no other arisen.

The group lined up by the gate of the tower. Fin turned to ask Reza if she wanted him to go ahead and scout the tower before sending the whole group in.

"No. We all go in," she said, letting out an involuntary shiver while looking up at the structure, mumbling, "I've got a feeling whatever evil stayed behind resides up there."

A few heavy clouds had just begun to drift over the desert city, the sun occasionally winding its way through to shine off the curiously moist petals of the exotic floral wall crowding the path towards the tower's entrance.

As she walked the path, Reza couldn't help but notice the transplanted beauty of the vegetation that grew there—their aromas lending a pleasantness to a dour mood.

A glint off to the side of the trail, brighter than a drop of morning dew could reflect, caught Reza's eye. Approaching the small metal object in the grass, she picked it up. A chain dropped a talisman down, spinning until she cupped it with her other hand.

Everyone stopped to see what Reza was so interested in.

"Her talisman," Reza whispered.

Reza gazed upon it for a while before looking back up at the tower, her concern for the path before them deepening.

"What if we're too late?" Fin said, breaking the solemn silence.

No one chose to answer his question, each keeping their thoughts to themselves, save for Reza who gave him a tired scowl.

"I know nobody wants to think about it," Fin continued, "but really, what are we going to do if Lashik has puppeted Bede? Are we going to fight her if we must? Are we going to destroy her? We need to discuss this before we go in there. Hesitation at a decisive moment can cost the mission—it can cost lives."

Reza's fatigued scowl let up, now only showing forlorn weariness as she admitted, "You're right. Finding her talisman here is more than likely no coincidence. Lashik may be performing rites currently or has already completed whatever dark acts necessary to turn her to his purposes.

"If she is corrupted, do we attack and release her from her cursed imprisonment, or is there any way of reclaiming a turned spirit?"

Reza's question was directed at Zaren, who, getting questioning looks from the rest in the group, shrugged his shoulders, blurting out, "The domain of divine hexweave is not my area of expertise. I deal with enchantment. You're the only one here that actively worships a deity, are you not? You are a follower of Sareth, one of her very children if I correctly interpret the symbols you've worn. Can't you ask her?"

Looking down at the cobblestone path, Reza mumbled, "It doesn't work like that."

She knew Zaren's claim to be true. She was the only religious one in the group now. She knew the answer she sought for, if within any in the group's grasp, should be within her circle of understanding. But, though she was a saren, she, out of most of her sisters, had always been more detached from her faith than was normal for her kind.

Her sisters often looked down on her curiosity and drive to break from tradition. She had always insisted on exploring and learning the ways of the vast world rather than studying and gaining favor of their heavenly mother in monasteries, temples, and their most holy sites.

She regretted that character trait about herself now, though. She knew that any of her saren peers would know tomes-worth more about the arisen and their dark powers than she did, even with her being twenty-seven years old, having had plenty of time to utilize their vast libraries to become well learned on religious subjects.

Though she hadn't formal tutelage on the subject, she had field knowledge to some degree on the subject of the state of a soul after being chained to a dark cleric after death. Isis had been under Lashik's command, and broke free from it, but only through her stronger, preexisting enchantment that bound her soul to her ring.

She was no hexweaver, and though she figured a powerful enough hexweaver might be able to rebind Bede's soul to an object, she doubted Bede's order would condone that practice, Elendium being very much against prolonged life or magic that would alter the natural cycle of life and death.

"If we find her controlled by Lashik—we must do everything we can to put her soul to rest, and that means we must destroy her. There is no option for reclamation for her. Elendium would not approve of any, even benevolent, resurrection magic, and she wouldn't either, I'm afraid. She'd want us to set her free."

Fin's usual jovial disposition was considerably dampened as Reza gave her final verdict on the matter.

Hand over his forehead, shaking his head, he breathed, "Glad Cavok isn't here for this task. He'd be furious about what we're talking about doing. Gods be damned...."

Turning to Zaren, Reza motioned him over to her, the old man obliging.

"Would you take the lead? This is your tower after all. If there are any traps laid by Lashik, you would be best suited to detect and handle them."

Nodding his approval, Zaren called for Jadu, whispering to him to keep close, explaining to him in a hushed voice what he was looking for in terms of wards as they entered the building.

They had entered and ascended the spiral stairwell without any opposition, a deep sense of pending dread growing in each of their guts as they neared the top of the tower.

At the top of the stairwell now, Zaren nodded to Reza that it was safe for her to lead them into the upper loft of the tower. Allowing Reza, Fin, and Nomad to pass on the stairwell, the group ascended the last flight to the open hatch that led them into the Highstudy.

Standing at the threshold to the room, Reza looked down at Bede's talisman she had picked up at the base of the tower outside. Looping the necklace over her neck, tucking it away underneath her chainmail, she steeled herself as best she could to the task that lay before them before stepping into the room.

Advancing into the wide room shrouded in a deep-purple glow, Reza looked around, searching for a familiar figure, a mixture of hoping beyond hope to find her—and not to. The toxic mix of emotions and anticipation churned her stomach until she felt sick.

Seeing only stands, furniture, tables, and strange relics of every imaginable kind adorning the room, nobody in sight, she waved for Nomad and the rest of the group to come up with her. She walked silently further into the room, her eyes carefully scanning the scene.

Her gaze locked as she looked out the balcony past the wispy drapes dancing in the threshold.

A woman stood, her back to them, looking out over the city from the balcony, her hoary hair flowing in the breeze oddly in the opposite direction of the drapes, making the already strange image seem that much more out of place.

Draped in a black satin dress, hemmed in purple embroidery, the figure slowly turned, showing a face similar, but horrifically changed, from the one they knew and loved.

Bede stepped into the room, the drapes blowing out of her way as she entered, her jawline sagging slightly, skin a marbled pale blue and ash. Her face showed no emotion, but Reza noticed that her usual grayish-blue eyes were now a fiery mix of green and orange, the whites of her eyes turned to an unhealthy black and red, which matched her dark lips. Whether it was a grim lipstick she wore or a natural putridity causing the color, she did not know.

Reza thought for a brief moment that she saw the faintest sign of heartbreak, her eyebrows and sides of her lips dropping slightly, the aged lines along the side of her nose to her mouth trembling momentarily, perhaps in remorse for what she had become, perhaps in pity for what she was commanded to do to those who entered her master's chambers.

Within an instant, the expression had washed away, leaving Reza and the rest to realize that whatever Bede was to them in life was not what was standing in front of them now.

42

GRIM RENDEZVOUS

Bede stretched a hand forth, black tendrils of energy splitting the stillness of the chamber, blowing Jadu and Fin across the room, Jadu igniting in a burst of colorful flames as multiple bottles of alchemical components and liquids concealed in his robes shattered from the blast.

Skidding to a stop, both remained motionless, neither appearing to be conscious after the deadly impact. Worse off for Jadu was that his robes were still lit like a torch doused in oil from the combustible attack.

Reza, Nomad, and Zaren looked back to the two. Zaren rushed to Jadu's side, producing his blue marble, quickly drenching the little praven in water to extinguish the flames while Nomad checked on Fin.

Nomad pointed for Reza to deal with Bede as they made sure their allies were not slain from the attack.

The attack had happened so quickly and without warning that Reza froze for a moment, looking to Bede, who seemed to hunch over slightly, her face sagging a bit more after the powerful attack before straightening herself, once again raising a hand, this time towards Reza.

Reza jumped to the side just in time before another bolt of black lightning erupted from Bede's outstretched pale hand, cutting lines in the floorboards and desk that lay directly behind Reza, scattering lit paper everywhere.

Reza rolled off to the side, Bede's cold stare slowly turning to her, the grim woman lining up her fingertips with her prone target.

Bede was knocked off her feet as Nomad plowed into her, shouldering her over not a moment too soon, another blast of dark energy crackling through the room, narrowly missing Reza once more.

As soon as Bede was down, she rebounded, quicker than Nomad had expected, a demonic rage showing in her features from being denied her target twice now.

Nomad's sword was out now, and he stood over Reza as she got back to her feet. Even with the resolution that he had to destroy Bede, Nomad now had a clear opening of attack, sword at ready, hesitating to slash into his previous friend for only a moment before Bede took advantage of his delay.

Bede shot her hands forward once more, this time lighting up the whole room with a column of energy directed straight at Nomad.

Reza, on the ground behind Nomad, held her arm reflexively over her eyes to guard against the attack, but after a moment, realizing Nomad wasn't flying backwards like Fin and Jadu had from the blast, she looked up to see Bede's continued outpouring of energy being sliced to the sides of Nomad's gleaming, bright sword, his weapon's white aura canceling the darkness that pecked angrily along the aura's edges.

Bede's features contorted, her rage engulfing her once beautiful face. Reza barely recognized her old companion at that moment.

She knew what they had to do, and though at that moment she wanted nothing more than to leave the task undone and leave that horrible situation, she drew her seax, gripping the hilt hard, and stood up behind Nomad.

The dark pricks of energy engulfed them for a moment longer before Bede let up her deadly bombardment. Nomad's shoulders sagged as he lowered his sword, the glow dying out instantly after the assault.

Reza was out, dashing at Bede a moment later, driving the seax into Bede's unprotected torso, the blade going cleanly through.

She brought a foot up instinctively, kicking Bede's body off of her blade, throwing her to the wall.

Bede, black blood oozing from the slit in her dress, still stood, resting against the wall, looking a bit haggard from either Reza's attack or her own after unleashing on Nomad full tilt.

Reza advanced, short blade coming in once more to stab at her corrupted friend.

Bede didn't even attempt to dodge the attack, welcoming the blade, letting it sink deep into her chest again, throwing arms around her assailant, gripping her in a death-like hug, refusing to give even an inch to Reza, who began to thrash, trying to power her way out of the grapple.

Squeezing even tighter than she had been, she began to crush Reza, causing her to inwardly curse the fact that she was only wearing chainmail and not her usual breastplate.

She knew her already injured ribs were about to snap, the dead flesh demonically exerting more energy than it physically should have been able to. Her arms were acting more like a maniacal device than a living thing.

Jumping with everything she had, she managed to lift Bede off her feet, toppling the two, bringing Nomad into her view above them now, sword out and glowing again; but, before he even had touched Bede, she screamed in pain, releasing Reza abruptly, skittering away from her.

Looking down to what had been the source of Bede's anguish, Reza saw that her talisman had slipped out of her garments and was hanging freely over her satin tunic. It now glowed the same aura of color as Nomad's sword had.

Bede glared frighteningly at the talisman as Reza held it up. Reza took the moment of hysterical fear to stand up and slowly advance towards the scared creature, with Nomad close behind.

Bede, seeing the two advancing, was up and running for the window, turning once on the balcony to stretch forth her hands to blast a charge of dark energy at them both.

Nomad shot in front of Bede, his sword flaring up to take on the bolts of blackness, absorbing them, rushing forward with Reza at his side, letting down his blade just as Bede stopped her assault, looking to leap from the balcony from the duo.

Reza lunged at her, slamming her against the railing just before Bede jumped. She pressed Bede's own talisman against her former companion's chest. Silk melted away from the area as the warm metal of the talisman seared into Bede's flesh.

A hellish scream issued forth from Bede—tormented, desperate. The whites of her eyes, once black and red, were awhirl, taint leaving them, her skin becoming more ivory and less blue.

As if a gust of wind finally blew out a stubborn candle flame, the wracked demonic cries were snuffed out, leaving a visually changed Bede from the one they had just faced in mortal combat.

Reza now releasing the talisman, Nomad lowering his sword, they both breathed heavily as the two waited to see what had just happened, not sure if the arisen curse had passed from Bede for good, or if the moment of stillness was just a reprieve in the fight.

Bede's grayish-blue eyes opened slowly, the warm smile Reza knew so well accompanying her pleasant features.

"Bede!" Reza said, completely taken aback by the reemergence of her once-thought fallen comrade. Hope injected into her like a bolt of lightning.

"Yes, child," she said, her smile quickly turning to anxiousness. "Please make sure Fin and Jadu are alright."

Nomad squeezed Reza's shoulder before rushing back into the tower to check on the two.

"Don't worry, Nomad will take care of them," Reza soothingly said, grasping her cold hand.

"I remember everything. Everything I did. Oh, I'm so sorry," Bede said, black tears easily falling as she began to break down, Reza propping her up, hugging her tight, trying to comfort her.

"Don't worry about that. We're all fine. We're just glad you're back with us! That's what matters," Reza said, patting Bede's back. For the first time in their relationship, the old woman's back felt very much her age—frail and almost as if it were ready for the long journey home.

"No," Bede said, struggling to regain her composure momentarily. "My visit will be brief. I know the magic Lashik used to preserve me, and I know that without it, I am as good as dead, but rightfully so. I should have departed this world that night Nomad and I stood against the darkness. It was my time, and though I didn't leave then, I thank you dear for giving me that opportunity now—"

A weak fit of coughing forced Bede to stop talking, black blood issuing from her mouth. Reza held her closer, not knowing what else she could do to help her dying friend.

Holding up a hand to Bede's forehead, Reza took a deep breath, hand beginning to glow as she started to channel her life energy into Bede, attempting a healing.

Barely had she begun when Bede gripped her wrist, causing her to stop the healing process. Looking to Bede, she waited for her white-haired companion to speak.

"Don't," Bede said in a serious tone, "it won't help. You can't heal this kind of wound. I'm already dead."

Reza was dumbfounded, not sure what else to do for Bede, the old frame beginning to tremble, her breath slowing.

"My bond to Lashik is broken. He'll be coming here soon."

Bede stopped struggling to speak, laying back to rest at peace, breathing slowly while Reza tried to prop Bede up more comfortably against the railing, waiting for Bede to come around again.

She never did.

43

AT DEATH'S DOOR

Getting up after a few minutes of watching Bede's aged, ever-still expression, memorizing all of her features, Reza turned, tears in her eyes, to see Nomad standing in the doorway looking mournfully Bede's way.

Covering her eyes, wiping the tears away, she cleared her throat and asked, "How's Fin and Jadu?"

"They're back up—drained—but seem to be doing well. Zaren is working with Jadu. He was burned badly, and since it's alchemical fire and not a magically inflicted wound, there's little he can do right now to treat him."

Walking past Nomad, who followed her back inside, Reza came to Fin, who was resting in a chair in front of the desk that had been blasted by Bede. He looked ragged, no smile on his face where it usually resided.

"How are you?" Reza asked, voice still slightly trembling from the unsorted emotions that ran through her.

Fin attempted a smile at Reza, but his gaze drifted to the balcony as he asked, "Is she—"

Reza answered before he could finish.

"She's out there at rest. She thanked us for releasing her from Lashik's spell before she passed. You should go say your goodbyes. She said Lashik is on his way here."

Fin's attempt at a smile quickly vanished. He got up, slowly making his way over to the balcony, hesitating at the threshold for a moment before stepping out of the room.

Moving over to Zaren, who was finishing putting on a white salve along Jadu's hands and face, Reza kneeled down to Jadu's height, getting a raised eyebrow and grin as Jadu said, "Blowing up is easy. The tricky part is staying alive after the fact. Lucky this one didn't break," he said, swishing a small jar of clear liquid before Reza gingerly grabbed it from the little praven, placing it off to the side.

"That one would have brought the roof down. *Shoo*! that energy bolt sapped some kick out of me, but I'll be fine. What happened with Bede?"

Reza would have normally been displeased with how directly Jadu had asked the question about her longtime companion, but she was beginning to understand that it was simply beyond Jadu to respect the reverence of certain situations.

"Lashik's curse was lifted and she's passed now," Reza said as guarded as she could, knowing that Jadu or Zaren would not be treating Bede's passing with a healthy level of compassion.

To Reza's surprise, Jadu's mood spoiled, seeming rather distressed by the news. Murmuring more to himself than to anyone, he looked down at the floor and said, "I liked Bede," as a silence momentarily fell over the group.

A scream, distant, but dreadful, echoed up through the entrance leading to the stairwell, causing everyone, even Fin, who swept the drapes aside to reenter the room, to look intently at the entrance, listening for the sound again.

Another scream, this one sounding as though there might be a second person joining in the grim cry, echoed up to them. The screamers were much closer this time.

"Lashik—or his followers," Reza whispered, Fin moving to close the door, looking to Reza for orders.

Reza, though the screams offset her at first, now unknowingly ground her teeth and clenched her fist tight, realizing that Lashik, the one responsible for Bede's death, was on his way to them.

Showing her intentions to the group, she unlatched her Morningstar, resolve heavy in her smoldering eyes.

The battle-tired group followed suit, Fin drawing two throwing daggers from straps along his thigh, Nomad lightly placing a hand along his curved sword, and Zaren lifting Jadu to his feet, opening once again his battered, large tome.

"Zaren, is there any way down from this tower besides the stairwell?" Fin asked, not looking nearly as anxious as Reza to take Lashik and his forces head on.

"Wellll," Zaren said slowly, drawing out the word to bide for time while he considered their options.

"That lesser levitation spell I performed at the cliffs!" Jadu piped in hopefully, Zaren instantly giving a stink-eye to the response.

"We would still have the same problem of the spell only supporting me and you, though, and then they would be up here alone without our aid. And—" Zaren paused, lowering his voice as he quickly added in, "relying on you to perform that spell for us once was more than enough for me."

Fin, looking to the door as another screech sounded down the stairwell, pressed the point.

"I know you say you're still weak, but if we stay up here, well, you'll be casting a whole lot more than a levitate spell to defend us against Zaren. Are you sure you can't make it work?"

Pinching the bridge of his thin nose, Zaren closed his eyes and responded.

"That enchantment isn't as easy as it seems—well, I should rephrase. It's easy if you have the right focus and components. The last time Jadu cast it, that was the last inscription I had of that spell. If I wanted to cast it again, I'd either need a relic with that specific spell attached to it or I would need to perform a whole ritual *just* to inscribe the spell for use, which would require components and time that we don't have right now. Spells for enchanters don't just pop out of thin air—even seemingly simple ones. Everything must be prepared beforehand."

"There's no time left. The enemy approaches," Nomad cut in before Fin could belabor the subject anymore.

Everyone's attention now turned to the stairwell, the rustle and whip of cloth quickly approaching the threshold sounding just around the bend.

Just as Zaren handed his spellbook to Jadu, whispering for him to hold it for him as he prepared relics to spend, two dark forms shrouded in shadow and sooty cloth flew into the room, immediately being struck by two daggers, the blades sinking into the white, emaciated torso of the two floating skeletal beings.

The daggers, not slowing the floating figures in the least, came in fast at Reza and Nomad, who stood in the front to meet them.

Reza rose her flail, bringing it down at the lead wraith. It rushed to the right of the attack, just out of the reach of Reza's flail as the second came up to overtake her as she attempted to step back to regain her footing.

Nomad's sword flashed out of his scabbard, cutting into the whirlwind of shadow and tattered robes, forcing the thing back from his battle mate momentarily.

Its retreat was accompanied by two more daggers, which thudded into its center, the group catching glimpses of black ooze seeping out of the wounds.

Coming in fast again followed by hellish cries, both wraiths rushed in once more at Reza, forcing Reza and Nomad to go on the defensive, warding off the flying shadows. Boney claws and ivory fangs thrusted in at the two only to recoil just in time before a flail or blade came back in at them.

As they gave ground to the wraiths, Zaren and Jadu were the first to note the violet-robed figure stride into the room behind the vicious wraiths.

A long, black gilded dagger scabbarded at his hip, Lashik lifted a skeletal hand from the folds of his robes, revealing multiple illuminated rings, a half smile showing slowly on the arisen's half-bone, half-flesh face as his gaze locked on Zaren.

"*Zarlos calbor awl!*" Zaren shouted in a tone so deep and commanding that the others, even the wraiths, momentarily flinched, glancing at the source of the booming voice.

A fuchsia flash shot forth from a hexagonal ruby pyramid Zaren held between his fingers. A beam of light, so intense that all eyes averted from the ray, slammed into Lashik. The beam warped around a net of dark-purple energy that encased him, slowly absorbing into the field. The blast intensified for a moment longer before it suddenly cut off, leaving Zaren scrambling for another trinket in his folds.

"Not this time, old one," Lashik hissed, slowly taking the golden, spiked crown off his hooded head, lifting it high, his mouth agape as he looked up to the focus.

Everyone was looking to the spectacle as Zaren found what he was looking for, producing a white shell. Frantically uttering words into its curved interior, a white glow spread over him and Jadu just as an explosion detonated, blowing apart furniture and stone closest to Lashik.

Everyone in the room was leveled save Zaren, Jadu, and Lashik. The wraiths, Reza, Nomad, and Fin were back to the other end of the room within an instant, rock and wood shrapnel assaulting the downed group.

Jadu's hazardous jar, which Reza had placed on the stone floor, exploded upon being flung to the roof of the room, causing a second detonation to directly follow the first explosion, ripping a wide swath of destruction across the room, this one even more devastating than the first. The vaulted cone roof of the tower blasted away along with parts of the stone wall, sending large bricks and shafts of wood flying all across the city.

The cloud-diffused sunlight partially made its way down on the dusty scene of obliteration, the inner sanctum of the Highstudy now blasted wide open.

The exposed room was enveloped in a lingering dust that didn't seem as though it would settle any time soon. Amidst the settling sounds of the building, brick, and beams still slamming to the floor, a metallic clatter rang out close to Lashik's location. The rim of what Zaren thought to be the crown he had held and used to cast the powerful destructive spell from spun in circles, making quite the ruckus before wobbling to a stop.

"Jadu—" Zaren said, trying to find the breath to finish his sentence. "My book. A protection enchantment."

Jadu, thinking he understood what Zaren was asking for, started to thumb through the book that was almost half his size, searching for a chapter he had read through once that held incantations that would help guard against magical attacks.

A fallen rafter beam at the other end of the room shifted momentarily before a bony hand shoved it to the side, forcibly ripping itself from the wreckage, dust, pebbles, and splinters shaking from it as it rose as though from the grave. The flickering shadows that once surrounded its figure were gone, a plain, ratty burlap robe alone covering its torso now.

Looking around through the dust, the wraith's dead gaze landed on Reza, who was most exposed from the aftermath of the blast and cave-in, Fin being partially covered by rubble, and Nomad being completely out of sight of the hooded specter.

Both were unconscious, leaving the wraith to close in on Reza, raising its head momentarily to show its fangs as it went in for a bite at Reza's unprotected head.

Through the dust hummed a blade, entering into the side of the skeleton's chest, thrusting up through its ribs, slicing out through the back of the wraith's shoulders, black sludge spilling all along the floor.

The wraith looked over to Nomad, who almost seemed a zombie himself, barely standing to hold the blade in its new sheath.

The wraith turned, almost throwing Nomad off his feet, barely keeping up with the sudden jerk of movement.

Fangs that originally were meant for Reza now came down on the base of Nomad's skull, sinking in deep as Nomad reflexively lifted his head to dislodge the maw, failing to do so.

Broken claws swiped in at the hunched man, slamming him on both his left side repeatedly as the skull of the wraith kept him pinned in place, not even seeming to notice the blade that was fully enveloped inside its body, right until a burning light began to flow from the base of the sword, shining right up through the tip of the blade that was exposed.

Letting go of its vise-like bite, the wraith frantically attempted to retreat, but the sword that had impaled it held it in place as Nomad spiked the righteous aura through the blade, burning away the blackness that had drenched it. Black smoke enveloped the figure as the white light showed through its skeletal frame. Its shrouded trappings burst into flames, the wraith bellowing its last cry before sagging, its hollow frame going limp on the end of Nomad's bright blade.

Pointing his sword to the floor, the corpse slid off, awkwardly flopping to the floorboards as the blade's light died out, leaving Nomad standing still, head slumped so that his hair covered his face.

After a few moments of silence, save for Jadu reading aloud to himself in the distance, a monotone voice penetrated through the veil of disheveled hair that hung over Nomad's face.

The stream of strange, foreign speech gently roused Reza from her unconsciousness. Looking up from the floor, she could see Nomad standing slack, wraith dead at his feet as he droned out an incoherent slur of words in a tongue she had heard once before when he had attempted to treat her in the catacombs.

"Nomad—" Reza coughed, clutching her left side, feeling a sharp pain along her ribs as she attempted to move, not sure if her ribs were collapsed or just fractured and splintered.

Showing no recognition to Reza's pain, slowly turning back to the entrance where Lashik last was, Nomad sluggishly headed out of Reza's sight, into the settling dust cloud.

A foul voice slithered out from the entrance of the room, followed by a swift gust that quickly blew through the open holes in the wall and ceiling, clearing the lingering dust from the air.

Lashik, now with a clear view of the slumped enchanter and the frantically reading praven, raised a hand. The two rings he wore on his left hand glowed a menacingly deep crimson before eroding away, flakes of the metal and gemstone breaking down into a fine haze, swirling out in fine tendrils, licking their way towards the two.

"By the gods, Jadu! If you don't conjure a barrier this moment, that glowing sand will snuff us out in an instant!" Zaren spat out as quickly as he could.

Jadu, aware of the direness of the situation, stopped flipping through the book and hurriedly read aloud from the random page he had stopped on. The runic language he had recently become somewhat acquainted with gratingly made its way out of his mouth as a prismatic flurry of tiny winged shapes fluttered off the disintegrating page into the path of the glowing dust that stretched towards them.

The tome's spine hit the floor, Jadu collapsing on top of it soon thereafter.

The brilliant display of the clash of spells happening above him were lost on Jadu, but Zaren stared slack-jawed at the dazzling display, honestly not expecting Jadu to be able to cast a spell robust enough to ward off the deathly potent spell Lashik had just tossed at them. He knew, though, that if Jadu hadn't killed himself in casting the powerful spell, he had at least wiped himself out, knowing the little praven was out of the fight at the expense of the costly, momentary protection.

An evil laugh issued from across the room, Lashik's cackle easily displaying that he was enjoying the thought that his last hex had probably cost Zaren his pawn's life.

Zaren looked down to Jadu with a hopeful look, knowing Jadu to be quite the exception to the norm. Though most novices would surely have died in channeling such a rush of hexweave through them without the aid of a focus to help mitigate the taxing life drain from such a powerful spell, Jadu, Zaren hoped, might just surprise them with his ample supply of perky resilience.

"*Ugh,*" Jadu breathed, shifting from his position on the floor, moving slightly to lay on top of the tome to better cushion his face before falling unconscious again.

Jadu's snoring silenced Lashik's wicked laughter, quenching his victory over their last exchange. Raising his right hand, which held three more rings, he displayed them to Zaren, making sure the old enchanter knew of the seriousness of the situation before chanting in long, drawn-out syllables.

Zaren groaned, sitting up, having to pop a crick in his back before leaning forward to snatch his spellbook out from under his sleeping apprentice's head, sitting back and taking a deep breath before flipping open the tome directly to the page he sought, beginning a replying string of arcane words back at Lashik.

Both mages were fervently steeped in their incantations, burning through line after line of arcane speech. Neither noticed Nomad approaching Lashik until he was only steps away from him.

As soon as Zaren noticed the slow approach of the man with the glowing sword, he dropped his incantation, flipping to another page in his tome, rushing through its chant doubly fast, trying to make up time for the spell he had just abandoned.

Lashik, after taking note of the approaching, haggard man, looked back to his focused target, not hesitating or stuttering through a single syllable as he lifted his hand forward, finishing the longwinded spell, a gust of sweeping flames bellowing towards Zaren, blasting Jadu's limp body and Zaren back along the floor before another wave of cinder and heat swept over the two. This time the scorching cinders in the air singed both their hefty robes, the waves of heat and fire continuing to come, each shockwave becoming more intense, the first ring on Lashik's hand beginning to dissipate as the hex continued.

A point, pure and white against the darkening heat billowing out from Lashik's presence, attempted to cut through the net of dark-purple energy that materialized over Lashik's body as Nomad's holy blade snagged along the once unseen force.

Not paying attention to the attack in the least, Lashik continued holding out the hex that now was ripping through layers of cloth of both enchanters that lay on the floor, seemingly helpless to counter the onslaught.

Shouting now to hear his voice over the roar of the inferno he and Jadu were in, Zaren ended his spell, the page he was on not seeming to be flammable amidst the licking flames up until the very point of Zaren's last command word. The page dissipated in a blink, Zaren immediately closing the book. The old man dove over Jadu's unconscious body to protect the praven from the onslaught of heat that continued to pound into them, their sweat sizzling dry on their scolding exposed skin—steam and smoke visually pluming from what was left of their robes.

With the end of Zaren's spell, Lashik's hexweave shield dropped. Nomad's still gleaming blade jerked suddenly, sinking into Lashik like hot iron through wax. His torso almost sliced in half as Nomad lunged forward, barely catching himself to remain standing, a chant of foreign words still constantly droning out of his lips.

The torrent of fire ceased suddenly, Lashik crying out in surprise, stepping uneasily back away from the divinely keen blade.

Nomad, showing no emotion still, even after his successful, devastating blow, lifted his blade again, coming in at Lashik with another lunge.

Recovering quick enough to sidestep Nomad's tired attack, Lashik hissed, grabbing the hilt of his gilded spike-like rondel dagger, yanking it out of its scabbard viciously before plunging it down into the back of Nomad, the tip plunging deep in through the protective chainmail Nomad wore. The point sunk in through Nomad's shoulder before coming to a halt, and Lashik, feeling the full depth of the spike within his adversary's torso, grinned, tattered lips half smiling loosely over his bare teeth.

A darkness quickly formed around the blade, the wound pouring out foul smoke as Lashik twisted the blade inside Nomad, ripping muscle and scraping through bone as he dug further.

Nomad's chant quietly relinquished, head collapsing to the floor, limp. Whatever consciousness the man had held to, departed, leaving only the rank smell of burning flesh in the air.

Lashik threw the hilt aside as the blade began to melt into a black, smoking ooze.

44
REQUIEM KNELL

"Reza!"

Jerking awake once again from unconsciousness, Reza almost immediately blacked out once more from the heavy damage her body had taken from the explosion and collapse.

The voice called out again, louder this time.

"Reza! Get up!"

Not sure who was calling her name, she squinted, looking around her for a moment as she attempted to discern who was speaking.

"Isis?" she slurred.

"Yes, and you need to get up! Lashik now goes unopposed. Your friends are down. He will kill you *all* if you don't get up and fight!" Isis yelled, her voice wavering every now and then as if her connection to the realm still remained very tenuous.

Reza lazily blinked again, trying to focus on the standing figure across the room. She was halfway to him, and she assumed she had arrived there last time she had started towards Nomad, blacking out along the way, but even twenty feet seemed an unreasonable distance to demand of her body in its current state.

Putting a hand underneath her, pushing up, she planted a foot on the floor, the exertion causing her to let out a belabored grunt, trying not to breathe too deeply to avoid the sharp bite of her aching ribs.

"Up, up!" Isis cried.

Forcing her broken body to obey, Reza pressed through the pain that assaulted her so sharply just from the action of standing.

Reza was up on her feet. A pressure in her head was causing her vision to blur, patches of blackness spreading over what she could see. She was distantly aware of Isis' voice shouting orders at her, but Isis was fading, Reza no longer being able to make out what her spirit companion was saying.

She noticed that Lashik was watching her, his lips moving, but he thankfully was not making advances towards her.

She took a step forward, crunching along her side clearly audible where broken bone rubbed broken bone, which caused her legs to buckle. Pitching forward, she managed to catch herself from falling, knowing she would not be able to get back up again if she went down now. She was operating on the edge of consciousness, and she knew that the faintest blow would likely do her in.

For a moment, she heard Lashik's vile voice, causing her to look sideways to see him in her periphery, her vision now blotching out everything directly in front of her.

She could see a dark-purple aura wash over him, and she presumed that he had just constructed the protective hexweave shield he had been enchanted with in their previous encounter.

She rested a trembling hand on the handle of her seax, sliding it slowly out of its sheath before trudging forward once more.

She knew with Lashik's shield up that her weapon would do her no good. Even without his shield, she doubted she had much in her more than a single thrust before collapsing, but she also knew Isis to be right. She saw none of her comrades standing now. She was their last line against Lashik having them, body and soul, permanently. She knew she had to press forward, even if there was no hope in her cause.

She could hear Isis talking again, though her mind was having a difficult time making sense of her words. Amber golden mist floated from the ring and into her periphery and was blowing over Lashik's aura, slowly breaking it down until it was banished completely.

Lashik looked slightly concerned at first, but his demeanor quickly turned to smug amusement, cackling as Reza shambled ever closer to him as she readied herself for her all-in attack.

She stared blindly forward, facing the cackling corpse, grimacing through the constant pressure and pain in her head.

Just as she readied herself to lunge, she noticed Lashik's laughing cut short, a rustle at the doorway causing her to turn her view once more to try and see around her blind spot.

Cavok burst into the room, his booming warcry understandably causing Lashik to take a step back from the man.

Though Reza could barely make him out, she could see through her vision's haze that he was badly wounded, blood streaming from broken arrow shafts and gashes all along his side, arms, and back.

Despite his grizzly appearance, he heaved with fury, and Reza knew that it was a blind rage that must had born him all the way up that flight of stairs in spite of so many ignored injuries.

The man's blood-slick hand clutched his greatsword. He let loose a pain-filled roar, focusing all his rage solely on Lashik.

Reza could hear Lashik's insidious voice start up again, and she knew he had begun casting another spell, but Cavok brought his sword up and chopped through Lashik's shoulder, cleaving straight through to the floor, cutting off Lashik's left arm and a large hunk of rotten torso that sickeningly flopped to the floor.

Lashik shakily stood for a moment longer before Cavok brought up his sword again, swinging it sideways with a yell while it ripped through the air, spraying oily gore as it slammed into what was left of Lashik.

It passed easily through Lashik's neck and remaining arm, his head tumbling in the air before landing amidst what remained of his robes.

Lashik's glowing eyes remained alit for a moment as he looked unbelievably at Reza, but the moment was abruptly ended as Cavok's heavy boot slammed down on Lashik's head, crushing whatever life was left clinging to the perverse interior of that dark skull.

Cavok stood heaving, bloodlust still in control over his mental state until Reza called out to him.

"Cavok…" she said, her voice hollow—almost gone.

The small voice was enough to snap his attention over to Reza, his features softening considerably, concern showing as he raced to her, almost stumbling over her as he closed.

Falling into his arms, Reza let her friend hold her up, being too weak to stand any longer.

"Reza—" Cavok started, easily supporting her weight, looking down at her, asking, "How bad off are you? I can't see."

Looking down to her ring idly for a moment before looking over to the pile of robes on the floor that were collectively Jadu and Zaren, then over to the lump on the ground that was Nomad, she quickly brought a protective hand down in front of her side as Cavok gripped a little too close to her broken section of ribs, gasping as she and he repositioned.

"My ribs are broken," she breathed out through clenched teeth, adding, "and I think I took a bad blow to the head. My vision is partially gone."

Holding her now up higher, stooping over to allow her to sling her arm over his shoulder, he asked directly, "You going to make it?"

Pausing to consider the question for a moment, in too much pain to sort through and assess how dire her bodily injuries were, she said, "Yeah, I'll make it," simply to allay Cavok's concerns over her, not knowing honestly if she was or not, but knowing that the rest of the group on the ground needed his help much more than she did.

"The others?" Cavok asked, looking past her, his white-filmed eyes searching for her answer.

A drawn-out cough from Zaren's direction answered them, Zaren shifting about, his bony, heat-blistered skin showing as he worked on sitting up, the hair along his face badly singed.

"What happened?" Zaren asked, smoke puffing from his mouth as he spoke.

"Zaren, check on Jadu," Reza called before slapping Cavok's arm, feebly starting to walk them over to Nomad, saying, "Over here, Cavok. Nomad's on the floor."

Assisting her over to Nomad, yanking the shaft of an arrow from his muscled back on the way, Reza tugged on his arm as they neared, the two of them kneeling in front of Nomad, his body smelling of seared flesh.

Reza hovered her hand over Nomad's mouth for a moment, then rested a hand on his stomach, searching for any telltale signs of life from the man. After a moment of stillness, she felt the slightest rise and fall of his stomach as he breathed, his breath faintly feathering her fingers.

"He's alive," she said.

Having to look up to inspect his body from the side of her vision, she noticed a black liquid seeping out from under him.

"Flip him over, Cavok," Reza said.

Cavok groped around until he found Nomad's body and gently flipped the man over as Reza had requested.

Through a hole in his chainmail, the edges covered in a tar-like substance, Reza could see a stab wound in Nomad's back above his right shoulder blade. The puncture looked serious, but not deep enough to cause her to consider the wound fatal. What concerned her more, though, was the blackness that seeped from the wound.

Putting a hand over the infected hole in Nomad's back, she hesitated for a moment, listening to Zaren's mumblings in the background as he attempted to rouse Jadu, considering if she should do what she was deliberating on doing.

Though she had used her innate healing abilities before, multiple times throughout her life, in fact, the more difficult skill to master was to use regulated amounts of her energy to heal another. She knew she couldn't afford to completely heal Nomad's wound, as she was already in a dire condition as it was.

She had to decide, did she risk an attempt at a heal, mending Nomad's black wound just enough to make sure he was stabilized, or did she let him fend for himself and hope that his dark injury wasn't as dire as it looked?

As soon as she posed the question, she knew the answer.

Reza turned to Cavok.

"I'll take care of Nomad. I think Fin is still buried in rubble over there," she said, pressing her pointing finger to his arm to allow him to feel the direction she was pointing towards before adding, "Go make sure he's alright."

She didn't wait for his response, turning back to Nomad. Cavok hesitated a moment, grunting and plucking another arrow from his shoulder, dropping the shaft to the floor before starting over towards the rubble pile to search for his old-time friend.

Reza tilted her head, trying to see past her blind spots to make sure she knew where Nomad's wound was. Looking forward, she hovered her trembling hand over the black spot, considering the thought that she could be experiencing her last moments in this realm as the saren known as Reza Malay.

She looked at the man lying in front of her.

He had clung to her at first, seeming lost, lonely, in need of connecting with someone—anyone.

By fate, they had been thrown together, and she had thought nothing but annoyance of it at first; but, the longer they had traveled together, the more she had begun to realize that he had meant something to her—even enough to risk her life for.

She knew she was one to run from her feelings, figuring to sort through them later. She exhaled now, coming to terms with the fact that if she and Nomad did survive, it would be her turn to insist on Nomad's company on the road ahead, wherever that road took them. A path without him now seemed…a barren one.

Hand hovering over his back, she could almost feel him giving up the ghost, his energy seeping out of the black puncture wound. He was departing as she sat deliberating.

"Turn back from that place, Nomad. Please."

Steadying her hand a moment before her sacrificial healing, she let the warming glow flow through her to Nomad, lighting the darkness over him, delivering her from consciousness.

Part Four: Victory at High Cost

45

WINDOW OF REST

"Nomad, look! She's coming around!" were the first words Reza recalled upon waking from a long, dark sleep.

Groaning, Reza pushed herself up from the bed she was in. Sheets slipping down to her lap, revealing a bare torso only covered with wraps of cloth over wounds still being treated, her first waking image was that of Nomad sitting in the bed next to her averting his eyes from her exposed chest. It was a sight she couldn't help but smile over, remembering their first encounter going similarly.

Lifting the covers up to cover her chest, she looked around to find Fin by her bedside in what appeared to be a small infirmary, only allowing for two patients.

"There we are, old gal," Fin said excitedly, clasping Reza's limp hand.

"The nurse said you'd be waking today! Wow, you two took the longest to come around after what happened in the tower. We had both doctors and clerics from multiple sects in here attempting to heal you, but you two were being stubborn. Nomad only just woke about an hour ago himself."

"Where's Cavok and the others?" Reza asked, sitting back in her

269

bed against the headrest, her ribs beginning to ache, details now coming back to her of the battle at the top of Darendul Tower.

"He's fine. They're all here. I could go get Jadu and Zaren if you'd like. Cavok would come if I let him know you're up, but in the state he's in, he really should keep off his feet for a day or more at least. Those arisen thugs must have really done a number on him in his blinded state while he made his way through the streets to get to the tower. He's cut up pretty bad, even for Cavok."

"Where are we?" Reza asked, skipping subjects once more, trying to catch up with what had happened during her unconsciousness, placing a hand on her head while suppressing a wince as she began to notice an underlying headache she had, feeling a gauze pad taped atop a shaven section of hair.

"Lots of details to fill you in on later, but first, I think I had better let your doctor know that you've come to. I already filled Nomad in on most everything anyways, so you two chat while I go get the doc," Fin said, standing up, pausing for a moment to add, "Great to have you back with us," before squeezing her hand once before rushing out of the room.

"I saw you," Nomad said, taking Reza's attention from Fin to her chamber mate.

"I saw you in my dreams after I entered *oking detoko*, after all went dark—you were there with me."

Staring at Nomad, Reza tried to make sense of his statement, knowing whatever it was he was saying, that it was very important to him. His gaze was locked on her—his features undeniably somber.

"What is *oking detoko*?" she asked.

Nomad, finally blinking, looked down at his bruised and stitched-up hands and arms from the aftermath of the explosion and collapse of the tower's roof, and considered how to explain the cultural term.

"It's a state of being one, in my culture, that few return from. In your tongue, it translates to 'walking dead man.' It's a last resort, when the body cannot perform the necessary task, those who know the traditional trance can enter into this—" Nomad paused, struggling for the correct words, "blank state of mind. Pushing the body to walk when it shouldn't—fight when it should be dead."

Looking up to Reza, meeting eyes once more, he softly voiced, "I thought we had no other options. I entered the corridors of death—the hallway of ancestors. I was departing this life—when you appeared. You placed a hand on my back and turned me away from the archway of the afterlife. I heard you say, *Turn back from that place, please*."

Reza welled up, looking down, then over to the window, which let in a light breeze, the sunlight bathing a single flower in the vase on the nightstand next to the windowsill.

She had said those words as she had placed a hand over the black wound that had weakened Nomad so terribly. Her healing had apparently worked, though the details of what had happened after the start of her healing were details she'd likely never know.

What she did know was the simple fact that she was willing to die for the man who currently shared the room with her.

Nomad—the stranger who had only recently come into her life. A drifter from another land. He had made an impression on her quickly. He had showed loyalty to her readily, and he had followed her into places he did not wish to go. He had risked his life multiple times for her, and had asked nothing in return.

Perhaps those qualifiers would merit anyone a place close enough to her usually guarded heart that she would lay down her life for, but she didn't believe so. He was different—curiously so, in ways she couldn't quite explain—but uniquely and profoundly an exceptional person in her eyes. One that she doubted she would ever forget or wish to depart from on the road ahead.

He had touched a chord with her on a level she didn't completely understand, but she knew that their partnership now was bound by more than the need of skill on a dire mission or simply an allowance to the pleas from the rest of the group for him to be able to come along for the journey. He was now a necessity for her. She knew she desired him for a permanent adventuring companion if she could have her way—and she didn't know what to think of that realized admission of her heart.

"Reza?" a booming voice sounded from the hallway.

Cavok, his eyes no longer milky, stopped at the door with a huge grin on his face. He was hobbling horribly, but he eventually made it over to her bedside.

The man was clearly on the receiving end of a traumatic amount of abuse, thick-threaded sutures all along his bare body, only a thin and bloodily speckled robe covering his torso to the middle of his thighs.

Cavok's unrepressed joy at seeing her shook her from her thoughts of Nomad.

"Your vision, is it back?" she asked, looking hopefully into his eyes.

Trying to brush the subject aside, not seeming interested in talking much about himself, he replied, "Mostly. They had some eye doctor take a look at me and her treatment has been helping."

Reza smiled at the news, attempting to scoot over to offer him a seat on her bedside.

Seeing her making room, Cavok waved to dismiss the offer. "Don't worry about it. I'd probably split a seam sitting down like that. I'll stand."

"You look like you need this bed more than I do, Cavok," Nomad said from behind, offering his bed to the awkwardly standing man.

"Nonsense," Cavok grumbled, not pleased with the two's focus on his condition.

"I came out of that fight in much better condition than you two fair flowers."

His comment, though getting a chuckle out of both him and Nomad, visibly soured Reza's mood, she now giving him a half-mocking scowl.

Attempting to move past his teasing comment, Reza asked Cavok a question, trying to change the topic.

"So Cavok, where are we?"

"We're in Sheaf," Cavok said, shifting his weight while trying not to wince from the inconvenience of standing.

"You're in a private infirmary ward meant for higher-ranking officers and delegates. It seems Leith was left in charge of the capital while Metus was away to lead the war effort. As soon as she was alerted that we had returned, she admitted us here. It's relatively empty, but I suspect that's about to change as soon as Metus and the troops return later today."

Reza stopped to consider the news, asking, "He's returning today? Did they already confront the arisen army? How long have Nomad and I been out?"

Motioning for Reza to scoot over, Cavok mumbled, "Think I will take that seat, on second thought. I can see this is going to take a while."

Gingerly sitting beside Reza, the bed dipping noticeably under his weight, Cavok began to lay out what had happened while Reza and Nomad were unconscious.

"So, you remember when we were in the tower and you told me to go help Fin out of the rubble while you tended to Nomad?"

"Yeah," Reza replied, nodding slowly.

"I came back after dragging Fin out of stone and wood and you were slumped over unconscious on Nomad, the both of you barely breathing; so, I laid you out beside Fin and Jadu, who was also unconscious. Me and Zaren puzzled over what to do with the lot of you. Everyone was in pretty bad shape and in no condition to move without help and mounts. I must admit, it was looking pretty grim.

"Well, I decided to give it some thought and went to the balcony—that's where I stumbled upon Bede...."

Cavok looked down at his hands, as if searching for what to say, or not to say, about the memory.

"We carried her away from that awful place. She rests here in Sheaf now. I'll take you to her resting spot sometime when you're up for it."

After the somber moment, clearing his throat, Cavok pressed on, not wanting to linger on the difficult subject for too long.

"I became aware of some commotion below in the city streets. I could make out outlines of things, but I couldn't see anything clearly down below—could only hear what sounded like wolves ripping and biting. I called Zaren over to look for me and he said that Arie with the dolinger pack was below, clearing the streets of the remaining arisen.

"Sure enough, it was her. An hour later, she came up the tower and told us that she had patrolled the outer city, noticing a lack of defenses and saw the explosion on the tower top. She decided we needed help, so she rushed in and found the city to be massively undermanned, easily ripping through what small force was left behind to occupy the empty city. After which, she made her way to the tower and found us there.

"We got everyone mounted as best we could and headed for, what we thought was going to be, a war-torn Warwick, knowing that with you and Nomad as bad off as you two were, some of us might not have survived another backcountry trip directly to Sheaf.

"We made it to Warwick by the end of the day with Fin and Jadu waking up along the way. Those two weren't too bad off. Jadu was probably the worst out of everyone but you guys. His burns were pretty bad—still are—but he's got a chipper tune about him. He's shrugged it off well enough."

Reza shifted in her bed, asking, "Had the arisen army destroyed Warwick? Was Metus too late in getting the word to them?"

Cavok looked forward and answered Reza's question.

"So when we got to Warwick, we found it busy. There was a

panic among the villagers, but the town was unspoiled. We gathered from the locals that Metus and his army had routed the attacking arisen force, the battle taking place just to the south of Warwick.

"They were still pursuing, but the battle had happened earlier that morning and victory was claimed sometime just after noon.

"So with that, we purchased a coach and packed everyone up, including you two sleepy ones, and headed back to the Sheaf, Arie insisting on getting the best physicians here to be the ones to nurse Nomad and Reza since she correctly guessed that both Warwick and Viccarwood's infirmaries were soon to be flooded with soldiers that had been wounded in battle.

"We rode through the next day and made it to the Sheaf that morning where Arie reported to Leith and they got us admitted here. That was yesterday; so, to answer your question, you and Nomad have been unconscious two days now."

Looking out the window through the flowing curtains fluttering past the vase and flower to the white, puffy clouds lazily strolling across the bright-blue backdrop of sky, Reza let the story sink in. She was genuinely amazed that they had all made it out of their suicide mission alive and that Metus seemed to have been successful in defeating the threat to the Plainstate of the arisen army and its terrible master.

They all turned to the door as they heard Fin's voice sounding from the halls, entering the room alongside a woman dressed in white whom Reza guessed to be a nurse. Jadu and Zaren entered behind too, the small room instantly becoming a bit too cozy for the nurse's liking.

Weaving past Fin, helping Cavok to his feet, getting a grunt of suppressed pain from him, she discreetly lowered Reza's sheets to take a peek at Reza's side. Covering her up again, she asked her a few questions about how she felt as Nomad, Fin, Cavok, Jadu, and Zaren began chatting, greetings from Zaren and Jadu to Reza out-talking the frustrated nurse.

The nurse was just checking the bandage over Reza's skull when two more individuals showed up at the door. Arie squeezed her way into the room to take a seat at the foot of Nomad's bed with Leith staying at the door, not even bothering on trying to add more congestion to the crowded room.

Leith asked from the hallway, "Reza. Nomad. How are you two feeling?"

The nurse threw up her hands, giving up on the checkup, taking a seat next to the window in the guest's chair.

Reza smiled and called across the chattering room, "We're doing well. Just a few broken ribs and a cracked skull is all for me. We'll be up and moving in no time."

Nomad simply smiled, nodding to Leith's question, receiving a returning nod from Leith.

"Very good," Leith said, most of the room quieting as she continued. "We've received messages that Sultan Metus is expected to return today in a few hours as some of you may have heard. There is to be a small welcoming ceremony in the courtyard open to citizens of Sheaf upon his arrival to celebrate the victory, and to honor those who gave their lives for our people. I would hope, if you feel up to it, that everyone present might attend. The sultan would be very kind to the idea of having you all there, I feel. He is so fond of you."

The last statement, Leith had said as if directed mostly to Reza, making eye contact before bowing out of the doorway.

Calling over her shoulder on the way out, she added, "Uniforms will be sent to each of you. You can't be seen before the people of the Plainstate in naught but a thin sheet of cloth."

Just at the thought of getting dressed, Cavok mumbled, "Never been that fond of ceremonies."

"Come on, big guy," Fin chipped in, about to pat the man on the back, halting, not seeing a spot that wasn't a bruise or laced with stitches, adding, "You can manage to throw something over that used pincushion of a body of yours. Would be disrespectful of us not to be there to greet Metus home and congratulate him on the victory. We might have gotten him the info, but he did the heavy lifting. His troops likely saved thousands from slaughter."

Reza, clearing her voice, added, "Besides that, it's a ceremony to honor the dead in this battle. I know we all will be mourning Bede's sacrifice and passing in our own ways, but this would be nice to do together. I think she would appreciate the sentiment in her, and everyone else's, honor. They gave their lives for a cause—not for nothing."

The somber comment left the packed room quiet, none daring to break the silence. After a few moments, the nurse came back over to Reza's side with white tablets of some kind, piquing Jadu's interest slightly.

Jadu made his way over to the nurse, tugging on her skirt, asking in a whisper of a voice, "What kind of tablets are those? If they're pain pills, I've got some really potent ones I could go get for Reza. Made them myself. Pure stuff, really effective."

Jadu's jabbering broke the silence, the nurse arguing with the little praven while Reza intervened on the nurse's behalf, trying to get Jadu to drop the issue, assuring him that the nurse's treatment was adequate. Cavok then jumped in, asking Jadu if he could sneak him a few of his home-remedy drugs, out of legitimate need—Fin also putting in an order of the alchemist's drugs, not so much out of legitimate need. Zaren remained brooding in the corner while Nomad and Arie began chatting about details of Metus' short but successful campaign against the arisen.

The little room was quickly filled with liveliness and conversation once again, which floated out through the thin curtains of the window into the quiet streets a story below.

46
PLAUDITS AND EGRESS

Getting dressed had taken most of them longer than they thought it would have. Cavok and Reza limped out of their rooms with everyone else already waiting for them.

They headed off through the infirmary corridors and down a path through a rock garden that led to the main palace court. When they got there, the courtyard was packed, with more locals still flooding in from the wide main gate with every passing minute.

Choosing to stay on the fringe of the crowd, Cavok and Reza not wanting anything to do with the scores of accidental bumps amidst the congestion, the group took a seat twenty feet off to the side of the crowd. The long bench at the end of the trail allowed for a few in the group to take a rest while they watched the military begin to break a line down the middle of the crowd of hundreds of gathered civilians cheering and waving to the oncoming officers atop dolinger and horseback alike. No doubt the dolingers were helping to hasten the path through the crowd the officers were attempting to make to the palace steps.

Jadu, pointing out Leith, who stood up in the shade on the palace steps, prattled on to the rest of the group, begging them to move closer to the action for a better look at the proceedings. His pleas fell on deaf ears, however, as everyone else was quite pleased with their somewhat secluded spot on the sidelines.

Nomad was the first to notice a slender figure approaching them from the crowd.

Arie hurried up to them, waving an inviting hand, urgently calling for them to get to the palace steps. Leith was demanding their presence there.

With Jadu dashing off ahead of her into the crowd, and Nomad and Fin joining her without objection, Reza, Zaren, and Cavok reluctantly looked at the others and begrudgingly followed.

Arie ordered a path through the crowd for the small group with only a few listening to her demands; until, that is, they glimpsed Cavok, who looked like as battle-hardened a veteran as any of them had ever seen.

As they limped their way to the steps, Reza and Cavok doing everything they could to not show the immense pain each was in from the broken bones, contusions, and deep, stitched-up wounds they suffered from, Cavok, looming over the rest of the crowd, could see as they neared the steps that Metus and his elite guards were making their way up beside Leith.

The group broke from the crowd, Arie leading them to the side of Leith, who had taken Metus aside for a minute while the crowd cheered for the soldiers and sultan at the steps.

Finishing up her private conversation with Metus, Leith stepped back next to Arie, Metus stepping up on the stairs to gain a bit more ground for the crowd to see him as he began to speak.

"Citizens of Sheaf!" he began, lifting his hands to hush the hundreds of residents that had shown up for the event.

As the crowd slowly died down, Metus began speaking again.

"There has been an obscure shadow and threat that has been looming over us this past year, making borders, our towns, and our profitable trade routes uneasy by the swift fall of the city Brigganden.

"That threat, thanks to the courage, strength, swiftness, and unmatched faith in the kind gods and goddesses of the realm, has been defeated!"

Even before Metus had finished his proclamation, the cheers from the crowd all but drowned him out, the masses easily whipped up in a frenzy of excitement at the sound of the good news.

Holding up his hands once more, Metus attempted to lower the volume of the shouts of *hurrah*. After a minute of Metus wrangling the attention of the onlookers, he started up again.

"We are here unharmed, safe in our beloved capital because of those that went out to face that terrifying foe that we now know to be an arisen army."

A communal gasp at the mention of the arisen echoed throughout the courtyard, and Metus let the wave of shock settle in before continuing.

"One that we defeated, thankfully before the cost of war scarred our lands. We wreaked havoc amongst their ranks thanks to our foresight and preparation, casting what was left of their ruined army out of our borders, southward into the Badlands.

"Though ultimately we come home this day undisputed victors, there were many of our people that come home wounded, or worse, those that did not come back to their families, alive. We had losses, and to them, we must be forever in their debt."

For a moment, Metus paused, looking to Reza, holding her gaze for a short but powerful moment. Reza's thoughts drifted to Bede, seeing that Metus also shared her thoughts. Looking back up to the captivated crowd, Metus continued.

"When our people hurt, we all hurt. Honor those that have died so that you may live life safely in the borders of the Plainstate.

"May we mourn them this day—but may we also celebrate them this day, and celebrate life as well, for we are, and still remain, a land of safety and freedom!"

Cheers erupted as Metus turned to speak a few words to Leith, then to the head of his elite guard before beckoning Reza and the rest to follow him into the palace, the inner palace guards closing the doors as they entered.

"You look as ragged as I feel," Metus said, looking to Cavok with a tired smile, Cavok simply grunting in response.

Metus turned to the rest of the group and softly addressed Reza and the rest, the sound of the crowd now shut out by the heavy palace doors.

"I'll let you all get some well-needed rest, but first, I'd like to speak with you all while you're gathered. I have something for each of you. Come, let's converse in my study."

Reza and Cavok's wandering gaze drifted up to the second-story office door, Cavok letting out another grunt as they began the long walk up the stairway to walk to Metus' office, Arie staying behind until Metus shouted out for her to join them as well.

With everyone filing into the room, Leith closed the door behind them. Metus took a seat at his desk, pulling clinking bags from his drawer, which grabbed Fin's attention instantly.

Metus handed seven, fine purple purses to Leith, who handed them out to each in attendance, including Arie, who seemed taken aback by the gift.

As they each drew open the pouch, they were met with a large quantity of gold, and more impressively, an array of silvery metals. Fin, for one, recognized the metals as varying platinums, which were much more valuable than gold in most local regions.

"Gold, palladium, rhodium, platinum, silver. Total, this is well more than I had said we'd pay you for your service. Your mission was beyond a success, and I hope the bonus helps you make the best of whatever endeavors you choose to pursue next."

"Thank you, Sultan. Truly we are humbled by your gift," Reza softly spoke, drawing up the purse strings, placing it to her side.

The group's attention drifted to Zaren, who held his pouch forward, offering it back to Leith, who, after a moment, took it, everyone waiting for an explanation.

"I don't need metals. I have an alchemist for a student for goodness sakes," Zaren grumbled.

Reza gave Zaren a look as though she was about to slap the old man. Looking down as a small hand was placed on her arm, Jadu looked up concernedly at her.

"It's not that we don't appreciate your gift, Sultan," Jadu said, his attention now focused on Metus. "It's just that Zaren would like to return to his tower to begin the ritual to recall his people back to this realm. He worries about them quite a bit. But the doctors say I might need to stay here a while longer for skin treatment for my burns, and he doesn't want to leave me here alone. He's just frustrated about that, that's all. He means no disrespect to you."

Reza was flabbergasted by the unusual seriousness and tactful awareness shown by the little praven. His explanation on what conflicted emotions rode just under the crusty old enchanter's skin was an analysis Reza didn't know Jadu was capable of.

"Ah. How thoughtless of me," Metus said, seeming to completely sympathize with the plight Jadu had presented to him.

"Leith told me of Brigganden city being mostly abandoned and your wonderful work in purging most of the arisen that were left there. I wouldn't trust it to be completely safe, and we already have a large regiment on their way to reoccupy the city, but perhaps a more helpful gift would be to send a doctor with you, along with a small contingent of guards to help you return to your tower safely. Any supplies you may need to assist you there, be it food and drink, stoneworkers, carpenters, and laborers that could help with any repairs if damage has come to your grounds during the occupation, we will send the necessary support with you."

All looked to Zaren now for a response. Zaren, with arms folded like a child who was moodily mulling over if he was going to accept the offer or if he was going to refuse it out of pride, eventually nodded, mumbling, "That would be adequate."

Zaren, getting up from his chair, called back to Jadu.

"Come, Jadu. We leave as soon as the guards and doctor are ready. I've been gone from my tower longer than I promised I would be."

As Metus issued a quick command to Leith to help assemble the caravan they had promised to the old enchanter, Jadu got up without hesitation and began skipping to the door, stopping in the doorway as if he had just remembered something.

Turning back, looking to everyone individually, he said after a moment of silence, "Never did get to dissect an arisen. Shame," before turning to follow his new master down the palace steps and out the door with Leith quickly in pursuit.

Turning back from staring into the empty hallway, the group all looked around at each other, attempting to make sense of what had just transpired.

Though none of them had gotten too terribly close with the little praven, he had been an intimate part of each of their lives over the past weeks, sharing some of the most trying and difficult times together. Being through so much together, to them, seemed as though a bond should have somehow tied them together, at least for a little while after the completion of their mission. The abruptness of Jadu and Zaren's departure out of their lives piercingly betrayed that notion.

"Arie. Leith told me of your part in the siege on Brigganden. A very brave move. You are welcome to any position you wish in all of Plainstate, as always. I hope you know that."

Arie, bowing to Metus, replied humbly, "I enjoy working as a guide. It's just the right amount of seclusion while still being of service to you. The wild is where I feel most at home."

Metus nodded his head, accepting Arie's answer before turning back to Reza and the rest, who still seemed somewhat out of sorts with Jadu's and Zaren's sudden departure.

"My time is short, but there's one other thing I wanted to discuss with you all.

"I admit that without the aid of a host of priests, clerics, and most notably amongst the ranks of the faithful, prophet Henarus, who led the effort against the arisen's commander, the narrow victory we earned that day would have been a crushing defeat. I have no doubt that with the wicked might of that arisen king, his army would have plowed through Warwick and Viccarwood's militia and would have gained strength before arriving at Sheaf. Without the warning you gave us to prepare for war, the outcome might have been drastically different than it was, and to that, we have you to thank. And also for that, gold, silver, and platinum are nowhere near enough to pay you for your service to our people.

"I don't know if this is adequate compensation, but if there's anything any of you ever need, you will always have my ear. Call for help any time and I will do what I can."

Getting up from his chair, Metus made his way over to a line of bookshelves and glass cabinets covering the left side of his room, plucking various items up that lay on the shelves and in the large cupboards, coming back to stand before them in front of his desk.

"Fin," Metus began, holding out an elegantly curved dagger. "I know how much you appreciate a well-crafted dagger."

The gleam of steel caused Fin to inadvertently lean forward to get a better look at the weapon as Metus continued talking about the twelve-inch blade.

"Crafted from the haltia, Leithonel tells me. It's somewhat of an infamous blade, locally. Rumors have it that this blade has a way of evading the eyes of all but its master."

Metus flipped the blade over in his hands, inspecting it one last time before handing it over to Fin, mentioning as he did so, "We confiscated it with the capture of a renowned thief, but we've never been able to determine if the rumors of the blade live up to the tales associated with it. Perhaps it will find you a more worthy master than I or my servants—in any case, it is a pretty thing."

Fin accepted the blade with a bow before sliding it quietly into the folds of his loose garments, Reza struggling to make out the shape of where it should have been in his flowing robes before Metus stole their attention away.

"Cavok," Metus said, looking the large man in the eyes before handing him a brass medallion with multiple tear-shaped aquamarines socketed into it.

Cavok took the small medallion and looked over it with a puzzled look on his face as Metus explained.

"It's not the coin that's my gift. This is a token that's worth more than its meager physical elements. It's an item that a man that's in town will have interest for. What he can provide you with is my gift. Seek him at the Dragon's Flagon inn downtown. His name is Lecken. Last report before I was off to war informed me that he had planned to stay there for a while. Hopefully he's still there. He specializes in a skill none in this region performs. If his skill is what reports say it is, then you would be well served, in your line of work, to seek him out. If it happens that he has moved on, bring that medallion back and we'll work something else out."

Cavok, still with a somewhat bemused look on his face, bowed and pocketed the medallion, thanking Metus before he moved on to Nomad.

Metus, holding a ponderous hand to his chin, considering the man a moment before he began, said, "I did not ask you about your heritage upon our first meeting as time simply did not permit that pleasantry. But with a name such as Nomad, I suspect your home is far from here, and your road ahead is not soon ended."

Standing before Metus, who still looked over Nomad's foreign facial features, Nomad met the sultan's gaze. Metus looked down to a few small bolts of differing shades of fine turquoise fabric, handing the bundle over to Nomad.

"Fabric may seem like a strange gift, but this fabric you'll not find in any bazaar. It's called fluxlace. It's a type of cashmere, laced with tear, flame, and weather-resistant materials. Your friend Jadu, if he had stayed a bit longer, would have been able to tell you a thing or two more about this rare cloth. It even is said to grant some resistance to channeled hexweave spells. Zaren might have spoken more on that claim, but it is, regardless of that point, some of the best material obtainable, even for me. I've been saving it to have it made into something, but never could think of a reason for a garment for myself. It would be a waste of adventure-hardy material on me as the most adventure it would ever see is some heated bureaucracy."

Nomad concealed his perplexity at his gift much better than Cavok had, but Metus noticed the blank stare and added, "I'll have a tailor work the materials into whatever apparel you would like."

Bowing his head low, Nomad issued a *thank you* as Metus stepped over to face Reza, smiling fondly at her for a moment before turning his attention to the scabbarded longsword he had latched by his hip.

Unlatching it from his belt, he held it up, speaking as he drew it from its silver-tipped, black-lacquered scabbard. It had a red band of cloth tightly wrapped around its base, and its steel blade gleamed—its wide, double fuller attractively running up the length of the blade.

Handing the flawless leather-wrapped handle to Reza, she reluctantly accepted it as he spoke about the sword, pointing out key features here and there.

"This sword was a gift from a distant king. It's an exceptional sword; though, I've always preferred my curved sword over a longsword. I don't know why, but I took it instead of my curved sword to battle this time. I didn't use it, and actually, it's never seen battle to this day.

"The king that gave it to me told me that it's unbreakable."

Metus looked up with a slightly skeptical expression.

"I'll let you be the judge of that, but the steel of the blade was said to have been composed of meteorite. The king gave me an ingot of the same metal the blade was forged with for testing purposes. This meteorite in particular seems to contain a very well-balanced carbon ratio, and is a low-alloy steel. My top smith confirmed its purity. It might just hold up to that bold, unbreakable claim. I hope it serves you well."

Reza thanked him graciously as he handed her the scabbard.

Turning to look over everyone once, taking a calming breath, Metus said in a reverent voice, "Bede would be proud of what you accomplished."

Bowing to Reza and the rest, he finished with, "I hope that you'll all come and visit from time to time; but for now, there are many things I need to tend to, and you'll have to excuse me. Good journey to each of you."

Walking out the door, Arie, Fin, Cavok, Nomad, and Reza sat in the sultan's study, each considering, now that they had the chance to rest and reflect with their mission at an end, what everyone else was going to do, seeing already the group beginning to dissolve with the departure of Jadu and Zaren.

47
LINGERING DARKNESS

"Hiro! Hiro! Fight it!" Reza's trembling voice made its way through the dark downpour as she took her hand away from his back to see that black ooze had seeped out of his cursed wound that he had received at the hand of Lashik all those months ago.

She held him tight in her arms there in the street, his tainted blood turning the puddle that they lay in black as ink.

Nomad opened his eyes to see that he was observing himself from above.

He could see every detail: his fluttering eyes as the raindrops pounded down on his face, his disheveled hair slick across his face, his skin quickly losing any semblance of color, his trembling lips going blue—Reza's devastated head resting on his, her tears falling, streaming across his face.

His hands, though once weak, now fell limp. His chest ceased its constant labor of rising and falling. Whatever tension that was in his face now went lax.

His out-of-body self began to drift higher, away from a desperate Reza, who now held her breath, searching for signs of life from a body that showed none.

After seconds of holding on to hope as long as she could, Reza let out a scream. The cry of a soul so grief wracked that even through the boom of thunder and torrential downpour, Nomad could clearly hear every inflection of loss Reza let out with the cry.

It was dark, but no longer raining; and, instead of the crash of thunder, Nomad could only hear the fearful blare of his own voice shouting into the night as he sat up, yelling out in bed.

"Nomad! What is it?" Arie said, sitting up beside him, just coming out of sleep herself from his outburst.

"She—I—" Nomad began to huff out between catching his breath while looking around for an explanation.

A sudden pain in his back forced him to jerk his arm tight to his chest as he took in a sharp breath to hold back from crying out in pain.

"Your back, it's bleeding black again," Arie said worriedly, jumping out of bed to grab a basin of clean water and a hand towel at the nightstand, placing them beside him while she helped strip off his upper sleeping garment, dabbing the towel in the water, pressing it over the wound that he had sustained months before.

Nomad gritted his teeth as the cool water met his hot wound, arching his back as Arie pressed and wiped some of the black blood from the cut that had refused to heal, eating away the multiple stitches, ointments, and bandages the doctors and clergy had used on it to attempt to mend the wicked wound.

"My god. It looks worse than before, Nomad," Arie whispered, deeply troubled by the thought that the wound might not get better.

Catching his breath after Arie cleaned his wound, getting out of the bed they had been sharing for the past three weeks, Nomad walked over to the nightstand mirror and put what he could see of his back in view.

Of what he could see in the dark at an angle, the cut was still flayed open, the black stain within making it difficult to see any subtlety of the wound.

The visions had increased in recent weeks as the wound continued to get worse. Always it was Reza who was there with him in his dying moments, and always the wound seeped its constant taint before bleeding the life out of him completely. None of the professionals knew of what nature his wound was other than it was no normal or natural infliction. It was a special, hateful kind of wound from a very powerful, sinful blade.

"Nomad, you need to find out what this is. It's eating you alive!" Arie said, walking over, placing the water and towel on the table before standing beside Nomad, putting comforting arms around him.

Holding his tongue, he looked down at his hands that were supporting him along the nightstand. He wanted to yell at her that he had done nothing since the war but to seek treatment and help with his wound, but he knew better than to be angry at the one who only cared for his well-being. She was just worried for him, and he was just angry at the enigma that vexed him from within.

"There's only one hope remaining here in Sheaf. Prophet Henarus is the highest-ranking clergyman in the region. I have an appointment with him tomorrow. If he can't figure out what this curse is—"

Arie understood Nomad's point without him having to finish his thought, and there was not much she could think of to say in response.

After a moment of silence, she asked, "Will you try to sleep tonight? Your body needs rest."

Nomad's tight muscles, eyes locked on himself in the mirror, answered her question as a silence slipped by with no verbal answer.

"Then I'll sit with you through the night," she said, tugging his tense arm until it softened, Nomad accepting her beckons.

The two headed towards the bed. Nomad sat up while Arie leaned on his shoulder, stroking his arm. Together, they waited out the night as visions of his own death tauntingly haunted every last minute of starlight.

48
SOLIDARITY

The door to the palace residence wing slowly opened, letting in the evening amber-hued light, basking the regal carpet.

A very worn Nomad tiredly closed the heavy wooden door behind him, looking up to find Cavok, Fin, Reza, and Arie sitting on the lobby room's sofa. Whatever their previous conversations had been, stopped, all turning to Nomad now.

"So?" Fin asked, waiting for Nomad to give them the news of how his visit to prophet Henarus had gone.

"You told everyone?" Nomad sighed, looking sternly at Arie.

"No," Reza responded, adding strongly, "Only your closest friends that you surely, carelessly forgot to inform."

Knowing he wasn't going to win any arguments being so outnumbered by so many strong-headed opponents who didn't place an emphasis on the respect of personal space as he did, he looked back to Fin, answering his initial question.

"He did what he could," Nomad said, unlooping his loose-fitting cross blouse, showing a still dark, but healing, scar where his open, weeping wound had been the night before.

After covering the scar, he added, "The healing cost him a great deal of personal sacrifice, and he said he wouldn't be able to perform the rite again, and only did so due to my recent contribution to the region."

"Wonderful!" Arie said, jumping up to embrace Nomad, who sunk slightly at the hug. Arie and the rest of the group suddenly guessed that there was a catch to the good news.

Holding the tall woman at arm's length, he looked at her, then to the rest as he finished the details of his condition.

"The wound is temporarily healed, but Henarus assured me that it would reopen and grow. He thinks he knows what kind of hex was placed in me, and it's a very pernicious wound that I've suffered, it seems. The blade could have been made of illimoth steel."

Arie covered her mouth, her eyebrows bowing, the realization of what infected her lover's flesh hitting hard while Reza, Fin, and Cavok waited for an answer, having never heard of that type of obscure steel.

Seeing that most of his friends hadn't heard of the material, he explained, "It's a metal brought from the Planes of Ash, from Telenthlanor's realm. Few blades ever appear here as it takes a great sacrifice to transport it here, and the material is very unstable once in our realm, breaking down into a sludge upon touching liquids.

"It seems that Telenthlanor was in league with the arisen army and held great interest over their campaign; otherwise, they would have never possessed such a precious gift from him."

"What does the steel do, though?" Reza asked impatiently, wanting to know how serious Nomad's wound was.

Arie replied for him.

"An illimoth blade, once it licks blood, infuses itself into the flesh, slowly corrupting the host until the victim turns to darkness…."

The room grew still for a moment before Reza asked, "I don't understand, what does that mean?"

"It means, I'll become an underling. The same as that greyoldor we came across in the cave in Brigganden," Nomad cut in, wanting to get the talk regarding him and his condition all out of the way, seeing how worried and uncomfortable it all was making everyone.

"Not quite an arisen, but a slave to their ways. Most arisen don't have a deathly sensitivity to light, but underlings do. I'll begin to seek darkness, live in caves or the undercities. My mind will warp. I'll become cold, savage—and I'll hunger and thirst for flesh and blood. Wickedness and corruption will become me.

"In my land, we call underlings *Oni*. They are rare, but there are tales of them from centuries past, and they were horrible creatures of fear and destruction.

"The wielder of an illimoth blade only stabs those who they see as a powerful opponent or as a potentially useful ally.

"Telenthlanor is said to have a breeding pit of praven in his plane of ash, a hellish place where he breeds underling praven. They have their own name for praven-type underlings—greyoldors—which we all already know a bit about. He uses greyoldors for his servants in other realms. The greyoldor we fought was one of those servants, brought here to this plane to serve his master."

Pausing for a moment, a gut-churning look of disgust clear on his face, Nomad pressed on to finish his thought.

"Though Lashik is gone, it seems his mission of death is still afoot in me."

Reza, refusing to accept defeat over the dire explanation, said, "Well there must be a way to reverse its effects. Henarus showed us that it can be done. We just need to find someone with greater capabilities than he."

"Henarus is a prophet of Hassome—no small deity," Nomad said, frustration beginning to sound through.

"Even in my lands, we know of Hassome. The only ones in Henarus' order above him are the five seers. If the curse is reversible at all, it would require the aid of those with incredible influence in the realm of divine hexweave. Who else can I go to for such a tall request? Henarus had reason to grant audience to me, but to anyone outside of the Plainstate, I am but a wandering passerby—a nomad. I have no connections to gods and goddesses."

Dropping Arie's held hand, Nomad slowly made his way to one of the empty sofas, falling into its cushions for a soft rebound, the rest of the group giving thought to the difficult case against hope Nomad had made against himself.

Cavok's voice almost made the group collectively jump as he loudly proclaimed, "Just cut that chunk of flesh out."

Nomad's response was quick, as though he had already considered the option.

"The taint runs deep. Henarus told me during the cleansing that it remains momentarily dormant on the outer edges of its spread, which bores deep into my core. It seems I waited too late to come to him. He said that if I had visited soon after I received the wound that he might have been able to completely remove the curse, but now it's too prevalent."

Resting a sun-sapped hand over his eyes, trying to rub away the weariness from him from the short time he had been out in the blaring desert sun, Nomad let out a sigh as Reza took a stab at a solution to his condition.

"You may not have connections to the gods, but I do."

Meriting an interested look from everyone, Reza continued.

"Even the youngest amongst my kind have extraordinary healing abilities—that is what my people are best known for. Though I wasn't able to completely heal your wound, I am young, and to be honest, never focused my studies on my kind's innate ability to heal. I am still quite inexperienced there, but I know many in my order, and they, I'm sure, could help. I've never heard of an ailment that Sareth has not been able to heal."

Nomad looked up, a glint of hope in his eyes, daring for a moment to consider an escape from his doomed future.

"There is a monastery in the Jeenyre mountains. It's a month-long journey northeast of here, but it's the closest Sareth establishment I am known at. The high priestess there would grant me the favor of healing you if it is within her power to do so. I would make the trip with you. You, after all, trekked with me on my mission of your own free will. I am, to a degree, responsible for the weight of that wound you now carry. I'll do anything I can to help you see it removed."

Reza's tone was determined; her mind, Nomad could tell, already made up that that was the course of action they were to take.

"A month's journey there, a month back, perhaps more depending on the weather. Winter is coming on soon, and the Jeenyre mountains receive a great deal of snowfall during the end of autumn. That, along with recovery time, you might be stuck up there through the winter months," Fin offered, figuring through the details of the trek with the group.

"What do you mean, *you*? You meant *we*, right?" Cavok corrected.

"No," Nomad ordered, shutting down Cavok's offer for help, adding to try and soften the disapproval, "If I am to go, I prefer it to be only Reza that comes on that journey. You all have lives here now. Arie, you have a two-week-long expedition coming up in three days. Fin, Metus has been using you extensively to expose high-priority criminals and illegal operations. Cavok, you have rank in the military's ranger branch. You have people that rely on you, jobs that need doing. Reza and I are the only two that don't have obligations or duties currently. I could not ask a half of a year of your lives."

"Well, say the word and the military be damned. Too stiff a lifestyle for me anyways. We've got your back if you want us along. Just know that," Cavok replied, Fin giving a wink and a smirk to let Nomad know that he held the same sentiment.

The offer and ready response from his two friends left an unwitting smile across Nomad's face.

Slowly looking over to Arie, wondering how she was taking all the talk of the quickly developing plans and journey, he immediately saw that she was not pleased with some aspect of the discussion.

Her speckled, striking silver and green eyes were boring into him, calculating. Her usual playful, caring personality that she only rarely showed to others besides him, that he had come to so enjoy, was a distant trait, her keen haltia half figuring how she would respond to him.

"Arie, you should stay. Metus depends on you a great deal, and with luck, I will be back with Reza within a few months, healthy. I prefer not to ask the hassle of this trip upon anyone else," Nomad said, placing his hand in hers.

"Anyone else, but Reza," Arie was quick to add.

An uneasy stillness settled in the lobby, Nomad looking down for a moment before voicing, "Yes. If she is willing to show me to her superiors, then I will gladly accept the offer."

Arie, gently releasing his hand from hers, said, "Then perhaps it is best that you two go alone. I would hate for you to inconvenience any of your worried friends who willingly offer you their companionship."

Arie, departing even before she finished her statement, left the room once again in a stillness, which this time no one readily broke.

Looking over to Reza, a strain of gloom peeking through Nomad's attempt at composure, Reza leaned forward, somewhat awkwardly offering him a reassuring hand and a comforting look.

"Well," Fin finally said, getting up, Cavok following his lead, "if you reconsider your travel company, let us know. If not—well—best of luck to you, Nomad. We'll see you when you get back."

Walking out the door, the two men left Nomad and Reza alone in the lobby, Reza's warm hand still in Nomad's palm.

49

THE OPEN ROAD

"Ready?" Nomad asked Reza, standing before her chamber door, well before the sun had risen.

His disposition was actually bright for a change, she noticed. Anymore, the times that she had seen Nomad around the palace grounds, he was either continually warn out or depressed. It was a nice change to see him beaming.

"Yes, I packed last night. Let me grab some fruit for the road. I haven't eaten breakfast yet."

Rushing back inside, snatching a handful of figs and apricots, she threw some in her satchel before looking herself over in the mirror to double-check that she was wearing everything she needed for the long journey.

She had not yet taken Metus up on his offer for his finest blacksmiths to craft her a personalized plate armor set, but thankfully, she wasn't going to need it on their journey. They were not expecting battle, and traveling in plate armor was awfully cumbersome and unnecessary for travel along well-used roads.

She had, with a small portion of her reward from Metus, bought some durable traveler's garb. A fine, thick, compressed cloth gambeson covered her stomach and hips, creating a lower tunic, with her upper chest donned in a very light chainmail, fitting over a black velvet top upon which a thin, silver gorget rested, connecting to a pair of scale pauldrons.

Tugging on her long gloves and her thigh-high leather boots, securing her wide belt where her longsword that Metus had given her and a newly acquired dagger she had had crafted from the leftover ingot of the same steel the sword was made from to accompany the elegant sword, she hopped out of her door for the last time for months to come.

Her braided hair bobbed as she passed Nomad, who himself seemed to have also obtained a new outfit just for the journey.

She was used to seeing him in local, traditional-style apparel, usually loose, flowing silk that opened freely to show his toned, tan body, but now he wore a leather harness that was tied over his neck and chest, thick stitching weaving around key curves to accentuate a fine figure. Thick leather protected his shoulders and hips, large belt loops hanging down from his waistband to help carry plenty of extra pouches and gear. The harness seemed to take the weight of his load from his whole upper body rather than just his hips. From beneath his harness ran a handsome aketon and undergarment, trim and sloped downward in a V shape. His arms and legs were covered by regional loose, soft fabrics, his old sword still by his side, which she rarely saw him without, even when out and about in the city.

The two made their way to the city's borders, Nomad chatting with her a little here and there on the way, Reza noticing that his grasp of Callatum, the regional language, had over the past few months become more familiar and natural to him.

Leaving Sheaf on horseback, they trotted out along the hardened sand road to the north.

The last of the cool, pre-morning air swept over the two, the last remaining stars disappearing from the brightening sky, deep pastels accenting the red and yellow landscape that stretched out for miles before them.

They'd be crossing it all—all they could see and more before making it to the Jeenyre mountains so many miles and weeks away.

Their beginnings along the desert road had been quiet, neither saying much as they began the first few hours of their journey; but Nomad, just before the sun began to rise to their left, said something offhandedly.

"A fair night it was," he offered, looking lazily over to her, locking gazes for a moment before the newly cresting sun caught her eye, causing her to squint.

"The sun is not nearly as forgiving these days, is it?" he spoke in a low tone, grimacing through the brightness of the morning sun.

As he turned back to face the road, Reza could discern the slightest hint of discontentment at the coming of the new day.

Continue the adventure with Reza, Nomad, Fin, and the others in book 2, <u>Lords of the Sands available on Amazon!</u>

The corruption has seeped through.

Nomad, Reza, and their companions have been victorious in their quest to stop the demonic undead warlord Lashik and his army from conquering their lands—but at a high cost.

Nomad's wound festers with Lashik's corruptive curse. He bleeds black blood, rampages uncontrollably, and threatens to harm his friends who wish to help him. Reza must save Nomad from the darkness within him and those who wish to take his life before he falls into demonic hands.

However, the undead do not wait. Their army is already rallying from their recent defeat, slaughtering the nomadic tribes of the out-regions as they prepare to move in on the heartland of the Southern Sands. Reza, already pushed to the edge trying to save her dear friend, must defend her homeland against their vengeful campaign.

The Lords of the Sands is the second book in the Lords of the Deep Hells trilogy, part of the *Lands of Wanderlust* saga, with captivating heroes struggling against Lovecraftian horrors in a hellish world plagued by threats from the undead.

FROM THE AUTHOR

I've been dying to publish this novel from the very start of it. Somewhere around chapter five, I realized that this world, this cast of characters, this genre, was what I was going to stick with for a very long time. I became enchanted with the idea of this series and realm quite early on.

This first book is only the beginning, and that thought is an exciting one. I can't wait to see what comes of these characters, and what of the new ones that'll be introduced in the following books.

I hope you enjoyed the first novel as much as I did. You can find book two, _Lords of the Sands_, available on Amazon. Follow me at the links below!

Visit me online for launch dates and other news at:
authorpaulyoder.com
(sign up for the newsletter)

instagram.com/author_paul_yoder
tiktok.com/@authorpaulyoder
Paul Yoder on Goodreads
Paul Yoder on Amazon

Made in United States
North Haven, CT
31 October 2024

59672289R00186